The Herbalist's Son Trilogy

Karen Anna Vogel

Copyright © 2018 Karen Anna Vogel

All rights reserved.

ISBN-13: 978-1717585691

ISBN-10: 1717585698

The Herbalist's Son Trilogy

All rights reserved. No part of this publication may be reproduced, stored in a retrieval system, or transmitted by any means – electronic, mechanical, photographic (photocopying), recording, or otherwise – without prior permission in writing from the author.

This book is a work of fiction. The

names, characters, places, and incidents are products of the writer's imagination or have been used fictitiously and are not to be construed as real. Any resemblance to persons, living or dead, actual events, locales or organizations is entirely coincidental. Any medical advice given in the context of this book is not to used to self prescribe an herbal remedy and Lamb Books is not to be held liable if misappropriates. If ill, see a physician.

Contact the author on Facebook at:

www.facebook.com/VogelReaders

Learn more the author at: www.karenannavogel.com

Visit her blog, Amish Crossings, at

www.karenannavogel.blogspot.com

From the Library of

———————————————

Karen Anna Vogel

DEDICATION

This book is dedicated in loving memory of a real Amish herbalist in Smicksburg, PA, who many simply called Dr. Dan. and his lovely wife who keeps the herb shop open, busier than ever.

TABLE OF CONTENTS

For the invisible things of him from the creation of the world are clearly seen, being understood by the things that are made, even his eternal power and Godhead.
Romans 1:20

This trilogy was written in sections for a reason. We take a spiritual journey with Willow Byler from his shy, fickle self to spiritual maturity. It's a coming of age book for those who are pressing on to be all that they're created to be in Christ., scriptures in the discussion guides to help lead and direct.

Book One	1
Chapter 1	1
Chapter 2	13
Chapter 3	21
Chapter 4	31
Chapter 5	43
Chapter 6	57
Chapter 7	67
Chapter 8	79
Chapter 9	95
Chapter 10	105
Discussion Guide	117
Amish Recipes	121
Book Two	123
Chapter 1	125
Chapter 2	133
Chapter 3	143

Chapter 4 ----- 151
Chapter 5 ----- 163
Chapter 6 ----- 175
Chapter 7 ----- 183
Chapter 8 ----- 195
Chapter 9 ----- 207
Chapter 10 ----- 223
Chapter 11 ----- 239
Discussion Guide ----- 249
Amish Recipe ----- 253
Book Three ----- 255
Chapter 1 ----- 257
Chapter 2 ----- 265
Chapter 3 ----- 273
Chapter 4 ----- 283
Chapter 5 ----- 295
Chapter 6 ----- 307
Chapter 7 ----- 315
Chapter 8 ----- 325
Chapter 9 ----- 335
Chapter 10 ----- 345
Chapter 11 ----- 359
Epilogue ----- 369
Discussion Guide ----- 371

Amish Recipes -- 376

About Author Karen Anna Vogel ------------------------------ 379

AMISH – ENGLISH DICTIONARY

Pennsylvania Dutch dialect is used throughout this book, common to the Amish of Western Pennsylvania. You may want to refer to this little dictionary from time to time.

ach – oh
boppli – baby
brieder - brothers
bruder - brother
daed - dad
danki – thank you
dawdyhaus – grandfather house
Gmay – Amish church, meaning community
guder mariye. Good morning.
gut - good
jah - yes
kapp- cap; Amish women's head covering
kinner – children
Loblied - The second song sung in a church service, sometimes twenty-five minutes long.
maedel - maid
mamm – mom
oma – grandma
opa - grandfather
Ordnung – order; set of unwritten rules
rumspringa – running around years, starting at sixteen, when Amish youth experience the Outsiders' way of life before joining the church.
wunderbar – wonderful
yinz – plural for you, common among Western Pennsylvania Amish and English. A *Pittsburghese* word.

Karen Anna Vogel

The Herbalist's Son Trilogy

BOOK ONE
CHAPTER 1

"I never saw a discontented tree. They grip the ground as though they liked it, and though fast rooted they travel about as far as we do. They go wandering forth in all directions with every wind, going and coming like ourselves, traveling with us around the sun two million miles a day, and through space heaven knows how fast and far!" John Muir

*W*illow Byler gawked when seeing Hannah Coblenz striding down the path and turned his eyes to the dog biscuits being made on his tiny kitchen table. *She'll think I'm daft, making cookies for dogs.* He seized the tablecloth by four corners and ran into his nearby bedroom and shoved it in the clothes hamper. When Hannah opened the door, he realized all the mess in his four room house; taking good care of so many dogs in spring during birthing season, left little time to keep house. His heart raced. Hannah was a stickler for cleanliness.

Hannah flashed a broad smile. "I thought you'd like some homemade bread. It's still warm."

He hadn't noticed that Hannah's blue eyes had a hint of violet. Did he see tinges of green sparkling in them, too?

"Willow, are you all right?" Hannah said, placing the bread on the table. "Where's your tablecloth? I've never seen the table bare."

He gulped. "Ah…it needs washed."

She tilted her head. "Something wrong, Willow?"

He chewed on his bottom lip. "You don't work today."

"And?"

"You bringing a present and all, I –I… I… well…" His face burnt as he stuttered.

Hannah took a seat at the table. "Willow, it's me, Hannah. I'm like your sister. And I brought bread for a reason."

I'm like your sister. Those words deflated Willow quicker than a popped balloon. He made his way over to the icebox. "Want some iced tea?"

"*Nee*, I'm fine." She tapped the bread. "*Danki* for helping me over this past winter. Breaking things off with Freeman and all was rough."

"No longer sad, *jah*?"

"Moving forward."

Hannah's long brown eyelashes made his heart throb. Or were her lashes blonde, but a dark blonde? He continued to observe to decide.

"Willow, is there something on my face? Flour from baking?"

He struggled to find his voice. "*Nee.* I was just, ah, you know…"

She stood and took his hand. "Why so nervous? Tell me. I'm like your sister, for Pete's sake."

I'm like your sister for Pete's sake, kept flushing around and around in his mind. When he couldn't stop staring into her eyes, she flared, her eyes a darker, icy blue. "Willow Byler, what is wrong with you?"

"What?"

"I'd have to say for the first time in my life, you're acting…arrogant."

"Arrogant? I am not."

She huffed. "Why look at me with your nose up?"

Willow swallowed a glassful and then shook his head to focus. "Sorry. Lots on my mind." He winced as throbbing from the ice cold drink shot through his head at a pain level of ten. He clamped his eyes shut and opened his mouth to breathe in warmer air. Willow leaned over and put his head between his knees, holding his head in his hands.

He felt Hannah's hand gently rub his back, and the touch of her slender fingers made him melt. "*Jah*, I'm okay. Just a brain squeeze."

"A what?"

"Brain squeeze. That's what the *English* call them."

Hannah giggled. "A brain *freeze*, not squeeze."

He looked up and noticed Hannah's eyes were a lighter blue now. *Do not stare, Willow*, he admonished himself. "Well, squeeze makes more sense. Cold water makes the blood vessels constrict…and squeezes them."

She gave a wry smile. "You sound like your *daed*, so scientific. *Ach*, I almost forgot." She pulled a paper from her apron pocket. "Can you give this to your *mamm*? It's a knitting pattern I keep forgetting to drop off."

He remembered making bargains with Hannah while growing up. "Swap favors?"

"I already brought you bread," she said coyly.

"It's not enough…"

"Okay, what do you want?"

His mouth grew dry, but he spit it out. "Let me take you home from the Singing on Sunday."

Hannah's eyes turned dark again. Willow held his breath. *She's angry.*

She planted a hand on her heart. "You deserve someone better. I'm an old *maidel* and don't even go to Singings."

"I don't usually go either, but you're only twenty-four and should. I'm twenty-two."

She sat looking at him, eyebrows pinched. "Really? You're that old?"

"*Jah*. I'm not *Boppli Willy* anymore."

She laughed. "*Boppli Willy*. *Ach*, how we teased you."

Their eyes locked. Willow hoped the blue would turn pale, but it didn't.

"Willow, I just got over Freeman's deception."

"You d-deserve b-better than that," Willow hissed. "A real man doesn't lead a woman on to believe a lie."

Hannah's mouth parted. "Do all of Reed Byler's *kinner* speak their minds so freely?"

"*Jah*, we d-do," he fumbled, reaching out his hand. "You can trust m-me."

Her eyes pooled with tears. "You're my *gut* friend, Willow. Let's just keep it that way."

He nodded, not able to get out a word and refusing to stutter again.

~*~

Later that day, Reed Byler poured alcohol into a jar filled with crushed willow bark, covered it with a cotton cloth and twine and sat it in the dark spot in a corner cupboard. "You age here with the other ones," he said.

"Talking to herbs again?" a voice asked.

Reed jumped. "Willow, for crying out loud, you scared the wits out of me. Something wrong with the bell on the door?"

"It rang, but you were, like I said, talking to herbs."

Reed chuckled. "An apple doesn't fall far from the tree. When you tend to your dogs, you wouldn't notice if I came into your kennel."

"*Jah*, we have one-track minds." Willow cleared his throat and leaned against the counter. "Hannah looks at me like a *bruder*. She said no to a buggy ride."

Reed's heart sank. Willow was just like him in many ways. How painfully shy he'd been during his courting years. It took a loving heart like his Dorcas to steady him. He was sure Hannah would do the same for Willow. "Well, there's other fish in the sea," he said lamely.

"Well, maybe not here."

"*Gmay* is full of young women."

"None that interest me. And *Daed*, to be honest, I think the reason I even asked her to court was to…keep me Amish."

Reed thought he heard wrong. "Keep you what?"

"Amish. *Daed*, I'm still not baptized for a reason."

Reed felt lightheaded and took a seat in his new Amish rocker. "Son, what are you saying?"

Willow started to pace the floor, making a loose board in the middle squeak. "Now that Edmond's back from Haiti for the summer, we've been talking –"

"*Nee*!" Reed yelled, surprising himself. "I can't bear it. Not again."

"*Daed*, it's not Edmond's fault he's so…interesting. I know he almost led Cassia away from the Amish but that was two years ago, well, my case is different."

Reed shot up and paced the floor along with his son. "Cassia could have ruined her life. She's Amish to her core and hallelujah that Martin moved here to keep her on the straight and narrow." He snapped his fingers and pointed at Willow. "Six months they weren't allowed to see each other. Same for you. No talking to Edmond for a spell."

Willow stood firm and crossed his arms. "*Daed*, that's ridiculous."

"*Nee*, it's not. I'll talk to Edmond. He's leading you away from the flock and doesn't know it."

"I know what I'm doing," Willow huffed. "Broadening my mind about poverty in Haiti and Africa…like *you*. I want to travel *like you*, not Edmond.

Reed felt his left eyelid flutter, a nervous twitch he'd had for years. "Travel? I don't travel."

"*Jah*, you do. Go to Pittsburgh all the time for seminars. Took the train to New York plenty of times. Now word has it you want to go to Mexico!"

"It's for my research. Willow, you can travel by train, bus or car, you know that."

Willow went limp. "I meet people from other states, even Canada, but always here, when a dog's sold."

Reed felt a pang of guilt pierce his heart. He pushed the limits of the *Ordnung*, having a voracious mind for medicine. Travel brochures to medical conferences in Europe he'd leafed through, maybe drooling over the thought of going. He was a bad example to his son. "Well maybe I'm partly to blame, giving you travel fever. It's not normal. Being content where you are is the *Gut* Lord's will for us."

Taking a wooden chair, Willow plunked himself down. "Content. In this little town? *Daed*, I don't think I can."

Reed pulled at his brown beard speckled with gray. "No one said you had to stay here in Smicksburg."

Willow slouched, looking defeated. "I know you and the church elders are disappointed in me, not getting baptized last month."

Reed couldn't deny that. He was bitterly disappointed. "And this was the reason? Feeling too cooped up here?"

"*Jah.*"

"So you would have gone through with baptism if it wasn't for such a trifle?"

"A trifle? What's that?"

"*Ach*, Granny and Jeb Weaver talk about trifles. The little things in life that really don't matter. We go down the wrong road by tripping over trifles." He clapped his hands and threw them in the air. "Lord have mercy, Willow. Why didn't you just say something to the Bishop?"

He reddened. "*Ach, Daed*, I do have something against the *Ordnung*...after seeing Edmond's pictures. When I go down to Pittsburgh with Hannah and Cassia to help their knitting circle pass out gloves and whatnot, I feel…moved with compassion to help the *real* poor. And the *Ordnung* says I can't fly."

Reed made his way back to his rocker. "We Amish help the poor…and can take the train."

"Can't do that to Haiti."

"Haiti again! You think there's no poor folks in America?" Reed cried.

"I know there is. I see them when I go with the women to 'protect' them. How ridiculous. If someone came near the women, I can't even slug him."

"What are you saying, Willow?"

"I don't know. I feel useless, I suppose. I go with women to Pittsburgh to protect them, but I can't even do that since I'm a pacifist."

"And you're doubting that, too?"

"*Nee*, I don't believe in violence. *Ach, Daed,* I'm so unsettled. What's my purpose on this earth?"

Reed bowed his head, pained that his son who was always so steady was unraveling before his eyes. *His purpose? Willow should know what his purpose is. To glorify God! And get married and be fruitful and multiply. To raise his kinner to serve the Lord. It was the Amish way. Lord, help my son.*

~*~

Guilt panged Dorcas' heart. Overhearing through the door this confidential conversation was eaves dropping. *Lord, help Willow. He's so much like his daed. Introverted and a keen mind bent on one thing so much they didn't see the whole picture of life at times.*

When she heard silence, she turned the door knob and entered the herb shop. "Willow, are you staying for supper? Made two meatloaves."

Willow's eyes mellowed when they met hers. "Sure *Mamm. Danki.*"

"*Gut.* I miss you during spring, too busy with all the new pups. How many this year?"

Willow looked up, putting fingers in the air, silently mouthing numbers. "Twenty-one last count. Happy's going to have hers soon."

"That's Cassia's dog, *jah?*" Dorcas asked.

"*Jah.* Gave it to her when she was down in the mouth about her breakup with Edmond." He shifted and grinned. "Martin was the best medicine."

"It's *wunderbar* your sister found what true love is," Dorcas noted.

"*Jah.* It was all infatuation between Cassia and Edmond."

Willow's eyes dimmed, and Dorcas' heart sank. Hannah was still waiting for her ideal man. She'd overheard her talking at knitting circle about her expectations; the major one being he must be older. Older men were wiser, Hannah had said.

As the men made their way over to the oak table, the store bell jingled. Dorcas ran to see who it was and soon saw Granny Weaver and Jeb. "*Ach*, have supper with us."

Jeb pulled Granny close. "We ate at the Country Junction. This old woman's tired from puttin' in the garden."

Granny darted a glare at Jeb with her light blue eyes. "Jebediah Weaver, I'm not tired. Just wanted to eat something I didn't cook."

Dorcas laughed at this animated couple. "Jeb, go on in and sit with the men. I want a word with Granny."

Jeb pulled at his lengthy gray beard. "You look worried Dorcas. Can I help?"

"It's womenfolk talk, Jeb, but *danki* just the same."

Jeb nodded and went into the main house. Dorcas ran to hug Granny. "I'm so upset. Do *mamm's* ever stop worrying about their *kinner*?"

Granny pat her back. "What's wrong?"

"Hannah turned Willow down. And he's crushed." She released Granny and looked earnestly into her eyes, needing her sage opinion. "He loves her, although he denies it. Loves her so much he's running. Running away from the Amish."

Granny held Dorcas' hand as they took seats on a nearby bench set out for customers. "Willow's a steady fellow. He won't leave the Amish. I agree he's running, but the great Hound of Heaven will catch up with him."

Dorcas frowned. "Hound of Heaven?" She shook her head in confusion. "What do dogs have to do with this?"

"*Ach*, Jeb reads C.S. Lewis and got the phrase from him. Lewis was running from God but the Lord caught him. He'll chase Willow until he's a believer, too."

Dorcas felt indignant but didn't dare show it. "Willow's a believer already. He's just questioning some of our ways. But he never did until he fell for Hannah. And now he's running away. Wants to go to Haiti with Edmond."

"Fly in a plane? He's Amish," Granny gasped.

"He's not baptized. Should we forbid it or let out more rope?"

Granny slouched. "Don't know. Everyone's different. Maybe he needs someone who can outshine Hannah…"

"Hmm. Martin's sister may come down to help Cassia with the *boppli* but Martin says she doesn't have the funds for the long bus ride. Gasoline's gone up quite a bit."

Granny winked. "Our knitting circle's raised money for many causes. Maybe for a bus ticket?"

"But this isn't charity. Do you think it's right?"

Granny wrung her hands. "*Ach*, I get ahead of myself. Maybe we can sell some items in Suzy's store?"

Dorcas laughed at the twinkle in Granny's eyes. How this dear woman loved to see couples happily married. If she was willing to help her son, Dorcas wouldn't stop her.

Karen Anna Vogel

CHAPTER 2

Edmond stared at the entrance to the herb shop, memories flooding him. Being home from Haiti for the summer, everything shocked him. Culture shock is what he was forewarned about by the mission base. He used to think Reed's store was so tiny, but it was ten times the size of a regular grocery store in rural Haiti, which carried only rice and beans. Anger continued to soar through him as he saw the plenty in America, and all the complaining. He wanted to shout at some college students when he overheard how 'crappy' the cafeteria food was. Haitians cut sugar cane all day with a machete to buy enough rice for their family, he inwardly screamed, clenching his fists and perspiring profusely.

He entered the herb shop and expected Reed to be sitting there, concocting a new herbal remedy, but no one was in sight. He eyed the store in wonder. Why so many brands of each herb? Edmond pursed his lips and hung his head in silence, an attitude of prayer. *Lord, I can't take this. I go to the store and see one whole aisle just for toilet paper. Who needs that many choices?*

The door to the house opened and Reed appeared. He cleared his throat. "Hello, Edmond."

Reed's tone was flat as was his mouth; no smile to be had. "Did I come at a bad time?"

"*Jah.*"

Edmond expected Reed to invite him in as usual but he didn't. Why? They'd talked to the wee hours of the morning last week about culture shock. Was he driving him nuts? "Guess I'll come by some other time then."

"Wait, wait. We need to have a talk about Willow." Reed pointed to a chair and Edmond sat while Reed took his place in his new rocker. But as soon as he sat, he shot up and started pacing the floor, raking his fingers through his hair. "Now, you know you're like a son, *jah*?"

Edmond nodded, bracing for a blow. Reed always paced when upset.

He plunked himself down again in his rocker. "But not a real son because you're not Amish. And neither is Willow. It's not right to lure him away to Haiti."

"Lure him? Reed, are you serious?"

"*Jah.*"

Edmond cocked his head back as if evading a blow. "I don't mean to lure. Can you give me an example?"

"You going on and on about how rich we are in America and how *kinner* starve to death. Willow's tender hearted and wants to go help. I don't believe in that. I say train people to fish, then they'll catch their own."

"Our mission does that," Edmond defended. "We have men learning to be tailors, plant nurseries, lots of important work, and the children's hair turns from red to black again."

Reed snapped his fingers. "Iodine deficiency."

"Yes. Haiti has the least protein in their diet than any other country and the kids live only seven-hundred miles from Disney World. It's not fair." The anger mixed with sorrow erupted in Edmond and he found himself enraged again. Why he had no control over this was a mystery. God gave self-control and one of Edmond's favorite verses was about a man who could hold his temper was mightier than a fortified city. But he was crumbling. He swung his foot onto his knee and lowered his face as tears again unexpectantly erupted. He soon felt Reed's firm hand on his shoulder. And then footsteps and shuffling, but he didn't look up. He wanted to hide in a hole and not come out. Some days he wished he'd never gone to Haiti. *Ignorance was bliss!*

Reed squeezed Edmond's shoulder. "Jesus wept. It's okay, son. I think your zeal is contagious."

Edmond nodded. "Making Willow want to go to Haiti." He groaned. "I'll talk with him."

"I'd appreciate that."

~*~

Later that evening, Hannah chewed her lower lip and kicked a stone into a mud puddle as she walked to Cassia's house to babysit. *How awkward Willow had acted. Why did he care for her?* Fire burnt on her cheeks and in her heart. Could she trust another man after being so disappointed by Freeman? He'd led her to believe he'd turn Old Order Amish for her, but he only tried to get her on the slippery slope of leaving her People and be Mennonite

She straightened and took a cleansing breath, the lilacs wafting through the air as she stomped down the driveway to

Cassia and Martin's house. Would she ever marry? She and Cassia had kidded two years ago about being spinsters, making yarn and selling it with the sheep farm they'd live on. Hannah was now twenty-four, so she may as well face facts that she'd be a spinster for sure and certain.

As she rounded the bend in the driveway, the two-story white house came into view. She stopped and stared as if she was seeing it for the first time. Her heart yearned to have this picture perfect life her best friend embraced with a passion. Cassia was indeed a woman who adored her husband, and Martin cherished her. A tinge of jealousy Hannah secretly harbored, only able to verbalize it to Granny Weaver, her dear old friend at knitting circle, slithered in her heart.

Hannah knew when she fell in love, she'd know it. No matter how much Cassia told her that love blossomed over time, like her love grew for Martin, Hannah knew she'd at least be attracted to her husband in a romantic way. Many Amish married for convenience, but not her. Willow Byler didn't make her heart soar like it had with Freeman. But then the thud and many months of crying and depression over Freeman's so-called romantic love couldn't be God's plan for her either. Well, maybe him surprising her on Christmas with a proposal and confession: "Will you marry me and turn Mennonite?"

~*~

Cassia noticed Hannah standing in the driveway. Why was she staring at her house? She raised her hand above her head and waved vigorously. Hannah put up a limp hand and Cassia ached for her friend. *Wish she'd admit how lonely and unhappy she is.*

She skipped down the steps and onto the lush green grass, her toes telling her it needed cut. *I'll do it after I help daed in the herb shop. Mighty busy with spring colds and tinctures needing to be made.* When Hannah came into ear shot, she yelled, "So glad you can watch Rose. You're a life saver."

Stepping onto the stone path leading to the house, Hannah attempted a smile. "I love *kinner*."

Cassia held Hannah's blue eyes for a moment. A chasm was forming between them and it ailed Cassia. No herbal remedy for a fracture in a friendship.

"Are you mad at me, Cassia?" Hannah asked, eyes now down.

"*Nee*. What makes you ask such a thing?"

"Amish grapevine is faster than the *English* internet. Willow hasn't stopped by to talk to you?"

"*Nee*. Saw him walking real quick-like up the road to the herb shop. Does he have bad news?"

Hannah slouched. "I know I'm a spinster and all, but seriously, you and Granny have to stop this matchmaking. Does the whole *Gmay* feel sorry for me?"

Cassia stepped back and tapped her foot nervously. "Don't forget Granny found Moses a wife last year." After a long sigh, she asked, "So Willow got up the courage to tell you how he felt and you broke his heart? Willow is the finest man on the planet. How could you?"

Hannah's mouth unhinged and it remained open as hurt poured from her eyes. A robin chirped and then took flight from a nearby tree. Cassia ran to take Hannah. "I'm sorry. I said too much."

"Cassia Byler, you talk from the heart, real frank-like. Well, let me do the same. I can't court someone, not even your *bruder*, if I don't feel romance."

Cassia gawked. Romance? What Hannah had with Freeman was not only infatuation, she near worshipped him. Cassia mentally went through all the great books she could lend Hannah about what true love really was. When she thought of Jane Austen's *Emma*, she gasped. "Granny has me reading classic literature and there's a book I want you to read."

"What?"

"It's about a woman who married her lifelong friend. Friendship is the foundation of marriage."

"With no romantic feelings?"

Cassia's deep love for Martin swelled in her soul. "How can you love someone you don't really know, and how can you know him if you're not friends first?"

Hannah looked a bit dizzy. "Say that again."

"Remember when I thought I was in love with Edmond? I didn't know him as a friend first."

Blinking rapidly, Hannah said, "You've known him your whole life…"

"I admired Edmond. I had a schoolgirl crush on the handsome *Englisher*. Over these two years of marriage, there's a deeper love. A love that's settling and more satisfying. I can't explain it, but Hannah you must open yourself up."

"And go on a buggy ride with Willow? It would be giving him false hopes."

"Are you still helping him with his dogs?"

Hannah nodded. "*Jah*, it's birthing time."

"*Gut.* Talk to him. Talk from your heart so Willow can know the dear Hannah I love so much."

Hannah stepped back. "Cassia. You're my best friend, but I feel nothing for Willow. Understand? He pays me to help with his dogs like you pay me to babysit Rose." She paused. "Not to compare Rose to a dog. I'd babysit Rose for free, but you get my meaning. I can't be a burden to my *mamm*, now that *Daed's* gone to glory…"

Cassia flung her arms around her friend. "There's someone out there for you. Be patient and wait. He'll come along…or you'll see Willow in a different light. Come on in and I'll lend you the book I was talking about." She slipped her arm through Hannah's. "*Danki* my kindred-spirit friend, for babysitting so late. *Daed* asked me last minute to help in the herb shop."

"Kindred-spirit?" Hannah questioned.

Cassia laughed. "Reading *Anne of Green Gables* again. Like I said, Granny's got me hooked on all the books her circle reads. I'll lend you that one when I'm done."

Karen Anna Vogel

CHAPTER 3

Over the next few days, Hannah read *Emma,* only to find that her intended was much older. Yes, she was right about Willow being so young. He was wet behind the ears and she needed a more mature man. Cassia thought her husband too old at first, but their age gap ebbed away. Her mind turned to Andy Smucker. Why wasn't he married? The Smucker family, just having moved from Ohio a year ago, was a mystery to the whole community. Andy was so handsome and had set up a fine carpenter shop, so he was financially set to wed. Was he jilted long ago and never recovered? Was he so devastated that the family moved away? Or was it that he was so short, he didn't want a taller wife? She snickered at this outlandish thought. But then again, Andy was only a little over five feet tall. No dwarfism in the family that she knew of. Or was there? *Maybe that's why Andy didn't marry!* He knew he'd pass along this genetic trait?

She shook her head. Being a dwarf was considered something special by the People. God made them that way, but fatal genetic disorders that took babies home early was a new challenge to all Amish. She stared at the ceiling as she pulled the light summer quilt to her chin. As the room became dusky, Hannah imagined Andy's dimpled grin and pondered if the Lord above had put this idea into her mind. She'd been attracted to him since they moved to Smicksburg, but thought him too old, being fifteen-some years older than her. She held the Jane Austen book to her heart. "Just like Emma's Mr. Knightley."

But how to get Andy's attention? He didn't go to Sunday night singings, but neither did she. What would she need to stop by and talk to a carpenter about? Her face lifted into a smile. Sadie, his younger sister, still lived at home, just like Andy. Sadie did seem to have her nose up in the air and had no friends. Well, they had something in common; both spinsters. She cupped her cheeks, dropping her book. Why was Sadie unmarried? What mystery lived in the Smucker house?

~*~

With baby Rose down for the night, Cassia and Martin lay in bed, their noses in books. "Anne marries Gilbert after all!" She held the book to her heart. I just know things will work out between Hannah and Willow, childhood friends that one day see what's what."

Martin pursed his lips and gave her a wry smile. "And what are they to see?"

"That Willow is not Hannah's *bruder*. It annoys me she can't see him for the man he is."

Martin leaned his head against the headboard. "Remember when I was living with Willow? I knew then he was a man the way he could care for the sick."

"Exactly," Cassia groaned. "He's so encouraging and truth be told, I think Hannah doesn't deserve him."

"Whoa. Hannah's your best friend."

"She turned down Willow flat again for a buggy ride."

"*Ach*..."

"Hannah's made it real clear to him that she's not interested." Cassia glanced over at the little shelf Martin made her for the books she was collecting. Emma. Emma was a matchmaker. What would she do? And then she remembered what Granny Weaver suggested. "What about your sister?"

"What about her?"

"She could come live here after planting season. Help take care of Rose. *Daed's* work at the herb shop is more than he can handle. We practically live there and he needs more help."

"Since I was helped so much by herbs, I can't get enough of studying them. Do you know black fermented garlic kills cancer cells? Amazing. Read it the other day."

Leaning her head on his shoulder, Cassia near purred like a content cat. "You were skeptical of herbal medicine when you first came for treatment. How many husbands and wives can work side-by-side, sharing the same passion for the plants the Lord gave us for healing? *Ach*, sure wish Hannah and Willow's love for dogs could bring them together." She pinched Martin's black bearded face. "Anna likes dogs, too, *jah*?"

"She's a cat person."

"She loves all kinds of animals. I'll write and...hint at the fact that we need help and well, so does Willow."

He sighed. "Okay, but let God be the matchmaker. He brought us together so he does a *gut* job." He turned to plant a kiss on her cherry lips.

She laced her fingers behind his neck. "For sure and certain."

~*~

Edmond drove the long driveway back to Willow's tiny place, hidden from the road. *Lord, give me words. I don't want to lead him away from his Amish roots.*

He passed Cassia's house off to the right. Martin was out chopping wood, never having enough put up for the winters. To think this man was so ill, in a wheel chair due to Lyme Disease and Cassia, Edmond's former fiancée, found love in such a carrying man. Edmond was glad to be on good terms with him, no envy or bad feelings harbored. When he decided to be a single missionary, not able to deny the calling, he felt whole and complete, not needing a wife. Not just yet.

He spied Lily, the youngest Byler, picking wildflowers. Slowing down to a snail's pace, he yelled, "Need a ride? Going to Willow's?"

She turned, a bouquet in her hands, blue eyes twinkling. "Hi Edmond. How are you?"

"Hop in and I'll tell you what I've been up to." Edmond noticed how womanly Lily had become, being now eighteen. She was always pure sunshine when seeing him, just like Cassia had been as a teen. He hoped he didn't give Lily any cause to think of him other than her "*Englisher bruder*" as the Byler family adopted him as their own. A bond that wasn't legally binding, only bound by love.

Lily handed Edmond her flowers. "Hold these while I get into this thing. Why such a big truck?"

"It's Pastor Dale's, not mine. Only using it for the summer."

Lily's shoulders slumped. "So you're really going back to Haiti? Why?"

His mind raced and as did his heart. How could he explain to anyone how needed he was, some people dying of very treatable diseases? "Have you been learning herbal medicine in the shop?"

"*Jah.* See all the red clovers I found?" Lily turned her bouquet to show him this valuable blood purifier. "I like helping people who come in. This spring flu's been keeping *Daed* and *Mamm* busy."

"I see how happy your mom is helping in the shop. The whole family's involved, right?"

Lily tilted her head, eyes wide. "Does it make you miss your parents?"

Such an unexpected question threw him. "No, just… I think it's nice families can get along and work together. Don't see it happen much."

Lily seemed unconvinced. "*Ach*, Edmond, you're all alone in the world. I feel for you."

Stopping at Willow's place, he near gawked at her. "Lily, you've always been a sweet girl. I appreciate the concern, but I'm not lonely with hundreds of Haitians lined up for medical care."

"But you'll never marry," she pouted. "How can you be happy single?"

"For now I'm single. If God shows me otherwise, I'm open to marriage."

Lily's lips lifted into a broad grin. "*Gut.*"

He cocked his head back and laughed at her expression. Lily had always worn her heart on her sleeve and right now she was apparently very relieved that her 'big *bruder*' wouldn't be a poor lonely bachelor.

Willow came out of his kennels, up the hill from his little house, hands on his hips, appearing to be fuming. In no time, Lily ran to him, looking down, intent on listening to her brother. What a gem Lily was, and all grown up.

"Will, what's wrong?" Edmond asked, making his way to him. "Lose a pup?"

"*Nee*. It's personal."

Lily took him by the shoulders. "Don't clam up. Tell someone what's eating you up. It's obvious you're miserable about something."

"Will, let's talk," Edmond suggesting, motioning towards his little front porch.

"I go by Willow now. Not ashamed of being named after aspirin."

"Aspirin?" Edmond questioned.

"You're a doctor and don't know that aspirin is made of willow bark?"

Edmond grinned. "Oh, yes, I forgot. Now, let's talk."

Lily gave her brother a side hug. "You go on. Edmond is *gut* medicine for you." She waved at them both and continued her walk to collect wildflowers.

He was good medicine? Such admiration by Lily he was used to, but now she was a woman. *Lord, I cannot be attracted to another one of Reed's daughter's. Help me not see the sweetness in Lily, a little girl now all grown up. I can never be Amish!*

~*~

The cotton ball clouds cluttered in the blue sky as Willow and Edmond ended their conversation. "So what you're saying is if grass is greener on the other side, fertilize my side?"

"Yes. But do it within the rules of the Amish. *Rumspringa* or no, respect your parents. If you came with me to Haiti, it would crush them and I don't think you could handle it."

The tone in Edmond's voice told Willow much. "You can't handle it?"

Edmond took a sip of meadow tea. "It's coming home and the culture shock. I'm mad all the time, seeing how rich people are and how much they complain. Almost yelled at a kid in the store whining because his mom wouldn't buy him a stupid toy."

"So, are you going back to Haiti sooner or not at all?"

"Well, this is confidential, Will, so don't tell a soul."

"Willow's my name. But, go on."

"I'm taking the whole summer furlough to find God's will. I read about other missionaries and they seem to be able to go from poverty to rich places just like that. Mother Teresa went to talk in many countries, but all she saw was 'poverty of the soul.' She felt the saddest for wealthy people, because they were lonely, the worst kind of poverty."

"Whose mother is she? Someone on staff in Haiti?"

Edmond chuckled. "No. She's a Catholic nun who helps the poorest of the poor in India. Catholics call priests Father and nuns Sister."

Willow leaned back to sway on his rocking chair. "Was she from India? Used to the poverty?"

Groaning, Edmond started to rock nervous energy out of his system. "That's the point. No, she was from Eastern

Europe and only eighteen years old when she became a missionary."

"Wow, that's Lily's age. Awful young, don't you think?"

Edmond wanted to say he couldn't believe how Lily had matured over the two years he was gone, but instead he changed topics. "So, you're going to take Mr. Peters up and go to Canada to train his dogs? Being away from home gives you a new perspective. Maybe you'll see just how Amish you are. And, there's lots of fish in the sea. Hannah's sweet, but if she's not interested, stop trying."

"But don't girls like to be pursued?"

"And you've pursued Hannah for how long?"

Willow leaned on one elbow. "Months. But she sees me as Cassia's little *bruder*."

"Well, we've all known each other for so long, being childhood friends. Do you really care for her or just want to get married?"

"How can you tell the difference?"

"Being content to be single. If you're not content, I think it's time to court someone."

Willow guzzled down the rest of his tea. "Are you content being single?"

Edmond groaned. "Some days I'm tempted to settle down and live an easy life here in America."

"Maybe you're supposed to help folks with soul poverty, like that lady you were talking about. I see it. Folks come to see the Amish to learn about community. Some don't have any, only talking to their spouses. They work too much and don't have front porches, is what I tell them."

Edmond smiled. "The psychology of the front porch. People used to build houses with front porches just so they could visit. Now porches are in the back. Sad, isn't it?"

"*Jah*, it is." He nudged Edmond. "And I think you've got more in common with the Amish than you think."

Edmond put up a hand in protest. "I will never be Amish. Mark my word."

Karen Anna Vogel

CHAPTER 4

At the next church service, Willow, as usual, helped pack up the benches into the wagon, specifically made just to store them for two weeks, when the next meeting would be held. He'd ignored Hannah pretty much for a week now, even though they worked side by side, as dogs birthed their young ones. Hannah seemed like her mind was far away, and Willow didn't try to figure out where she wandered to. So, to see her coming over to talk to him was a bit odd. "Hello, Hannah. Something wrong? Did you get word a dog's in labor?"

Hannah shook her head, her prayer *kapp* strings floating. "I want to talk to you. Ask you something."

Concern was all over Hannah's face. Was she courting someone and wanted to be the first to tell him? But courting was done in secret. Maybe she felt guilty. But why? "Want to take a walk down the road?"

She nodded, crossing her arms. Willow jumped from the wagon, all the while asking if he could be dismissed since he'd done his share. His buddies smirked and chortled, obviously thinking he and Hannah were a couple. He observed Hannah and a blush line grew down her neck. Her mint dress with the pink made him crave watermelon, which was being served right this minute, but he'd forgo mentioning it would all be gobbled up if they left.

Hannah near marched to the road, Willow running to catch up. "Hannah, what's bugging you? You look mad."

"Well, Willow Byler, I am. When I said no to a buggy ride, you've been so quiet at work, I think it's to punish me."

Willow bent over to grab some red clovers and made a mental note of where so many grew in abundance. *Daed* would want to know.

"Aren't you going to talk to me now?"

Willow slowed his pace, and Hannah paused so he could catch up. He felt like one of his dogs that put a tail between their legs when scared. "Hannah, I've never seen you so mad."

"I'm not mad. Well, I mean I am, but… I listened to the sermon and, well, what did you get out of it?"

"Well, ah, it was about correction and how a man was wise who took a rebuke. I remember that."

Hannah sighed. "What I got today was how we're to walk in harmony. Live at peace. If I'm going to work for you with the dogs, you'll have to be nicer. I miss the old Willow."

Old Willow? I haven't changed in two weeks. And then it dawned on him. "*Ach*, Hannah, I've had my mind elsewhere. Didn't mean to be rude."

She frowned. "What's your mind on that you can't talk about?"

Did he hear jealousy in her voice? He had been talking quite a bit to Susanna Miller after church. Oh, what wishful thinking. "My trip to Canada. I forgot to tell you about it."

She crossed her arms again as if not wanting to hear his news, so he looked ahead, dumbfounded.

After an uncomfortable silence, she said, "Willow, why're you going to Canada and how long will you be there?"

"*Ach*, thought you wouldn't be interested…"

She slowed her pace. "Of course I'm interested…"

"Well, remember Mr. Peters who came down with his wife and *dochder*?"

"How could I forget," Hannah recalled, "The *dochder* flirted with you to no end."

Willow smirked. "It's your imagination."

"*Nee*, Willow, she was a flirt. But from what I hear, Amish men are considered more grown up than *Englisher* young men, so she must be looking for someone older."

"I am older than her. She's only eighteen. And her name is Cheri."

Hannah snickered. "Cherry? She'd fit into your family, all names coming from plants or trees."

Willow observed her blue eyes dancing and he couldn't look away. "It's not pronounced like a cherry, but shur-*ree*. Have to roll the "R" since it's a French name. Accent on the second syllable, too."

Hanna sat down on a grassy bank. "Willow, you're all lit up. Are you going there to see this Cherry woman? Tell me it's not true."

Willow readjusted his straw hat. "She's not Amish."

"You're not baptized since you have travel fever. Cassia told me all about it." Hannah picked a daisy and started to pick off white petals one by one.

"Why do you care?" Willow asked boldly. "I was just your dumb little *bruder* not long ago."

"I never said dumb. But I am concerned. Why are you leaving, and how long? And is it because of me?" She lowered her head, avoiding eye contact.

"It's not because of you, Hannah. I never expected you to say yes to courting."

She put a hand on his shoulder. "So you understand?"

"*Jah*. I do. I need to get away from this little town. Not sure I want to be confined to the Amish, either. Edmond's told me so much about missions. I'd like to go to Haiti and help really poor people."

Hannah put a hand up as if to stop from hearing his voice, but he continued.

"*Daed* wants me to go train one of Mr. Peters' prize hunting dogs to get traveling out of my system. But it won't work. Unless I like Canada and decide to stay. I mean, there're lots of Mennonites up there. Maybe I'll fit in with them."

"Stop! I can't take this. Willow, are you joking?"

"Not at all. I'm a man now and need to find my purpose, and living behind my parents raising dogs isn't it."

"But you help on the little farm. Maybe you need to learn a trade, like carpentry or buggy making. We don't have a maple syrup farm in Smicksburg. You'll inherit land, *jah*?"

Willow stared at her in disbelief. Was she trying to keep him close by? He knew better than to flatter himself. "I need to do this. Can you watch the dogs while I'm gone? I'll pay more since it'd be a big responsibility."

"For how long?"

"I'm still getting it all worked out, but I'm staying for a month."

Letting her head fall into her open hands, Hannah moaned. "A whole month?"

"Or two...depends on where the *Gut* Lord leads me. Takes time to know yourself. Funny that you live every waking hour with yourself and don't know what's in the heart."

Hannah mumbled something under her breath for quite a spell. A cool breeze brought the aroma of freshly cut grass. Two yellow finches darted playfully among the shrubs in the meadow across the street. "Are you mad at me or something? I can find someone else to work for what I pay."

Hannah darted an exasperated scowl at Willow. "You realize what you just told me? You're moving far away and are thinking of leaving the Amish."

"So? Why do you care so much?"

"Willow, this is serious. Where will you live?"

"Don't know yet. *Daed* and *Mamm* want me to find an Old Order Settlement up there, but I need to be up early with the dogs; it seems reasonable that I'd live with the Peters."

Hannah sprung to her feet and ran. Willow ran after her, but she was as swift as a deer. Baffled, he turned to head to his place to talk to his *daed*. Women were a mystery, for sure and certain.

~*~

Mr. Peters,

After some thought, I'd like to take up your offer to train your dog to retrieve ducks out of your lake and much more. We can discuss details when I arrive. But the price you want to pay me is too high. If you can find me lodging not far from your dogs, and feed me three meals a day, it would be more of a retreat for me. I wouldn't mind living in a tent, it being summer and all.

As you know, I'm Old Order Amish. My parents want me to live in an Amish community. I told them I'd ask if there was one near you, even though I think it best if I stay near the dogs. I'd get the job done much quicker.

Let me know when I can come and I'll buy a train or bus ticket.
Thanks for this opportunity,
Willow Byler

~*~

Hannah pinned up her long blonde hair, positioned her prayer *kapp* and sat in the chair near her window for morning devotions. Her bookmarker was placed at Proverbs 20 and she read:

Verse 1. Wine is a mocker, strong drink is raging: and whosoever is deceived thereby is not wise.

This was so true. How many Amish had secretly gone to the bottle? She recalled how Willow walked a mile once a week to check on Ezekiel, his life-long friend, to help him beat his addiction. He kept it all secret, too, not wanting the praise of the People. If Cassia hadn't told her, she'd never know.

Verse 2. The fear of a king is as the roaring of a lion: whoso provoketh him to anger sinneth against his own soul.

Hannah thought of the wrath of kings mentioned in the *Martyr's Mirror*, something her *daed* used to read to the family. She was so thankful to not be living in Europe when long ago thousands of Anabaptists were tortured and killed for their faith.

Verse 3. It is an honour for a man to cease from strife: but every fool will be meddling.

Here she was thinking of Willow again. She'd wanted to pick a fight with him after church, truth be told. But he was as cool as a cucumber.

Verse 4. The sluggard will not plow by reason of the cold; therefore shall he beg in harvest, and have nothing.

She thought of some lazy Amish men, although few and far between, who burdened the *Gmay* with needs that were preventable if they'd just gone out and worked harder.

Verse 5. Counsel in the heart of man is like deep water; but a man of understanding will draw it out.

Willow was the deepest person she knew. It irritated her how she had to drag things out of him, but in the end, she got good advice.

Verse 6. Most men will proclaim everyone his own goodness: but a faithful man who can find.

Hannah wanted to throw her hands up in surrender. *Lord, why am I thinking of Willow so much? Because he's the most faithful male friend I have?* But after Freeman's deception, she appreciated a loyal honest man more. *But, Lord, I want to marry a man, not a boppli!*

Verse 7. The just man walketh in his integrity: his children are blessed after him.

Annoyed, Hannah closed her Bible. Why she was thinking of Willow so much was a mystery, but she had to admit that he'd make a good father, just like his *daed*, being so close with his *kinner*. Reed Byler would be her father-in-law if they wed.

"For Pete's sake," she murmured. "I'm not marrying Willow. Why am I thinking like this?" She'd arranged her day to visit Andy and Sadie Smucker today on her way over to

Katie's Greenhouse. It being Memorial Day, the *English* would buy out all the plants before the Amish could get to them.

~*~

With a buggy loaded down with flats of vegetable and flower plants, satisfied with her purchase at Katie's Greenhouse, Hannah slowed down as she neared the Smucker's. *Providence! Oddly, they're on the front porch!* She waved, and Andy hollered out if she wanted some ice cream. It was in the middle of the day during planting season. Most likely they were taking a break, but Hannah took it as a sign she was to get to know Sadie…and Andy. *Lead my path, Lord. I want a mature man.*

When she pulled into their gravel driveway, Andy was quick to meet her horse and lead it to a hitching post. Taking the reins from her, his dimples deepened, as did his blush. "Buy all the plants over at Katie's?"

"I was glad to get some. Slim pickins' already, even though she doubled the size of her greenhouse. Can't blame the *English* for looking for a bargain. Only a dollar for a six-pack."

Andy was more than interested in her purchases, taking out a flat of bearded pansies. "Ever see one of these pressed in a phone book? Comes out like a butterfly wing. *Mamm* used to sell dried flower pictures."

Having never had a conversation with Andy, he was sweeter than she'd imagined…and taller up close. She was only an inch or two taller. "I'd like to see some of her work. Maybe I could learn and sell them for the benefit auction in August."

"She doesn't do it anymore," he said, his countenance falling, placing the flowers back on the seat. "Come on over and have some ice cream. I made it myself."

Hannah gawked. *He made ice cream?* "Do you bake?"

"*Nee*, only make ice cream," he said as they walked the stone path to the porch.

When she said hello to Sadie, oddly she stuck her nose back in her book, brows furrowed. Andy had to tell her to say hello to their visitor for Sadie to look up. "*Ach*, I'm sorry. I'm at the best part." She shut the book quickly. "We have lots of toppings. I canned berries from last year and our strawberries are coming in."

"I'll get you a bowl," Andy offered, soon leaving Hannah alone with Sadie

"So, where's the rest of your family?" she asked.

"*Mamm* and *Daed* took the bus into Indiana. Told Andy and me to get things done, but it's too hot." She flung a ladybug off her three-quarter-length sleeve. "Sure do wish we didn't have to wear such hot clothing compared to…"

"Compared to where you used to live?" Hannah prodded.

"*Jah*. Out in Ohio."

Sadie's green eyes lost their sparkle and Hannah found herself drawn to her. "I'd miss Smicksburg heaps if I left. Why did you leave Ohio if you liked it so much?"

Sadie's eyes darkened. "*Daed* chose to leave."

Andy soon appeared with a white bowl in hand. "Now, don't be shy. Take as much ice cream as you want. Plenty in there."

Shy? Was she blushing? She didn't think so. Taking the bowl, Hannah made herself a feast of vanilla ice cream, strawberries and chocolate syrup. But there was no place to sit except by Andy on the porch swing. A porch swing made for two.

As if reading her mind, Andy rose and got a spare fold up chair and motioned for her to take the swing. When Hannah tasted her sundae, she couldn't help but lick her lips. "Yum. This is the best ice cream ever."

"A recipe handed down in our family for generations. *Mamm* won't give it out," Andy said with a chuckle.

"She got first place at the State Fair for her pickles," Sadie added, and then covered her mouth. "Oops."

Andy darted a wide-eyed gawk at his sister. "*Mamm's Englisher* friend helped her and took the pickles to the fair." He turned to Hannah. "Don't you think it's odd that the Amish aren't allowed to go to the State Fairs?"

Hannah shrugged. "We can go but not enter our animals or goods. Competition isn't in line with our ways."

"But," Sadie added, "It's a *gut* way to make money. How else will people hear where they can buy good livestock?"

"Word of mouth and local papers, of course," Hannah said. "Some have orders a year in advance. My friend, Willow, raises hunting dogs and there's a waiting list. And we all know that Katie doesn't advertise her greenhouses, but folks from Pittsburgh come up."

Andy leaned back on his chair. "You're right. Now, are all those plants for your kitchen garden?"

"*Jah. Mamm* and I will be planting it tomorrow."

Sadie snickered. "So-called woman's work, but Andy's got a green thumb and does ours."

Hannah gaped. "You put in the garden for your *mamm*?"

"She has a bad back," he was quick to say.

"She's on the couch too much," Sadie groaned.

Again, Andy eyed his sister and Hannah knew for sure there were secrets in this family. No Amish talked down about their parents in public. Something was very mysterious about this family and it got the best of Hannah, wanting to unravel the mystery. "If you have time, can you two come over to my place tomorrow and help me put in the kitchen garden?"

A smile slid across Andy's face, his green eyes glowing. "I can help."

Sadie raised an eyebrow and snickered. "I think I'll be needed here."

Andy reddened. "What time?"

Hannah, flattered to the high heavens that Andy seemed to take such a liking to her, blurted, "Noon. Or, ah, well, before the noon meal, unless you want to eat with us. How about nine and then eat at noon?"

"I'll be there at nine," he said as he got up to take Hannah's empty bowl. "Want more?"

"Sure," she said, hoping this wasn't a dream. Andy had taken quite a shining to her.

Karen Anna Vogel

Chapter 5

Reed turned over the black dirt he'd been nurturing since March, when the weather was milder, and he was pleased to once again be planting his extensive herb garden. Dorcas was in the little plot next to his, tying twine to posts to mark a straight line. As he stared, she was in her twenties again, confident and dedicated to her faith. She'd taken him, shy as he was, with all his eccentricities, and she never tried to change him. He longed for Willow to find such a woman to complement him, and he believed it was Hannah. The young woman's faith was unwavering, breaking up with Freeman, refusing to leave Old Order ways. Hannah could keep his flip-flopping son on the straight and narrow.

"Did you hear me?" Dorcas asked, nearing him.

"*Nee*, suppose I was deep in thought. What is it?"

"Marigolds. Do they really keep rabbits out of the garden?"

"*Jah*. It's in the Farmer's Almanac. Place them six inches apart and –"

"I know that. I just didn't get any this year. Sold out everywhere." She leaned on her spade. "Maybe Cassia has some. I'll ask her when she comes to work."

Reed nodded and continued turning the earth.

"What's wrong?"

"Nothing."

"Spit it out."

Reed's eyes slowly met hers. "It's Willow. What if he goes to Canada and loses his faith? A steady girl like Hannah is what he needs."

"Our son needs to find out for himself how Amish he really is being among the *English*. And it won't last forever."

Read groaned. "What if he meets someone up there who's Mennonite, or worse, *English*?"

Dorcas took his hand. "He needs to fly, *jah*? Look at all the nests and the little ones faltering, plummeting down. I think they'll break their necks, but they don't. I think Willow's our youngest son and we've kept him too near the nest."

"It was his idea to have that house and the dogs…"

"And who lent him the money? Gave him the land?"

Reed scoffed. "We did. I like having family nearby."

"I know, Love, but we need to give Willow over to the Lord. Our plan for Willow may not be God's plan."

He embraced her. "Since when do you call me 'Love'?"

She pushed him away. "I suppose Granny and Jeb are rubbing off on me. Would you rather I call you 'old man'? Granny calls Jeb that, too."

Reed's eyes misted. "We are getting old, aren't we? Soon all the kids will be out of the nest."

Dorcas went on tip-toes to kiss his cheek. "I'm kidding. We're not old. You've been so emotional. It has to be something more."

"Edmond. He's thinking of leaving early for Haiti. Culture shock is too much and he said he wants to fulfill his call to be a single missionary for a while. Maybe he's being tempted to marry someone."

"He was out talking with Lily on the porch the other night..."

From the center of Reed's core bubbled up emotions of joy and anger mixed into a sloppy soup. "For goodness sake. He needs to stay away from my girls."

"He knows that."

"How do you know?"

"I can read between the lines. Edmond's work is so important and he needs to obey the Lord. God's grace keeps in pace with what we face. Edmond's miserable back here in America."

Reed bent down and kissed his wife tenderly. "I love you, Dorcas Byler."

She leaned into him. "Love you, too...old man."

~*~

Running to beat the band, Willow yelled out to Hannah as he rounded the corner into her yard. "Birthing time for Daisy and Daffodil!" He shielded his eyes from the sun and ran to the back door. He knocked, knowing it was noon and folks were eating. Hannah's *mamm*, Esther, yelled come in and he did just that. Through the utility room and into the large kitchen, he tried to catch his breath. When he saw Andy Smucker at the table, he wondered what this picture perfect house needed a carpenter for. "Hi Andy. What're you doing here?"

Hannah shot up. "Willow, what's wrong? You're panting."

"Two dogs in labor. Need help. Can you come over?"

Hannah glanced over at Andy as if to ask permission. What was going on?

"I'm tied up here. Can't your *daed* or Martin help?"

Willow's head snapped back as if he'd been slapped, as it dawned on him as he took in Andy sitting at the table with food before him, and Hannah's furtive glances between him and Willow. "Never mind," he said as he spun around to leave when Andy called after him that he'd help. Hannah said she'd come now too. Now this irritated him more than ever. Willow motioned for them to follow him and started to sprint back home. Not hearing them nearby, he looked back. Andy was handing a few wildflowers to Hannah. *She was courting Andy! He was over at her place to visit, not work.* What a fool he made of himself. Indignant, Willow stopped until they caught up. "You know, the more I think about it, I'll ask Martin. *Gut* idea, Hannah." He avoided eye contact with Andy because jealousy was coursing through his veins.

"Don't be silly," Hannah shouted, running passed him. "I hear Daisy wailing. She's my favorite."

So the three entered his kennel, Hannah making a beeline to Daisy. "It's okay, girl. *Mamm's* here."

Andy pat Willow's back. "We've bred dogs before. Where do you need me?"

Willow could handle Daffodil alone and his mind blanked out. Shrugging, he pointed to a row of dog leashes. "Can you walk some of the dogs? It's getting mighty tense in here and the less dogs the better."

Andy nodded. "Anything to help."

Staying away from Hannah would help, he wanted to say. So this was why she was making a big issue about his age. She was courting a middle-aged man. Andy must be near forty with little to show for it, still at home with his parents, no wife or *kinner*. That he had his eye on Hannah was obvious and Willow knew what he'd be doing tonight. Writing Mr. Peters to move the date of his arrival up by a few weeks.

~*~

Over the next few days, Cassia noticed how down in the mouth her brother was. Leaving for Canada before Anna's arrival was ruining her matchmaking efforts. No matter how hard she tried, Willow couldn't be pried open, but he certainly walked faster than a roadrunner and was mighty quiet.

Cassia poured oil into the tincture bottles and sat down to find a recipe in *Back to Eden* for morning sickness. She hadn't told anyone but Martin she suspected there'd be another *kinner* at her house come autumn. As she took a seat, the bell on the door jingled. "Hannah, so *gut* to see you."

Hannah, basket in tow, grinned. "I've been wanting some alone time with you and knew you worked today."

"Take a seat. Neither of us has been to knitting circle due to planting time and that's when we had more one on one time. So, what's new?"

Hannah repositioned her white prayer *kapp*. "Nothing really. Got the garden in. Looks real nice."

Cassia eyed her friend. "And?"

"And? Why do you say 'And'?" Hannah took a nearby brochure to fan herself.

"*Ach*, what else do you want to tell me? What else would 'and' mean?"

"Andy?" Hannah exclaimed.

Cassia studied her friend. She was clearly nervous. "I heard Andy Smucker helped with the dogs. Was surprised because he's never come around here. But I don't think Willow will keep him on. Personality clash or something…"

"Keep him on? Did he offer Andy a job?"

"Well, that's what I thought. Willow's been silent as the grave, not to be morbid. He's leaving early for Canada. *Mamm* and *Daed* might be able to change his mind. Haste never was a *gut* thing." She crossed her legs. "That girl keeps writing him about her dog and it scares me to no end she may catch his eye."

Hannah clasped her hands together, resting them on her lap. "Willow and I have been quarreling. He may be leaving over that."

"Willow's so easy-going, just talk to him and make things right."

"I, ah, may make things worse…"

Cassia didn't know this dear friend of hers sitting next to her. Hannah had become so mysterious. She was too emotional. "How can you make things worse?"

"I'm getting to know Andy Smucker and…"

"And what?" Cassia clenched her book tight. "Andy Smucker? You're courting him? He's ancient!"

"He's only thirty-five, Martin's age," Hannah defended. "It just happened so fast. I didn't have time to tell you."

"*Ach*, Hannah, you're not healed over your break-up with Freeman."

"*Jah*, I am." Hannah straightened. "And not long ago you were mad I turned down Willow for a buggy ride, so you know I've moved on. What's wrong with Andy?"

Cassia wanted to scream, 'He's not Willow!' Couldn't her friend see what a treasure he was? But she silently prayed for words and the image of Anna came to mind. "Martin's sister's coming down for the summer. Maybe Willow will stay longer when he finds out."

"Cassia, don't change the subject. You should be happy for me. Remember when we thought we'd be spinsters, sitting around with our cats spinning wool?"

Cassia closed her eyes. "How long have you been so-called courting Andy?"

"He came over to help plant our garden and we're taking a buggy ride this weekend."

"One little outing and now you're talking marriage? You don't really know Andy."

Hannah shot up. "Cassia, I didn't say marriage, but, I like what I see and he's given me hope. Hope that a mature Amish man still exists who's never been married."

"*Ach*, now your back on that maturity thing. Willow's more mature than you." Cassia covered her mouth and stared into Hannah's hurt eyes. "I'm sorry," she said, grabbing Hannah to embrace her. "Where's our friendship going?"

"Not in a *gut* place," Hannah said with clenched teeth.

Cassia took Hannah's hands and searched her eyes. "We need to knit together."

"It's summer time. Too much to get done."

"So? If we don't make time for each other, I fear...I'll lose my best friend."

Hannah's eyes clouded. "You have to stop trying to make a match out of Willow and me. I read *Emma* and she learned to not put her nose in everyone's business, *jah*?"

Cassia didn't want to mention that Granny Weaver had paired many happy couples but shook her head in agreement.

Willow came in from the farmhouse and upon seeing Hannah, he turned to head back in.

"Come on in, *bruder*. It's not private."

"*Jah*, Willow, come visit," Hannah encouraged.

Willow's face contorted as he crossed the shop to grab a bottle. "I have a headache. Getting some Devil's Claw Root."

Determined, Cassia took both Hannah and Willow's hands. "We've been childhood friends. Feelings have been hurt, but we all move on, *jah*? We all want God's will. He has a plan and we need to follow it."

Willow stared at the floor. "*Jah*, you're right."

Hannah's chin quivered with emotion and lunged at Willow to embrace him. "I'm sorry if I hurt you. Don't leave for Canada because of me."

Cassia, seeing the two embracing, wanted to shout a hardy 'Amen' like her Baptist friends, but just watched in awe.

"I'm not leaving because of you," Willow said, patting her back. "I got that travel fever *Daed* talks about and like I said, I need to leave to see if I'm Amish."

Hannah withdrew and smoothed her apron. "Okay, but when you're up there, you'll write, *jah*?"

He nodded. "And you'll be taking care of the dogs along with Martin and *Daed*."

"And Anna's coming, Willow," Cassia added. "She can help, too."

Willow's eyes twinkled. "Hope she doesn't talk their tails off. When's she coming?"

"Next week," Cassia informed.

He scratched the back of his neck. "Maybe I can stay a week longer to train her."

"I can train Anna." Hannah sighed. "We really don't need her."

Cassia noticed how their eyes lingered on each other. Hannah seemed a bit touchy about Anna coming. Cassia was elated.

~*~

Reed stared in wonder at basil sprouting. It was a miracle every time. A dead seed coming to life. It was like the resurrection and he pat the little plant in holy reverence. *Danki Lord for the earth that provides our food. Foods that can heal.* "Help me find the right tincture for Mrs. Eberly to help her arthritis."

"You do it, too?"

"What?" Reed asked, turning to see Edmond.

"Talk to plants," Edmond said, plunging his hands in his jean pockets.

"Didn't hear you pull up. Give up your car?"

"No, not yet. Thought about it."

"Son, you're becoming more Amish than you think. What's going on?"

"Can we talk? Have time to spare?"

Reed's heart warmed. "Always for my *Englisher* Son. Let's go get a glass of iced tea and sit on the front porch."

"Lily's there, nose in a book. Just like Cassia."

The hair on the back of Reed's neck rose and a chill rippled down his spine. He felt the familiar need to pace. Pacing worked nervous tension out. Reed nodded as to motion Edmond to follow him and he hastened his walk around the big farmhouse to see Lily on the porch swing. "Lily, you need to help your *mamm.*"

"She's at the knitting circle," Lily said, eyes wide.

"Then, well, go and help clean the house."

"Just mopped down the floors, *redd* up the whole house and have everything ready for the noon meal."

Reed slowly closed his eyes. His daughter was mature beyond her years. "Well, how about making some iced tea for Edmond and me."

She smiled at Edmond. "You like meadow tea. Just made a gallon."

Reed darted a gaze between his daughter and Edmond. Was it his imagination or was there romance in the air? He shook his head to clear it. "*Danki*, Lily, we'll take a pitcher full."

She was soon out of sight and Reed took a seat on his rocker while Edmond took the swing. A robin chirped and then flew up on the rafter to her nest.

"You're like Saint Francis, the animals not afraid of you," Edmond said. "Most fly off the porch when I come."

"You come? On this porch? When?"

He fumbled. "L-Lily and I talk a lot out here. She's been pretty helpful. Lots of insight."

The screen door slammed behind Lily and she struggled to carry the pitcher and glasses. Edmond jumped up to take them from her. "Was telling your dad how the birds never go to their nests when we're out here."

"*Nee*, the fly away. Three little nests making new families right here on the porch." She held her middle. "God puts the lonely in families."

Reed felt his blood boil. "What are you saying, Lily? You think Edmond's lonely and needs to marry?"

"Maybe. Not normal to stay single."

Edmond's countenance fell as he plopped down on the swing. "You may be right. It's why I'm leaving for a while. Find time to seek God. I'm headed to a nature camp for troubled youth. Nature has a way of putting things in perspective."

Reed threw his arms up. "You live in the boon doggies. More cows than people. And you're a medicine man. Don't you have paperwork to get done, like you said?"

Edmond slowly nodded, his jaw set firm. "I have it done. I'm a real doctor, just like I've planned for years, but don't care."

Lily sat next to him. "You've been finding so many things vain, *jah*? You sound like King Solomon, 'vanity of vanities! All is vanity.' Edmond, I hate seeing you so discontent."

"Vain?" Reed barked. "Edmond, we've worked hard on you being a doctor for a reason. Help the sick. It's your calling. Do you think I get up every day and skip into the herb shop?"

"You don't?" Edmond blurted.

"Of course not. I get travel fever and drool over medical conference brochures. My restlessness may last for a few days, but then that settling comes."

"That 'knowing'?" Lily asked. "You just know that you're supposed to be doing something."

"*Jah*," he said. "God's not unstable. He doesn't lead us to be a doctor to go off and help troubled youth."

Edmond slumped and twiddled his thumbs. "I know I'm in the way over at the Adam's. They're nice enough to let me stay for the summer, but they need a break."

Lily beamed. "You could stay here! There're lots of spare rooms."

Reed gawked as his daughter smiled so broadly, it looked unnatural. "*Nee*, Edmond, you best be going to that camp. If you made the commitment and all." He eyed Lily. "Now you skedaddle. We have men talk."

"I'm not a *boppli*."

"Did I say a baby? *Nee*, I said men talk."

She grinned at Edmond. "*Gut* seeing you. And I'm done with *Moby Dick*. What else can I read?"

He snickered. "I'll find something. Can't believe you like adventure books."

"I like romances, too, if it's *gut* and clean," she twinkled.

Reed put a hand over his mouth to hold it shut. Watching the two of them brought back memories of Edmond and his other daughter's secret engagement and break-up. Cassia was depressed for eons and he wouldn't let that happen with his Lily. But he couldn't accuse Edmond of flirting. Nor being a charmer. When Lily was gone from sight, he wagged a finger at Edmond. "Stay away. She's only eighteen and you're not Amish."

He hung his head. "It's why I'm leaving. I'm ten years older, but she's grown up. Has a real good listening ear and will make some Amish man happy."

"*Jah*, she will. But I'm in no hurry for her to wed. She's a *gut* teacher. Always finding time to read stories to pass on to the *kinner*."

Edmond shifted. "She must be lonely during summer break."

"Not so lonely that she has to spend so much time pouring over books with you. Edmond, it's how you and Cassia got tangled up. Can't you find a nice missionary *English* girl?"

Edmond bit his lower lip. "I'm praying on being single still. God calls some to remain single since having a family's a distraction. But it's hard. There aren't many called down this road."

Reed understood. He was a misfit among the Amish, being so highly educated and traveling if he got permission. A keen mind for learning is what God gave him, but it came with 'Mad Doc' jokes. "I'll be praying for you, Son."

CHAPTER 6

When planting season was over, the herb gardens fenced in to ward off deer and rabbits, Reed put his feet up on the footstool under the new arbor he'd put in for shade and to give Dorcas her dream. An English ivy covered space for lawn furniture where the two of them could enjoy morning coffee. He opened his Bible. 'Water for the soul' as he called it, and since Willow was heavy on his heart, he read Ezekiel 17, the verses from which he and Dorcas had picked their son's name.

He also took a seedling from the land and planted it in fertile soil.
He placed it beside a broad river, where it could grow like a willow tree.
It took root there and grew into a low, spreading vine.
Its branches turned up toward the eagle, and its roots grew down into the ground.
It produced strong branches and put out shoots.

Willow trees grew fast, their roots routing out water, so thirsty they were. Reed and Dorcas wanted their son to thirst after the Living Waters, the Lord God above. But Reed's objection to the name was that willow trees could be blown over easily, not like the majestic oak that took longer to grow. He smiled, remembering her face when he suggested 'Oak' or 'Maple'. Dorcas had one humdinger of a fit. *He can call himself Will if he doesn't like Willow. I'll not have my son be named Maple!* she'd reasoned. *And we'll pray he thirsts all the more for God and gets plenty strong. He'll look to God and get wings like an eagle.* Reed picked up Dorcas and spun her around, so thrilled he was that they'd agreed. And their son went by Will until recently, requesting he be called Willow.

Something about this trip to Canada didn't settle right with Reed, but he couldn't hold him back. He wouldn't hold him back because Willow needed to find his bend. *Lord, cause my son to thirst for you. Keep him by streams of living water where he can grow and bear fruit and not wither up. Keep his faith strong.*

A harmonica sounded off in the distance and Reed chuckled, knowing Lily could play better than anyone, but would so-call 'faint' if anyone knew she played outside the comfort-zone of their land. Three houses on the property with many acres gave them the privacy to be the so-called eccentric Bylers that they were. "Creative," he said. "Lord help the Amish if creativity is squelched. You created, Lord, so why shouldn't we?"

He heard someone clearing their throat to make their presence known. "*Jah*, I'm talking out loud to God. Who is it?"

Willow played a quick run up his harmonica. "Didn't you hear me playing?" He took a seat next to his *daed*.

"Thought it was Lily."

"She can't play as well as me and she's so shut up inside reading all the time, I haven't heard her play in a while."

Reed cracked a knuckle. "She misses teaching." A slight breeze wafted over his face and he closed his eyes, taking in the scents of this June day.

"Too tired to talk, *Daed*?"

"*Ach, nee*. I can smell better with my eyes closed. It's scientific, you know. One of our senses takes over when others are shut down."

Willow raised his brows. "Now that's something to think about, but I wanted to, well, confess something to you while I have the nerve."

"What is it?"

"Well, I got my picture taken for the passport. I know the Amish can go through loopholes and all, but I wanted to do it all legal."

Reed's eyes bulged. "We are exempt. You just need other evidence, tax records and whatnot. Willow Byler, what's gotten into you?"

Willow stood his ground. "*Daed*, I'm not baptized, and I guess I wanted to see how it felt to be *English*."

Reed shot up. "And how do you feel?"

"Stupid. I can't get my passport for three weeks now, and that's with it being expedited. Sure do hope Mr. Peters still wants me to come up."

Reed's arms flailed about, but he had no words to say. He couldn't force his son to be Amish. But having his picture taken, knowing he didn't have to, was a brazen move. *Lord, help me. I cast this on You.* He slowly sat down and picked up his Bible, opened to where it was marked and began to read.

"Is this some kind of shunning?" Willow asked lightheartedly. "I'm in *rumspringa*."

He raised a hand. "Don't want to say something I'll regret."

"*Ach, Daed*, are you sore at me?"

"Son, we measure our words, *jah*? Right now, I don't have any. Let this old man calm down." He took a swig of meadow tea and out of the corner of his eye he saw Willow swing a foot onto his knee and pull a little book out of his vest. "What are you reading?"

"The Bible Edmond gave me. A new translation more understandable."

Reed tapped his Bible. "He got me one, too. This here Bible is something we have in common, son, forever. It's the rock that doesn't move, even if we do. Even if you leave." He lowered his straw hat and bit back tears.

"*Daed*, I think I'm Amish, but need to be sure. Don't cry."

He coughed. "Who's crying? Must be allergies or something."

~*~

Hannah purled one, knit one to make a seed pattern while Cassia sat next to her. The silence was actually a sign that their friendship was on even keel again. No nervous chatter to fill the spaces. With baby Rose asleep in the bassinette next to her *mamm*, she wondered if Cassia just appreciated silence all the more. "You look real content. So happy for you about the new *boppli*."

"We're excited," Cassia said. "I have been awful nauseated, though, so Anna coming today will be a relief. Martin's happy to have kin around, too, being so outnumbered with us Bylers."

Taking in a deep breath, Hannah hadn't felt this relaxed in a while. "Knitting sure is *gut* for the nerves."

Cassia eyed her. "Things not going well with Andy?"

"*Jah*...okay. He's real nice."

"And?"

"Mysterious. Their whole family baffles me. It's like they tempt God. Our *Ordnung* is clear about owning some things, but I see them in their home."

"Really?" Cassia blurted. "Like what? A television?"

"*Ach, nee*, nothing like that. Sadie has a cell phone. She said she only reads books on it, whatever that means. Phones were allowed when they lived out in Ohio..."

"But not here. Does Jeb Weaver know? He's the bishop and wise. Maybe he's letting them ease in?"

Hannah knit all the faster. "I doubt it. But that's not the worst of it. They have a camera. I saw it with my own two eyes."

Cassia put her knitting to her chest. "What?"

"I asked Andy about it and he said they were allowed in Ohio, too. He takes pictures of images in books customers want him to carve."

"Why can't they just leave the picture?" Cassia asked.

"That's what I suggested. He doesn't want to take the chance of using expensive books while carving. I guess he doesn't want to ruin something so valuable."

"Hogwash," Cassia groaned. "We have old books. They're not worth twisting up our People's ways."

Hannah knew her friend was right. "Maybe I should tell Jeb and he can have a talking to with the whole Smucker family. Martha, the *mamm*, runs a mixer. They have free natural gas and they somehow figured a way to have a few electric appliances."

Cassia held her stomach. "Don't tell me anymore. I feel a flutter."

"The *boppli?*"

"Don't know. Could be my nerves now. Hannah, the Smuckers are playing with fire. Jeb does need to know." She leaned towards Hannah. "And why don't they ever fellowship with any of us?"

Hannah shook her head. "I don't know. Maybe their secrets would get out."

"But the best part of being Amish is fellowship, sharing life in community. I never see anyone over there on an off-Sunday."

Hannah sighed. "I know. What I think is that they may have been Beachy Amish out in Ohio and are having a time with being Old Order. Andy hinted that his parents are struggling."

Cassia reached for her hand. "You're my kindred-spirit friend. I couldn't bear to see you hurt again. Maybe they were Mennonites and trying to be Amish and not making it. *Ach*, Hannah, Freeman broke your heart, trying to lure you from our ways. Don't see Andy anymore until you talk to Jeb."

Hannah saw love in Cassia's chestnut colored eyes. *And she never brought up Willow.* "*Danki*, dear friend. I'll talk with Jeb."

~*~

Later that night, Anna arrived and although she was a chatterbox, it was all catching up news about Marathon, New York and things not mentioned in letters. But Anna appeared to be more mature and didn't rattle on non-stop. Cassia was feeling pretty satisfied with herself. She'd made a meal without burning a thing, not giving Willow any room to tease her, and right now she saw her *bruder* near gawking at Anna. "Willow, help me slice up dessert."

"Girls do that."

"*Ach*, Anna's our guest and I need help."

"I'll help," Anna offered. "I'm not tired at all." A smile slipped across her face. "I've missed my *bruder* and his little family."

Martin's mellow brown eyes misted. "You can stay as long as you want. Built this house big enough for company."

Cassia put angel food cake on plates as Anna passed them out. "Martin, it was only two years ago you were in a wheelchair and now here you are, in this beautiful house you've built."

Martin pointed to Willow. "He did the most."

"You had a whole crew," Willow protested. "I just live close-by and it wasn't a bother."

"When you're running as big a kennel as you have, customers coming down this little back road with license plates from across the country, I say you sacrificed time, and I'm thankful." Martin took a bite of cake. "Now who made this?"

Cassia grinned. "I did."

Willow bust out laughing. "Cassia, you did not. *Mamm* made it."

"Willow Byler, I made that cake. When will you realize I learned to bake last year? I'm not laughing at your burnt offering jokes anymore."

"Calm down, Cassia" Martin encouraged. "Remember…doc said you need to keep calm."

Cassia felt heat rise from her neck to her the roots of her hair in no time. Silence hung in the room until Anna broke it. "Cassia, you're having another *boppli*?"

"*Jah*, I am," she said, feeling like crying and laughing at the same time.

"*Ach*, Cassia, another Byler running around," Willow quipped. "Hope it's a boy so we can do men things."

"He'll be a Miller, too," Anna corrected. "Is that why you asked me to come down? Not just to help with Rose?"

Cassia wanted to get back at Willow. Wanting to scream he needed a woman in his life. But she just gazed at her *bruder* and coyly said, "*Ach*, many reasons. Willow, why don't you show Anna your dogs? She'll be helping you, *jah*?"

Willow's glare could bore a hole in Cassia's head, but she didn't care. She smirked and said, "Better do it before it gets dark."

The next day, Willow's head was in a whirl. Anna was as sweet as iced tea. Respect for all he did with his dogs was evident, too. Respect. Something Hannah lacked. She took for granted what a hard worker he was and thought she could run the place all by herself. His breath shortened. That's it. Ask Hannah to be in charge of the dogs when he's gone. Give her the pay he'd give three and then she'd see what he really did.

But Anna was so eager to help. Put her in charge to boss around Hannah? "Someone younger," he moaned. Needing to talk to Jeb about his final plans and mixed up emotions, he decided to take the family buggy over to see the wise bishop. He snapped the reins and off he went, into the sweet morning air. Misty fog swirled and Willow saw little tornados. How he loved to see images in the clouds, but here he was, seeing tornadoes. Would he ever be able to care for someone else besides Hannah? He'd kept his love for her a secret for years, but something had changed: his need to settle down and start a family. Did seeing his sister with a family make him yearn for it? Maybe he did need to leave to meet more people. *Can't tell a gut coon dog unless you've tried a few.* To him, a family always included Hannah at the helm. "She's bossy enough," he murmured.

His horse snorted as if in agreement. God talked to Balaam through a donkey; maybe this old girl was smarter than he thought. "*Jah*, she's bossy."

He was soon on the heels of another buggy headed in the same direction. He could see though the tiny square window a white prayer *kapp*, so it was a woman. But the horse was white, and with that realization, he moaned. *Hannah*. A turtle could beat her; such a slow poke she was. If buggies had horns, he'd honk it.

When he rounded the turn and could see for a mile straight, he pulled over to pass her up. As he did, he waved and yelled a 'hello'. He raced up his horse and felt the wind blow his hair up, almost losing his straw hat. Half-way up the hill, he let the horse walk, not wanting to strain the animal any further. "*Gut* girl," he said. "*Gut* job."

Willow noticed the red winged blackbirds for the first time this summer. He'd been too cooped up with the dogs to appreciate spring. He hadn't even gone out in April to see the trillium, such a rare flower that bloomed too infrequently. *Lord, I need to adopt the pace of nature, like Daed always says. I'm too restless, in a hurry on the inside and out. Edmond feels the trip to Canada will give me perspective and broaden my understanding of human nature. Lead me.*

He turned around a sharp bend and heard the clatter of metal tires. Surely Hannah's not racing him! Not on this turn. He pulled over and let her pass in his lane. "Slow down!" he yelled, but Hannah was basking in all her glory, waved and called out "Slow poke!"

"Slow down," he cried. "Head strong woman!" Willow lingered behind, but when he saw her pull into Jeb Weaver's place, he gripped the reins. Most likely she was doing some knitting with Granny and talking about her new-found love for Andy Smucker. Her horse, now exhausted, was slow as molasses in January. The dirt road leading to the Weaver's was narrow and he was boxed in. He yelled out, "I should walk. I'd get there sooner!"

Laughing reverberated from ahead. "Go ahead, Will. Free country."

So she was being feisty. He liked that. He pulled the buggy over to a nearby tree and roped it up and then sprint on down the road. Being a fast runner, he was soon ahead and he egged Hannah on. "I'll get a carrot out of Roman's garden and maybe your dumb horse will pick up some speed."

She had that same old childhood, broad-faced, missing tooth grin. "Better watch out or you'll get trampled."

"Don't think so…."

In a flash, the horse was upon him and he jumped off the road. Hannah let out a victory cry and left him in a cloud of dust. He burst into laughter.

CHAPTER 7

They ran up the steps to the Weaver's. "I win!" Hannah cried, touching the screen door.

"*Nee*, I did."

"It's a tie?" she giggled.

"We both win. I'm here to see Jeb and you Granny, *jah?*"

"*Nee*, Jeb. Important matters…with the *Ordnung*."

"You doubt it, too?"

Hannah gawked. "Heaven's no. Willow, do you?" She felt her mouth grow dry. "Maybe you just don't understand it."

"Come on in," Jeb's voice was heard through the screen door. Opening it, he offered them meadow tea, which they both accepted and in no time he had two glasses full at his long oak table. "Now, what do *yinz* want to talk about? I think I know but want to hear it straight from you two." He folded his hands with satisfaction. "Deborah's been praying for this day, but she's out picking berries with Lizzie"

Hannah sipped her tea. "I came to talk to *you* private-like."

"Me, too." Willow gulped down his entire glass of tea.

Jeb looked up as his eyes danced. "Can't fool me. I have plenty of courting couples come here for advice. Let's kill two birds with one stone, like the saying goes. Now, Willow, what's bothering you about Hannah?"

"She's bossy and shows me no respect."

Aghast, Hannah exclaimed, "I said we're not courting!"

Jeb ignored her. "Well, looks like opposites are attracting and sparks are flying. You know that was me and Deborah back in the day. I was raised too strict and she was a liberal Amish woman, in my opinion."

"Granny, liberal?" Willow chuckled. "You straightened her out then?"

Hannah felt like her face would catch fire. "Straighten her *out*?"

"Well, like the Good Book says, 'iron sharpens iron'. We near killed each other, our tongues sharp towards each other, but she opened my eyes to new ideas and other Amish ways."

Hannah forced herself to breathe evenly. "She was from Ohio, *jah*? From a Beachy or Mennonite background?"

"*Ach*, Old Order," Jeb quipped. "But she wanted a clothes dryer back in 1963. Her beau turned Mennonite and tried to lure her away with all the new modern contraptions." His eyes landed on Willow. "A *gut* woman speaks her mind, not timid-like, but wants the best for you. Makes the best *of* you, even when it hurts."

"When do you know to give up trying to change someone?" Hannah asked.

Jeb's brows creased. "Is Willow beyond repair?"

"We're not courting," Hannah said evenly. "I'm meant Freeman, my beau who led me to believe he'd turn Amish."

Jeb wagged a finger. "Someone who loves you never leads you to anything but the truth. Didn't you see in Freeman his resistance? How many times did he cancel to come talk to me about baptism?"

Hannah lowered her head. "Countless, I suppose." She blinked back tears, embarrassed about how naïve she was. A hand on her back startled her. She looked over at Willow. *What was he doing?*

"You were patient with him is all. Nothing bad about that."

"Of course not," Jeb said, "but he did lead her to a falsehood."

Hannah stared hard at Jeb. "So, watch behavior closely and don't make excuses for stepping outside the *Ordnung*?"

"Hannah, of course," Jeb blurted. "Willow isn't baptized yet, so him going to Canada for a spell won't hurt a thing. Love can grow while apart."

Willow looked at her love-struck, and Hannah had had enough. "Jeb, I'm not upset about Willow leaving!"

"Then why are you yelling?"

"Because I came over here to talk to you about Andy Smucker, not Willow!"

Willow ambled off the bench and headed out onto the porch. Hannah's heart sunk. Now she'd done it; hurt her friend after a two-week smooth patch.

"I can see I've been a fool," Jeb groaned. "Deborah prays so hard about couples being together, I figured you were, well, an answer to her many prayers." He cracked a few knuckles. "So you like Andy Smucker?"

"We've been talking and he's mature. *Jah*, I like him."

Jeb reached for her hands and grasped them. "Eyes wide open, *jah*? No more excuses?"

"His sister has a cell phone and there're other modern conveniences in the house," Hannah despaired. "Why?"

Jeb's lips parted but not a murmur came out. He bowed his head and it appeared he was in silent prayer for a spell. "You stay away from him until I get to the bottom of it all."

"So you think they're living outside our rules?"

He wagged a finger. "Of course. And I'm glad you had the sense to talk to me. Already you've learned to not overlook faults and see everything through rose colored glasses." He pointed to the door. "Except for Willow out there; now you need to put those kind of glasses on and stop counting his faults."

"He's two years younger," she protested.

"*Humph*. More mature than most elderly Amish men. Takes after his *daed*."

Hannah felt fully rebuked and put in her place. Did everyone in the whole village of Smicksburg think she was supposed to marry Willow? Why? "Well, I best let Willow have his time with you. Guess he has a question…" She rose and took her empty glass to the sink. "When's Granny getting back?"

"Not sure. Hopefully not until later because that'll mean more berries…and pies."

"I should be out picking. Maybe Sadie Smucker would like to see the best patches…"

"Stay away from the Smuckers until I talk to them," Jeb reminded her.

Hannah nodded and made a beeline to the door. Willow sat on the rocker, slouched and looking defeated. "I'm sorry to hurt you, Willow."

"A little bit of bacon makes a dog take his medicine."

"What?"

Willow rolled his eyes. "You could use a dose of sweetener like…."

Pressing fists into her hips, Hannah exclaimed, "Anna?"

"*Jah*, Anna. I read Dale Carnegie's book, *How to Win Friends and Influence People*, and she has it nailed. She'll be in charge of talking to customers. You can…keep the dogs clean."

"What?" Her eyeballs bulged. "I'll quit before that happens."

"Give me two weeks notice and help train Anna. Okay?"

This pricked Hannah to her core. So Willow liked Anna, preferred her. Not being the apple of Willow's eye hurt more than she expected. Speechless at Willow's directness, which made him strangely seem more mature, she only nodded and ran to her buggy.

~*~

Jeb groaned as he stared at Willow from across the table. "She said what?"

"Do I have to repeat it again?"

Taking a handkerchief, Jeb wiped perspiration off his forehead. "How old is this girl?"

"Eighteen, and her name's Cheri." Should he have told Jeb his suspicions on what a flirt she was? Writing letters already about wanting to take him to parties full of alcohol, which led down the wrong path.

"Are you telling me everything? Don't hold back."

"Well, that's about it. Her language is fowl, I know, but some Amish swear, too."

Jeb swatted at the air. "But it's not accepted, and we have correction. *Englishers*, not all, but most, don't like being corrected, especially at eighteen."

"I'll stay away from her. Going to camp out by the dogs and seek God. Edmond Ledger suggested it. 'Know thyself,' he said. An ancient Greek saying that means to not pay so much to what others think and…find yourself."

"*Ach*, Willow, that's *furhoodled* in the head. The Bible says to forget yourself and serve others."

"*Daed* says we all have a natural bend or talent that's God-given. What's so *furhoodled* about that?"

Jeb groaned. "If it leads you away from the Amish?"

Willow didn't flinch. "You left the *Swartzentruber* Amish and found yourself here in *Smicksburg, jah*?"

Jeb lowered his gaze. "*Jah*, you're right. Hurt many I loved, but I couldn't go with such a strict *Ordnung*."

Willow finished his iced tea. "So, you're still okay with me going?"

Jeb blew air onto his gray bangs, making them flutter. "Promise me if you find this girl leading you into sin, you'll leave or call for help. Be like Joseph in the Bible and run for your life?"

"*Jah*, I will." A smile slid across Willow's face. Jeb Weaver was one animated man. "The other thing I came to ask you about is Martin's sister, Anna."

"Nice girl. Pretty, too."

"*Jah.* I've thought for ages Hannah would be the one for me, but now I see how sassy she is and doesn't respect me. Anna does, and it feels *gut*. Is that wrong?"

"Men need to be respected. We thrive off it. Maybe that's why Hannah gets under your skin. She sees you as Cassia's little *bruder, jah?*"

"*Jah*, and she's becoming less appealing to me. I think I need time away to know my mind about what makes a *gut* wife and if I can bow my knees to Amish ways."

Jeb's eyes softened into deep turquoise pools. "Know thyself, Willow, and I'll be praying for you. Write me if you need anything."

Willow, at this moment, didn't feel confined by Amish rules, but loved by his dear bishop, a man who wanted him to walk with God more than any set denomination. "*Danki*, Jeb. I'll miss you."

~*~

Willow kicked a stone down the dirt road leading to his little house. His comfort zone for too long. To the right he spied Anna running down the hill from Cassia's house. He swallowed. Should he ask her to take a buggy ride? Jeb's advice was sound and his *daed's* was too. He straightened and headed towards her to meet at the white fence. "Hello, Anna. How are you?"

"*Gut*. Want to come in to play Dutch Blitz? The more the merrier."

As the sun was setting far off on the horizon, magenta ebbing through the trees, he pointed towards the heavens. "I like being outside in summer. Want to go fishing?"

"Fishing?" she asked, clasping her hands.

"Fishing. *Jah*, they bite when the sun's down. We have a fishing hole we stock, so you're sure to catch something."

"*Ach*, I love to fish. I've gone with my *daed* on the ice up in New York."

"Ice fishing? Are you serious?"

"*Jah*. I didn't pack my pole, so I'll need to borrow one."

"I have a rod you can use and lots of earthworms."

She spun around and ran back up to Cassia's, yelling back, "I'll be ready in a jiffy."

Willow felt his heart skip. She was saying 'yes', but did she think it was an *English* date, not being a Sunday Singing and all? Why the Amish only paired up after Singings bothered him to no end. All cooped up in a barn, young people gawking at each other. He often thought he should get up and auction off girls to the highest bidder.

Willow pulled a tall reed of grass and positioned it between his thumbs and blew through it. A loud whistle bellowed out and some of his dog's must have heard. "*Ach, nee*. They'll yap until I go pet them. All ten of them."

Anna hummed as she ran down the hill and then looked at Willow, dumfounded. "Something wrong with your dogs?"

"I whistled through this stupid grass and it's one of the signs I want to play."

Anna's white teeth actually glimmered in the moonlight as the sky became inky. "Let's pet them then. Can't get enough of your dogs."

"But you want to fish, *jah*?"

"Let's do both," Anna shrugged. "It's only eight-thirty. Plenty of time…to spend together."

Willow caught her meaning. One thing he liked about Anna was she didn't put on airs, like Hannah. He felt like taking her hand but didn't. Maybe as the night crept on, he would. He jutted his chin towards his house, some thirty feet away. "Let's go calm down the pack. Which one's your favorite?"

"Well, I like Australian Shepherds, the black, brown and white ones. They remind me of those old-fashioned dogs that carry barrels under their necks to save people."

"*Ach*, those were Saint Bernard's. Legend has it that the monks of Saint Bernard gave brandy to dogs with barrels attached for search and rescue. They didn't know back then that alcohol made hyperthermia worse."

"That's interesting, Willow. So, are dogs used today for search and rescue?"

"For sure. People still get lost in cold places or lost and such. I never really cared to train my dogs to rescue but I might have to when I go to Canada."

Anna hung her head, staring at the ground before her as they neared his house. "Cassia told me you were leaving. How long will you be gone?"

"I'll be here for two more weeks and then I'm off. Need to find myself, I suppose. You know I'm not baptized."

Anna took a seat on his front porch. "Dogs seem to be calming down. They hear our voices."

He nodded and sat on the other chair. "Maybe I spooked them. We can just go straight to fishing."

She crossed her legs. "I understand about finding yourself. When I came down to see my *bruder* when he was sick, I learned lots. A new place gives you new perspective."

"Seriously? I noticed you're, well…"

"Not a chatterbox?" She laughed. "I was nervous, always trying to please everyone."

"So, how'd you learn to be calm down here?" Willow asked.

"Well, we thought Martin would die when he came here. We didn't know he had Lyme Disease and your *daed* and Cassia would cure him. When I was here, I saw Cassia's love for Martin. The whole community, actually, and it got me thinking about the healing power of love. Does this sound corny?"

"*Nee*, go on," Willow urged, taking in Anna's beauty, inside and out.

"Well, we live more rural in New York, houses are far apart. Down here, neighbors can walk to each other's houses and it amazed me how much they did. Granny Weaver, the sweet lady, taught me tons about love and community and I put into practice her advice."

"Which was?"

"Be slow to talk, eager to listen, and reach out to others who are hurting. It was hard not to talk so much at first," she laughed, "but when I paid attention, really caring about other's pain, I wasn't needing to think of what I was going to say next. I did that a lot. Pride, I suppose, thinking I knew it all."

Willow leaned his chin on his hand as he stared at her. "I don't think you're proud at all. Some girls around here need put down a wrung or two." He groaned, hoping his anger towards Hannah wasn't too evident. He slapped his knee. "Best get those fishing poles."

"Cassia's upset Hannah, too. I think Hannah's hurting, don't you? Maybe jealous? She's Cassia's age and doesn't have a husband and *boppli* yet."

Dumbstruck, Willow stared ahead. "How did you know I was talking about Hannah?"

She stood up and pressed wrinkles from her apron. "I listen, remember? You're upset with her for other reasons, though."

Feeling challenged, he rose to meet her gaze. "She's hurt my sister, but also acts all puffed up."

"Said no to a buggy ride, *jah*?"

"How did you know?"

With huge sympathetic eyes that drew him in, she said, "I overheard Cassia and Martin talking." She took his arm and steered him towards the door. "Now, enough of this and go get those poles. I love to fish."

Willow obeyed, with a skip in his step. Anna actually seemed happy that Hannah turned him down, and there'd be no other reason for that then if she liked him. He wanted to throw is straw hat up, but contained himself.

Karen Anna Vogel

CHAPTER 8

Hannah crossed Willow's place and sighed with relief that he was nowhere in sight. She hastened her step as she was already late to visit and play Dutch Blitz. But she heard a scream in the woods. Willow! She dashed towards the path that led to the fishing hole. Images of him drowning made her heart race. "I'm coming," she yelled.

But as she neared, she heard a female voice...and laughter. *Cassia and Willow were up to their childhood ways again.* How many times had they taken the rope and splashed in that pond? And of course Willow could swim, he wasn't drowning. It being a muggy hot night, she too would jump in, like old times, leeches or not.

The full moon cast a warm glow over the pond and she almost made her presence known until she heard Anna squeal, swinging from the rope. *Anna? Anna and Willow?* She wanted to laugh and cry at the same time. Were they horsing around or was this a secret romance?

As Anna splashed into the pond, Willow swam near her and she couldn't make out what was going on. Were they talking? Surely not kissing? Were they? Feeling like a complete idiot, she stayed a spell, watching the two. She heard chatter. Lots of chatter coming out of Willow Byler's mouth. He never chattered on with her. Was Anna's chatter swallowed up by Willow? Or did she bring him out of his shell?

The longer they stayed in the water, the more irritated Hannah became until indignation sprung up full force. How could Willow ask her to court not long ago and as soon as Anna came, he acted like she was leftover meatloaf? Hurt pierced her heart, but she didn't know why. She didn't give a hoot for Willow, but she did fear she'd be an old *maidel*.

~*~

Cassia pulled Hannah away from the Dutch Blitz game, dragging her to the front porch. "What is it, Hannah? You've got to open up."

Hannah bit her lip and then pressed them together.

Why was her best friend a stranger? "Hannah, don't you trust me anymore?"

"*Jah*, I do. But you can't relate to me like you did. You're married and...."

Taking Hannah's face, she turned it towards her. "Look at me. Now, faithful are the wounds of a friend, *jah*? The Bible says that? I'd rather tell you the truth than flatter you with lies. Now, Hannah, you've got to stop acting like everything is perfect in your life when you're so sad. Let others see the real you."

Hannah pulled her face from Cassia's grip, and crossed her arms, brows furrow deep. Very deep.

"Hannah, why do you act better than others? There, I said it. You're not perfect."

"I never said I was."

"Not out loud, but you do give airs like the *English* sometimes."

Her face deepening into crimson red, Hannah glared at her friend. "Like the *English*? Me? *Nee*, that'd be you, Cassia, with all your book learning about herbs and science stuff. Have you cooked a meal for Martin that's not burnt?"

"'Course I have," Cassia pounced, being insecure as a cook. "Willow comes over to eat with us sometimes."

"He doesn't have sense God gave geese, so how would he know?"

Cassia sprung up. "What did you say?"

"*Ach*, it's in a book I read. Willow acts brainless at times. Do you know what he's doing right this minute? Swimming in the leech-filled pond with Anna."

Cassia forced herself to frown, but the edges of her lips soon lifted high. "He is? Anna and Willow? *Ach*, I'm so happy for him." She spun around with delight. "So, I was right."

"Like usual," Hannah huffed.

"And you're jealous, Hannah. That's what got your goose. One of these days, and maybe when it's too late, you'll realize my *bruder* is the best single Amish man in town."

"You think you know everything, Cassia Byler, even me! Better than I know myself."

"*Jah*, I do. You're shutting life out and becoming as prickly as the Spinster Yoder Sisters. You can see how grumpy they are, but they can't see it."

Hannah jabbed her fists into her hips. "The Spinster Yoder Sisters? *Ach*, rub it in, Cassia Byler. I *am* a spinster. Shout it from the rooftops. Well, at least I didn't leave the Amish like your *bruder*. How can I say yes to courting Willow when he's not even baptized and leaving for Canada to 'find himself?"

Cassia saw it. It was not her imagination. Hannah loved her *bruder* but was afraid he'd turn *English* or Mennonite because of his doubts. How horrible for Hannah! "*Ach*, Hannah, I'm so sorry. You care for Willow but you're afraid you'll get hurt, like you did with Freeman."

"N-O." Hannah stomped her foot. "Cassia, you are no Granny Weaver, a matchmaker. Stick to your herbal stuff."

Cassia gingerly sat on the swing. She knew she was right but didn't want to lose this dear friend. "Let's not quarrel, Hannah. When we get together to knit, let's pray out loud together like the Baptists. I saw twenty or so of them praying together and Janice and Suzy say it makes you closer. We can't drift away from each other. You're like a sister."

Her face softening, Hannah sat next to Cassia. "You've got to stop pushing Willow on me."

Cassia wanted to defend herself. Hannah brought Willow up, not her. "Okay, I'll stop. And if his name comes up, we'll pray for him. I am concerned about this *English* girl's letters. She seems like a loose goose."

"A what?" Hannah asked.

"It's an *Englisher* saying. It means a girl who's too willing to kiss and…more."

Hannah pat Cassia's knee. "You need to give Willow more credit than that. He's not the type to fall for a charmer."

"Something about his trip to Canada bothers me to no end."

Hannah took her hand. "We'll pray for him."

Cassia's heart warmed as the old Hannah emerged. "*Jah*, and write often. Make him give a daily account of what he's doing."

"We'll learn lots about dogs," Hannah said with a smile.

Cassia put an arm around Hannah. "You'll meet the right man. We'll pray about that, too. Someone who deserves my best friend."

~*~

Sweet, freshly cut hay wafted through the scrubbed down barn used for Sunday service. Hannah felt refreshed inside and out, Cassia finally understanding her. Their 'heart' talk lasted into the wee hours of the night last Tuesday and her *mamm* panicked that she got in so late. Andy had stopped by to say hello and she'd missed him. Well, that was *gut* due to Jeb's admonition to stay away.

But as the service ended, all baptized members were asked to stay. Cassia looked back at her, seated before her as she was a married woman, and motioned for her to come sit by her. Hannah scooted up a few rows and asked, "Do you know what this is about?"

"*Nee*," Cassia said, gently rocking Rose. "Maybe Old Joe Miller's come back to repent."

"That would be a shock." Hannah looked outside the barn and saw Willow talking with Anna. A knot formed in her stomach. Must be hungry, she told herself. But she studied Willow real careful like and he seemed to talk more than a woman. He didn't go on so with her.

"We have a family among us that wants to confess breaking our rules," Jeb's voice boomed out, echoing off the barn rafters. "Come forward."

When Hannah saw the Smucker family go to the front near Jeb, Cassia gripped her hand and she squeezed it. Her best friend was lending strength, once again.

Jeb motioned to the family and they got down on their knees. All was silent for a while until Mr. Smucker began. "When my wife got the flu last winter, I panicked, and got a cell phone in case she needed rushed to the hospital. And a few other modern conveniences. Took a piece of the forbidden fruit, and well, Jeb confronted us and we're here to ask forgiveness. All modern contraptions are gone."

Andy had shame written all over his face as he looked over to Hannah. The room seemed to dim as the basket was passed for votes to be cast, either to forgive or leave it as a warning. She seemed to be falling into a hole, a dark place where deep in her heart she could trust no Amish man. And she wanted to stay there and hide. Yes, to hide since she'd rather be single than marry a fake Amish man. She'd tried to lower her standards, but no more. Andy had kept secrets during their short-lived courting time, which would end today. She wrote "forgive' on the provided paper and pencil and threw it in the hat as it passed by.

Lord, just when I was starting to really see a future with Andy, just like Freeman, he was a fake. He kept secrets and lived a lie. He was a hypocrite.

She could tell Cassia was staring at her. "What now?"

"All of us have sin, Hannah. No man is perfect."

"The Bible says all have sinned and fall short of the glory of God, but in the epistle of John it says you cannot make a habit of sin and be a Christian."

Cassia gaped. "Don't you mess up at least once a week? Have an evil thought? Jealous of someone?"

"Why would I be jealous?" Hannah whispered.

"Just an example. Gossip, slander, looking down on someone, isn't that all just as bad as the next sin?"

Hannah nodded and pretended to agree with Cassia, that she was being too hard on the Smuckers, but her heart changed that day. She made a resolution to not marry. Edmond Ledger was called to be single, so maybe she was, too. The only problem was it wasn't acceptable among the Amish. 'Be fruitful and multiply.'

A plan formed in her mind. Andy was thirty-five and maybe he didn't want to marry either. By them so-called courting on a friendly basis, nothing romantic, the pressure would be off from every Amish woman she knew from Smicksburg to Lancaster County.

A more sinister thought slithered into her mind. She was hurt by Andy. Maybe she could hurt him. Give him false hopes? As soon as she thought this guilt or her conscience came banging down hard. *No, Hannah, that is wrong,* and she agreed. She liked Andy and would just be good friends. Very good friends.

~*~

That night, Hannah read another Jane Austen book, *Pride and Prejudice*, by oil lamp light on the front porch. Thankful that the trying day was over, she flipped open to the first page. *'It is a truth universally acknowledged, that a single man in possession of a good fortune must be in want of a wife.'* "Well, I'll steer clear of any such man," Hannah said to the orange tabby cat that rubbed up against her ankles. "Come on up here and sit on the swing."

She soon rubbed her fingers through the soft fur, and it quieted her heart. *Was this how Willow felt around dogs?* she wondered. Willow. He'd divided the chores at his kennel between her and Anna, not letting Anna be in charge. Was he sensitive that it hurt her or did he feel Anna incapable?

Anna and Willow were near joined at the hip after church, walking around the Miller farm, back to the pond. She kept watching to make sure they didn't jump in. Someone had to keep the young couple in line. Were they a couple? The Amish grapevine said yes and some elderly women praised God, saying it was their dying wish to see Willow married, such a shy 'boy' who was too involved with his dogs to get a wife. Now Willow was animated and full of life. Cassia mentioned he didn't want to go to Canada now, but needed to keep his word.

The clip clop of horse's hoofs and a dangling lantern to the side of a buggy caught Hannah's attention. She waved, as usual, to the buggy, but after it passed the house it turned into their driveway. She recognized the chestnut mare; it was Andy's. *Lord, oh no. I don't want to talk right now. I just need some time to hide in a book.*

Andy hollered a 'hello' and tied his horse up to the hitching post and sauntered over, his hands dug into his pockets. "Nice night, *jah?*"

"*Jah,*" Hannah agreed. "I love to read outside on such nights."

"Maybe we can catch fireflies and make a mason jar lantern." His eyes were fixed on her as he neared, taking her cat, Pumpkin and rubbing her belly as he sat next to Hannah. "And we can find more fireflies if we go on a buggy ride."

Hannah felt her resolve weakening. Andy Smucker was one good-looking man. "I'd rather just...read. Not to be rude, but it's been a trying day."

He nodded. "*Jah*, sure has. Our family's mighty surprised at how forgiving the People were today. We've never really experienced that before."

"What do you mean?" Hannah asked.

"Well, Old Order Amish we figured were less loving, more judgmental and whatnot. My folks really want to stay on the straight and narrow with all these new branches of Amish popping up."

"And what about you, Andy? Are you as committed as your parents?"

Andy grinned. "Our family moves as a four horse team. Some think it strange, but we get along. Some feel we need to start splitting up, Sadie and I making our own families. I'm finally at the point financially where I can do that."

A single man in possession of a good fortune must be in want of a wife, Hannah had just read. "So, you waited thirty-five years to get married because of finances? It's not the People's way. Surely the community where you lived helped. Men apprentice at fifteen."

"And women as pretty as you wed before twenty." He nudged her playfully. "Why aren't you married?"

Hannah stared "There's a big difference between twenty-five and thirty-five."

"Men marry later, *jah*?" The cat jumped off him and he rested his head behind his hands. "I suppose we've both courted others and just never found someone we'd want to spend our entire life with."

He understood her. "*Jah*, and stay Amish. I could have married outside the order to Old Order Mennonite or Beachy Amish, but I…well, I can't explain it."

"I'm eager to learn the ancient paths, the old ways, the Bible talks about. Feel a tug in my heart when I read *The Martyr's Mirror*, those willing to give their lives for their faith."

"*Jah*," Hannah said. "Some think I'm too serious about our heritage, thinking it morbid, so many martyred, but my *mamm* thinks we're related to someone in the book."

"Isn't that something. Ever think he prayed for his offspring and you're an answer to it, preserving the old ways?"

"It was a woman, but maybe you're right. God's blessing is for a thousand generations. I never thought of it. Maybe I'm not a stick in the mud and too serious like Cassia says."

"The herb lady? Well, you can see they've teetered near the edge of the *Ordnung*."

"What do you mean?" Hannah asked.

"Not many Amish travel to medical conventions and are so cozy with the *English*. And isn't the son leaving Smicksburg to train dogs somewhere?"

Hannah nodded. She'd never seen this before. The Bylers almost lost Cassia to the *English*, and now Willow. "I'm sure Willow will come back," she near whispered.

"You care for him like a *bruder*?"

"*Jah*, I care for him. Like a *bruder*."

Andy took her hand. "Let's take a buggy ride." He kissed her cheek. "I like talking to you Hannah Coblenz."

Hannah let *Pride and Prejudice* slip from her fingers as Andy enveloped her in his arms and kissed the top of her prayer *kapp*.

Dear Willow,

This will be my last letter since you'll be with us next week. I can't wait to show you around and meet my friends. My friend, Jimmy, got an old corvette and made it run somehow. He made it go over 100 mph. How fast does a buggy travel? I'm glad you've decided to come live in the 'fast lane,' no pun intended.

Like I said in my other letter, we'll meet you at the train station. We'll have our Lab, so you should be able to pick us out. Can you bring a straw hat and wear suspenders to look like the Amish guys on TV? Never met a real Amish man, but they sure are cute, the ones on television.

Oh, Dad did the background check on you. Thanks for giving all the info and the picture. You're drop dead gorgeous.

See you soon,

Eager to meet you,

Cheri

Willow reread the letter. Guilt plagued him as he wasn't totally truthful with his *daed* as to why he needed a photo. "Drop dead gorgeous". Was that a compliment? It made him think of road kill. Was he pale like most Germans were? But why call him gorgeous? That was what you'd call a girl. Did she think his hair was too long, his traditional bowl cut with bangs cut straight across? He planned to get his hair cut like Edmond as soon as he got there. The need to not stick out like a sore thumb possessed him. Willow was shy by nature, but Anna sure did unleash his tongue. What a sweetheart she was. So beautiful and supportive. Respectful, looking up to him.

Well, the afternoon changing of the dog water and helping his *daed* out in the herb garden awaited him, so he slid off his desk chair and took his straw hat off the peg and left the house.

But an awful cry sent shivers down his spine. What was that? A cat fight? Willow soon saw a ball of orange fur. *Ach, nee.* Hannah's cat. He darted towards it. and as he got to the cat, he realized its back end must have gotten hit by something since it could only move its front. But there was no blood. He took off his hat to scratch his head, when Hannah came panting.

"Willow, have you seen Pumpkin?" She stopped short when she saw the cat, now listless before her. "*Ach*, what happened?" she cried. "Was she hit?" She gently stroked the cat's head. "Willow, what do you think happened? She can't move her back."

Willow read all he could on animals and feared a blood clot in the spinal cord. But he didn't have the necessary equipment to treat the cat. "You go get a basket and blanket. We'll take her to Doc Fox."

"It's too expensive," Hannah said, chin quivering.

"He owes me a favor," Willow lied. "There'll be no charge for a visit."

Hannah relaxed and ran to her house. Her mint green dress swayed and he remembered the first time he saw her in that color. Her eyes looked turquoise, and they argued about her true eye color till the cows came home. It was the first day he saw Hannah with different eyes, ones that grew to adore her. He shook his head. What was he thinking? He was courting Anna. Anna had gorgeous eyes.

The cat gave a low meow as if to say, *Hurry up. I'm in pain.* Hannah whizzed around her kitchen garden, a wicker laundry basket and towel in hand. "I got a towel instead. All we have are quilts and *Mamm* would be mad."

"Fine, let's get Pumpkin ready." Willow slid the towel under the cat and raised it into the basket real gentle-like in case she had a broken bone.

"You have such a sweet way with critters," Hannah whispered.

Willow grabbed the basket and ran back towards his house, yelling for her to keep up. Doc Fox closed early on Fridays and they needed to skedaddle. Placing the cat in the back seat of his buggy, Hannah slipped in alongside the cat and off Willow flew for the next mile on dirt roads until they saw Doc Fox's little clinic built off the side of his house. Once inside, a large mutt made a low growl, and Willow stood in front of Hannah. The cat made an awful cry and the straggly dog gave a threatening bark. Willow put a protective arm around Hannah. The dog's owner pat it's head, saying what a nice dog Petunia was.

"Bring your dog in here, Joe," ordered Sally, the doctor's secretary, pointing to a small room. Shutting the door behind them, she wiped her brow. "That dog needs anxiety meds."

"I agree," Willow said, relaxing and taking a chair. Hannah sat next to him. "You're such a *gut* friend, Willow. Willing to risk your life for…Pumpkin."

"That dog could have bit your leg off," Willow snapped.

Hannah was quiet for a spell, rubbing Pumpkin behind the ears to calm the creature down.

"Sorry for shouting at you. You treat me like a little kid sometimes, though."

"Now how did you get that idea? I was trying to say *danki*."

"You were surprised that I could stand up like a man, but never mind. I don't care that you treat me like a *boppli*."

Hannah looked over and their eyes locked. "Why's that, Willow?"

He chewed his lower lip, wanting to measure his words. "I know what real respect is now, so I don't need it from you anymore."

Her eyes misted with tears. "Willow Byler, that was a spiteful thing to say."

In utter shock, he pat her back. "Spiteful. I'm just saying…I put too much importance on your opinion of me."

She got a handkerchief from her apron pocket. "Because Anna respects you, *jah*?"

He had to nod in agreement. Anna was easy to get along with, too, not flaring up or crying out of the blue. But he kept his trap shut as they waited for the doctor.

~*~

The next day, Hannah yanked ardently at weeds in the kitchen garden, throwing them into the wheelbarrow. Pumpkin needing to spend the night at the vet's made her nervous, and pulling weeds was a remedy for pent up anxiety. The cat had been a comfort to the family for ten years, helping her the most when her dear *daed* passed on to Glory. She never told a soul, but she believed Pumpkin could feel her heartache. Volunteering over at Willow's kennel until he offered a wage, she was used to being accused of getting too attached to critters. She'd go back to doing it for free if the financial burden hadn't been so keen at home. But they managed, pinching pennies, selling raw cow and goat milk to *Englishers* and working endlessly on quilts. Hannah missed going to knitting circle with Granny Weaver so much, she wondered if she should go back. Maybe she'd be more energized if she could not only knit more but be encouraged by women fellowship. Yes, she was lonely.

"Hello, Hannah."

She knew Willow's voice and when he was nervous. "Hello. Did you get to see the vet like you said?"

He bent down to pull at a dandelion. "*Jah*, just talked to him. Nice of him to talk on a Saturday, since he's closed. He did some tests and isn't sure, but he thinks it Aortic Thromboembolism, or ATE." He rose and took Hannah's hands. "Most cats don't survive past forty-eight hours once…"

She gripped his hands. "Once what?"

"Once paralysis and pain come on. It's real quick-like. Really a heart problem and Pumpkin has a blood clot. Now, the doc said there're all kinds of treatments but…"

"But?"

"It costs a fortune and most cats don't survive after treatment. I reminded the doc of our arrangement, bartering my services for payment, but he said the cat was in great pain. Sometimes it's a mercy to euthanize."

She tried to grasp all Willow said, but all she could think of was a life without Pumpkin. She gasped and then let the tears flow. Willow drew her to himself and his strong embrace gave her strength. "Let me talk to the doctor. I can make enough quilts to pay him."

Willow rubbed her back. "We'll need to take Pumpkin to Pittsburgh for treatment, since Doc Fox won't do it."

"Well, then let's go," Hannah cried out.

"Okay. I'll go with you. I know how much Pumpkin means to you."

CHAPTER 9

Janice Jones glided into Doc Fox's driveway. "Hannah, as a pastor's wife, I don't go around town saying I'm praying for a cat. Some people have odd notions that it's sacrilegious, but God cares about the sparrows. When you see your cat, know God sees it, too, and cares."

Hannah forced a smile. "*Danki*, Janice. Sure miss seeing you at knitting circle. Seems like I only see you when we need a driver."

"Well, you and Willow were quite the team, taking all our projects to the homeless. We sure would like to have you back." She turned to Willow. "Both of you."

"Headed to Canada, remember?" Willow said.

"Running from the obvious," Janice said under her breath.

"I heard that," Willow blurted. "What's obvious?"

Janice flashed a smile. "I'm sorry. Some pastor's wives let their husband's rub off on them, giving advice when it's not welcome. Now, you two go on in. I've got you on the clock."

Hannah laughed because Janice never charged for a short ride. Willow led her to Doc Fox's side door, since the clinic was closed, and rang the doorbell. "Such a nice place, *jah?* Don't know why Amish can't have brick homes."

"Willow," she chided, "we have all things in common so as not to cause jealousy or competition."

Willow hit his chest. "It's in here that we overcome temptation, not avoiding them."

Hannah wanted to argue, but the door opened and Doc Fox seemed grave, but maybe it was her imagination. He invited them into his living room, two little Pomeranians soon skirting around them. The Doc put up one finger, and the dogs sat instantly. "Good girls. Now go see Mama."

On cue, the dogs ran out of the room, their plumy tails erect. Doc Fox motioned to the overstuffed floral sofa and Hannah took a seat next to Willow. The vet situated himself across from them. His eyes, full of compassion, settled on Hannah. "I'm very sorry. We did all we could, but Pumpkin passed away this morning, an hour ago."

Rage and sorrow mingled together made Hannah scream. "*Ach*, God, why? Why?" She sobbed. "She's all I had," she repeated several times as she struggled to breath.

"You have me." Willow took her hands. "You have the whole community. My sister's your best friend and –"

"Let her cry," Doc Fox corrected. "She's had a great loss."

"I can get her another cat," Willow protested. "Hannah, how about I find an orange tabby like Pumpkin?"

She wailed all the louder. "There is no cat like Pumpkin. I'll never have a cat again, only a barn one. Give your heart to something and it dies or runs off."

Willow hit his knee. "I'm sorry. I forgot your goat died last month."

"Goat? Who cares about a stupid goat?" Hannah spouted, her face crimson.

Doc Fox put a hand up. "Sometimes silence is all that's needed to help someone in grief."

"How much do I owe you, Doc?" Hannah asked in a calm, resolved tone.

"We have an agreement, right Doc?" Willow interrupted.

The Doc stared at Willow and then fumbled for words but ended up sputtering out, "Yes, we do. Willow and I have it all set up."

Hannah saw the wink Willow gave the Doc and suspicion filled her. But it was short lived when Willow darted up. "Janice is waiting. Can you give us the cat to bury?"

"Yes, yes," the doctor said, scurrying out of the room.

Hannah doubled over, sobbing again. Willow kissed the top of her prayer *kapp*. *Such a nice gesture of friendship*, she thought.

~*~

Reed gazed around the noon meal table. His beloved wife, Lily and Willow, a small foursome. Maybe in a few years it would be only himself and Dorcas. Bowing his head, he led in silent prayer. *Lord, thank you for the time I have with my kinner. I cannot bend Your will to mine, and I set my last two free to do Your will in their lives. Danki for Dorcas, Lord. Love her more each day.* He grunted to signal the end of the prayer and rubbed his hands together briskly. "Now, this is what I call a feast, Dorcas. Greens, greens, and more greens. More studies showing that cancer can't live in a body filled with greens."

"Our kitchen garden's a bumper crop this year," Dorcas said. "With corn coming on already, this meal was free."

Reed noticed the sparkle in Lily's eyes were dim. "Lily, are you tired? Reading books all summer will make you lackadaisical."

"I don't read all day, *Daed*. This big old house gets cleaned since *Mamm's* in the herb shop with you. And I'm working on lesson plans for school. It's August, you know."

"Where did the summer go?" He passed the massive salad to Willow. "Son, Mr. Peters is only being careful, doing that background check. No information on the internet and all the complaints about puppy mills among the Amish is just making him cautious."

"A little too cautious. He was here and saw my kennels. Television shows about us make us out to be cruel and stupid. How many *Englishers* have puppy mills compared to the Amish, I'd like to know. They sure do charge more for a dog."

"You'll get to go on a train ride when the leaves change," Lily encouraged. "And I'm glad you won't be leaving until Edmond gets back."

Dorcas coughed after sipping meadow tea. "How…"

Reed ran around the table and pat her back. "Go down the wrong pipe?"

She nodded in agreement. "Lily, Edmond's coming here? How do you know?"

"We write real regular-like. He sure loves working with troubled youth, but, well, I can't say. He'll tell you when he comes back next week."

After plopping down in his chair, Reed felt the room spin. Lily wasn't baptized and she was writing to Edmond and they were keeping secrets. "Why the secrecy, Lily?" He pursed his lips together. "Do not tell me…that…you and Edmond…" He gripped the table. "I won't have it! I can't!"

Willow ran next to him and put water to his lips. "*Daed*, you look so pale."

Lily's eyes brimmed with tears. "I just said Edmond had a surprise."

"Edmond writes to me, too," Willow told his dad in a reassuring voice. "You're having PTSD. Lily isn't Cassia."

Dorcas wiped her brow with a napkin. "But, Lily, I've known you to have a crush on Edmond for ages."

"*Ach, Mamm*, who wouldn't? He's everything a man should be."

"Except Amish!" Reed mustered enough energy to bellow out.

Reed could see Dorcas clearly now and the room stabilized. "Lily, I'm your *daed*, but not God. God has a plan for you. Your *mamm* and I raised you in the Amish church, but at eighteen, you too are not baptized. I blame myself, having my nose stuck in medical books –"

"*Nee*, Reed, you provide for us by that shop," Dorcas said. "I'm her *mamm* and if she goes *English*, it's my fault. I take her to knitting circle with *Englishers* and let her sleep in until eight because she's up late reading."

Willow raised both hands. "You're great parents, is what I think. You let us know our own minds. How many get baptized just to make their parents happy? Or never letting up on the pressure to bow the knee?"

"*Jah*," Lily followed. "I do have a mind to read a lot and I'm thankful to have parents like you two. I have so many interests and the reason I'm not baptized is because I just had a few more questions is all."

Reed studied Lily. "Questions? What do you mean? Questions about the *Ordnung*?"

"Okay, I do have another secret. I go over to talk to Jeb and Granny quite a bit. They say I overthink everything and that the apple doesn't fall far from the tree." She grinned at her *daed*. "But no more. I'm Amish from the tip of my head to my toenails. And I'll be making the vow come New Birth Sunday, next spring."

Reed blinked as tears blurred his vision. "Seriously, Lily?"

"*Jah*, I don't know why I waited so long." She reddened and laughed. "Maybe a wedding next fall?"

"You mean in over a year from now, *jah*? Not this year," Dorcas gasped. "And to who?"

"She has too many after her for me to figure out," Willow chuckled. "Nathan Hostetler? Ezekiel Miller?"

"It's a secret," she giggled like a little school girl.

"Of course he's Amish, *jah*? Already baptized?"

"Not baptized…yet."

Reed threw his hands up. "Secrets! Why on earth do Amish court in secret? That's something I think I'll bring up when the *Ordnung* gets a review. It makes parents go crazy!" But inside his heart was leaping. *The Lord God is my strength, and He will make my feet like hinds' feet, and He will make me to walk upon mine high places.* Obviously the little flirtation he saw or imagined between Lily and Edmond was all in his *furhoodled* mind. The Good Lord led his children, not really children anymore, though. They were adults. *Glory be.*

~*~

Hannah found herself on the porch, reading by lamplight again, the second floor engulfed in stifling heat. In tow was the little cream kitten with a gray face and tail. Willow found the cat and knew she'd open her heart to a new kitten again, but this cat seemed different than any stray she'd ever seen: long fluffy fur and blue eyes. It almost looked like a fancy *Englisher* breed.

She reclined on the swing, an embroidered pillow from her hope chest fluffed under her head. Why waste a work of art? Why have a hope chest with no hope left to be married? Tired of Jane Austen and happy endings, she decided to read a book recommended by Granny Weaver. *The Hiding Place*, by Corrie Ten Boom, a prisoner at Auschwitz, a Nazi concentration camp; her only crime was hiding Jews during the holocaust. The story was riveting, but what Corrie said about getting bitter, Hannah did not want to hear. Oh, she wasn't shutting Andy out completely, going on buggy rides and whatnot, but something inside was broken, and she knew it. Was it her heart? Still? Freeman! But how could she even respect someone who led her to believe he'd be Amish? The Bylers, all so frank, called him a liar. That was too harsh, though, and she left lots of room for empathy. Maybe the empathy was causing the bitterness? *You think the best of others, but then you face the truth*, Cassia had said. Cassia's romance with Edmond Ledger had ended with a thud, and her dear friend suffered. She called their relationship for what it was. *Infatuation*. Was she to call Freeman a liar? A liar who needed her forgiveness? Did she, like Corrie Ten Boom, need to purposefully give forgiveness? Should she write to Freeman? Say she holds nothing against him?

Yes, that's what Corrie would do. Scooping up her kitten, Hannah scurried back inside to gather paper and a pen and then resumed her cozy spot on the swing.

Freeman,

I'm only contacting you because I need to say I forgive you fully for not being altogether truthful about wanting to be Amish. I hope you find someone Old Order Mennonite you can share your life with. I'll pray for you.

She reread the two lines and wondered if it was too short. Too abrupt? *Did she sound angry?* Cassia cautioned her that she gave the impression she was better than others. No, she felt lower, putting up a front. She needed this letter to be kinder. She added:

I hope your parents and sisters are doing well. I pray for your cousin who's battling such an illness. Cancer. Will there ever be a cure? Someone here is taking the train to San Diego and will be picked up to go into Mexico to be treated by alternative medicine. You should write Reed Byler and get the information. It's not expensive across the border.

Well, again, say hello to everyone.

Hannah

"Now that's a friendly letter," she told her kitten. Stroking its soft fur, she wondered what to call the little thing. It had followed her around like a shadow for days. *Shadow?* She kissed the kitten's nose. "I'm trying to love you, but I miss my Pumpkin." She willed back tears. What would she have done without Willow during the whole ordeal? He'd shown such strength, supporting her, protecting her from the dog at the clinic. *Ach*, she was being spun closer to him like wool was spun into yarn and she'd miss him dreadfully. But he wasn't leaving for a little while yet. *Maybe I won't have to work with Anna.*

Anna. Just the mention of that girl's name made her annoyed. She was pretty and knew it and…it was obvious she wanted to marry her *bruder's* relative, making another marriage between the Bylers of Smicksburg and the Millers from Marathon. Hannah's heart sunk. She was becoming a bitter old spinster! A *jealous* bitter old spinster. What a mess she was becoming.

Karen Anna Vogel

CHAPTER 10

Edmond surveyed the Byler family around the table. His Amish family who became like kin when his parents were taken in a car accident when seventeen. Reed had encouraged his medical studies and to follow his passion. He had to tell them. "I learned something about myself at the camp," he started. "The Bible is right. It's not good for a man to be alone."

Cassia put a hand to her mouth. "You met someone?"

Edmond felt his eyelid twitch in nervousness. Could he go through with this? He knew Reed Byler's temper. "Have you ever read *Little Women*?"

Willow bellowed out a laugh. "Not me. It's a woman's book, *jah*?"

"I sent it to Edmond to read," Lily quipped, her light blue eyes blurring as she stared at Edmond. "It's about a man who thinks he loves one of the older sisters because the youngest hasn't grown up yet. He goes away for a while and comes back to find the youngest sister is a mature woman, and she's his match."

Reed's knife scraped the plate as he dug too hard into the meatloaf. "Why are we talking about this book? Fiction is *gut* in moderation. All things in moderation."

Dorcas came around the table and applied pressure to the side of Reed's head. "I think a stress headache is coming on, *jah?*"

"*Nee*, but that feels *gut*. Got a crick in my neck, too."

"Reed, our *dochder* told me something, and I believe it will make you very happy," she said with confidence. "You have one Amish son unmarried and you may have two."

The way Dorcas could read her husband was admirable. "*Jah*," Edmond tried to say with a strong Dutch accent to lighten Reed's mood, which appeared to be stormy, his eyes like a hawk on prey, staring at him. "What I learned in Haiti is that America has a different kind of poverty. 'Poverty of the soul,' like Mother Teresa said. Kids at camp made me realize how troubled families are in America. I also realized the luxuries I had here. I came back and yearned for a simple life, and well..." His mouth growing dry, he took a swig of meadow tea. "I want to be Amish and I want to marry Lily."

Silence hung in the air. A cool breeze from the open window cooled Edmond's brow. *Lord, help Reed not to explode.*

Reed ambled out of the chair and made his way to Edmond. With open arms, he embraced him. "Are you sure?"

As if in a dream, Edmond methodically said, "Talked to Jeb Weaver. Read about the Amish while in Haiti. And I love Lily." Did this man really love him like a son to have this reaction? He'd always said it, but now he felt it. Be a part of the Byler family.

Lily slipped an arm through her *daed's*. "What do you say, *Daed*? Do I have your blessing?"

"He needs to be Amish first, of course. Go through a lengthy process. May take a year."

Edmond's heart felt too full. "Or less. Jeb said me living in a rural place with no electricity and no car could count as a proving time concerning modern conveniences."

Reed kissed the top of Lily's head. "Bless you, my youngest *kinner*. I prayed much all summer while out on the porch at night. This is more that I could ask or dream of."

Edmond smiled at Lily, the little sixteen-year-old when he left, now a mature woman, and one he dearly loved. What the Lord had done in working out their love story was so unique, he couldn't wait to tell it to his family to come.

"You can't travel or be a doctor," Willow blurted. "Edmond, you Amish? There're too many limitations."

Reed wagged a finger. "Things are changing. How many of our people go regularly to Mexico for cancer treatments? That was unheard of when I was young. And relief work has expanded and I'm sure Edmond would like to help with natural disasters and whatnot."

"I would," Edmond said eagerly. "I'd still be a doctor, able to help…the People. My People."

Cheers and laughter echoed off the walls, but Edmond noticed Willow grabbing his hat off the peg and dart outside. Curious, he ran after him.

~*~

"You're…sick," Willow snapped at Edmond. "First Cassia and now my little sister? Do you love Lily or just want to be a part of our family?"

Edmond clamped his hand on Willow's shoulder as if to calm him down, but it was soon shoved off. "You're in shock. I know you're not thinking clearly, it's the body's way of not taking in too much stress or change."

"Stop the doc talk. My mind's clear it's yours that needs checked out." He shoved an index finger in Edmond's face. "You better not mess this up. You better be serious about loving Lily and being Amish." Feeling his face burn, he took off his straw hat to fan himself. "I was raised Amish and even I'm not sure I can take the vow. You're a proud, arrogant man."

Edmond charged Willow and secured him in a headlock. "Now listen to me. You're not mad at me, but yourself. You know what you need to do."

Trying to wiggle free, he was defeated. "Stop the doc talk."

"No, I won't. You're mad at yourself, not me. You can't make up your mind. You flip flop all over the place. When I left for camp, you were set on Hannah. I come home and you said yesterday you might not go to Canada because of Anna. Now, if you shut up, we can talk face to face, but I won't let you keep insulting me and your sister. Lily's as mature as Mother Teresa."

"*Ach*, the *furhoodled* Catholic nun?"

"Shut your mouth, Willow Byler. That woman changed millions of lives and knew herself when she was eighteen. Jealous? You're much older and don't have a clue. Now, can we talk?"

Willow had erupting anger like he'd never experienced, but being a pacifist, he had years of experience in turning the other cheek. "*Jah*, you can let me go, but I don't want to talk."

"Okay, we just stand like this all day."

Willow heard a red-tailed hawk screech overhead. He could outrun Edmond any day after a one-minute talk. He did owe his so-called *Englisher* brother that much. "Okay, you have one minute. All I can stomach." When he was released, he stomped over to a nearby cedar chair. "One minute."

Edmond leaned on the porch rail. "When I came home, I was restless, like you know. My mind was going crazy. So, I took a job, running from what I felt the Lord was leading. I never wanted to be Amish, but my whole perspective changed when I lived in Haiti. Families depend on each other for survival, just like the Amish. They have extended family all around a strong community. I didn't want to come home. And then I do, and I see it in the Amish. Seeing Lily took me back. Willow, she's a woman, wise beyond her years. I became attached to her and so I left. Never wanted to hurt your dad ever again. But I leaned on the scripture 'Commit your way to the Lord, and your thoughts will be established'. It took all summer, but I've never been more settled. And it's why you need to go to Canada. You're not."

Willow's heart hammering against his ribcage eased a little. "Maybe Anna's for me. She's pretty and I'm just stubborn. Travel fever came from you, but maybe I'm ready to make the vow and be baptized."

With a coy look, Edmond said, "Too many 'maybes.' You need to be sure. It wouldn't be fair to Anna...or Hannah."

"Hannah's just a friend," Willow groaned. "She's seeing Andy Smucker. And she doesn't respect me deep down. Anna does."

"One minute's up," Edmond said evenly. "Willow, you need to leave to seek God and get more perspective. I'll be praying for you."

~*~

That night, Willow took a stroll over to Cassia's place. There was either a Dutch Blitz match or a bonfire going on, but what he wanted was to see where he stood with Anna. Was this love? He just couldn't believe a beauty like Anna would give him the time of day, now courting him. Only seeing her to ride home from a Singing was only Sundays and he needed to move quickly. Maybe he'd make his baptismal vow, forgetting about travel fever, and settle down with Anna. No one could really agree on every single thing in the *Ordnung*, they just had to abide by it.

As he neared the front porch, all was silent but he spied the glow of the oil lamp in the living room. Upon entering the house, he saw Anna, alone, reading a book. "Where's everybody at?"

"Celebrating Lily's engagement over at your parents. Didn't you know?" Anna said, setting the book aside. "I'm babysitting."

"Well, I came to see you anyhow," he said, not knowing exactly where to sit. But Anna pat the seat next to her. "Come. Sit down. What's on your mind?"

Sitting down, he stared straight ahead. "Oh, nothing. Just seeing how you were." Chiding himself for chickening out on making a marriage proposal, he clenched his fists.

"Well, truth be told, I'm really homesick. I like Smicksburg and all but could never live her permanently. It's so hot in the summer."

Willow's heart sunk. "So, when you get married, you wouldn't even consider living anywhere but Marathon?"

She shook her head. "I'd be depressed and wouldn't make a *gut* wife. I'd always be needling my husband to move to Marathon."

Willow crossed his legs. "But Amish move all the time. A man needs to make a living."

"*Jah*, I know. But Martin's so far away and I fear my *daed* wouldn't be able to handle it if I left, too. He's old, you know. Much older than my *mamm*. And over the past two years I've seen the decline. *Nee*, my responsibilities are in Marathon."

Willow brows were a single line, this information so shocking. "Anna, do you consider us a courting couple?"

Smiling shyly, she nodded.

"Courting leads to marriage. I live here. I'll inherit land and…"

Anna's head turned to meet his. "You'd never leave here? Not for me?"

He gulped. "I was going to ask the same. I'm the head of the house."

"The Bible says a man shall leave his mother and father and cleave to his wife. It's the man who leaves, just like Martin did. He'd be selfish to ask Cassia to leave her family here. It's harder on women to move away."

Willow shook his head, confusion saturating him. "I've never heard anything like this. It's common for a couple who love each other to find the best place to live. You need to cut the apron strings if you…marry me."

Her eyes bulged. "If you loved me, you'd be sensitive to my need to be around my *daed*." Her voice became raspy and

Willow noticed her face contort. "Willow, you're being so rash. Talking about marriage when we're still getting to know each other."

"I need to know where I stand before I leave for Canada."

Her left eyelid twitched. "Remember when I said I notice things now that I listen and pay attention more?"

"Jah."

"Well, you're being hasty-like with me because you're running away from Hannah. You love her and I can't go on courting a man who loves someone else." Her eyes met his, painful as it was for her. "I say we be gut friends and leave it at that."

"*Nee*, I don't. *Ach*, Anna, *nee*. I don't love Hannah. She's like a sister."

She pursed her lips then forced a smile. "I see it and so does everyone."

Willow looked away, Anna's piercing eyes seeming to be like a mirror to his inner thoughts. Did he love Hannah? Did everyone see it?

Anna rose. "I can't marry someone who doesn't love me. You won't cherish me, and I want that in my husband." She nodded. "I best check on Rose."

"And I, well, better get on over to the party at my parent's." He turned, hoping strong emotion would compel him to hold Anna, tell her she was mistaken. If she'd have him, he'd be Amish, even move to Marathon to prove his love. But his conscience pricked him. It was a lie. He was trying to love Anna and she knew it. *Commit your way to the Lord and your thoughts will be established,* Edmond had quoted. *Lord, level my thinking.* He heard Anna's footsteps tapping up the steps. A perfect picture of Hannah's face came into his mind's eye, irritating him. "She's not the one," he muttered, charging through the screen door, letting it bang shut. "Maybe there are greener pastures in Canada among the Mennonites. He didn't have to be content to be in tiny-little Smicksburg.

~*~

The few days later in early morning, Willow found he'd fallen asleep at his kitchen table. Lifting his head up, he stared out the window. It was daylight, so it was passed seven o'clock. Through the mist being burnt off by the August heat, he saw an image of a woman. *Ach, Cassia's bringing me cinnamon buns*, he thought. But he soon realized it *was* Hannah. His heart leapt into his throat. Having slept in his work clothes, he lifted up to sniff his armpit. He reeked. His mind whirled until he saw baby wipes he kept around in case he needed to change Rose's diaper. Grabbing them, he raced to his bedroom and tried a little too fast to undress and wipe himself down. As he tumbled, the house shook.

"Willow, are you hurt?" Hannah's called out. "Where are you?"

It wasn't the morning heat that made his face beet red. "I just tripped in here. Overslept."

"Have you had breakfast?"

"*Nee*, not yet," he tried to say calmly as he pulled up his trousers and started to button his shirt.

"I know where everything is. Want two eggs or three?"

"Four would be *gut*."

"Four? You're not a spring chicken anymore. Need to watch your cholesterol. Not that you're over the hill, but you need to make better eating habits." The banging, clattering and closing of cabinet doors, and then, "Willow, you have so much junk food. Do you live off this stuff?"

"If I don't go to my *mamm's*."

"Which is how often?" Hannah inquired suspiciously.

"Don't want to wear out my welcome." He looked in his tiny mirror. *Ach, nee.* The vinyl tablecloth imprint was embossed on his forehead. As Hannah continued to make small talk, he got a wash cloth and rubbed his forehead vigorously, only to see it made the mark all the more red. "Hannah, I think I'm sick."

"I'll take care of you."

Such a bossy older sister figure! "*Nee*, it may be contagious. Was around Cassia and must have caught something."

"What are your symptoms?"

"*Ach*, nausea and a stomachache," he lied. Well, not exactly a lie. His stomach was in knots right now.

The rattling of pans and then Hannah laughing. "You can't catch morning sickness from your sister, Willow Byler. Now, I need to know exactly what I'm to do when you leave next week. It is next week, *jah*?"

"*Jah*."

"Why isn't Anna here? Isn't she supposed to be the boss?"

"The boss? Anna? Why would you think that?"

"Because you said it," Hannah informed.

"Well, you'll be the boss. Anna's not…qualified. You along with Martin and my *daed* can handle it."

There was a moment of silence. "So Anna's not helping at all?" Hannah quipped.

Was that sheer delight her heard in Hannah's voice? He'd noticed she was distant from Anna, but then again, she was busy. Or was she jealous? He shook his head to dislodge the thought. His dream of marrying Hannah had turned to dust. He was moving on and soon. Maybe he'd make new friends in Canada and settle there.

"Willow, are you okay? Why aren't you answering? You're hurt, *jah*?"

"*Nee*, be out in a second." The smell and sound of crackling bacon lifted him a bit. Hannah knew he loved his bacon. He rushed around to straighten up his room, throwing the covers of his bed up, which was never made, and flinging his clothes in the hamper. He raked a comb through his blond bangs straight down as best he could to hide the red mark and entered the kitchen.

"Goodness, Willow, you have a rash on your face? Did you get bit by a tick? Lyme Disease starts with a rash. Let me see up-close. There still may be a tick on you." She lowered the gas oven and sprinted to him. "Now, sit down here and I'll check this out."

Pushing his bangs back, she leaned close to examine his forehead. The scent of peppermint mouthwash made him notice her lips. They were always cherry colored, not pale, like other girls. And then he noticed something he'd never seen: freckles. *Ach*, they were little brown dots that accented her nose perfectly.

"I can't find anything. But those buggers can hide. Let me check your hair."

The touch of her parting and ruffling through his locks tempted him to grab this girl and kiss her. Show him what a man he was. But he knew Hannah. Ever strong, sensible

Hannah would be appalled. But the desire increased, and he took her hands. "I'll find it. Or my *daed* will."

Looking offended, Hannah backed away. "Okay, but make sure you have it looked at. That rash is nasty."

His eyes locked onto hers and the desire to kiss her overwhelmed him. "That bacon smells *gut*. Let's eat."

She slipped over to the door and demurely held up a package wrapped in white tissue paper in one hand and a pastry bag in another. "Something to eat on the train and…I made you something to keep you warm in Canada."

His face reddened as heat grew up his neck. "*Danki*." He glanced up and found Hannah watching him closely, a peculiar smile on her lips.

"Willow, that rash is spreading down your neck."

"I'll be fine."

"That's what Old Abe Stoltfus said when he got bit. Messed his knees up *gut*. Lyme Disease isn't something to sneeze at."

Willow peeked in the pastry bag. "Maple Oatmeal Cookies. My favorite. Love maple syrup, you know."

"Jah, I do."

What was Hannah trying to say by such kind gestures? He ripped open the gift to see a long multi-colored scarf. "*Ach*, Hannah, *danki*. I'll be like Joseph with the coat of many colors."

Hannah laughed. "Too fancy?"

"*Nee*, just perfect. I'll think of you when I'm wearing it."

"Write to me?"

"*Jah*, sure will," he assured her, ignoring the longing to hug her, never wanting to let go.

DISCUSSION GUIDE

Dear Readers,

In this trilogy, we'll take a journey with Willow Byler as he 'finds himself'. He's full of *self*-doubt and low *self*-worth.

1) Below each character trait, think back to where in the story this is clearly displayed and discuss:

Self-consciousness:

Haste:

Fear of people:

Quick temper:

2) Reed thinks back to the scripture that his son's name was derived.

He also took a seedling from the land
and planted it in fertile soil.
He placed it beside a broad river,
where it could grow like a willow tree.
It took root there and
grew into a low, spreading vine.
Its branches turned up toward the eagle,
and its roots grew down into the ground.
It produced strong branches
and put out shoots.

Willow trees are seen planted next to ponds and streams in rural Pennsylvania, sucking in water continuously to survive. Read the Parable of the Sower found in Luke 8:11-15. What are the dangers of a plant growing too fast?

3) Willow gets his picture taken and Cheri says he's "Drop dead gorgeous" but Willow thinks first of road kill. Is he that naïve or is he showing pride flipped upside down, self-pity?

4) If you were to sit down and talk with Willow, what advice would you give him?

5) Hannah teases about being a spinster, but we know her heart's desire is to be married and have a family. Do you see fear holding her back? Are there any areas in your life where fear has a grip, holding you back from all God has called you to?

6) Willow is furious with Edmond when he announces he's staying put in his hometown of Smicksburg. Why such strong emotion?

7) When Hannah's cat dies, she seems to lean on Willow. Do you think it's an eye-opener to her that he's mature and strong to lean on?

8) What do you think of Anna? The once chatterbox we met in *The Herbalist's Daughter Trilogy* has put James 1:19 into practice:

Understand this, my dear brothers and sisters: You must all be quick to listen, slow to speak, and slow to get angry. (NLT)

We all have different personalities, some more outgoing, but this scripture tells us there's wisdom in listening fully to others. This is engrained in Amish culture, it being so important, they have a word for it: *Gelassenheit*. It actually means 'quietly waiting'. How does *Gelassenheit* benefit Anna? How can it benefit you?

9) If you look back at Lily in *The Herbalist's Daughter Trilogy*, she was fifteen going on sixteen. Now at eighteen, she's very mature. Edmond considers her because Mother Teresa left home to change the world at eighteen. Do you think young adults are pampered too much? Can an eighteen-year-old be more mature than someone twice their age? Read Proverbs 14: 26-27.

10. What good character traits do you see in Willow that would make him a wonderful husband?

Ponder this:
Have you ever tried to feed a baby? My grandson didn't like carrots, so all things orange he cringed at, his chubby chin tripling as he cocked his head back. When given a dab of peach cobbler, he first stared in shock, and then licked it up. Not all things orange are gross!

Do you find the Bible boring, hard to understand or digest? Try reading Psalms 119. It will whet your palate to read the scriptures. We can see how willow trees break for lack of water. The scriptures water us and keep us fueled up. If you lack the desire to read them, be honest and tell God. I've done this countless times. There are so many distractions. C.S. Lewis says:

"It would seem that Our Lord finds our desires not too strong, but too weak. We are half-hearted creatures, fooling about with drink and sex and ambition when infinite joy is offered us, like an ignorant child who wants to go on making mud pies in a slum because he cannot imagine

what is meant by the offer of a holiday at the sea. We are far too easily pleased."

I don't want to be too easily pleased.

In the next book, we'll see Willow is forced to see what kind of metal he's made of as temptations abound. Will he bend like a willow tree or turn into an oak?

AMISH RECIPES

Hannah's Bread

5-6 c. flour

3 T. sugar

2 tsp. salt

2 pkgs. yeast

2 c. water

¼ c. canola or vegetable oil

In large bowl combine 2 cups flour plus dry ingredients; sugar, salt, yeast. Mix well. Heat water and oil until warm, 120-130 degrees. Add warm liquid to dry ingredients and beat with wire whip for 3 minutes. Stir in the rest of flour slowly. Knead for 10 minutes. Put in greased bowl and let rise until double in size. Push down and let rise again. Put in 2 loaf pans, let rise and bake for 30-40 minutes at 350 degrees.

Hannah's Maple Oatmeal Cookies

1 c. sugar

1 c. brown sugar

1 c. butter

2 eggs

1 Tbsp. milk

2 c. flour

2 c. quick oats

1 tsp. baking powder

1 tsp. salt

1 tsp. vanilla

1 tsp. baking soda

1 tsp. pure maple flavoring

Mix shortening and sugars. Add eggs and milk. Blend. Add all remaining ingredients to mixture. Drop by rounded teaspoon onto lightly greased cookie sheet. Bake at 350 degrees for 10-12 minutes, or until golden brown.

Enjoy!

The Herbalist's Son

BOOK TWO

But they delight in the law of the Lord,
meditating on it day and night.
They are like trees planted along the riverbank,
bearing fruit each season.
Their leaves never wither,
and they prosper in all they do.
Psalm 1: 2-3 NLT

CHAPTER 1

Reed cuddled closer to Dorcas, the breeze from the porch swing giving this autumn day a nip, and listened as she read Willow's letter:

Dear Mamm and Daed,

The train trip up was colorful. The leaves are at their peak in September, some trees already bare, it's hard to believe. I envy the green you still see, but not in a bad way. There're more pines here. Indiana, PA is the Christmas Tree Capital of the World, as lots of folks in Smicksburg are proud of, but the Canadians I think beat us. And if you can believe, I saw my breath when I got off the train. Pulled the scarf Hannah made out of my luggage and swung it around my neck a few times.

The Peters seem like real decent folk. Mr. Peters is a teacher and his wife is a dentist. Daed, can you believe the woman makes more than the man? I've never seen or heard such a thing, let alone a woman going out to work half an hour away from the house by car.

Their house is three times the size of ours. Seems like there's more windows than walls, but the view of the lake and the boathouse is spectacular. Mr. Peters said the lake's stocked and will take me ice fishing if it freezes up in late November.

Mr. Peters has seven dogs, not just one. He has huskies that pull a sleigh. Truth be told, I've always dreamt of riding a dog sleigh.

The family's taken me out to restaurants they sure don't have in Smicksburg. Last night we ate on the twenty-eighth floor of a building in Toronto. It took us a little under an hour to get there, but I had lobster for the first time. Mamm, I love your cooking, but I've never tasted anything so good. For dessert, there was a separate menu., I didn't know what some of the things were, but when I saw pie, Mamm, I thought of you and ordered cherry. Hands down, your cherry pies are better. Maybe you should try selling them. I know Hannah likes to bake and since Cassia's so busy and Anna went home, she'd be right good company for you. I'm sure Lily's with Edmond a lot.

How's Edmond's proving time coming along and his baptism classes? I know him. He'll come over and you'll tutor him like you did with herbs. I still shake my head that he's giving up being a real doctor to be Amish, and I'm furhoodled over how we could have missed Lily's love for Edmond for so long. Lily wrote to Edmond for two years and I always knew she took a shining to him. Remember how she cried when he left for Haiti? But she was sixteen and being the baby of the family, we treated her like one.

Well, I best get going. Write me about what's new at home, and Daed, I'm worried about my dogs. Are you sure Hannah can handle being in charge? She acts all confident and all, but she's not. Can you keep an eye on the dogs along with Martin? Course, Lily can help, too.

Your loving son,
Willow

P.S. UPS order should be coming next week. More stuff for the kennel, so keep an eye out for it. I told Hannah what to do with the things when they come.

"He mentioned Hannah how many times?" Reed asked.

Dorcas scanned the letter. "Four."

"Poor kid. He went there to forget her."

"He went there to forget Anna you mean?"

"*Nee*, Anna was a decoy."

She crossed her legs and arms. "A decoy as in a wooden duck decoy?"

"Well, you know, her pretty face drew him, but Hannah's the real duck and Willow knows it."

Dorcas snickered. "You do have odd ways of saying things at times. I think Willow's only up there to see how Amish he is. And I have a peace in my heart. Get up at night to pray for him now and then, having a hankering something's wrong, but I'm not fretting. Are you?"

"*Nee*, me fret? It does no *gut*, only gives me indigestion. Concerned, but not fretting."

She yanked at his beard playfully. "What's the difference?"

"I'm not all worked up and fearful. Willow's a straight shooter and knows who he is. It's the Peter's daughter."

"And what's wrong with her?"

Reed groaned. "She's a decoy and a prettier one than Anna."

"You met the girl?"

Reed nodded. "Peters came when you were visiting the *kinner* in Troutville. She was a right out flirt with Willow."

Dorcas clucked her tongue. "Then why'd you

encourage him to go?"

"*Ach*, he needed no encouragement. He's wanted to travel, remember?"

She pressed her foot on the floor, stopping the swing. "He wants to get married, too!"

The sudden fear in his dear wife's eyes made him naturally pull her close. "He's been planted in *gut* soil for twenty-two years. He'll survive the winds."

She nestled into his embrace. "He'll be twenty-three in November. He better come home for his party. We always make a big to-do."

"You do make a nice home here." He pinched her cheek. "Still having parties for all the married *kinner*, and *grosskinner*. How many cakes do you make in a year?"

"Lost count. Maybe thirty-some, but it's well worth the effort to make someone feel special and get some of the family together."

"Sure am glad you believe in homemaking. Can you imagine if you worked all day as a dentist and then came home to cook? You'd be no *gut* to anyone, always tired."

She pinched his cheek. "*Nee*, I'd lend you my cookbook."

A yell coming from around the side of the house startled Reed as he was about to kiss his dear wife. Soon, Hannah ran to them, shaking. "What is it?"

"Dorcas, come with me. It's Cassia. I think she's losing her *boppli*."

~*~

That night, Hannah held her best friend's hand, willing her to stop sobbing so. Never in all her life had she seen

Cassia wail in grief. What should she say? *You can have other boppli? Nee,* the wee boy lost was something to be grieved. "I'm here for you…"

Martin came into the bedroom, his face sullen. "I'll sit next to her. You must be hungry."

She was famished and heard Granny Weaver and Jeb downstairs. Granny never went anywhere without a pie or meal. "Let me know if I'm needed, Martin. I'll stay the night if you'd like."

Cassia howled all the louder. "*Jah,* Hannah, *jah!*"

Sorrow filled Hannah's soul. How she loved Cassia since first grade. They were true bosom friends. How glad she was that Cassia had suggested knitting together to mend their friendship. *And all because of my jealous heart,* Hannah chided. No, everyone has pain in their lives and how she wished she could carry it for Cassia.

She padded down the stairs to find not only Granny but the entire knitting circle. "How did *yinz* know what happened?"

Janice tapped her gold wristwatch. "It's seven o'clock, dear. Granny was over at Forget-Me-Not Manor to teach the girls how to cook. Word got to her and she brought lots of stew and biscuits."

"And they are good," Suzy, quipped. "Let me get you a bowl full."

Hannah collapsed on a nearby chair. "What are we going to do? Cassia's so broken."

Granny held a handkerchief to dab her tears. "We need to knit together once Cassia's up to it. *Yinz* know how much it's helped us all."

Heads bobbed in agreement.

"With winter coming on in a month or two, we'll be cooped up again," Hannah said robotically. She surveyed the room. "Where's Dorcas?"

"She's lying down with Rose, the *boppli's* fussing for her *mamm*," Granny said. "She'll need to knit, too."

Hannah tasted the stew Suzy set before her, the aroma of beef, carrots and potatoes with lots of pepper made her mouth water, so she dug in. "When?" she asked.

"Well, we meet Thursday afternoon," Suzy informed. "I close the store at noon and then it's tea time and knitting."

Granny cleared her throat. "So, it's Thursdays at two o'clock. It being Friday, that gives Cassia near a week to recover…" Granny covered her face with her handkerchief.

Suzy rushed to put an arm around Granny. "Still brings back memories?"

"What memories?" Hannah wanted to know.

"Granny had a stillborn baby girl," Janice said as she massaged Granny's shoulders.

A hush whisked through the room. Hannah stared at the wide plank oak floor. She'd thought Granny never had a care in the world. To have this pain so fresh after so many years, was shocking, and she realized her weakness: *fear of hurt*. Granny embraced life, the good and bad and believed God made all things work together for the good. How could she be more like Granny? Not run away from pain, for starters. Her plan to keep Andy at a distance; was it fear of pain? Shame filled her; she was like a cat, always wanting to purr. *In this world you will have troubles*, Jesus had said in the Gospels. Why was she such a coward?

Karen Anna Vogel

Chapter 2

*W*hile writing a letter home, Willow felt a tickle on the back of his neck and swatted it, thinking it was a bug, only to find a slim, soft hand. Dumbfounded, he turned to find Cheri. "What are you doing in my room?"

"Door was open," she cooed, running a finger across his suspenders. "Want to go to the mall with me? Get you some new clothes?"

Willow had decided he'd dress Amish, feeling so uncomfortable in blue jeans on the trip up. "I have clothes. No sense in wasting money."

She twirled around, her skirt flowing up as she began clicking her boots and clapping her hands. "You need some dancing clothes. I'm taking you Line Dancing this weekend. Need boots, a flannel shirt and more jeans."

"D-Dance?" he stuttered, trying to avoid staring at her shapely legs. "Amish don't dance."

Cheri tapped her boot heel a few times and then danced towards him, sitting in his lap. "You're not Amish, jay?"

Her fragrant perfume intoxicated him as she brushed aside his bangs. "A new haircut, too, jay?"

"W-Why are you calling me Jay?" he asked as she turned his head from one side to another.

"You say it all the time, jay?"

A nervous laugh erupted. "That's Pennsylvania Dutch for yes. We say *'jah'* not jay."

She giggled. "You have so much to teach me if we're to get to know each other better. I say you get your hair cut short on the sides and longer on top. It'll fit your cute face." She yanked him up. "Now, put your hand around my waist and I'll teach you some dance steps."

He thought his head would catch fire, half embarrassed and half burning with desire. Cheri was prettier than Anna.

"Come on," she cooed. "Time to throw off the Amish and have fun."

He ignored the comment and as if spellbound, he was following her lead, Cheri very near as they tapped toes and heels and clapped hands for a few minutes. When it was time to take a twirl, she wrapped her arms around his neck and pulled him into a kiss, whispering "You are so adorable."

Willow backed away, passion flaming in him in a way he'd never known existed.

She took his hand. "Let's go shopping, I want to show you off at the dance."

"Show me off?"

"*Jah*. It's about time this small town knew what 'drop dead gorgeous' meant. You know you are, right?"

"*Nee*, I don't. And it's what a person's like on the inside that matters...."

Cheri twirled around again, her panties showing. "Do you think I'm gorgeous?"

Willow said yes before thinking and she was soon too near him again, lacing her fingers around his neck. "Your mouth is perfect." She kissed him hard and then her lips moved down his neck.

Something inside him told him to run for his life, but this new sensation made him weak and powerless. Self-control he knew was important to keep his integrity, but this was a power he'd never known could bring a strong man down. Willow, raked his fingers though her silky hair, until he thought of Hannah, and shame filled him. Pushing her away, he said he felt weak and was maybe coming down with something. Cheri didn't care, but Willow managed to get her out of the room, and he locked the door.

He laid on his bed, sensations tingling through him. *Lord, forgive me for what I was thinking. You know my thoughts, and it was beyond kissing, things married couples do. And I don't want to do it with anyone but my wife. Lord, are you tempting me? Testing me? Do all men go through this?*

Trying to regain his composure, he took a pen and paper on his nightstand and started a letter to Martin, a man in the past who taught him the Bible and lived out his faith when in such suffering. He'd give him wise counsel.

~*~

The next few days he was a hen hiding from a fox. When Cheri drove to college, he went to work with the dogs and found Mr. Peters nice company. The man was in his fifties, but lifted weights and ran, trying to be fit to race his dogs.

"When the snow really flies, I'll teach you how to use the sled," Mr. Peters said. "For now, the team needs exercise and my Labs need to learn to track a scent. I'd like Lucy here to be a search and rescue dog."

Willow leaned over to rub the dog behind the ears. "You're a sweet girl, Lucy. Labs are smart, for sure and certain."

"Before you set to work, you'll need some winter clothes. A down jacket and overalls. Don't need to change from your Amish clothes if you don't want to. They'll do fine, but outer gear up here is essential. How about we go into town and get you fixed up?"

Low on cash and not being paid yet, he shook his head. "Next week, when I get paid."

Mr. Peters dug into his pocket and pulled out five bills. "Here's five smackers. Like to pay in advance. Sorry I forgot."

"*Danki*...I mean thank you."

Slapping Willow on the back, Mr. Peters said, "I like you, Willow Byler. You're like an old-fashioned man of integrity. I'd never let a non-Amish man live in my house with my daughter. Glad Cheri's commuting to college so you can get to know her."

Willow gulped. "What's she studying?"

"She wants to be a vet tech. She loves dogs as much as I do, so she's specializing in small animals. Said they can't fend for themselves, or something like that."

Willow listened to him tell of the types of birds Cheri nursed back to health, setting them free when healed, as they hopped into his pickup truck. "Yes, she even tamed a deer once. Folks didn't believe me until they came and saw it for themselves. Cheri would get up at the crack of dawn when she was around ten and whistle and before you knew it, the deer would come out of the woods."

"Really? Never heard such a thing," Willow said, admiration for Cheri rising.

"She's a certified animal rescuer for all types of animals, but right now, I told her school came first and settling down. She's got a wild side to her like the animals and it's time to put away childish ways."

Willow recalled a Bible verse saying something similar.

As they drove down the hill away from the mansion perched on hill, a red-tailed hawk flew above and Willow arched his neck to get a better view.

"Cheri tamed a raven, I kid you not. It was an old bird, only lived a few years, but that bird flew where Cheri drove when she got her license. She'd open the sunroof, raise her hand, and the bird would swoop down and perch on her hand."

Willow chuckled. "Now I know you're pulling my leg."

"It's the honest to God truth. I'd swear on a Bible. She wasn't driving fast when the bird perched, but real slow. She only did it on back roads where there's little traffic. When that bird died, you'd have thought she lost a family member."

Willow took this all in. Was Cheri affectionate by nature, kind to critters and overly affectionate near strangers? He could still taste her cherry lipstick. "Why doesn't a girl like Cheri have a fiancé by now?"

Mr. Peters clung to the steering wheel. "Engaged? *At eighteen?*"

"*Jah*, it's common among the Amish."

"Well, she's not Amish. But truth is, we all thought she might be making plans with Jason Ingersole, but when he headed out to college in British Columbia, he dropped my Cheri like a hot potato. She cried day and night. I had a notion to go over to the Ingersole's and blacken that boy's eye, but you can't make someone love your daughter like a dad does."

"How long ago was this?"

"Oh, several months ago. I have to say, she's cheered up quite a bit since you've come. Well, I have a confession, really. I love all I read about the Amish, so pure and wholesome. When we came down to your place, I thought a nice young Amish man could show Cheri what a real gentleman was like, so I got the notion of you coming to work for me."

Shame filled Willow. He'd kissed up a storm with Cheri and Mr. Peters wanted him to be a good example. Well, at least now he knew where her pent-up passion came from. Cheri missed Jason Ingersole and he was the rebound. How could he teach her what a gentleman was like when he felt so ungentlemanly-like around her? He hoped Martin got his letter and would reply as soon as possible.

~*~

Lily tapped her toes when nervous, and now, watching Jeb Weaver's hawk eyes on Edmond, she felt like a baby rabbit on the run. But she was ever so confident that Edmond could overcome this hurdle.

"Reed Byler's going to Mexico. Why can't I?" Edmond asked. "We can bring back knowledge about alternative medicine and at the same time, help children, sometimes saving their lives."

Jeb pulled at his lengthy gray beard while Granny put a plate of homemade whoopie pies on the table. "Sometimes things go down better with some sugar," she said, glancing at her husband. "Lots of Amish traveling these days."

Jeb plucked up a chocolate whoopie pie. "Old woman, you have the advantage and you know it."

"Advantage?" Lily asked. "Of course, she bakes better than you, Jeb?"

He swooshed his hand as of shooing a fly. "I was raised in a strict Amish sect and Deborah a liberal one."

"Who's Deborah? Someone who was shunned?" Edmond asked sincerely.

Granny chuckled. "That's my name, along with 'Old Woman.'"

Lily reached for Edmond's hand. "I hope we're like you two when we're old." She cupped her mouth. "I mean older than…we are…when we've been married a long time."

Now Jeb laughed. "Why so nervous Lily? We're old and know it. "Not spring chickens anymore. And it makes me all the graver to keep the Old Order Ways going smoothly."

"Like Jeb was saying," Granny added, settling next to Jeb. "He came from a strict Amish Order that wasn't even allowed to take a ride in a car. They still exist, some coming to the auction in August clear from Cambria County, some fifty miles away, by horse and buggy. Now, I came from not a liberal, but a more lenient sect in Ohio." She slid closer to Jeb. "Iron sharpens iron, as the Good Book says."

"But what does that really mean?" Edmond asked. "Like when two knives are sharper when rubbed together?"

"*Jah*," Jeb and Granny said in unison.

"Sounds like war, not a marriage. Lily and I agree on most things."

"But, you need to agree with the *Ordnung*, Edmond," Jeb said. "Would you give up this monkey business of leaving the country to study to abide by the *Ordnung*…to be able to marry Lily?"

Edmond bit his lower lip, his eyes piercing the table.

The pendulum clock ticked, and the scent of dried corn and apples drifted through the open window. Lily examined Edmond closely. He was clearly torn. After all he'd said, would he give up being Amish just to take a trip to Mexico? What was wrong with her *daed* and *bruder*? What was this travel fever all about?

Jeb cleared his throat. "Let me talk to Reed. He's the one who put this monkey business –"

"It's not monkey business," Edmond snapped. "Kids die for lack of medicine. They line up for miles to get shots that will help them make it to be five years old. Amish can travel by train, so what's the problem?"

Jeb's eyebrows arched so high, they slipped behind his bangs. "We move slowly, Edmond. What we do as a

People has been handed down since the seventeenth century."

"I know but –"

"Are you willing to bend the will? Or as an *Englisher* said in a book, 'It's not about me'. *Jah?* It's called *Gelassenheit.* It means humility and putting one's own desires aside for the *gut* of the People. Can you do that? If not, there's no sense in going any further in your baptismal classes."

Lily withdrew her hand from Edmond. Her life was being held by a thin thread, like Rahab, who put out a scarlet thread to save herself and her family. *Lord, help me if Edmond says no.*

Karen Anna Vogel

CHAPTER 3

Willow,

This may not be my best letter. Cassia had a miscarriage and we're grieved to the core. Your parents may have tried to call, so I don't know if you know. It's been tough here. Cassia's blaming herself for not resting enough, but we had Anna here to help. Cassia thrives at the herb shop and it did our boppli no harm. We named him Frankincense, Frank for short. Prayer's been a big part of my life, especially when sick with Lyme Disease. I wanted my son to be a man of prayer. Frankincense, as you know, was burnt in the Temple in the Old Testament as a symbol of prayer. His Bible verse would be "Psalm 141:2. Let my prayer be set forth before thee as incense; and the lifting up of my hands as the evening sacrifice."

This is his life verse, even though he lived a few minutes, but went to be with Jesus. Some say he looked like me. Imagine that.

So, I'm not up to par to give advice. Flee from sin. You and Hannah are good friends. Maybe she can help you understand this young woman. I'll write back as soon as I get my wits about me.

Martin.

"*Ach*, Cassia!" he blurted. "And I can't be with you, so far away." Helplessness enveloped him and then homesickness. Family and community helping mourn a death by sitting with the family, not speaking, but sitting. It was their way. Was the baby old enough to be embalmed and then viewed at the family home? Was there food being taken over?

He reread the letter as tears spilled over it. *Flee from evil. Maybe Hannah can help?* What was Martin thinking? He had Cassia, Lily and a *mamm* to talk to if he wanted womanly advice. Feeling frustrated, he knew he needed to be by the dogs who always calmed him down. He rose from his desk to see a little red car pulling up the driveway. *Cheri*. Why was she home? She had an afternoon class. Trying to avoid her was becoming harder and Willow grabbed his new coat and ran out of the massive house on the opposite end of the garage. He hid behind a colossal oak, feeling ever like an idiot, until he saw movement in the house through the many windows. Cheri was inside. No one was home, so she'd look for him. *Lord, I don't want to be lured like a fish.*

Snow crystals sashayed onto him as he speculated what to do. Should he hide behind a tree or go in and see if she was sick or something? Cheri took her studies so seriously; she may be ill. Knowing the answer, he started for the house. "Cheri, you okay?"

She appeared behind the granite countertop that encircled the open kitchen. "I'm sick. Barely made it home." She lifted a can of soup. "Going to make this."

"I can do it. Go lay down."

She tried to smile, but was so pale, she nodded and went over to the leather couch in the living room. "Sure is cold in here."

"I'll make a fire in the fireplace and have your soup to you in no time."

She wrapped herself in a wool blanket. "You're sweet."

Willow didn't want to give Cheri the wrong impression. He wasn't falling for her charms, but truly felt sorry for her. "I'm moved with compassion," he said, knowing it sounded out of place.

Her teeth chattered and as soon as he had the soup going, he ran to the fireplace and threw some kindling in, and then a few logs. Striking the match, it soon caught fire.

"I love the s-sound of c-crackling w-wood," she chattered.

Willow knew she had the chills and should put his lips to her forehead to check for a fever. But was it wise? "Do you have a thermometer?"

"Can't you feel my forehead?"

"My hands are cold."

She moaned. "Then use your lips."

Flee from evil? No, this was necessary. He pressed his lips on her forehead. "You're burning up. I'll call your mom. She'd want to know."

Cheri rolled her eyes. "She's working and I'm n-not a b-baby. G-Get me some medicine."

Willow ran to the first-floor bathroom and rummaged through the medicine cabinet, grabbed a few bottles and rushed back to her. "Here, take this. The liquid will get to your blood stream faster." He poured the gooey syrup into the cup and held it to her lips.

Cheri sipped it down and groaned again. "Willow, I'm so achy all over. Can you hold me?"

She was suddenly so dependent and childlike. She wanted comfort, but how? Dogs. "How about I bring in the lab I'm training? He'll be a *gut* comfort."

"Dad doesn't want the dogs in the house."

"Why don't you have a cat?" he asked out of pure frustration.

"Don't yell at me. I'm sick."

"*Ach*, I wasn't yelling." Before he knew it, he was sitting next to her, his arms around her, trying to sooth her. She shivered for a spell and then calmed down enough to say, 'thank you' and fell asleep. Willow looked out of the wall of windows and thought of his sister, so far away, needing his embrace more than Cheri. He thought of dependable Hannah. He'd write to her to make sure she took care of her best friend.

~*~

Hannah sat between Dorcas and Cassia at knitting circle. She brought four embroidered handkerchiefs, two already given to the grieving *mamm* and *grossmammi*. As was their way, someone sat with Cassia since the burial, and now, with *English* friends.

Suzy cracked the door leading to her living room. "Janice called. Has the church flu and I think I do, too. I'll keep my distance. *Yinz* know where the tea is and whatnot. And Granny may show up yet with a treat."

"Hope you feel better," Cassia said in a hollow voice, not looking up.

Ach, the pain in Cassia's heart. Hannah hoped Granny would show soon, the elderly woman having just the right words to say. This room always being full of cheer and lots of chatter, was silent. *Ach*, what to say? She cleared her throat. "So, what are you making with all that black yarn, Cassia?"

"My mourning shawl," Cassia said in monotone.

How stupid of me! Hannah turned to Dorcas, who was continuing a blue alpaca project. "Well. I'm finishing up the little *boppli* sweater I was making…" She held it up limply. "Just need to make the sleeves."

Cassia burst into tears, her body shaking. "I can't knit. Making mistakes."

Hannah hugged her friend, taking Cassia's black yarn. "How about you crochet? I can knit you a shawl."

"Would you?" Dorcas added. "Cassia's tired of seeing black, I'm thinking."

Cassia nodded in agreement.

Hannah handed her mint green yarn. "Finish this scarf. Making them for the homeless and it'll be outright chilly soon."

"*Jah*," Cassia said. "Knitting for charity… helps me, too."

"Blessed are they that give," Dorcas said flatly. "Anytime I need a touch from above, I give to someone. Somehow it lifts my burden."

Hannah heard the little bell on Suzy's yarn shop. Relief swept over her. *Granny is here!* "We're in the back."

Heavier footsteps than Granny's were heard. To Hannah's shock, Andy leaned on the Dutch door, the top being open. "Andy, do you need...yarn?"

"*Nee*, came by to see you. Your *mamm* said you were here."

Irritation slithered down her spine. This was her bonding time with women friends. "Is something wrong?"

He curled his finger towards him. "Need to ask you something."

Heat on her cheeks, she inwardly rolled her eyes and went into the yarn shop, closing the top of the Dutch door. "What is it?"

"Well," he started, his eyes twinkling. "Finally heard back from my driver. Can you go out with me for dinner in Indiana tomorrow? I've missed you." He took her hands. "I know Cassia needs you, but we're courting, *jah*?"

"*Jah*," she said. Hannah knew she had to try to rid herself of fear of hurt, of men, but Andy seemed a bit too smitten with her. This was all happening too fast. She'd only agreed to court last week. "Cassia's mighty down. I don't know."

"She has plenty of family. I'm sure she won't miss you one night. And you need a nice relaxing dinner, *jah*?" Andy probed.

She did need a rest, after cooking meals to take over to Cassia and Dorcas. Lily was a big help, but busy with teaching. "*Jah*, okay. I would like a meal I don't have to prepare."

He kissed her cheek, the rim of his black wool hat hitting her in the eye. "Ouch," she moaned, flinching.

He removed his hat. "*Ach*, sorry. I'm so clumsy." He pulled her to him and planted a kiss on her lips.

She pushed him away. "Don't steal kisses," she chided. "Don't be hasty."

"*Jah*," Granny said, standing in the door frame.

Hannah was now red as beets. "Granny. I didn't hear the bell."

She wagged a finger. "Courting's done in secret, but I suppose yours is out. Andy, I know Hannah, but not you. Save such kissing for marriage."

He straightened. "It was a mere peck."

"Looked like Hannah couldn't breathe, for Pete's sake." Granny eyed Hannah. "Do you encourage this?"

Filled with indignation, she said evenly, "I'm not a *boppli*."

"*Ach*. I see." Granny challenged. "You've courted in secret and will wed soon. When will you be published?"

"Married?" Hannah gasped. "We just started courting. A week ago."

"Slow down then."

Hannah robotically nodded her head, but Andy stepped forward. "I'm thirty-five. My own *mamm* doesn't talk to me like I was born yesterday."

"Well, maybe she should," Granny snapped. "Now, I need to give the girls their treats." She huffed. "Walnut kisses of all things. Hannah, will you be going back to the tea room? *Now?*"

"In a minute," Hannah informed, wanting to confront Andy on how rude he was to Granny.

Granny, tapping her umbrella on the wooden floor, jutted her chin and entered the back room.

"Andy, Granny's your elder. You don't speak to her like that. It lacks…humility."

"She was being rude!"

"She was being protective of me. Granny knows how Freeman broke my heart and how hard it's been to move on. To trust men."

He nodded, setting his hat back on. "I didn't know that. I'm sorry." His green eyes were moist and filled with pain, as if he was carrying her burden. She wished right now he would steal a kiss.

CHAPTER 4

Hannah picked a rare daisy that wasn't killed by the autumn frost. How odd it was there, alone, white petals with a bright yellow center. Was this her 'He loves me; he loves me not' daisy to pick apart? She slipped it into her apron pocket. No, she was not going to turn it into a fleece before God. She wasn't going to depend on a flower to tell her if she was loved. Truth was, she didn't know if she wanted Andy's love. Her *mamm* told her she was a flower that opened slowly. Andy was pulling a bit too fast at her petals lately, and it made her want to run. But, as Cassia had said, pain is a part of loving. Her pain was nothing compared to her best friend's. She was more afraid of the future, of trusting a man, of being a spinster and having the entire community pity her. *Lord, help me.*

As she neared her house, she decided to check the mail. Maybe her pen pal from Montana wrote. She riffled through bills and junk mail until she saw a letter from Canada. *Willow!* She ripped it open to read:

Hannah,

How have you been? I'm settling in up here best I can.

Martin wrote and told me about Cassia's miscarriage. I may as well be the man on the moon, so far away and can't be there for her. Can you have her call me? Stupid me, I didn't give out the Peters's phone number.

Can you do something for me? Cassia loves fudge over at the Village Sampler. Can you get her a pound of chocolate and I'll pay you back? If you can think of anything she'd like better, you're her best friend so pick something else. I'm willing to spend fifty bucks.

So how are my dogs? How are you?

All my contact info's on the back of this letter. Write back,
Willow

She blinked back tears. Willow was the sweetest brother ever. But the tone of his letter concerned her. He seemed so homesick and unhappy. Or was he being mistreated? *Stupid me?* He never called himself stupid. Were the Peters treating him dumb like some *Englishers* do, knowing the Amish only go to the eighth grade?

She looked up as the moon slightly appeared, as the dusk set in. Willow was far away, and she missed him. She'd never admit it to a soul, but her little *bruder* was up there among the *English*, and that flirty girl. That girl that could lead him down a path of destruction. Was she making him feel stupid?

"This is ridiculous," Hannah spoke out to the moon. "I'll just call him from the phone shanty before it gets dark." She pulled tight her shawl and ran onto the path leading to a shed set in the back of a cornfield. The cornstalks, all dried and leaning together to make little mountains was one of her favorite scenes of autumn. She recalled the time Willow took a ladder up the corn mound and slept on it. He was only eight, and no one could find him. Cassia was spitting mad when she discovered his refuge and he refused to come down. He'd tied one leg down in case he rolled over at night. His parents thought it was funny and let him sleep under the stars for a week, until he missed his bed.

Reaching the phone shanty, she wrote in her name, the number and put five dollars in the jar. But she only had a quarter, so she called collect. A female voice spoke, and she asked, "Hannah who?" Hannah quickly said she was Willow's friend.

The voice mumbled something under her breath and Willow was put on. "I'll accept the charges," he said. "Hannah, is that you?"

"*Jah*, it's me. Just got your letter. I'll get Cassia fudge and some yarn I know she has a hankering for. Are you all right?"

"*Jah*, sure. Are my dogs okay?"

"*Jah*, fine."

"So you called to say you got my letter? Why not just write back?"

Why didn't she just write back? Feeling like a fool, she blurted, "Are you okay? Are they treating you *gut*?"

"*Jah*. I'm only sad about Cassia's *boppli*."
Silence.
"I miss you, Willow. You've never been away."
Silence.
"I should get going, *jah*?" Hannah uttered.

"*Jah. Danki* for calling."

Hannah's chin shook, but she managed a "*Gut nacht.*"

"Hannah, you crying? Is Cassia worse than everyone's saying?"

"*Nee*, she's knitting again, and time will heal her sorrow."

"If I need to come down, I will."

"Don't worry about Cassia. She's strong. And she has Martin."

"*Gut.* Well, *gut nacht* again, Hannah."

Why was she crying now, in a full blubber? She coughed, grunting a good night back, and near threw the phone back into the cradle. "Hannah, what's wrong with you? Such a *bopphl*! You got homesick when staying over at Cassia's when twelve! Grow up," she chided herself, reaching for a handkerchief, but pulled out a daisy, and threw it in the field.

~*~

A week after Cheri was bedridden with fever, it was a mystery to Willow how quickly she rebounded and was again pouncing on him, eager for all his attention. How he let Cheri talk him into this country line dancing was a mystery. She was so good at…tugging at his heart. That's what she did. Used her misty eyes begging for male attention to lure him in like a fish, and before he knew it, he'd bitten the worm. He sure was a fish out of water here. A bar with neon lights, advertising all kinds of beer, girls in skimpy shorts twirling around, and Cheri making eyes at him to beat the band.

"Come on, cowboy, let's dance like we rehearsed."

Yanking him onto the dance floor, he stepped to the tune of *Cotton Eye Joe*. He kicked his foot forward two times, and then back twice, and then more tapping and twirling. Some shouted and out a 'heehaw' and Willow soon got to feeling 'fancy free,' as Cheri said to him at times. *I'll make you fancy, yet, Willow. Foot loose and fancy free.* He danced up a storm, waiting for the next song.

"I love this song! *Shake it for Me!*" Cheri shouted, as she playfully shoved Willow off the wooden floor. "Watch me."

Having never heard this one, he took a seat. A burly man asked him if he wanted a beer, but he declined. But the man persisted, daring him to guzzle it down, *Amish boy*. But he was wearing a plaid shirt, jeans and boots to fit in. "Not Amish," he retorted.

He threw up both his hands as if under arrest. "Cheri said you were. No offense."

Willow slouched and watched Cheri as she danced and indeed, shook her hips, making eyes at him. He gulped. Cheri was one gorgeous creature. He stared until the song was over and she ran to sit in his lap.

"Did you like that?" she asked, kissing his cheek.

He nodded, her perfume penetrating his senses. "You dance *gut*."

"*Gooood*. Not *gut*. Remember, Fancy Free's your name now." She entwined her finger behind his neck. "You can do what you want. We can go up in the hay loft."

She jumped up and yanked at Willow. "Follow me, Fancy."

He was a sheep before the shearers, not saying a word. But when he looked out of the open barn doors, a light shined on something across the street. *Lord's Mennonite Church.* Willow's knees near buckled. What was he doing? He needed to get to church and fast. *If anyone thinks he stands, take heed lest he fall.* Willow remembered the Bible verse and his *daed's* shaking finger, warning him of the wayward women in Proverbs.

Instead of following Cheri up the ladder, he walked out of the barn and across the street and knocked on the door. Did people knock on church doors? Who would answer? Did *Englisher* preachers live inside? But the door opened, and in he walked into the scent of pine. Pine floors and benches lined towards the front where a pine podium stood. And on the pews were people his age, dressed plainly, praying with people who were wearing cowboy hats, flannel shirts and boots. The burly man who offered him a beer had his head down praying. A man had his hand on his back, and they appeared to be praying out loud. How odd.

"Can I help you?" a sweet voice from behind asked. He spun around and wasn't prepared for what he saw. A woman pretty enough to be on a cover of one of those Amish fiction books he saw at Walmart. Her dark hair was more exposed, her prayer *kapp* only big enough to cover her hair put up in a bun. And he could see through it. "Hello," he managed. "I'm Willow. Nice to see some plain folk around."

Her eyes widened. "I'm Betty. Are you thinking of joining the plain people?"

"I'm Amish," he answered.

"Amish. Really? *Wo kommen Sie her?*"

"Smicksburg." He took off his cowboy hat and fidgeted with the brim. "Why are you speaking German?"

"Because I can. How about you?"

"Pennsylvania Dutch."

Their eyes met and held, but soon Betty's laugh lines showed. "Thought you were kidding. You really are Amish? For real?"

"*Jah*, I am. Working up here training dogs for the Peters. Know them?"

Her face fell. "Did Cheri Peters take you to the dance?"

Willow nodded, observing the concern etched on Betty's face. "Why do you ask?"

Betty's eyes seemed to catch fire. "You run for the hills from that girl. Flee from evil," she warned, her voice low.

"She's one hurting girl," he retorted. "Only out for attention."

"The wrong attention," Betty snapped. "You look old to be on *rumspringa*, but if you haven't decided to stay plain, at least don't go down the broad road that leads to destruction."

Willow felt heat rise from his collar and he loosened a button. "*Danki*. I saw that sign and…"

"No need to explain. We're open when the dancing goes on. There's not only dancing going on, if you know what I mean…"

Where were the men? Willow wanted to shout. Men minister to men, not women, especially about touchy issues.

She handed him a little book and church bulletin. "Come to church tomorrow. You'll find help."

"You sure it's this Sunday or the next?"

She grinned. "Every Sunday. If you come early, we have Sunday School."

"Every Sunday?"

She laughed infectiously. "*Jah*, every Sunday. Amish go every other Sunday, right?"

"How'd you know that?"

"I was Amish," she said, her hips ever so slightly swaying, her long mauve skirt flowing.

~*~

That night, Cheri gave Willow the cold shoulder, until it was midnight. The door opened, and in slithered Cheri, taking off her robe to reveal a see-through night gown. And Willow saw through. "What are you doing?"

"We're going to finish what we started."

Willow jumped out of bed, glad to have worn pajamas instead of just boxers. "Get out, Cheri. You're better than this."

"Oh, I'm good all right."

"*Nee*, you're a better woman than this. Women who seduce men aren't respected."

In the dim light of the moonlight sloping in from the window, her shoulders slumped. "What did you say?"

"Men use you. Men don't want to marry a girl who's been used. Understand?"

She covered her face. "They love me."

"*Nee*, they don't. Like I said, they're using you for their selfish lusts."

"You don't know anything. You're an inexperienced Amish boy."

"*Jah*, I'm pure, if that's what you mean, and I plan on staying that way until I'm married."

"You're kidding," she hissed.

He turned from her as his eyes adjusted to the dark. "Listen, Cheri, you need to talk to someone. Do you want to go to church with me tomorrow?"

"Where?" she asked, her defenses seeming to diminish.

Baffled at her emotional ups and downs, he told her about the Mennonite Church.

"Dress like an Amish freak? No way."

"But there's a nice woman there I know could help."

She put up her nose. "You're trying to convert me? No, way. I'll convert you one of these days, Fancy Free. Make you a real man."

"I'm already a real man," he retorted.

When she glided out, Willow ran to lock the door and collapsed on the bed. What should he do? Tell her parents? Leave? No, he made a commitment to Mr. Peters and most likely, he wouldn't believe him about Cheri's behavior. If he wrote his *daed*, he'd be telling him to run for the hills, straight south back down to Smicksburg. *Edmond.* He was considered a handsome man by women and probably encountered such a woman as Cheri. Maybe he could make an herbal tincture to make Cheri's brain work better. "Leave out passion root," he mumbled.

~*~

Hannah shouted to Willow, "Run! Run from that Jezebel!" But Willow stared at the woman in white, seduced by her beauty. "Run!" she screamed. "She'll kill you. Run, Willow!" Now she was on a bumpy buggy ride, being tossed by her *mamm's* erratic driving. "Slow down, *Mamm.*"

"Wake up," Esther cried out. "It's a nightmare."

Hannah gasped for air and shot up in bed. Seeing the concern imprinted on her *mamm's* brow, she tried to even her breathing. "Sorry. I..."

Feeling Hannah's forehead, Esther proclaimed no fever. "You were telling Willow to run."

"He needed to... in my dream."

"*Ach*, honey, I've never seen you in such a bad way. Do you think it's a warning from God?"

"A warning to Willow?" Hannah asked. "I don't know. It was so real and when I talked to him today, he sounded bad."

Esther planted both hands on Hannah's shoulders, leaning down to make eye contact. "And you called him because?"

"Because his letter was odd. I got concerned. He's like my *bruder*, you know. And ever since *Daed* passed, we've gotten closer. Him coming over to chop wood and whatnot."

A smile slid across Esther's face. "You miss him, *jah*?"

"Of course I do. Like I said, he's like a *bruder*."

"Only a *bruder*?" Esther raised an eyebrow. "I know Willow asked you to court and you turned him down. I think my *dochder* cares about Willow but is afraid of pain."

"*Mamm*, no disrespect." Hannah said, taking her *mamm's* hands. "I know you care, but I know my heart. Only I can know it, *jah*?"

"*Mamm's* have a way of seeing things. Freeman disappointed you, broke trust. You try to care for Andy, but you don't. But you called out Willow, are concerned that he's being tempted by another woman?"

"How did you know that?"

"You yelled out, 'Run from Jezebel' or something like that."

"Well, the Peters daughter is a flirt."

Esther pat Hannah's cheek. "And why would you care about that? You've always said Willow's shy and needs someone to bring him out of his shell."

Hannah gripped the bed sheets. "Not a Jezebel."

Esther rose and looked out the window. "Full moon tonight. What a soft glow it has. But you know, it's just made of rock, no light."

Hannah appreciated her *mamm's* love of nature, especially astronomy. "Can you see Mars and Venus?"

"*Nee*, not tonight. But like I was saying, it's funny how the moon has no light of its own, only reflects back the light of the sun."

"It is amazing," Hannah said.

"And some people just glow when they're around someone who brings out the best in them." She pulled her shawl tighter. "Sure do miss your *daed*. He did that for me, you know, bringing out the better part of me, character and talents I didn't know I possessed. Take astronomy, for instance. I thought I wasn't too smart, the universe is vast, and he urged me to learn all the constellations in the Almanac."

Hannah hugged her knees. "You miss him at night?"

"*Jah*, for sure. He was my best friend."

Hannah knew her parents were childhood friends who fell in love one day when he pushed her too hard on a tire swing. When she flew off, the wind was knocked out of her and he thought she was dead. It was then that her *daed* realized he loved her *mamm*.

"The right man brings the best out in you…I like Andy…but, not familiar with him. Need to get to know him if you're courting. He does treat you like a child at times, but he is older."

She was right. That's what bothered Hannah about Andy. He treated her like a child. But she could barely stay awake to admit it to her *mamm*. "We'll talk tomorrow."

Esther pressed a hand to her chest. "Sounds *gut*."

CHAPTER 5

Reed paced the wooden floor in his little shop, trying to calm himself, but it wasn't working. "Edmond not go to Mexico? We have it all planned. He was looking forward to it."

Jeb pulled his gray beard. "Edmond needs to show he can live simple. I see in him too much of a free independent spirit. I'm afraid he'll dart."

"He won't. Take my word for it. I know him like a son."

"Well, I don't, and Edmond's fickle. First he said God told him to be single and now get married. I don't think God's double-minded."

Reed raised a hand. "Single for a spell, not forever. Edmond never said that."

"Well, it's only been two years ago he said he'd be single. Aren't you concerned?"

"*Nee*, I know Edmond. Never thought he'd stay single. Now I never once thought of Lily for him, her being nine years younger. Thought he'd marry someone on the mission field, truth be told." He commenced pacing. "I think it was a test. Was he willing to be single to serve God? Was God first place in his heart? Edmond passed that test…"

"Hmm, you have something there," Jeb admitted. "Guess I'm being a bit cautious, but I'd like to see this travel fever be over and done with before Edmond's baptism."

Scratching his head, Reed paused. "Dorcas will be awful disappointed. Said the knitting circle's making things for the poor children over the border. Need help distributing it all."

Jeb threw up his hands in surrender. "*Ach, you* can go. You're not on a trial. But Edmond can't go with you. Best cancel his train ticket or take someone else with you who could be of use."

"Have anyone in mind?" Reed asked.

"Not at the moment, but I'll think on that."

The little gold bell jingled, and Janice Jackson popped her head in. "Looks like a serious discussion. Should I come back later?"

Reed grinned. "*Nee*, I just got an idea."

Janice slipped in. "Getting cold out there."

"How would you Baptists like to join some of us Amish on a trip to Mexico?"

Jeb's arms flailed. "Now, that's a *gut* idea. They can drive cars down there, *jah*? Would save you money."

Janice put two fingers in her mouth a blew out a whistle. "Wait a minute. Who said we Baptist's are going to Mexico?"

"Don't you think it's a *gut* idea? You know all about our trip."

"But to organize a full-fledge missions trip is work. We'd need to raise money. And our church has ministries it gives to."

"Well, this is a medical mission. Any medical people who might want to go?"

Janice's eyes soon appeared too big for her face. "Alex Newhouse. He's a physician's assistant who's been itching to go on such a trip."

"Will you talk to him?"

"Absolutely," Janice chimed, raising a finger to her cheek. "But, why not take Dorcas? She *'mans'* the store when no *'man'* is working."

Reed caught Janice's meaning. Why hadn't he thought of taking Dorcas! How foolish of him, thinking only men could go.

~*~

Edmond face was so stiff, he appeared inhuman. Jeb feared he'd pushed him too hard but it's what the elders had decided upon. "There's safety in a multitude of counsels," Jeb encouraged.

Granny lifted a piece of pie. "Maybe we can talk about it? Want some coffee, Edmond?"

"Alex Newhouse is an old friend of mine, you know. Fun guy to hang out with." He swiftly crossed his arms. "So the Baptist's encourage him to go, but not the Amish."

"Do you take cream and sugar, Edmond?" Granny asked.

"Yes. Please."

The cuckoo clock tweeted out the time and Jeb wished they had a large grandfather clock, the large pendulum such a calming tone. The tension in the air hung like a heavy fog. "Edmond, why compare the Baptist's ways with the Amish? We all have rules. Life is full of rules. You can't go 65 miles per hour in a 45-speed limit zone."

"*Jah*," Granny sighed. "Some of our drivers do that. I tell them to slow down, but they don't. No wonder there're accidents."

Edmond kept his head low, twiddling his thumbs. "Okay, I won't go to Mexico. If this is part of *gelassenheit*, I submit my will in order to be Amish."

Granny ran to him and slipped her arm through his. "It's painful, I know. I gave up a clothes dryer for life. You've only been asked to give up one little trip."

"*Jah*," Jeb quipped. "Maybe you can go on others, just not this one while under the proving time."

"It's okay," Edmond said, his face softening. "It's hard to be a dying person."

Granny stared up at him. "Edmond, are you ill?"

Edmond wrapped an arm around the dear woman. "No, I'm fine. As a Christian we're called to do God's will, not our own. It brings out the fruit of the Spirit. Love, joy, peace, patience kindness, goodness, faithfulness, gentleness and self-control. The next verse says we need to kill our flesh or pride daily to have this fruit."

Jeb reached over and clamped a hand on Edmond's shoulder. "When we draw the lot to see who's to be a minister in the church, I'm going to be tempted to put the paper in the book you choose."

"What?" Edmond looked truly perplexed. "That's a common Bible verse."

"It's connecting the two that would be a *gut* sermon. We can't be patient if we always want our way, so we need to crucify our flesh daily, like the Apostle Paul said. Is that the next verse?" Jeb ran to his book shelf in the living room to retrieve his Bible, perusing the pages as he plunked himself at the table. "Here it is. Galatians 5."

"But the fruit of the Spirit is love, joy, peace, longsuffering, gentleness, goodness, faith, meekness, temperance: against such there is no law. And they that are Christ's have crucified the flesh with the affections and lusts."

Granny hovered over Jeb, reading along. "Lust meaning like a lack of self-control, a strong longing towards something, *jah*?"

"*Jah*," Jeb said. "Well, well, I never knew a baptismal candidate could make me think deeper into the why of our ways. We sure do know our ways, but the why's not so much."

Edmond grew solemn. "It's common in Haiti. The Christians there have nothing but the Bible, so there aren't too many distractions. We're rich here in America in material things, but they're rich in the spiritual. And out of necessity they have to agree and depend on each other for survival."

"How about that," Granny said reverently. "How about that."

~*~

Willow gazed around the quaint living room. The stuffed furniture had a few too many pillows, but a crackling fire place, and floral wallpaper was appealing. Mennonites are indeed fancy, he discovered. The circle of young people, both male and female, sitting beside each other, not segregated was another oddity, but then again, this wasn't church, but a Bible study. As he recalled, at the church building, families sat together, which he found rather reasonable. Parents could help their *kinner* flip through their Bibles and find passages, or the *boppli* could be passed along to the father if cranky. Willow found much of what he'd seen of the Mennonites over the past weeks normal, as if he'd have arranged things this way himself. And he liked the change of clothing styles, especially among the women, who took pride in their small print dresses and skirts. Ever so modest, he wondered why Old Order Amish only allowed solid colors, even the hues stated in the *Ordnung*.

As they were instructed to get their cookies and hot chocolate while it lasted and take their seats in a few minutes, Willow made a beeline to the delicious cookies, bumping into a fellow, nearly toppling him over. A hardy laugh rang around the room. From the floor, the young man laughed. "You Amish are mighty aggressive, or you like cookies more than us Mennonites."

Willow offered a hand up. "Sorry about that. And I'm not Amish and we're not aggressive."

Betty laughed as she neared them. "You're Amish on *rumspringa* for now, Willow. Why not wear jeans?"

He'd missed his Amish attire for some reason but didn't know how to explain it "Feel at home in my old clothes." Willow ambled over to the cookie table, piling cookies onto two plates. He turned and eyed the man he knocked down. "I'm Willow Byler. You pick which plate you want."

"I'm Lee Angler. And I pick the one with the most chocolate chips," he quipped, taking a plate. "So, Willow, Betty told us you're from Pennsylvania. Are you homesick?"

"*Nee*, why do you ask?"

"You said you felt more at home in your Amish clothes. I felt that way before I made the leap."

Willow wasn't sure what Lee meant. "Do you mean you're not from these parts?"

"I was born fifty miles away but was Amish. Converted to being Mennonite before baptism."

"I thought I recognized a German accent," Willow said. "Where are the Amish up here?"

"Quite a bit away. Fifty miles, give or take a few. I hear you're staying with the Peters. How's that going?"

Willow wanted to crawl under the braided rug. Cheri threatened to make up stories about him making passes if he didn't give in to her passions. "What Cheri says isn't true," he blurted, feeling heat rise into his ears.

Betty stepped away. "I'll let you two talk," she said in a knowing way.

Lee clinched a hand on Willow's shoulder. "Run for your life. That girl's got one bad reputation. She's like Potiphar's Wife."

Willow nodded, remembering the wife who seduced Joseph in the Bible, him having to flee. "I want to keep up my end of the deal with Mr. Peters."

"But you're not as strong as you think, right? Remember, we all have feet of clay." He lowered his voice. "Is she really that bad? I mean, does she…you know, act like Potiphar's wife?"

Willow gulped, trying to get the image of her in a sheer nightgown out of his mind. "*Jah*, she is. I feel sorry for her, though. Her boyfriend dumped her when he went to college."

"Which one?" Lee asked. "She's had a string of them."

"Mr. Peters said she had one. One she hoped to marry."

"Well, he probably sees her through rose colored glasses. She's the biggest flirt in Ontario."

Willow nibbled at a cookie. "But why? Something makes a girl promiscuous. Maybe she's starved for attention."

"Whoa. You're taking this too light. Remember in Proverbs where it talks about loose women? She's one of them and it says to turn and run, or you'll ruin your life."

"But I have to stay there to work."

Lee snapped his fingers. "I can ask the Yoder family who's hosting me if you can board. They're former Amish and help others who want to leave."

Willow scratched his chin. "Don't know if I respect people who badmouth the Amish, if that's what they're doing."

"No, they're more respectful of the Amish than most. No pressure to leave since they know the consequences; they've been shunned." He grinned. "I'd rather take up Betty's folk's offer to stay with them, but it wouldn't be proper."

"Why not?" Willow asked.

"Kind of like her too much. Such a sweet girl."

Willow looked past Lee to observe Betty. "*Jah*, she is…"

~*~

Hannah wiped clean the last dog dish, went into Willow's little house to *redd* up, and then grabbed her wraps to walk home. Snow was spitting from the skies and she tried to catch a flake on her tongue. Willow was the best 'snow gobbler' as she recalled. He'd made up that name when in grade school. He could pounce to a flake and then snatch it with his tongue. What a sweet man Willow was, ever so trusting. When the older boys dared him to put his tongue to the frozen water pump, telling him he could warm it up for all to take a drink, Willow did it, his tongue stuck until the teacher set him free. She noticed tears in Willow's eyes, but Cassia turned him so no one would see. "Willow was tenderhearted since birth," Hannah mused to the cardinal that swooped down onto the fence post.

She heard a familiar meow, and soon Shadow made her usual trek up the alley way behind the houses to greet her after a day's work. Hannah scooped up the fur ball and held it tight. "Getting nippy out here, *jah*?" She stroked the cat as it nestled into her. "You purr as loud as an *Englisher* lawn mower. *Ach*, I'm so glad to have you, even though I miss Pumpkin sorely." The image of Willow rushing the cat to Dr. Fox's and his concern for her after the cat's death had touched something deep within. She couldn't put her finger on it, but it made her miss him. Why she panicked about his safety was irrational, and the more she prayed about it, the more the fears subsided.

When she rounded the bend to her house, her arms went limp, but she caught Shadow in time. "Freeman? What are you doing here?" Hannah held the cat close, as if to guard her heart. They were finished. No man had hurt her like this former fiancé.

"Please hear me out, Hannah. I made a mistake."

His handsome face drew her in, but she froze up. *The pain this man caused me…*

He offered his hand, but Shadow only pawed at it, leaving a scratch. "That's one feisty kitten."

She may sense fear, Hannah wanted to say, but she remained mum, too stunned to utter a word.

"Can we talk? I can take you to the Country Junction for coffee."

His eyes were pleading, but a pit lodged in her stomach. "*Nee*, Freeman. We best let things in the past stay there. I've moved on."

"There's someone else so soon?"

She could say Andy, but she was so unsure about him. Men. So controlling. She decided it was best to treat Freeman like a shunned man, ignoring him. She held Shadow close and walked past him.

"After reading your letter, I've decided to turn Amish for you."

Hannah stopped and then turned, incredulous. "Again? *Ach*, Freeman, you're like a…"

"Yoyo," he said with a winning grin. "I know. I've been off kilter and had no peace." He touched her face. "I've missed you. Can't imagine a life with you not in it, as my wife."

Memories flooded her, their first time holding hands. A spring breeze blew through her mind. She was in her garden, the scent of peonies perfuming the air. His hand on her cheek made her weak. He was a gentleman, never forcing a kiss, but ever so tender. "So you want to be Amish?" she found herself asking.

"Yes, I do. And I'll live here in Smicksburg, like we planned."

She shook her head. "I need to think, Freeman. This is too shocking."

"I've already talked to Jeb Weaver."

"What?"

"I wanted his blessing before seeing you."

"And he gave it?" Hannah croaked out.

"Well, I read between the lines. He didn't say no."

She eyed him with suspicion. "Jeb would never tell you to suggest marriage until you were baptized Amish. It was a mistake to listen to you last time. I took you at your word, Freeman, and you broke it."

"I'm sorry. I talked to Jeb about baptism classes and –"

"Talk to me after you're baptized. I will never leave the Amish."

A frown creased Freeman's forehead. "There's someone else, isn't there?"

She clenched her fists and oddly thought of Willow. "*Jah*, maybe there is. A woman's heart is to be won over by *gut* character. Maybe I appreciate someone more because I recognize...I don't even know the word. Integrity? A man who keeps his word?"

Freeman stepped back as if to avoid a slap. "I'll prove to you I am all those things."

"*Jah*, you do that. Until then, keep your distance."

He reached for her arm. "Hannah, what's happened to you? You're so bitter."

She scoffed. "Maybe I am. Is it any wonder? I can't trust a man enough to marry him because my former fiancé deceived me."

His countenance fell. "If I'm the cause, I'm awful sorry, and will keep you in my prayers."

"You do that," Hannah snapped, spinning around, breaking free, and darting into the house. Once inside, the tears fell like a waterfall. She felt arms around her; her dear *mamm*.

"I'm proud of you, Hannah. Freeman was awfully bold to show up here."

Again, words failed to come, but Hannah realized what a comfort it was to share a home with this dear woman. Maybe it was her place in life to simply care for her widowed *mamm*. Maybe they could take in a child from Arbor Creek and create a home in a different way.

"Commit whatever you do to the Lord, and your thoughts will be established, Hannah. God gives us firm ground to walk on, *jah*?"

Hannah let her *mamm* continue to rub her back. "I'll do that. Is that in the Bible?"

"*Jah*, in the Psalms somewhere. When your *daed* passed, the Bible became ever so precious to me. It's sweeter than honeycomb. You can find a refuge in it. Read it."

"I will," Hannah said. "I will."

CHAPTER 6

The next day, Hannah made time before tending to the dogs to get advice from Cassia. Ever so close again, she was thankful she had a kindred spirit friend in this time of confusion. She'd read Psalms last night until she fell asleep, 'trust in the Lord' recurring in her dreams, as the Good Book said. But she was still as numb as her fingers were becoming, a chill straight to her bones. She began running the distance to Cassia's, leaning into the wind. Rushing up the porch steps, she found the door opened, Cassia there to greet her.

"*Ach*, Hannah, what a bitter cold day, *jah*?"

"*Jah*," Hannah said, rubbing her hands together. "Should have worn mittens."

Cassia pointed to her basket of yarn near the settee. "Almost done with another pair. Can finish them while you're here, if you can stay a while."

Hannah knew her friend had a way of seeing to her soul, so she avoided eye contact, looking around the living room as if she'd never seen it. "You moved the furniture. I like the rocker near the window."

Cassia tapped her foot. "It's been there for months. What's wrong, Hannah?"

"*Ach*, nothing. Just came by to get some advice. Freeman came back," she blurted.

Plopping on a chair, Cassia was as stunned as a deer in headlights. "What?"

"Freeman came back. Said he wants to be Amish."

Staring at the floor, Cassia growled. "He's like a see-saw. Up and down he goes, jumping off and leaving you with a thump. Hannah, *nee*, he's not steady!"

"I know," Hannah sighed, taking a seat near the yarn. Picking up the mittens, she knew this pattern by heart and started to work the project. "I still can't believe it."

"Did you tell him to take a hike?" Cassia barked. "He hurt you before, deceived you. Guard your heart, please!"

Hannah knew what Cassia said was true, but… "What if he's changed?"

Cassia clenched the armrests. "Do you still love him? I thought you were courting Andy?"

"I was planning on breaking things off. He's too pushy." Hannah frowned as she continued to knit. "Plan on being single. All the jokes of being a spinster seem rather appealing right now. *Mamm* needs me; we're two peas in a pod. Ever so cozy at home."

"Safe, you mean."

"Safe and cozy seems *gut* to me."

"So why are you asking for advice about Freeman?" Cassia asked in an ever so gentle tone. "I know my kindred spirit friend and she wants a family of her own. Your *mamm* can live right next door in a *dawdyhaus.*"

Hannah felt exposed around this friend of hers. Could Cassia read her mind? "What should I tell Freeman? He wants to marry me after his baptism."

"He's not baptized and had no right to say that."

"That's what I thought. And Cassia, please don't tell a soul, but he seemed different somehow, not as appealing. That's my question. Do you think his breaking my heart has tainted me towards him?"

Cassia nodded. "*Jah.* When Edmond broke things off with me, the cat and mouse game was over, the thrill of the infatuation was gone."

"What? Cat and mouse…"

"*Ach*, we hid our romance. Forbidden fruit's always more appealing. When everything came out, after a few months, I saw the same dashingly handsome Edmond Ledger, but my heart didn't thump out of my chest." Cassia smiled. "Is that what you mean? You didn't swoon over Freeman?"

"I never swooned in the first place," Hannah defended. "But to answer your question, *nee*, there was something gone. Romance or whatnot. I feel numb, truth be told."

"It's shock and your normal emotions toward him will come back. Maybe not the romance feelings, but the real feelings. Just take it one day at a time and keep doing what you were doing. God meets us there."

Hannah set down her knitting. "Something Martin taught you?"

Cassia beamed. "*Jah*. We have devotions at night. He said King David wouldn't have fallen into sin with Bathsheba if he was on the battlefield where he belonged at the time. I think God blesses us when we're doing what we're supposed to be doing minute by minute. For you, it's being a *gut* companion to your widowed *mamm*, tending to the dogs, farm chores your *daed* did and whatnot."

Hannah met Cassia's earnest brown eyes. "I'm so thankful for you, dear friend. I'll do just that. There's no pressure to change a thing, *jah*?"

"*Nee*, not at all. Move in pace with nature as it changes ever so slowly." Cassia pulled out paper from her apron pocket. "Got a letter from Willow. Want to hear it?"

Hannah's mind sharpened. "*Jah*, for sure."

Cassia licked her lips and read:

Dear Cassia,

I think of you so often, I'm thinking of coming home for a while. How are you dealing with the loss of your wee one? My prayers are with you, sweet sister. And how is Martin taking it? That little one saw no tears or pain on this earth but went straight into the arms of Jesus, just like the moms of the Nickle Mine School shootings said so many years ago. You'll see your little one again.

The more I'm up here, there's more decisions. Too many choices. I know you didn't tell mom and dad about me attending the Mennonite church, but it saved me really. Cheri is one out of control woman, desperate for attention. A flirt like her I've never seen. Don't women realize that when they flirt, they look unattractive? Maybe that's why Martin fell for you, ha ha. I remember how stand-offish you were. I'm so happy you found such a solid Amish husband.

Back to the Mennonite church, I'll go when I'm up here, no Old Order Amish around, but when I read Martyr's Mirror, I feel like it's calling me to carry the torch. Not that I want to get burnt at the stake, but that I have a responsibility to stay plain, to be Amish.

Betty, my new friend, is a great girl, but I won't be wishy washy about my stance and she won't be Old Order. But I've only known her for a short time. When we talked about religion, it seemed like she was recruiting me to the Mennonites, like those people who come around with pamphlets asking if we found Jesus. Remember how dad would tell them, 'Is he missing?" I miss dad's wackiness, not to be disrespectful, but he sure is himself. Mom helped him be that way. What a match. Someday I'll find mine.

Think I'll be taking the train down and will be home for my birthday. It means so much to Mom. Can you put a bug in her ear that I have a craving for her cooked icing? If she gave me a bowl-full for my birthday present, I'd be one happy man.

Say hello to everyone and let them know I'll be home for my birthday 'til Thanksgiving. I think Hannah will be happy to have some time off at the kennel.

Take care, sister,
Willow

Cassia put the letter to her heart. "I'm so excited. Never thought I'd miss him this much and feared he'd like Canada and stay. He's been one constant in my life I've taken for granted."

"Who's Betty?" Hannah croaked.

"Betty? I suppose the Mennonite girl he likes, or liked. He never mentioned her before. Maybe he wanted to be certain of his feelings before saying anything."

"That is *gut* news. I'll make him a cake for his birthday with cooked icing. Maybe give him a bowl full like he asked for."

Cassia grinned. "That's a great idea."

Hannah returned to her knitting. *Willow didn't say anything until he was certain.* He had something she couldn't put her finger on, but it was something ever so right.

~*~

That night, Reed read Willow's letter to Cassia over and over by the glow of the oil lamp. "I knew he'd be homesick."

"It doesn't say that," Dorcas teased, nestling up to the side of the bed. "Seems like he's taking his time to figure something out."

"Well, he's going to be Amish, praise be."

"He's weighing it out, Reed, don't you see? He likes this Betty but doesn't want to break her heart like Freeman did do Hannah. *Ach*, he's back and will break her heart again. What did Jeb say when he was over?"

"Well, he's perplexed. Planning on talking to the Mennonite Church Freeman left to see if there's a scent."

"A scent?"

"You know, when a *gut* coon dog goes out on a chase, it starts with the scent of the raccoon. Maybe there's a stench in his past. Seems to move around quite a bit…"

"Broke Hannah's heart is what he did. Hope Jeb finds something, some scent, like you say, to make him seem mighty disagreeable to Hannah."

Reed took her petite hand. "Now, what's gotten your dander up about Freeman?"

"He could steal Hannah from you know who."

Reed kissed her cheek. "You'll never give up, *jah*? You're a matchmaker like Granny Weaver?"

"Not as *gut*," Dorcas quipped, "but I saw Hannah today and she was pining."

"Pining? Over Freeman?"

"*Nee*, over Willow. When she brought the letter over, she talked about Willow's birthday cake. Who does that but a wife? And she's making him one just for himself, a bowl full of cooked icing to boot. What do you think of that?"

"Makes me want to get out of this bed and heat up a cinnamon roll. Any left?"

She slapped him good-humoredly. "*Nee*, all gone. I'll make you some tomorrow."

Reed cleared his throat. "Love, I have another request." He pulled her to himself and held her tight. "I want you to take Edmond's place on the medical mission's trip to Mexico."

She tried to wiggle from his embrace, but he only pulled her closer. "Mexico? For Pete's sake, it's a foreign country. I don't have travel fever, don't forget. N-O!"

"We all know from Willow you don't need a photograph to get a passport, so why not? A long train ride across the country? See the Rocky Mountains? *Ach*, Dorcas, it would be such an experience for you."

"But I'd need new shoes."

"New shoes? Buy them. Buy new clothes!"

"I sew my clothes, Reed. We can't afford it. Who would watch the store?"

Reed leaned his head on hers. "Want to hear a secret?"

"I suppose," she whispered.

"I'd be homesick for you. Three weeks without my Dorcas. I couldn't handle it." He tilted her chin up and kissed her softly. "We've never been apart for that long. I can't sleep without you nearby."

She rubbed her cheek on his. "So, Willow being homesick is your fear, too?"

"Maybe. Is that childish?"

She laced her fingers behind his neck. "Not childish at all. But who will run the shop?"

"Cassia. She needs her mind taken off the miscarriage. She appears strong, but Martin says she cries herself to sleep many a night. *Ach*, busy hands are what's best when in grief."

She sighed. "Our *grandkinner* in heaven before us. It's not natural…I've struggled with it, you know. Maybe a trip for me to Mexico, helping the young mothers learn about nutrition so their *kinner* can grow up to live past five years old would help."

"I'm sure it will. So, you'll come with me?"

"What if Cassia needs help with Rose? And will we be home for Christmas?"

"We'll leave right after Thanksgiving and be home by December twelfth, plenty of time for you to make me all those gingerbread men."

She snickered. "There's one cinnamon roll left if Lily didn't eat it for a bedtime snack. Go on down and get it. You have one powerful sweet tooth."

Chapter 7

Hannah missed reading out on the porch, but the glow of the oil lamp was soothing as the wind rattled the wooden house. Shadow kept pushing her nose in front of her Bible and Hannah stopped reading to pet the little gray fur ball. Peace washed over her, giving her strength of mind when reading Psalms. King David said so many honest things that she couldn't say out loud to God. But her heart resonated with him when he asked for direction, justice and wisdom. When confusion ruled over him, he admitted his need for help. This did not come naturally to Hannah, ever the self-sufficient one. Who else would seriously thinking of being single? She had that 'pull yourself up by the bootstrap' mentality her *daed* had had. Maybe it was why men turned from her, not needing a man to complete her. It was odd how some girls lived for and obeyed their husbands without question. Hannah found this type of mindset insipid. *May as well be a doll on a shelf,* she thought.

A light flickered in her window, revealing huge snowflakes. What in the world? No one shone a flashlight in her window except Freeman. *Ach*, Lord, I'm not ready to talk to him. She lowered the wick of her lamp to make the room dark, giving a big hint that she was asleep now. She snuggled Shadow under the covers with her and closed her eyes. The Psalm she'd set to memory, Psalm 1, recited in her mind, but the light kept flickering, sending out light bursts over the walls. She clamped her eyes shut for a spell, nearly drifting off, until a gentle knock on her door jarred her.

"Hannah, someone's outside to see you," her *mamm* informed.

"*Ach, Mamm*, it's Freeman, and I'm not ready to talk. He'll leave soon."

"I see a buggy, not a car. Maybe it's someone else."

"Maybe he's got a buggy already. Needs to go through the proving time."

"Okay, *dochder*, I'll just pull down my blind. Can't sleep until he leaves."

"Sorry, *Mamm*. I'll tell him tomorrow not to come around."

"No worries," Esther said.

Hannah tried to sleep, humming to her kitten, as it made her purr. The purring of a cat was like a lullaby. But the light kept flickering and Hannah now thought it rude. She wanted to go down and give Freeman a piece of her mind. Flipping back the three heavy quilts on the bed, she edged her feet into her knitted slippers and grabbed her thick robe. A work bandana was good enough to cover her hair and off she ran down the stairs in a huff. She opened the door and yelled, "Freeman, go away!"

"It's Andy," she heard as she slammed the door shut. Andy? Opening it, she motioned for him to come inside. "What on earth are you doing out there in this snowstorm?"

He rushed the steps, took off his black woolen hat, holding it to his heart. "I may chicken out if I wait." Taking her hand, he said, "Hannah, I love you. Everything about you from your sweet mellow eyes to your spirited nature. I like a woman who can stand up to me."

The room being dim, Hannah could only go by his tone of voice that he was serious. She needed to see his face, so she pulled away to light an oil lamp. She studied him. He was showing such eagerness and humility, as if he'd be so honored if she accepted this proposal to be his wife. Could she learn to love him? And what about Freeman? Come to think of it, Freeman never said he loved her. Always implied but never said. *Ach, for Pete's sake, you told Cassia you were on the verge of breaking things off with Andy.* "I need time to think, Andy. *Danki*, but I can't say yes tonight."

He slumped. "I suppose you'll pick up where you left off with Freeman. Met him today and he talked about his hopes for the two of you. That's when I realized I love you."

This side of Andy she'd never seen. He'd been too confident and, well, a bit controlling, but now he was like a lost child. Rejection was carved into his countenance. "*Ach*, Andy, it's not because of Freeman. I'm just not sure I love you."

"I'll give you the best home ever. Have lots of money put up and we can…raise sheep so you can spin the wool." He forced a smile. "I'd do just about anything if you'd take me as your husband."

Andy's green eyes, ever so tender, had made her want to fall over when she first met him. He was appealing in every way. What was holding her back from loving someone? Past hurts or was she heartless? Was she supposed to be single for a while, like Edmond Ledger?

"You think about it, Hannah. Will you at least do that?"

"*Jah*," she said out of sympathy. Maybe Andy would make a *wunderbar gut* husband if he continued to show this humility. Maybe the other Amish sects he'd been raised in were liberal and pride wasn't considered something to squelch. "Would you like some hot chocolate before heading back home?"

His face lit up, a schoolboy smile sliding across his handsome face. "I'd like that."

A thought came to Hannah. Since she'd liked Andy from the start, maybe she needed to backtrack and get to know his real character. Eating together bonded people or it showed any personality flaws. "Andy, how about you come over for dinner once a week and we can see where the *Gut Lord* leads?"

He ran to her, enveloping her in an embrace. "*Danki*, sweet Hannah."

Hannah pushed him back. "Your jacket's like ice." She smiled. "Hot chocolate will warm you right up."

~*~

Hannah couldn't sleep that night. *Ach*, three men circled her mind. Freeman, Andy, and of all people, Willow. Surely, she was only concerned for Willow's predicament up in Canada. This Betty could lure him away from his Amish roots. Didn't he know about Jacob and Esau in the Bible and how ungodly wives pulled Esau from the One True God? She needed to set him straight but good when he came home this weekend. That he wanted cooked icing, a bowl full, showed he was still such a *boppli*, his *mamm* treating him as such. *How I treated him as such*, she thought. Willow would be twenty-three soon, only a year older than her. *They were eighteen months apart, not two.* Somehow Willow aged in her mind.

She shook her head. Why was she thinking of her best friend's *bruder*? Her employer, too, and maybe she was a tad bit nervous that he wouldn't think she kept the kennels in tip-top shape, as was his expectation.

Expectations. Andy and Freeman sure had theirs. How confused she was at times, her mind like a volley ball bouncing back and forth. Continuing her study of Psalms, she returned to Psalm 23, where it said, 'The Lord is my shepherd; I shall not want.' She didn't want for anything if she was single. She had a roof over her head, and maybe it was wrong to want something. Just accept life as it is.

She reread verse one:

The LORD is my shepherd; I shall not want.

So, was it wrong to want anything? To be a *mamm* like Cassia? She did want to be a mother. Hannah pulled her Bible dictionary, approved by the bishop, out of her nightstand drawer, and flipped to the meaning of 'want.' It said, 'Lack, to be in need.' What? You have to want something to know you lack it? How odd. Truth be told, she felt like her whole life was lacking. God didn't want this, did He?

She continued to verse two to see if it made more sense:

He maketh me to lie down in green pastures: he leadeth me beside the still waters.

Granny had sheep and they were timid creatures and not too intelligent. Jeb joked that turkeys were smarter. When one was butchered, the others left behind called for days, but the sheep didn't even notice if one in their fold was missing. She tapped her fingers on the book. So, God's people needed guidance. She loved the book *Far From the Maddening Crowd*, it being so rural, but the shepherd lost all his sheep as they followed each other over a cliff, all dying from fright. So, sheep were dumb and timid. That's how she felt when it came to men. *Lord, help me to be wise with men. I've made so many blunders out of fear of being an old maid.* She read the next verse:

He restoreth my soul: he leadeth me in the paths of righteousness for his name's sake.

Restoreth popped out at her. She needed to be restored as bitterness was beginning to choke her. Jealousy, envy, fear.... Riffling the pages of her dictionary, restore meant 'to turn back, return.' Return to what? Hannah wondered. And then Cassia's concern about her bitterness and mistrust rang through her mind. *Ach, I need a tender, trusting heart. Now gullible, but soft enough to notice the Lord's gentle nudge, to hear his voice as sheep do.*

My sheep hear my voice and they follow me, she recalled.

She closed her eyes and prayed:

Lord,

My heart's like a rock at times, stone cold. All this saying I'm so cozy here at home is a bluff. I'm afraid is what I am. And I've turned from You, the one who has the answers, but I can't hear Your gentle voice because my voice is always screaming through my mind in a panic. So, forgive me and give me ears to hear and eyes to see. Open me up, no matter how painful it is to let go, white-knuckling my life and letting you move me along with Your plan. I commit my way to You so my thoughts will be established.

Amen

An oppressive weight she'd carried for ever so long lifted. She actually felt lighter. *Danki, Lord. Is this why Granny preaches so much to cast our cares on You because You care about us?*

~*~

A few days later, Hannah decided to get some oil of oregano for a cold she'd been nursing. When entering the herb shop, Lily was behind the counter. "Hello. I didn't know you worked here."

"I do after school," she sighed. "*Mamm* and *Daed* are both going to Mexico, you know, and I need practice helping customers. School was called off since so many *kinner* are down with a bad cold."

Hannah swiped her handkerchief under her nose. "I came to get something for *Mamm* and me. We've got the sniffles."

Lily grinned. "I thought maybe Andy would be tending to you... *Ach*, Hannah, maybe we'll both be married women in a year. How about that?"

Hannah squinted. "What are you talking about?"

"The news about you and Andy being engaged." She leaned forward as if to tell a secret. "Cassia's mighty upset, but she'll get over it. Treats us both like *bopplis* since she's on old married woman, *jah*?"

"Lily, are you joking?"

"*Nee*." Her brows pinched. "Cassia thinks Andy's not the one for you, at least not yet. You just started courting, *jah*? Or it could be that she wanted to hear it from your own lips."

Hannah clenched her fists, wanting to scream. But she took in a deep breath, and thought, The Lord is my shepherd, I shall not lack. Lack self-control or sympathy. *Maybe Andy's confused.* "Are you telling me Andy told your *daed* we were engaged or is it the Amish grapevine?"

"*Nee*, Andy's telling everybody, seems like. They knew over at the tack shop. Edmond's getting his horse and buggy and told me."

Hannah felt pressure on her face as her heart raced. "But I never said yes to his proposal."

Lily leaned one elbow on the counter. "Did you encourage him? Body language is eighty percent of communication, you know."

Did she say yes with her eyes? A nod? Did she nod in agreement? "*Ach*, I've got to set him straight."

"So you won't marry him?" Lily asked.

Her head spinning, Hannah took a seat. "I didn't say that. *Ach*, Lily, do you have any herb for my predicament?"

Lily giggled, always seeing some bright side to life. "Passion Root. Maybe you need Passion Root to see Any in the right light? He's so handsome. Almost as handsome as my Edmond, but it's not why I love Edmond. It's his inner strength, tenderness to others and –"

"Lily, please. My nerves are fraying. Get me some valerian root and oil of oregano. I have to run."

"What's the hurry?" Lily prodded.

Hannah's attempt to squelch her temper was becoming a losing battle. She gritted her teeth, counting to ten like Granny Weaver had told her to do, when the little bell on the door jangled. In walked Freeman, cheeks red and eyes aflame. "Hannah, I came to talk to you. Lily, do you mind?"

"*Jah*, I'm running the store. And how did you know Hannah was here?" Lily asked, eyes wider than full moons.

Freeman just stood there, eyes stern on Hannah. "Her *mamm* said she was getting herbs. Hannah, my car is warm. Can we take a ride?"

Lily handed Hannah two bottles and helped her from the chair. "Hannah's sick. She'll be taking a nap on our couch."

Confused, Hannah met Freeman's sorrowful eyes. "Is something wrong? Do you need me for something?"

"Lily, can we have a few minutes of privacy?" Freeman near demanded.

Lily's lips became a thin line. "A minute. Hannah's not well and I don't like your tone."

Hannah gasped at Lily's own tone. She was reprimanding Freeman for something. But Lily closed the door to the house and there they stood, all alone.

"So, you accuse me of being deceitful and here you are engaged to Andy Smucker." His eyes watered. "I thought you'd have the decency to tell me I had no chance."

Hannah felt fatigue plunge over her and she plopped back down on the chair. This was a nightmare, a bizarre dream. One of the Fruits of the Spirit was self-control, and determined to have a softer heart, she clasped her hands in prayer. *Lord, help!* "I think there was a misunderstanding. Andy asked, and I said I'd pray about it. Need time."

"I'm willing to be Amish for you! I thought we had some kind of understanding."

What Janice would call a red flag waved in her mind. *Be Amish for me?* "Freeman, you shouldn't be Amish for me, but because you're called by the Lord to do it. If you try to be Amish with your own will-power, you'll fail."

He flinched. "What?"

"Didn't Jeb tell you? Being Amish is something that has to come from here." She pressed her hands to her heart.

He sped to her, knelt at her feet and took her hands. "Wait until I'm ready. We care for each other."

If he'd done this last Christmas, she'd have been pleased as punch. But she felt numb, with no feelings of love towards him. Somehow, she knew he wasn't the one for her. Was this an answer to her prayer? For the Lord to lead her? "I'm so sorry. I feel nothing."

"We need to spend more time together…"

For the life of her, Hannah didn't want Freeman to feel the pain, the rejection she'd endured after their break-up. "Freeman, you know you're not Amish. You would have converted before and not let me go."

"It was a mistake."

"Reed Byler told me anyone who truly *loves* someone will never let them go. Freeman, do you really *love* me or are you lonely?"

"I miss you," he said, kissing her hand.

She flinched. "You care for me, miss me, but never once have you said you loved me."

"I thought you understood my feelings."

She shook her head. "Out of the abundance of the heart, the mouth speaks." She rose and headed towards the door leading to the Byler house. "Find a girl your heart can be full of, Freeman. It's not me."

"Wait, Hannah."

"Good-bye, Freeman." She turned the doorknob and calmly entered the Byler's kitchen, which was oddly empty. She leaned on the door, glad to close this chapter with Freeman. And she felt no lack…

Chapter 8

Hannah opened her eyes to realize she was in Cassia's old bedroom and foggily remembered Lily telling her to take a nap. But it was dark out, so she'd slumbered for a while. When she swallowed, pain shot down her throat. *Ach, nee. I need to get to Mamm. She must feel the same.* Climbing out of bed, her joints stiff, she slipped on her shoes and headed for the stairs. She stood a while to let her eyes adjust before going farther. As she did, she heard Cassia laugh, Reed clap his hands and give out a hearty 'amen' and then Willow…Willow was home! She braced herself on the banister and let her feet feel their way down the dark steps. Heading into the kitchen, the light from bright lights shot pain into her eyes. She covered them and stepped back into the dark corridor.

"Hannah!" Willow yelled. The scraping of a chair and footsteps nearing. "Hannah, are you feeling better?"

Feeling dizzy, she said nothing, trying to regain her strength.

"*Ach*, Hannah. You look sad. Why the tears?"

"What?" she was able to get out.

He put his arm around her. "Are you okay?"

"I'm sick. Eyes…it's painful."

"*Daed*, I think Hannah needs more of those herbs you gave her."

Lily spoke up. "I'll get it."

She gripped Willow's strong arm. "My *mamm*. She's ill, too."

"*Mamm* went over to check on her. Lily told me you had a fever and all, so we thought it best. Your *mamm's* fine and wants you to stay the night."

Leaning her head on his shoulder, she muttered. "*Danki*, Willow. I missed you."

"Missed you, too, Sister."

"Sister?" Hannah repeated, heart tense.

Willow tapped her head. "*Ach*, we're like *bruder* and sister, *jah*?"

Hannah's heart sank. Why? She'd called Willow her *bruder*. Did he fall for that Mennonite girl or worse yet, Cheri? Where was the wooing in his voice she was used to? "Are you home to stay? Realize you're Amish, *jah*?"

"Talking to Jeb. Making sure my path is sure. But I'm going back."

Lily appeared next to them with some capsules and a glass of water. "Here, Hannah, take these. Now, Rose is in the dining room, so I'll bring you up a tray of food. Can't be having the *boppli* around you."

"*Ach*, for sure," Hannah agreed.

Willow released her. "Hope you get better by morning."

"*Danki*, Willow. So *gut* to see you." Tears filled Hannah's eyes most unexpectedly.

"Hannah, what on earth? You're crying?"

She covered her eyes. "Light's so bright."

~*~

Later that night, Lily came into the room, the oil lamp dim. "Are you awake?"

"*Jah*, I am. Peering up at the full moon."

Lily lay next to her on the double bed. "Cassia liked to watch the stars, so her bed always faced the window. Now, tell me why you barely ate anything from the tray and why you were crying."

Hannah wanted to lift her head and protest, but any movement hurt the back of her neck. Swollen glands, Reed had said. "I'm sick is all."

Lily sprang up to get another pillow and fluffed it behind her head. "I'm not little Lily anymore. Tell me what's wrong. Upset with Freeman or Andy?"

Hannah let the glow of the moon calm her. "Neither of them. I'm not upset."

"And I'm not engaged to Edmond."

"*Ach*, what happened?" Hannah asked.

"I'm joking, silly. Let me rephrase. And I'm not Amish. Now spill the beans or would you rather go through the torture of Cassia dragging it from you?"

"Cassia's my dear friend and patiently waits to hear my woes. Does she drag things out of you?"

Lily snickered. "She can't. I loved Edmond since I was twelve. No one believes me but I did. All along when he was courting Cassia, I loved him. When they broke up, I loved him more and had hope. And his two years in Haiti, I wrote faithfully, because I loved him. Cassia never knew."

"You wrote for two years? Even when he said he'd be single?" Hannah asked.

"God put this hope in me for Edmond. At first I thought it was a childish crush, but I've courted plenty, and always thought of Edmond. Hope doesn't disappoint. Hope gives us direction for our calling."

As tired as Hannah felt, this sounded like *wunderbar gut* advice. "What do you mean? Hope gives you direction?"

"Look up hope in the Bible. It's like fuel that keeps us going and God gives it to us. Faith, hope, and love will always abide, so it must be important, *jah*?"

"*Jah*," Hannah whispered. "I suppose."

Lily leaned towards her. "That doesn't sound very convincing. Did you break things off with a beau?"

"Told Freeman there was no future. I suppose I had no hope about him after all."

"Because you love Andy, *jah*?"

"*Nee*, I don't. Not yet at least. Maybe it's coming. He's the only man who's said he loved me."

Lily played with her prayer *kapp* ribbons. "When Edmond told me he loved me, I didn't sleep all night, it was too *wunderbar*. I kept thinking I dreamt it, if I dozed off, so I stayed awake," she said with a laugh. "Since that day I've had more energy, as you can maybe tell. Am I talking too much?"

Hannah was glad the room was hazy as tears trickled down her face. She coughed and cleared her throat to hide the force of emotions. "Happy for you. But I'm mighty tired."

"What is it, Hannah? You're crying again."

Hannah covered her face. "I don't know. Maybe I've lost hope. Hope of being loved."

"Let it out, Hannah. Cleansing tears, like Granny says."

"I must be unlovable, *jah*? Hannah, the old spinster crank."

Lily caught the tears with her slender fingers. "Listen to me. If anyone was a crank, it was Cassia. Remember how horrid she was when Edmond left? And look at Martin's steady love for her. It mellowed her into a purring kitten. Love changes us."

"I don't believe Andy loves me," Hannah blurted, "or I'd be…I don't know. I'd be up all night at the wonder of it all, *jah*? But I'm not."

Lily hugged her. "Give it time, Hannah. Cassia did. Remember when we laughed at the notion Martin was the one for her?"

Hannah remembered that day vividly and started to laugh and cry simultaneously. "We teased her so."

"It was fun," Lily laughed. "And here I am, marrying someone nine years older."

"Andy's a decade older." She hugged Lily back, feeling encouraged. "I need to be patient."

"And he may not be an old man, but young in spirit," Lily quipped, as she skedaddled to the oil lamp. "I forgot. I need to help *mamm* with a few chores before lights out. Good night, dear Hannah. *Gut* to talk woman to woman, not as Cassia's little sister."

"*Ach*, Lily, you're a sweetheart."

"I take after my *bruder*, *jah*?"

As Lily closed the door, Hannah was baffled. Why did Lily mention Willow and not Cassia? She meant Cassia, Hannah reasoned.

~*~

That night, as all the lights were out except the lamp between him and his dear son, joy mixed with concern filled Reed's heart. "Son, so *gut* to see you. But you've changed. Tired?"

He nodded and sipped his hot cocoa. "*Mamm's* big meal stuffed me, but I'm *gut*."

"*Nee*, I mean your soul seems weary… tired."

Willow hovered over his mug. "I see things differently."

Reed arched. "Are we that boring down here?" He let out a chuckle. "Sorry about that." Willow stared into his mug and Reed knew a serious talk was coming on. His son needed pried open, not like his daughters. "What so different? Comparing our ways with the modern world? Those fancy Mennonite friends appealing to you? Betty in particular?"

Willow shook his head. "She's nice, but…"

"But she's Mennonite and you want to be Amish?"

Willow shrugged and grunted.

Reed raked his fingers through his graying hair. This was going to take a bit of patience. "Do you want to tell me?"

He nodded and took another sip of cocoa. "*Jah*, *Daed*, but it's no use."

"Why? You think since I'm old I don't have *gut* advice?"

"*Nee*, you have more wisdom with age, but…"

Reed raised his hands in surrender. "Okay, we'll play hangman." He leaned back and grabbed a piece of paper from the China closet. "Put down lines and I'll guess a letter."

Willow slowly looked up and laughed. "No need. I'll tell you." He cracked a few knuckles as if to let out tension. "Hannah. She's engaged to Andy Smucker. For the life of me, I can't get over why I care for her so much."

"*Ach*, I did hear at the tack shop something of the sort. Andy's blessed to get her. Do you write to Anna?"

Willow glowered. "*Nee, Daed*, she's definitely not for me."

Reed bit his lower lip to control it, not wanting to suggest a host of available Amish girls at *Gmay*. After biting his lip too hard, Reed blurted, "Have you thought of all the younger girls at *Gmay*? How about we invite some to your birthday party? Your *mamm* loves to make big cakes…Have you considered Sarah Miller? She's nineteen and sweet as they come. Then there's Rachael Weaver, a girl eager to learn herbal medicine, coming in here with all kinds of questions. She spunky like Lily. How about a big party full of available girls?" He clapped his hands in animation. "Could be like an Amish Cinderella story."

"Who's Cinder…what?"

Reed leaned forward. "Don't tell anyone, but Lily brought home a big book of stories. Called *Grimm's Fairytales*."

"But the Amish don't read fairytales."

"Lily didn't know. It was in the history section of the library and had an old-fashioned cover. Well, it was forbidden fruit and I sinned. Confessed it to the Almighty, but I learned something from the story."

Willow shook his head, a smile sliding across his face. "What?"

"There're girls in ash heaps, you know. Girls whose lives are sad. They long to find a man who will cherish them. Women need to be cherished. Now, they're fine until marrying age. Look at Lily, such a little bird, happy as a lark. But now, all grown up, and wants to get married." He rubbed his hands together. "What happened in the story was that the father saw his son needed a wife and asked all the fair maidens to come to a ball."

Willow chuckled. "Fair maidens? A ball? What?"

"He asked single women over to meet his son. His son was a prince, so they had to come. Now, I'm your *daed* and I say we have a big birthday party, ask lots of girls from *Gmay* and you pick one."

Willow covered his mouth, laughing. "*Daed*, are you serious? It's hard to tell with you."

"I'm serious! You need to just go out and pick a girl. Don't be shy!"

"Like you were? *Mamm* told me."

"*Jah*! Don't be like me, for pity sake."

Willow's eyes mellowed. "*Daed*, I wish I was more like you. Meeting lots of folks up in Canada, I think you're the best *daed* ever. You know what's going on under your own roof and you care. The Peters' daughter, Cheri, is so secretive. The Peters' have no idea about her double-life."

Reed remembered Cassia secretly dating Edmond for years, right under his nose. "It's hard being a parent when your kids are holding back. I'm glad you told me about Hannah. I'll tell your *mamm* to make a big cake enough for ten people? Lily has at least ten single girlfriends."

"*Daed*, I don't want a party full of girls. I've come home to see the family."

"I'll have Lily invite a few friends," Reed insisted with a wink. "Now, remember, deep roots and look up like the eagle." He grabbed the Bible that lived on the table. Flipping through the pages, he read:

He also took a seedling from the land
and planted it in fertile soil.
He placed it beside a broad river,
where it could grow like a willow tree.
It took root there and
grew into a low, spreading vine.
Its branches turned up toward the eagle,
and its roots grew down into the ground.
It produced strong branches
and put out shoots.

Tapping the pages, Reed said, "Ezekiel 17:5. Your life verse. Now, I know I've never been a minister, but I can preach like the best of them. I'm not being prideful, only truthful. Some books are so watered down these days, so lukewarm I'm sure it makes the Lord want to spit them up. Now, I see a son who's being tested to be sure he wants to be Amish, *jah*?"

"I want to be Amish, *Daed*," Willow informed.

"But you're not certain, I can tell. Just look at how excited you were about the Mennonites when you talked about them at dinner."

"Well, they study the Bible more and can drive cars and whatnot."

"Bingo, so you're being tested, like I said. Now, do you think I'm ever tested?"

"To be Amish? Of course not."

"Wrong, Son. When I go to Mexico with your *mamm*, I'll be tested with fire. I'll be tempted to move there and help the poor. I feel confined here at times, you know. But I learned long ago that I have limitations. I can't be all things to all people, even though my heart wants to help the world. So, I'll battle discontentment, once again."

"Again?"

"*Jah*, I'm human. But I've found firm footing over the years. Now, when you go back to Canada, we'll write and pray for each other." He scratched his head. "I wonder how much postage is from Mexico to Canada. We'll both be out of this country."

~*~

As sleep evaded Willow that night, he got up to throw a log into the woodstove of his little house, kept so immaculately clean by Hannah. She even sewed new white curtains, he noticed. And the walls seemed brighter. Did she paint them or wash them? "*Ach*, Hannah, why marry Andy," he murmured. He noticed the mail piled up on the table, sorted by sales fliers, dog magazines, and letters. But what was *Family Life Magazine* doing there? He hadn't subscribed. Must be Hannah's to pass on to him. Grabbing the letters, he noticed two from Canada. Already? He'd only been gone a week. How could letters get delivered so quickly?

Ripping open one, he saw it was from Cheri. He rolled his eyes and read:

Dear Willow,

I had to tell you before I popped. Dad was right in bringing you here to straighten me out. He told me his plan. What a good dad I have. I visited the Mennonite church. I'm reading my Bible now and see how sinful I was. You must think I'm a slut. I'm not, only really like you a lot. Don't live with Lee. Such a nice guy and a friend for you up here, but it would be harder for me to see you.

Write back and let me know what you decide.

Love,

Cheri

Willow blinked in amazement. Had his straight and narrow view of purity changed Cheri Peters? If so, she'd turn into a woman someone would marry for the right reasons. She was going to the Mennonite church? Was she dressing plain? To think he'd influenced her made his heart soar. Was this the reason he was led to go to Canada? Help Cheri?

Pushing the image of her beauty out of his mind, he opened the other letter and read:

Hi Pal,

Just a quick note to ask a question and tell you the latest. Yes, you can live with us when you get back. Plenty of room for Ex-Amish here in town. Seems like they pity us and are happy we're out on our own. More choices with the Mennonites.

Also, I think your sweet on Betty. She's grown on me over the past few weeks. If you like her, I'll steer clear. But if not, I'd like to ask her out. Be honest when you write back. Lots of fish in the sea, like the saying goes, but Betty's really something.

See you in a few weeks after Turkey Day.

Lee

Oddly, Willow had mixed emotions about Betty. But he was Amish and she was Mennonite for sure and certain. It wouldn't work. *Look up and grow roots*, his *daed* had admonished. He was an unstable tree right now, any wind blowing him over, not toughening him up. He'd write Lee back to say he had no intention of dating or courting anyone.

He flipped through junk mail and threw it in the stove. That left dog magazines and *Family Life Magazine*. He picked up *Family Life*, and flipped through it and noticed Hannah had circled a recipe for cooked frogs? He pondered the fact that since Hannah's *daed* had passed, rumor had it that the family was pinching pennies mighty hard. How bad off were they if they were eating frogs? Surely the *Gmay* knew if they were in need.

CHAPTER 9

In a few days, Hannah was over her sickness, Reed Byler saying it was due to stress, which she dismissed entirely; Hannah decided to head back to Willow's to take him the little cake and bowl full of cooked icing as a birthday present, even though his party wasn't until tomorrow. Hannah dodged icy spots along the path to Willow's place, a white pastry box repurposed from the Village Sampler, decked with a red ribbon tied around it, containing Willow's cake. As she neared, she heard men's voices. Was he with a customer? No car in sight, she rapped on the front door.

To her complete shock, Freeman opened it. "Come in, Hannah," he said coolly.

Hannah's eyes rounded as she saw on the table a book called *Glimpses of Mennonite History and Doctrine*. She put the box down and slammed the other book shut to read the title, *Mennonite Hymnal*. Glaring at Freeman, she barked, "What are you doing? I thought you were turning Amish?"

"Not anymore. I've only been here a few weeks and I see the control. Jeb Weaver went snooping over at my old church to find dirt on me. How pathetic." He clamped a hand on Willow's shoulder. "He looks better, happier than ever, since he's been set free."

Hannah could barely believe Freeman's turn in character. He wanted to marry her less than a week ago.

"I didn't ask him to come share all this," Willow pled. "He was shopping at the herb shop and walked back to see the dogs."

"See the dogs my eyeball! He came back here to convert you." She inched towards Freeman and looked him squarely in the eyes. "Why? Why do you want Willow to go back to Canada?"

Freeman's face reddened, and his face contorted, as if in pain. "I already explained it."

"*Nee*, Freeman, I see you're threatened by Willow. Why?"

Freeman grabbed his winter coat from the rack. "I'm leaving. Willow, you read those books and make up your own mind. Don't let others control you."

Aghast, Hannah grabbed the books and shoved them at him. "He doesn't need them. He can think for himself."

"Why do you care so much what Willow thinks, Hannah? You're engaged to Andy Smucker."

Hannah clenched her fists, saying over in her mind, *I am a pacifist, not given to violence.* "I'm not engaged to Andy! Quit spreading it all over town!"

"Andy's doing it, not me. And I suppose he's a reliable source," Freeman scowled. "Old enough to be your dad."

"He's only ten years older than me..." Hannah said evenly.

Willow took a seat at the table, ignoring them both, and Hannah decided she'd best do the same. Visions of pouring the bowl of icing on Freemans head kept replaying. "You best get going, Freeman. When are you leaving town?"

"I don't know. Might stay a while."

"Why?"

"Enlighten Amish in bondage. Maybe help *you* see the light of day!"

So, he never intended to turn Amish! What a liar. He came to win her to Mennonite ways and get a bride. *Men. Could any of them be trusted?*

"Stay away from Hannah," Willow warned. "She's baptized and would be shunned if she broke her vow."

Freeman zippered up his coat, met Hannah's glare with mellow eyes. "I do care for you."

She plunged her fists into her hips. "Leave! Please!"

He lowered his head in defeat and closed the door behind him. Hannah plopped down on a chair at the table. "What a...can't say the word. *Ach*, he's so deceitful."

Willow's eyes misted. "Glad you can see that."

She pushed the box near him. "Your birthday present. Guess what it is."

Willow's eyes looked watery almost to overflowing. "Don't know."

Hannah had never seen Willow so emotional. Was he so torn between being Amish or Mennonite? "Willow, what's wrong?"

He pulled his hanky from his pant pocket and blew his nose. "Must be getting a cold. Nothing's wrong." A smile slid across his face, despite him trying to hide it. "I'm touched by the present."

She put her hand on his. "No, you're not. I know you."

He clasped her hand. "I thought you were engaged to Andy and…"

Hannah's heart near burst with satisfaction, like a feeling of coming home. "*Nee*, I'm not."

"But you're courting him, *jah?*"

"*Jah*, I suppose," she said limply. Hannah saw in Willow for the first time how genuine he was, how mature and steadfast. He'd cared for her for so long, yet she'd overlooked him because of his age. Right now, he had a more established heart than Freeman and Andy put together.

He withdrew his hand. "You suppose?"

She grabbed his wrist. This was the time Willow was supposed to be bold. To ask her to go on a buggy ride, like he did last spring. "A girl can court two men at once and see where it leads…"

He lowered his head. "I'm going back to Canada next week. Need to keep my word to Mr. Peters."

Hannah, not knowing where to look, or what to say, got up and *redd* up the little house. Letters strewn on the little couch caught her eye. A letter written in lovely cursive made her heart lunge. She grabbed it to see the signature was Cheri. As Willow just sat there, saying nothing, she scanned the letter. Cheri was turning Mennonite. Fury burned in her. "Willow, are you seeing this Cheri girl?"

"*Nee.* She wrote me to say she wants to walk the straight and narrow. I think it's part of my mission to see her settled in her faith."

Hannah crumbled up the letter and threw it at Willow. Shocked at her behavior, she burst into tears. "Willow, how could you? Turn Mennonite...for her?"

"I'm not. Like I said, I'm going back to keep my word to Mr. Peters like an honest Amish man would." He shot up and ran to her. "Hannah, I don't give a hoot about Cheri. But why would you care?" He forced a smile. "I'm only a *boppli bruder, jah?*"

She leaned into his embrace. "You've grown up somehow."

He held her head to his chest. "Hannah, what are you trying to tell me?"

"I don't know." Tears sprang to her eyes. "I'm so *furhoodled.* Andy saying we're engaged, Freeman showing up and...I've missed you something fierce. Scared to death that Cheri will lead you away from..."

"From what?" he prodded.

"From the Amish," she said, shyness sealing her lips.

~*~

That night at Willow's birthday party, after cake was gobbled up, Reed eyed the group of young people, especially the young eligible Amish girls encircling Willow. *Ach, it's working.* After what his son told him about Hannah's so-called *furhoodled* behavior, jealous of the *Englisher* girl in Canada, he knew the key to use to get Hannah to be Willow's wife. *Jealousy, Lord forgive me*, he confessed. Dorcas would tan his hide if she knew of this

Cinderella plan, to begin with, but the story took an unexpected turn. Clearly Willow did love Hannah and she did him, but she was harder to open up than Willow. A clam shut tight, but a pearl inside if pried open. A pearl of great price, and an excellent woman for his son.

Hannah was holding Rose, giving Cassia a break, but she was distant from Willow. Sulking, if he saw it right. As the girls begged Willow to take out his harmonica, he obliged and played a tune Reed had never heard. He tapped his foot to the beat and whipped out his juice harp and Willow nodded as if to say, *Danki*. This was totally improvised music, something Reed and his son had loved to do, making up songs as they went along. He recognized the easy Key of C and just stayed clear of any flat notes. Some of the girls' hands clapped, as they gawked at Willow and then him. When the attention turned his way, he decided to back away and take a seat.

Dorcas entered, Granny and Jeb on her heels. She waved a hand in front of Reed, concern etched on her pretty face. She pointed to Granny and Jeb, but Reed swooshed her concern away. How many times had their family played lively syncopated rhythms? Yes, the Amish church service was solemn, but he recalled his courting days, singing lively Christmas carols.

When the song died down, Jeb cleared his throat. "Willow, where'd you learn that song?"

Willow hit his harmonica clean against a cloth, ready for a new song. "In Canada. They sing it there."

"The *Englishers*?" Jeb prodded.

"*Nee*, the Mennonites."

A hush fell over the crowd and then whispers. Reed heard doubt in many a girl's tone that Willow would be Amish. That he was going to jump the fence to be Mennonite. One by one, they withdrew into little groups, and Willow's face grew solemn. "Don't see anything wrong with having fun. We're not dancing, too."

Granny covered her mouth after crying out, "*Ach, nee.*"

"Do the Mennonites dance to music?" Jeb asked, eyes round as buttons.

"*Nee*, they don't." He straightened. "They have a mission across the street from the barn dance held on the weekends where lots of young people drink alcohol and go down the wrong path. I did go to the barn dance, since I'm on *Rumspringa*, and it was the Mennonites that kept me out of a heap of trouble."

Now he had everyone's attention, all seats taken.

"*Jah*, I wanted to fit in somewhere and went to a dance. I was being tempted to the quick, when I saw a sign outside the open barn door; 'Lord's Mennonite Church'. One guy that bullied me went across the street and found Christ." He shot up a hand. "No disrespect, but the joke Amish tell of 'Jesus not being lost' isn't funny to me anymore. I saw this guy crying like a *boppli*, holding a Bible in his hands. The Mennonites point the way to the Savior, and…." he shoved his harmonica in his pocket. "Maybe I agree with them more than I thought." He nodded to Dorcas. "Sorry, *Mamm*, but I had to get that off my chest."

Granny went to Willow, reaching up to cup his face. "We point to God, too."

Willow nodded. "I know. Lots on my mind, I suppose."

Reed groaned. *That's what you get for reading fairytales!*

~*~

Hannah passed a wet plate for Lily to dry. "Willow really said he liked my cake better?" she asked softly, so Dorcas, also in the work line, couldn't hear.

"*Jah*, he said that," Lily whispered. "Think he likes the baker better." She grinned. "I know you think Willow's too young for you, but he's changed, *jah*? Speaking up so in front of the whole group."

"I couldn't believe it. His leanings towards the Mennonites concern me," Hannah confessed. "They can lead him from the People."

"*Nee*, I don't think so. The Amish are changing, reaching out like the Mennonites. Look at how my *mamm* and *daed* are going to Mexico. Willow knows he's not too confined."

Abigail Fisher, a pretty redhead, asked Lily if she needed a break, and Lily sighed. "*Jah*, I do. But my *mamm* needs one more. You can ask her."

"Well," Abigail began. "I actually wanted to ask you something." She glanced at Hannah. "Private-like."

"Hannah can hear what you have to say," Lily said, looking over fondly at Hannah. "She's like a sister."

Abigail squeezed between the two of them. "Lily, is your *bruder* going to jump the fence?"

"Become Mennonite? *Nee*, he just got all riled up about music and whatnot. Why do you ask?"

"Well," she began, her voice softening. "You invited me here and he's been talking to me real sweet-like. Do you think I stand a chance?"

Lily spun around, her towel flapping like a flag. "Abigail Fisher. Every man in the *Gmay* likes you. Are you saying you like my *bruder*?"

"Willow's twenty-three and more mature…"

Hannah felt jealousy grab her unaware. She should be glad that the beauty of Smicksburg, as some called her, a girl pretty enough to be on the cover of an Amish novel, liked Willow. But all she wanted was to tell her to stay away.

"And Hannah, look how much older Andy is than you," Abigail continued. "What's it like to be engaged and the whole town knowing it?" She snickered. "Why not keep it a secret?"

Hannah's chest enlarged with a deep breath. "We're not engaged is why."

"What? It's the talk of the town. Are you serious?"

"*Jah*, I'm serious. I need to set Andy straight. He's been gone a few days to Ohio to visit kin, but when he gets back, he'll know."

"How old is he?" Abigail asked?

"Thirty-five," Hannah informed.

"Is he a widower? I mean, he's so handsome to be single."

"*Nee*, not a widower. Just waiting to find the right one."

Abigail put an arm around Hannah's shoulder, giving her a squeeze of encouragement. "And he found the right one here in Smicksburg. You'll see eye-to-eye and make things work. You look *gut* together."

"Do we?" Hannah asked. "How so?"

"*Ach*, I've seen you with him on buggy rides. I hear laughing and lots of chatter. Isn't that what makes a *gut* romance? Communication?"

Hannah pondered this. "I suppose. I'm praying and waiting on God. Marriage is the biggest decision I'll make."

Soon Willow made his presence known. "Any cake left?" he asked his *mamm*, who was at the sink.

"*Nee*, Son, all gone." She handed Willow a washcloth. "It's your turn. Only the baking pans need scrubbed and I'm worn out."

Abigail spoke up. "It's his birthday. I'll do it."

Hannah turned to study Willow as he handed the rag to Abigail. Was it her imagination or was he blushing?

"Did you have a *gut* birthday?" Abigail asked him.

"*Jah*, real nice. Wasn't expecting such a crowd. Usually just my family, but this was nice." He peered over at Lily. "Did you arrange all this? Lots of your friends here."

"*Jah*, I did. *Daed* said to make it a real party full of young people. Had to invite Granny and Jeb, of course, since they're like family."

The kitchen door opened, ushering in chilly air. "There's freezing rain out there," Cassia called out, rubbing her hands together. "Best wait for the salt trucks to go down the road."

"Glad I can walk," Hannah said without thinking. "Getting tired and need to check on *Mamm*."

Willow caught her arm, bubbles spurting onto her dress. "*Ach*, I'm so clumsy."

Hannah laughed as he took a dry towel and rubbed her arm. "It's okay. Water never hurt anyone."

He leaned closer to her. "Can I walk you home?"

Stunned, she met his earnest eyes. "*Jah*, that would be nice."

His eyes danced. "Don't want you to fall on the ice..."

"Don't want an old lady to break a bone, *jah*?"

He winked. "*Nee*, wouldn't want that to happen."

~*~

Willow flipped the page. "A dog like this one."

Hannah leaned toward him. "Sheds too much. You need to raise Labradoodles."

As she neared him, inching closer on the settee, Willow fought the urge to reach over and hug his beloved Hannah. No girl would ever come close to her, a ruby beyond price.

"What're you thinking? Please don't say beagles. They stink to high heaven."

"*Jah*, they do, but *gut* hunting dogs." He nudged her. "Won't you work for me if I raise them next spring?"

"Will you be here?" Hannah was quick to ask.

"Of course. What would make you say a thing like that?"

She slumped, her prayer *kapp* shifted to one side. "I know you're leaning towards the Mennonites. Look how you talked about them tonight. I could barely believe it was you, so bold and sure of yourself."

"I am more confident, but is that wrong?"

"*Nee*, not at all." She tapped his hand. "You up there in Canada, being forced to meet new people, live with very strange people. A strange teenager girl..."

"She never would have considered a different path if it weren't for me. The whole town has her pegged as a loose woman, and it's turned her away from Christianity."

"Turning your head," she mumbled under her breath.

"She has not. Well, she has, but I…never mind. Not important."

"Cheri's turned your head how?" Hannah pounced.

He met her glare, blue eyes afire. "I've asked before, but seriously, Hannah, why do you care?"

"I'm like one of the Bylers, *jah*? I care about everyone over at your place."

"Little *boppli bruder, jah*?"

"*Nee*, Willow. You're a man now. But…"

"But?"

"I'm afraid you're going to be Mennonite. You're a cooked frog."

Willow cocked an eyebrow. "Come again?"

She shifted, facing him straight-on. "I left an issue of *Family Life Magazine* over at your place. The story of the cooked frog was in it…"

Willow let out a loud 'Phew' and then said, "I thought you were eating them."

Hannah grinned. 'Some do, but not us. I wanted you to read the article, but I'll tell you what it said in a nutshell. If you put a frog in a big old pan of water and set it on the stove, what does he do?"

"Jump out."

"*Nee*, frogs love to be in water. It's their habitat. You're thinking of a toad. Now, that frog just sits there in the pot, having a *gut* time, swimming around in the nice clean water.

What it doesn't know is that the water's being heated. He doesn't feel it and before he knows it, he's one cooked frog. Dead!"

Willow flinched. "Doesn't sound right. It would have to be one dumb frog to stay in hot water."

Hannah shook her head. "The water's heated gradually and the frog can't feel it."

"Like I said, that's a dumb frog."

Their eyes locked, Hannah screwed up her face, and then burst into laughter. "*Ach*, Willow, maybe it is dumb. Never thought of that but let me get my point out." Looking down, now pensive, she continued. "You're in the water up there in Canada and the heat's turning up. You don't see it. Others do and we're afraid you'll be…cooked dead."

"Others? Who?"

"Granny Weaver for one. And she's as wise as they come. We talk at knitting circle about you. Sure do miss you going with us to Pittsburgh to hand out scarves and hats."

He couldn't believe how turquoise her eyes appeared. Or were her pupils so dilated, due to the poor lighting of oil lamps? "Hannah, I love…that you care so much about me. Not many have such a *gut* friend."

She took his hands. "Please don't go back. It scares me to pieces what might happen. I have an awful feeling about that Cheri girl."

He rubbed her thin hands with his thumbs. "I have to. Anyhow, you have Andy to keep you company."

Her chin quivered. "Not too sure I'll be keeping that relationship going."

Willow held his breath. *Please say you love me and that's the reason!*

"I don't know. It's confusing. He said something from his heart no man has ever said. Maybe it's a sign from God."

Willow knew how much Hannah wanted to be cherished. Andy must have been doing a pretty good job or Hannah would have dumped him. If only she'd give *him* a chance to cherish her. Was he leaving a sign that he didn't care? Did he need to stay home to show her he was Amish and marrying material? Her eyes said something altogether new. She respected him and saw him as a man.

Hannah sat back and flipped through dog books. "Ever read *Where the Red Fern Grows*? Cried my eyes out at the end."

Willow raised two weary eyebrows. "Is it by Jane Austen?"

She grinned. "*Nee*. It's written by a man, I think. About two hunting dogs, Old Dan and Little Ann. They're quite a pair, very attached. One night, they see a mountain lion and it attacked their master. Old Dan saves his owner's life and dies. Little Ann loses the will to live and won't eat. She dies of starvation and is found dead on Old Dan's grave."

For the life of him, Willow did not understand women. Why was she telling him this story? What was she trying to say?

"Later on, the family sees a red fern growing between the dog's graves. Only angels can plant a red fern, according to Native American legend, so the family could move on in life. Balled my eyes out." She yawned. "Lily read it to her students and cried, too."

"Lily cried? She's so chipper."

"It was when she was missing Edmond that she read the book."

So, Hannah read this book after the break-up with Freeman? he wondered. Feeling too fatigued to ask, he slouched next to Hannah as they shared a dog breeder book.

Karen Anna Vogel

CHAPTER 10

"*W*hat on earth?" Hannah jumped, eyes popping open to see her *mamm* in her bath robe. The winter morning light cast shadows across the living room to reveal that she was in Willow's arms. "*Ach, Mamm.* We fell asleep reading." She nudged Willow. "Wake up."

"Cheri…"

Hannah, not fully awake, thought she heard *Cheri*. Willow's head was back, snoring up a storm.

"*Mamm*, did he say Cheri?"

Plunging her fists into her sides, she nodded. "*Jah*, but the question is, what's going on with you two? Aren't you engaged to Andy?"

Hannah roused Willow until he was fully alert. "*Mamm*, we can talk later. Willow, we fell asleep here all night."

Esther just stood towering over them. "All night. It's not right."

Willow rubbed his eyes. "Sorry about that."

"Well, do you want some breakfast?" Esther offered, crossing her arms.

"*Jah, danki,*" Willow said, his eyes half shut.

"I'll help, *Mamm*," Hannah said, needing to collect herself. *He said Cheri? Was he dreaming of her? Ach*, he was one cooked frog.

"I don't want anyone to know about this, understand?" Esther cracked eggs and whipped them vigorously in a glass bowl. "If Andy finds out, he may break things off."

"*Mamm*, I'm not engaged to Andy. It's a misunderstanding..."

"Honey, I see how he looks at you. I know it's supposed to be a secret, but the man just couldn't keep it in, *jah*? His sickly *mamm* is beaming to beat the band. But he's sensitive about Willow, remember?"

"*Nee*, I don't remember anything of the sort," Hannah said.

"Ever see the look of jealousy come over him when you talk about Willow?" "Andy gets jealous over any man I talk to. It's not a *gut* thing, *Mamm*."

"He loves you is why. It's a *gut* thing. Even God is jealous of anything that takes his place. We're called the Bride of Christ and –"

"*Mamm*, no disrespect, but I need some coffee. Can we talk about this later?"

Esther dumped the eggs in a skillet and made a clamor tossing and flipping. She grated some cheese and then took a knife out to cut an onion. "I'll be talking to your parents Willow Byler," she informed, a blade pointed at him.

He raised his hands as if under arrest. "We only read, nothing more. I swear."

"You swear? Amish don't swear," Esther said, nearing Willow, the knife an extension of her pointed finger. "'But above all things, my brethren, swear not, neither by heaven, neither by the earth, neither by any other oath: but let your yea be yea; and your nay, nay; lest ye fall into condemnation." Esther stopping just to inhale, she continued. "Where'd you hear such tomfoolery?"

"M-My new friends say it." Willow straightened. "Some Amish say it. My *daed* does. Says its *tomfoolery* to be rash…and rude." He crossed the room and yanked his coat off the rack. Slamming his black wool hat on his head, he nodded to Hannah. "Lost my appetite."

Hannah felt like she was in a nightmare. What should she do? Run after Willow? Despite her *mamm's* protests, she wrapped herself up in her outer garments to go after him. When she met up with him, she begged him to slow down, but he didn't. Never in her life had she seen Willow act indignant. He was rude to her *mamm*, too. "Willow, why are you so mad? What's come over you?"

He spun around. "For starters, I'm not even awake. But your *mamm* was treating me like a *boppli*. And she's too concerned about what Andy thinks. She places him so high up on a pedestal. I sure hope he doesn't fall. Might crack his head open."

Hannah huffed. "*Mamm* sees Andy loves me. She sees a future for us."

Willow turned and motioned for her to get away. "Go marry Mr. Perfect then," he growled.

Ice crystals blew off the farmhouse onto Hannah as a horrid chill froze her heart. Willow was far away from the People to act so rude. *He said Cheri. He dreamt of her.* And he didn't care if she married Andy. *Willow. You better turn around and come back…*

She waited a spell, refilling the birdfeeders and sweeping the little snow that fell on the sidewalk. A cardinal came to the feeder. A bright red male. A female soon appeared, pale brown with tinges of red on wing tips and chest. The male hopped next to his partner and broke out in a song. To Hannah it sounded like the bird was saying, *hurry, hurry, hurry.*

Wind slapped her face. Was she so tired that birds seemed to be talking to her? Should she hurry, hurry, hurry after Willow or go inside? Filling her lungs with air, she slowly let out with a sigh, "Go back in. Men pursue, not women." Turning, she wondered why the traditional rules of courting couples sprang to her mind. "Tired, is all," she groaned, rubbing her hands together. *Hopefully Willow will wake up, needing a few cups of coffee, and come back over and apologize.*

~*~

Upon opening his eyes, Willow could see by the shadows in his bedroom it was late morning. *What on earth?* Here he was, fully clothed, collapsed on his bed. He cupped his cheeks. "*Ach*, I was so rude to Esther! To Hannah." He tossed the quilt off, but then decided to pull it back over him. *Awake in the morning with your thoughts turned to God.* This little tidbit out of *Rules of a Godly Life* had saved him from many a woe. Trying to say a quick prayer in the morning, giving the day back to God as He gave it as a gift, he wanted to make it count. *Lord, Danki for this day, a gift from You. Number your days so that we can apply our heart to wisdom is in your Holy Word. So, on this day, I'm...asking for direction and boldness. Direction because I don't know if I'm really Amish or not. I say I am, but can I vow that to You? Boldness because I have to apologize to Esther and Hannah. I'm not afraid of them, but Esther seems right set that Hannah should marry Andy and...I'm afraid. Afraid that I'll spill the beans about what's in my heart. I love Hannah. Afraid that I'll lose my temper if Esther praises Andy to the hilt again. I just don't see Hannah happy with him. Something's not right. Clear my path, Lord. I give this day to You.*

A knock on the door startled him. Was it Hannah? If so, his kitchen was a mess! Dishes from two days ago piled up, and his table! Receipts covering it, needing to be filed away. *Hannah can't see that!* She'd end up taking over accounting for the business! Willow blew out a breath. She was just about able to run the show by herself.

Willow yelled that he was coming in a minute as he splashed water on his face and shook his hands over the basin that lived on his dresser. Taking the handheld mirror, he made a quick over with his hair, and grabbed his hat to cover the mess. Now to open that door!

He found Edmond there, watching the birds at his feeders. "You sick?"

"*Nee*, just, ah, well, just got up."

"It's ten o'clock." Edmond steered Willow back into the house. He grabbed a log from the little pile on the porch and threw it into the woodstove. "Now, sit down and stick your tongue out."

"What?"

"I'm a doctor, and you look sick. Pale…or is it…I don't know. You don't look good."

Willow crossed the room to make coffee. "Need some joe is all."

Edmond chuckled. "Remember when you didn't know coffee was called 'joe' and you kept asking me why I needed 'joe' so much?" Edmond slid onto a chair. "You taught me a lot."

"You mean you taught *me* a lot. How to speak fancy."

"And look who's going plain. Who would have thought it? Lily had to grow up and I needed a way to see how much I didn't need modern conveniences, my last hold out to being Amish. Not going to Mexico with your folks is hard, but it's a test. Tests are good, I suppose."

"Feel like I'm in one now," Willow glowered. "Who would have thought I may be Mennonite?"

"I thought you had that all figured out. You said at your party you did."

"And look at how I acted. Ruffled some feathers with my harmonica."

"You pushed it with some songs and you know it. Sounded like rock music."

"Rock music? *Nee*, it's contemporary Christian. I felt happy so that's what I played." He pursed his lips. "And look at how the Amish acted," he grumbled.

Edmond put a hand up. "The Amish? Since when do you call your family and friends 'the Amish' in that tone of voice?"

"I'm tired. Didn't sleep right."

"I'll bet you didn't."

Willow poured the boiling water into his coffee maker and an uncomfortable silence echoed around the walls. "What?"

"Stopped over to see Lily early. She said you stayed the night at Hannah's."

Willow blinked rapidly in shock. "How'd she know?"

"Esther came by early to the herb shop to tell your parents. Pretty upset. Are you two secretly courting? Did she dump Andy?"

"I wish," Willow admitted. "We fell asleep reading dog books. She's seeing Andy. Not me." Willow thought back to his morning prayer. Was Edmond an answer? He needed direction. Memories of following Cheri to the barn loft, images of her in a sheer nightgown haunted him in his dreams. "Need advice. Went to a line dance and…"

Edmond glared in disbelief. "You went to an *Englisher* dance?"

He nodded. "Lots of bad stuff going on in there."

"Any drugs?"

"Don't know. Well, maybe there was something in the air. I got intoxicated, but not with alcohol, if you know what I mean."

"No, explain." Edmond was at full attention now, on the end of his chair.

"Women. Understand?"

"That kind of intoxication…"

"*Jah*. Me, your little *bruder*, almost fell into sin. And you can't take this kind of sin back."

"No. Sexual sin can't be taken back. We can be forgiven, but it's something we don't soon forget, and neither will our future spouses."

"Have you…?"

"No, but it's hard. I'm pushing thirty but a virgin. Saving myself for someone special, and Lily was worth it all." He sipped some coffee and then his face looked grave. "So, this girl you're tempted by, don't tell me it's the girl you're living with. You asked me to pray before you left about this girl being a flirt."

"She's the one." Willow narrowed his eyes. "She was like Potiphar's wife in the Bible. Came into my room in the middle of the night half dressed. Actually, I could see through –"

"Stop! Get that image out of your mind right now. It could make a permanent groove." Edmond stared at the floor. "If I'm being harsh, well, maybe you need this. Men are wired by sight and once an image is in, and we think about it, it makes a real change in our brains. It's like making a sliding board slippery when we were kids. The more you go down the faster it becomes, right? That's why men have to stay away from immoral thoughts. One thought, then two and then you're hiding porn in your house."

Willow stared at Edmond. "Do you have a problem with this or something?"

"I've battled it. Staying pure in your mind for a man is hard."

Willow was relieved to hear this. The images of Cheri made him feel filthy. Gulping down his coffee, he prayed again for boldness. Could he tell Edmond? He popped a few knuckles and then knew he had to. "I almost gave in and I think of her sometimes. Makes me feel like less than a Christian."

"Oh, no, Willow, we can have bad thoughts. We're human. Just don't feed those thoughts is what I'm saying. Take your thoughts prisoner, like the Bible says. And stay away from that girl."

Guilt he'd been carrying seemed to lift. "Thinking something isn't a sin?"

"Don't think of a pink elephant in this room. Don't do it. You see it floating by."

And that's exactly what flew through his mind. "So? I see a pink elephant."

"Don't you see?" Edmond asked. "It's human nature to want to eat the forbidden fruit. It's in our nature. The more you try to not think of that girl in Canada, you think of her all the more. It's why I used the pink elephant experiment on your mind."

Leaning both elbows on the table, Willow moped. "How do I get the picture out of my head? It's been floating in there for months…"

"By filling it with scripture. When the thought comes, say out loud if you have to, 'I can do all things through Christ who strengthens me' or 'God hasn't given me a spirit of fear but of power, love and a *sound mind.*' A sound mind is an undisturbed mind."

"Undisturbed, *jah*? Peaceful?"

"Yes. Christ died for our peace of mind, you know. The chastisement of our peace was upon Him."

Willow knew this scripture, but he'd never had to really believe it. "Do you think God brought Cheri into my life to tempt me so that I'd grow as a Christian? Exercise my faith?"

Edmond's eyes were orbs. "God doesn't tempt you. He's the same. He hates sin. We get stronger going through hard times, but God doesn't tempt. It's the old serpent in the garden." He shook his head. "You cannot ever live in the same house as that girl. You cannot ever be alone with her. Understand?"

This sounded too harsh. "She wrote and said she was going to the Mennonite church. Said I changed her."

Edmond's index finger shot into Willow's face. "You're not as strong as you think, and she's not going to change overnight. If she really did commit her life to Christ, great. But she'll be battling lust for a long while if she propositioned you in her own house."

"She doesn't know the love of men in a right way…"

"Stop it, Willow. Stop defending her and downplaying the danger she is." Edmond shot up and paced the floor, something his *daed* did when deep in thought. "I don't think you should go back there. Call up the family and get a refund for your ticket."

"Edmond, we Amish keep our word. Mr. Peters is going to run his sled dogs in a race and he hired me with good pay."

"Good pay? Seriously, Willow. Listen to yourself. Is it worth the risk just for money?"

Willow hadn't seen Edmond this fired up in a long while. He slowly got up and embraced his friend, patting him on the back. "*Danki* for caring. I'm living with a family who takes in Ex-Amish, so don't worry about it. I'll keep my word to Mr. Peters."

"Willow are you serious?"

"*Jah*, why? It's better than staying in the same house as Cheri."

Edmond plummeted down again, making the table shake. "People who take in Ex-Amish are against the Amish. *Messed im Kopf. Leichtgläubig!*"

He was not messed up in the head and gullible, Willow wanted to say, but didn't. "I'm not sure I can be Amish. I still have a few doubts and they keep growing the more I'm here."

Edmond now had a uni-brow, his frown was so deep. "When I went off to teach teens, I wanted to get away from Lily. And I needed time to see if my love for her grew or diminished. So, being away for some people is good. Joseph Hummel, gave me good advice since he was *English* before Amish. I memorized a verse:

"Thus saith the Lord, Stand ye in the ways, and see, and ask for the old paths, where is the good way, and walk therein, and ye shall find rest for your souls.

"Joseph said to stand. That means don't move, right? So, take things very slowly. Old paths are basically rules we think are old-fashioned, but the Bible is always relevant. And then ask God for the good way and walk in it." A smile slid across Edmond's face. "I waited at the camp and the desire, pure love, for Lily grew. It was the good way for me."

Willow's heart warmed when he saw the almost reverential love Edmond had for his sister. To think that Lily had a crush on this man even when he was dating Cassia in secret. Lily never gave up. Hannah's lovely face was set like a centerpiece in his mind. Lily said she never lost hope of marrying Edmond someday. Hope gave her strength to wait. He needed this hope. There had to be a reason why despite everything, he still loved Hannah. He'd go up to Canada like a retreat, seek God and the good way. The plan God had for his life.

Edmond glanced out the window. "Let's take a walk."

~*~

Hannah rolled the pie dough a bit too thin. Squishing it up in a ball, she tried to not take out her frustrations on the pastry. Hours had gone by without Willow coming back over to apologize to her *mamm*, and tension filled the house. Esther had been out to the chopping block, stacking wood like a man. After attempts to offer to help, Hannah decided to bake.

Maybe she should open a bakery? Be like a character in an Amish romance novel. She'd be there putting out specialty items, pray, and the right man would walk in, and he'd fall in love with her over pastries. "Hannah, where's your head?" she said to Shadow, always near her feet. The gray cat seemed to notice her sour mood and wanted to calm her. "You're a good pussy. Willow did a *gut* job picking you out."

Willow. She was a teeter totter over that young man. Yes, he was a man now, all grown up. Just like Edmond seeing Lily as a woman for the first time, what a discovery she'd made about 'wee little Willow'. Hearing loud voices, she followed them to see three Amish men bantering on the road. Through the light snow, she could make out that Edmond was between the two that seemed to be arguing. One's man's arms flailed about, the other one had his head down. How ironic that a man like Edmond, in his proving time to be Amish, would be the peacekeeper.

What she saw next seemed downright comical. Her *mamm*, axe in hand, went out to meet them. Hannah chuckled. What a fright her *mamm* must appear if she hadn't worked out her bad mood by chopping. When the men turned towards Esther, Hannah gasped. "Willow? Andy? What?"

Edmond slowly took the axe from her *mamm* and Esther soon jabbed a finger into Willow's jacket. Willow seemed so dejected. Could he lower himself anymore into the road? "*Ach, Mamm*, we fell asleep on the sofa. You're being too harsh."

She ran to get her wool cape and outer bonnet and dashed out to defend Willow. When she could make out their voices, Andy's grew mighty loud for an Amish man.

"We're engaged, you know. Staying over could ruin her reputation."

"Hold on now," Hannah said in a huff.

"*Nee*, Hannah," her *mamm* said, clasping her by the elbow. "Let Andy say his fill. He has every right."

Hannah listened in horror as Andy degraded Willow about being careless about her reputation. But when he accused him of making advances towards his so-called fiancée, Willow said nothing, only nodding his head.

"So, you are after Hannah?" Andy growled.

"Stop it, Andy!" Hannah pleaded.

"I love her," Willow said through the crisp clean air. "Always have and always will."

Hannah's heart swelled with love. *He loves me?* Could this be true? And there was no mistake that he meant romantic love, not sisterly. She wanted to run to Willow, her heart so full, but her *mamm* kept her back. "She's engaged to Andy."

"*Nee*, I am not," Hannah said. "*Mamm*, I am not a child." She withdrew, embarrassment overcoming her, and darted away, fleeing back into the house.

Her *mamm* was close on her heels as the door opened and slammed shut in quick succession. "Hannah, how could you say such things? Andy's never been married. He's your best chance yet. Do you want to marry a widower? One with a ready-made family?"

She clenched her fists. "Has it ever occurred to you that Willow is one of the best men on God's green earth? And he just said he loves me."

Esther's countenance fell. "*Ach, dochder,* I did hear that and it's very touching, but he's not Amish. Can't you tell by the change in him?" She sat on the sofa, patting the seat next to her. "Come, let's talk."

Hannah reluctantly obeyed.

"Who wiped your tears about Freeman?"

"You did."

"And my heart was just as broken, I dare say. From what the People have been saying, Willow's going back to Canada and will be Mennonite. Is leaning towards their ways." She took Hannah's hand and pet it. "Now, Andy is baptized and said he loves you, *jah*? And you were so happy, *jah*? Can't you see the writing on the wall?"

Hannah wanted to say she didn't love Andy, but her *mamm* would just lecture on how love grew over time. That she's only been seeing Andy for such a short time; give him time. He has a *gut* job. And he's Amish, through and through. Their family was devout, giving up the conveniences they were used to in the liberal sect out in Ohio, and it was to their credit they wanted a stricter Order.

Thankfully there was a knock on the front door to break the silence. "I'll get that." When Esther opened the door, she beamed. "Andy, come in."

"I came to see if Hannah was all right," he said, his eyes soon meeting hers. "*Ach*, Hannah, I lost my temper in front of you. I'm sorry. But what's happened got all over town."

"They fell asleep reading dog books," Esther informed. "I'll let you two have some privacy," she said, soon back outside, most likely to chop wood.

Andy took her hand, his green eyes pleading. "Forgive me. I don't get angry like that unless provoked, and Willow's a fool."

"He is not a fool. He's my best friend, next to Cassia. The Byler family is mighty tight with ours."

"He didn't respect you enough to deny he slept on the couch with you."

Hannah near exploded. "All we did is read books and fall asleep? We didn't sin."

Andy rubbed her hand with his strong calloused thumb. "I always imagined waking up to my bride, never anyone else. May sound silly." He raised her hand to kiss it. "Hannah, say you'll marry me."

Hannah couldn't process all that just transpired.

Andy shot her a glare. "Do you love Willow? Are you falling for his charms?"

Stunned at Andy's change in temperament, she pulled her hand out of his. "Honestly, sometimes I wonder if men are worth the bother. Isn't love patient and kind? I don't see that in you."

He slid closer to her. "I'm sorry. I'm jealous."

Hannah shot up. "Love is not jealous."

"Hannah, *ach*, I know. I admit it. I'll work on my temper. Do you forgive me?"

She nodded, but when he wanted to resume the conversation, she refused, saying she needed to bake a dozen or more pies. And after that, she would knit another scarf, a warmer one…for Willow to take to Canada. She let Andy see his way out as she scooped up Shadow and nestled her face in the gray fur. *Willow, why aren't you coming over to apologize to my mamm…like a gut Amish man? Are you leaving me for the Mennonites?*

Chapter 11

A few days later, the Byler house was near bursting with commotion. Willow, wrapped in a crocheted blanket Cassia made him to take back to Canada, hovered near the woodstove. He admired the women dropping off shoes for his parents to give to those in need in Mexico. His *mamm's* face tightened as she explained she couldn't take so many boxes. Medicinal herbs were paramount on their list and then money. Money to buy items in Mexico for a fraction of the cost. When Granny Weaver explained she bought special orthopedic shoes for elderly women, Dorcas consented.

Reed came near, pressed his hand against his son's forehead. "Temperature's come down. A little warm though. Best stay put."

"But *Daed*, I need to say good-bye to...someone."

Reed sat near him. "Everyone knows we're leaving from here to Timbuctoo. Hannah will show up."

"Hannah? *Ach*, who said I wanted to see her?"

"Edmond told me what happened out on the road. Mighty proud of him for keeping the peace." He gripped his son's shoulder to lend courage. "He gave you *gut* advice. Now, go up to Canada while we're gone, and we'll cross paths in a month. Home for Christmas, *jah*?"

"*Jah*, of course. I suppose…"

"You suppose? Do you lack money for the train fare?"

"*Nee*. Mr. Peters pays well." He didn't want to admit he wanted to stay in Canada and hide. Hide away from the inevitable; Hannah would marry Andy. When God closes the door, he opens a window, Edmond had said.

"And these people you'll live with aren't enabling Ex-Amish, trying to paint us all out to be cuckoo birds?"

"*Nee*. I've met them once."

"And this Cheri will leave you alone and if not, you'll flee, like a *gut* man should?"

Willow could tell his *daed* was nervous about leaving for Mexico with his *mamm*. She'd chattered long into the night, giving Cassia strict instructions on not burning the Thanksgiving turkey. Soon they'd be eating over at his sister's and he prayed she'd listened. "*Daed*, you'll be okay and me, too. And I love you, too."

Reed's eyes misted. "*Jah*, that's what I'm trying to say. Those Mennonites helped you speak up about what's in here?" he asked, pressing his heart.

"*Jah*. They're more open in their conversations with others. Outsiders, too."

"Loosed your tongue enough to tell Hannah that you love her. Still can't believe you said it, but I'm proud…in a *gut* way. You've gotten bold."

"But she hasn't come over. Look what *gut* it did me."

Reed twiddled his thumbs a spell and then said, "It hasn't sunk in."

"*Ach*, I'm sure it's sunk in and Esther's making sure it stays there."

Arching his back, Reed guffawed. "Then go over there and make it clear."

"You said I may be contagious."

Dorcas came over, offering a hand to Reed. "Come help. We have thirty pairs of shoes to fit into our luggage." She wiped her brow and turned to Willow. "You feel any better?"

"Kind of. Why? Want me to head on over to Cassia's to see if the turkey's black?"

She grinned. "Cassia's become a *gut* cook."

"Thou shalt not lie, Dorcas," Reed said, wagging a finger playfully. He stood and put an arm around his wife. "Best get back to work." Placing his hand on Willow's forehead again he winced. "Son, I think you best get in bed. *Ach*, it's Thanksgiving and I know everyone wants to see you, but you need to do a fast and cleanse."

He put up a hand. "*Nee*, not today. Burnt turkey or not, I'm headed over to Cassia's."

"*Nee*, there'll be wee ones there and if you're sick, the young and elderly are at risk. Granny and Jeb will be there and that's that. Now, follow me into the shop and we'll get a *gut* cleanse going."

Willow, feeling weaker by the minute, couldn't keep up the conversation. He yearned to crawl into bed but limply followed his *daed*, paying no mind to anyone along the way, those wishing him farewell as he left for Canada tomorrow.

~*~

Hannah thought arrogance in Willow had taken seed, but now here it was in full bloom. The nerve of him walking right past, ignoring her as she tried to say goodbye. And no response to her *mamm*? An elderly woman he failed to ask forgiveness for his rude behavior?

"Proud young man," Esther whispered in Hannah's ear. "Andy would never be so rude."

Tired of hearing the praises of Andy, Hannah gripped the gift bag. "*Mamm*, Dorcas will hear you."

"I don't think these Bylers follow the *Ordnung*; going to Mexico of all things. Back in my day, we were content to be at home."

Hannah took her *mamm's* hand, pulling her to a corner, the room too full of Amish and *English* who might overhear. "*Mamm*, Jeb Weaver gave them permission."

"Jesus never traveled two-hundred miles from his house."

"What?" Hannah asked, shaking her head, trying to gain understanding.

"It was in a poem Granny's knitting circle read. *One Solitary Life*. Jesus never went so far from home, so we shouldn't either."

"There were no trains or planes in Jesus' time. *Mamm*, I've never heard you talk down the Bylers before. You and Dorcas are like bosom friends, *jah*? What's really wrong? Nervous the turkey will burn before we get home?"

A smile slid onto Esther's face. "*Nee*, because Andy and his family are tending to it. Andy puts my nerves at ease like no other."

"He's a human being, *Mamm*," Hannah said evenly. "We all have our faults."

"Name one in Andy. One that would prevent you from saying yes to a marriage proposal? Something I pray for without ceasing. Just last night, I couldn't sleep, and I got on my knees and prayed to the Lord above you could see Andy as I see him. Perfect for you."

Hannah stared into her *mamm's* earnest eyes. With no *daed* alive and no uncle to step in to take charge, her *mamm* did have a lot on her shoulders. "I'm sorry to make you worry…"

"Then end it all and tell Andy yes. Look at how much I've aged as a widow. I may not be here to see you get married."

Although dramatic, her *mamm* was right. How many girls in their mid-twenties were single? Her hope chest was full of fine China, crocheted table runners, embroidered pillow cases and essentials to make for a beautiful home. Why was it that there was no hope in her heart? But she kept hoping for Willow to be his old self again and be kind, his best character trait. He said he loved her, yet he was leaving for Canada and just snubbed her and her *mamm*.

"Is this a secret meeting?" Granny Weaver asked as she caught both by the hand. "I talked Dorcas into taking the shoes the Baptist's bought. The church will pay for the extra boxes. Trains do that, you know. I'm sure Janice will be on it right quick to get a discount for charitable purposes."

Hannah's heart smiled as Granny went on, her light blue eyes dancing with delight. Granny had turned down several marriage proposals. She'd seek advice from Granny.

Dorcas soon joined the little circle of friends tucked away in the corner as the room cleared out. "I'll miss my dear friends. Scared to death to cross into Mexico. Can you imagine me, Dorcas Byler, Old Order Amish, stepping foot onto a different country?"

"It's not like you're flying," Esther snapped.

Silence hovered over the four for a spell until the sound of shuffling boxes and Martin and Reed's heavy footsteps sounding like racing horses echoed around the walls. Dorcas turned to go, but Granny clasped onto her hand. "Now, Dorcas, I don't think Esther meant what she just said. What she's trying to say is that it's awful strange to think of you in Mexico, but you're not breaking the *Ordnung*."

Meekly, Dorcas met Esther's gaze. "You're not approving, are you, Esther?"

Esther's mouth dropped. "Just like a Byler. Saying whatever comes to their mind."

Hannah, shocked to no end, tried to stop blinking. "*Mamm*, this is not our way. We are not to judge."

"*Nee*, we aren't. Dorcas, I have to confess I'm upset with your son, like I tried to tell you. Since he's been to Canada, he's been mighty rude to me. Is this the fruit of all this traveling?"

"Willow? Rude?" Dorcas stomped a foot. "Never seen it in my life without correcting it. But right now, he's sick in heart and body." She jutted her chin, near poking it in Esther's face. "You know he loves…you know who. But…you know who is interfering."

"Willow's sick?" Hannah blurted.

"*Jah*, he is. Reed just took him to the herb shop." She pulled a handkerchief from her apron to wipe her brow. "I'm sorry, Esther. My dander got way too high. Willow's been ailing something fierce and we leave tomorrow. You know how *mamms* fret."

"How long's he been sick?" Hannah asked, her heart pounding in her ears.

Dorcas avoided eye contact with everyone but Granny. "Ever since he stood out in the snowstorm, sweating to beat the band."

"Was he jogging?" Granny asked. "The *English* do that, funny thing."

"He was with Edmond and *jah*, sometimes they do run back in the woods like *kinner*, but *nee*, he was out on the road and…was upset. Best keep my mouth shut." She turned to Esther. "Amish are taught as wee ones to mind their elders, but there are limits."

"Limits?" Esther crowed. "Limits to Amish teachings?"

Dorcas edged her way near Esther. "*Jah*, limits. If you provoke others to anger, you're just as much at fault."

Reed and Martin yelled over, saying they were headed to Cassia's. *I need to see Willow!* Hannah wanted to scream, so she left the circle and drew up to Reed. "Can I see Willow? I hear he's sick. I could help him."

Reed's face reddened slowly but surely. He cleared his throat. "Don't think anything will help him now but the snow cleared from the back of the herb shop to the outhouse." He leaned over and whispered. "Just gave him a cleanse."

Understanding his meaning, Hannah shoved the gift bag at him. "Can you give him this? And I can shovel the steps and path."

As she turned to go, Reed chuckled. "Hannah, it's all shoveled. And you are not to see Willow today. Stop by tomorrow."

"He leaves tomorrow, *jah*?" A hole the size of Pennsylvania made a hollow in her heart. "And I won't see him…again."

Reed's brows furrowed. "Looks like that would just about break your heart, *jah*?"

She nodded, refusing to let tears spill out. "*Jah*, it would."

"Now why would that be?" Reed asked, studying her.

Her chin trembled, and she looked down to readjust her prayer *kapp* strings that were never tied, but she was tending to them now. "He's like a *bruder*."

Reed gave her a side hug. "Don't hold it in. Crying cleanses a body just like herbs."

Hannah knew she had the willpower to squelch her emotions. Wasn't self-control a fruit of the Spirit? "I'm not crying or going to cry. I just thought I'd be the one giving Willow that." She pointed to the bag. "You give it to him and tell him I said good-bye."

Reed peeked in the bag and pulled out a long colorful scarf. "It's like Joseph's robe of many colors."

"I made the one Willow wears now, and they're almost identical, but this one's warmer. Thicker, longer and made with an alpaca and wool yarn mix Granny spun."

"He'll treasure it like he does the maker," Reed said with feeling. "I'd let you in to talk to my son, but I fear it's contagious. If he still has a fever tomorrow, he won't be leaving for the train station with us. You might just catch him yet." He pulled at his beard. "Dorcas and I are headed south of the border and Willow north. Sure do hope in time we're all settled right here in Smicksburg. No other place on God's green earth closer to Heaven."

Hannah was too choked up to speak. She nodded and got out a 'safe travels' and then had a sudden yearning to crawl into bed with a good book. To escape from the dinner with Andy's family; lately her *mamm* being worse than Mrs. Bennet in *Pride and Prejudice*. How prejudiced she was against Willow and how her pins would pop right off her dress if she was the one chosen to marry Andy. Hannah heard laughter and turned to see her *mamm* embracing Dorcas, tears running down both of their faces. *Ach, life isn't supposed to be this confusing when you're a grown up!*

~*~

Willow fingered the scarf Hannah made him as he sat watching married couples take their seats on the Amtrak train. *God, bring Hannah and me together if it be your will. I'll be standing at the crossroads and wait for your direction up in Canada. I'll look for the good way, the path you promise to pave, and walk in it. But, Lord, please, this love for Hannah I can't squelch. It must be from you. If not, take it away.*

Discussion Guide

Dear Readers,

Willow Byler is taking us on a roller coaster ride with his emotions, confident one day, doubting the next. Hannah's on a tailspin journey as well. Granny Weaver and Jeb, wise elderly counselors, seem to help with their well-seasoned advice

The story opens with Cassia having a miscarriage and Granny is overcome with emotion over her stillborn daughter. Hannah recognizes that Granny truly believes in Romans 8:28

And we know that all things work together for good to them that love God, to them who are the called according to his purpose.

Granny is a much-loved character who finds herself into many of my books, bringing hope to many. Have you had a tragedy, difficult time or an experience you're keeping to yourself? Notice that Granny not only gives love (teaching the single moms at Forget-Me-Not Manor how to cook) but also receive it from her knitting friends. 'Mold grows in the darkness' Granny has said. 'Bring things out into the light." I think we forget that 'all things work together for the good' and we need friends and community to remind us. How can you implement this scripture into your life? Do you have a friend who can keep you mindful of this truth?

1.) You my experience fear when reaching out to share your deepest hurts. Read 2 Timothy 5:7 and discuss fear. What does God give us to overcome this joy stealer?

2.) Willow is sorely tempted by Cheri, but he feels sorry for her. He seemed to see the good in everyone. Do you think Willow's kind or gullible? Can you be too nice?

3.) Consider this exchange between Hannah and her mom:

"Commit whatever you do to the Lord, and your thoughts will be established, Hannah. God gives us firm ground to walk on, *jah*?"

Hannah let her *mamm* continue to rub her back. "I'll do that. Is that in the Bible?"

"*Jah*, in the Psalms somewhere. When your *daed* passed, the Bible became ever so precious to me. It's sweeter than honeycomb. You can find a refuge in it."

"I will," Hannah said. "I will."

Do you agree with Esther's advice? One of my favorite authors is Joshua Choonmin Kang. His book, *Scripture by Heart: Devotional Practices for Memorizing God's Word* is very insightful as to why and how to memorize scripture. I highly recommend it. Scripture truly is sweeter than honeycomb.

4.) What do you think of Andy Smucker? He's only known Hannah for a several months. Can he really be in love in such a short time? Hannah finds him controlling, a fear many women have will develop in a relationship. Are her fears valid or irrational?

5.) Edmond Ledger realizes he loves Lily while being away and seeking God. Her relies on a scripture Jeremiah 6:16:
"Stand ye in the ways, and see, and ask for the old paths, where is the good way, and walk therein, and ye shall find rest for your souls."
Rest for the soul. Who doesn't want that? How does this scripture speak to you personally?

5.) Lily says hope gave her strength to wait for Edmond when all hope was gone. Hope means to have an expectation, to trust, have confidence. The Bible says three things will remain: faith, hope and love. (I Corinthians 13:13) Deep in your heart, what are you hoping for? I don't mean a new car or temporal thing, but something of substance. Maybe a relationship to be reconciled? More confidence like Willow? Direction about a major decision? Believe God and have hope…and patience. Romans 8:25 says, *'But if we hope for that which we don't see, we wait for it with patience.'*

6.) Reed Byler says after reading Grimm's fairy tale, *Cinderella*, "There're girls in ash heaps, you know. Girls whose lives are sad. They long to find a man who will cherish them. Women need to be cherished." Does anyone come to mind? If so, let her know in a special way that she's cherished by God. What can you do for her? A gift? An invitation to talk over a cup of coffee? Discuss and share ideas.

7.) Do you agree that Willow needs to leave Smicksburg to 'know himself'? Does getting away from your usual routine and surrounding give you more perspective?

8.) Edmond Ledger is turning Amish. Does this surprise you? Do you believe there are seasons in life for singleness and marriage? Read Ecclesiastes 3 and discuss.

9.) Do you think Willow fits in more with the Amish or Mennonites? Why? If he's more Mennonite, is it right to return home to Smicksburg for his love for Hannah? Should he be Amish for Hannah, like Freeman said he'd do, or should he be called by God?

AMISH RECIPE

Granny Weaver's Walnut Kisses

2 c. sugar

6 egg whites

3 tablespoons flour

2 cups walnuts chopped

Beat egg whites until stiff and dry. Mix flour and sugar and fold in stiffly beaten egg whites. Add walnuts. Drop by teaspoon onto a greased cookie sheet making sure they are about 2-inches apart. Bake at 325 degrees for 10 minutes and then let cool.

The Herbalist's Son

Book Three

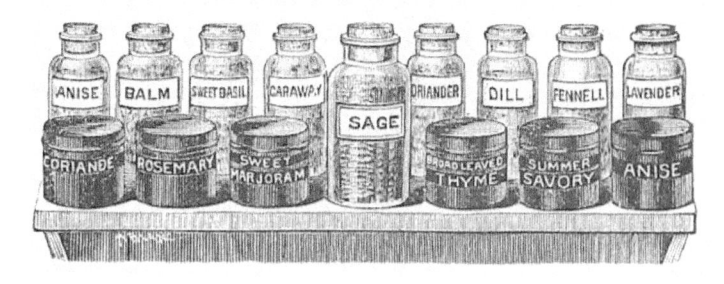

*"I believe in Christianity
as I believe that the sun has risen: not
only because I see it,
but because by it I see everything else."*
C.S. Lewis

Chapter 1

Son,

Our arrival to Mexico was as colorful as a crazy quilt. Crazy in that I couldn't believe, little me, an Amish woman from Smicksburg was standing on Mexican soil. I have to admit, it was a breath of fresh air. I understand your travel bug, as your daed calls it. But, Willow, to live here, in such dire poverty, the other side of me is full of pain. Edmond said Haiti's much poorer, but I can't imagine it. I read about it in Christian Aid Ministry newsletters, but you have to be here in person to understand. The hopelessness of the children in the orphanage your daed's focusing on, makes me want to adopt every one of them. The parents who leave them here they believe are doing it for their good, and I'm not judging, just saying I could fill the house with these children.

You see, Son, once the wee ones know God's not mad at them, they lighten right up. When I told them Jesus loves them, a shadow crossed their faces. I wondered why and a man in charge said it's hard for them to believe. They think bad things happen to bad people. So I say, "Jesus loves you" like the English, out loud and bold, and I must say, they're like plants being watered. I see the power of the tongue, *used for healing. Your daed found out the boys needed to learn a trade to raise a family. He's teaching basics about having nutritious soil and in a nutshell, they'll get a crash course in herbal medicine and growing herbs as well. Your daed smiles from ear to ear, very much alive in Mexico. I think the kinner here are doing just as much for him. For both of us. With all the kinner marrying (you will, too, someday) it's nice to have a mission in life, to feel needed. We're already talking about our next visit down.*

How was your train ride up to Canada? I do hope you'll come home for Christmas and stay until the new year. You've kept your word to Mr. Peter's and well, I fret about you. Jumping over to the Mennonites is what I fear, but God's will be done.

Much love,

Mamm

Cheri placed the letter on Willow's nightstand. "Does that cheer you up? Make you feel any better?"

He groaned, as pain shot up his back. He never should have left Smicksburg so sick. "Fever," was all he could get out along with "Lee. Where is he?"

"You're staying here. Dad insisted, you know. Said the family who was taking you in was really trying to get Amish to leave their faith."

She lay next to him, with her skinny jeans and short top, Willow finding it hard to divert his eyes. *Flee from evil*, Edmond had cautioned, but how? With a temperature of one-hundred and three, burning up one minute, chilled the next. She snuggled up against him, the feel of her body sending shock waves all over. Desire. Lust. *Ach, Lord, help me.*

"I'm a bit chilly," she purred.

"G-get a sweater. T-too cold for summer clothes."

A laugh foreign to Willow's ears, one that mocked, rang in his mind as she kissed his earlobe. "You came back for me, jay?"

"*Jah*, not jay," he groaned. "And *nee*, I didn't come back for you, but your *daed*. I thought you'd changed, being Mennonite."

She undid a few buttons of his pajama top, slipped her hand in and rubbed his chest. "I tried to be holy like Betty, but I can't. You're so irresistible and right now, you need a massage right here. We're afraid of pneumonia."

Though weak, the desire to kiss her, her breath the smell of peppermint, intoxicated him. *Flee from evil!* He pushed her away, redid his buttons while slipping out of bed. "You need help." The room spun, and he was soon flat on his back, her voice wafting pleasantries into his ears. Suggestions most men couldn't resist. *Men dream of things like this.* His mind ran towards his *mamm's* letter. Did Cheri pursue men so hard because she didn't know God's love? "It hurt you that your beau broke things off, *jah*?" he managed to get out.

"He wasn't a man like you," she murmured. "You know how to love a woman in every way."

"Every way? *Jah*, when I'm married I will." The image of Hannah hovered over him. Was he getting delirious? "I told you I'm saving myself for my spouse."

That laugh again pierced his heart. It had wicked intent, the seducer talked about in Proverbs, and the one who followed her would be led to a road of destruction. Although she was now laying on him, he pushed her back with all his strength and rolled out of bed again. Hitting his head on the nightstand, he let out a howl, but was glad to hear noise outside the door. Mr. Peter's was asking if he was okay. Cheri put a finger to her lips as she raced to hide in the closet. "I'm okay."

The door opened, and he looked around the room suspiciously. "I heard you talking." He crossed the room, demanding he put the thermometer in his mouth. While he waited for a reading, Willow wondered what could make Cheri so promiscuous? He'd never met anyone like her, but then again, he was sheltered. Hannah's goodness and purity made him long for her all the more. But she didn't even say good-bye, only leaving the new scarf with his *daed*. *She'll marry that jelly-spined Andy*, he thought and immediately repented of his thought. Andy was a mystery, appearing to try too hard to live by the *Ordnung*. Just how different was the *Ordnung* in his church in Ohio?

"Still one-hundred-three. Get dressed. We're heading into town," Mr. Peters informed, starting for Willow's closet.

"I can get my own clothes," Willow blurted.

Mr. Peter's threw up his hands. "Do it fast. Throw on a sweater I got you."

"I'm dressing Amish," Willow informed.

"But, I got you alpaca sweaters. Mighty cold up here."

"I have a wool jacket…and a new warm scarf."

~*~

The next few days, Willow was stuck at the Peters, Cheri testing him at all hours of the day. Was he being tempted like Jesus in the wilderness for forty days and nights? But thank goodness Betty and Lee showed up to give him a talking-to.

"You can't live here," Lee commanded. "Cheri tried her flirting on me when I got here. Run, my friend."

Willow fluffed the massive couch pillow in the Peters' family room. The fire flickering in the fireplace, casting shadows up against the icy glass walls was a dichotomy; like Cheri. "I pity her, really," he said. "Something's missing in her life to be so immoral."

Betty batted her lashes, an almost matronly smile upon her face. "That's what I *love* about you, Willow. You see the good in others."

"Aren't we supposed to?" he asked, searching Lee's stern face. His crossed arms told him he wouldn't be listening to any of his naiveté. Flee from evil, was Edmond's plea, and the images of Cheri he'd shared with Edmond had become alive again in dreams that made him blush. "I'll get my things and leave tomorrow."

"Today," Lee stated. "It's a guy thing," he said, turning to Betty.

"Must be since I feel sorry for Cheri, too. How can we help her see that God loves her? It's the cure for immorality."

"Really?" Willow asked. She was sounding like his *mamm*, saying the love of God helped children in poverty. Did Cheri have that poverty of spirit Edmond had told him Americans have?

"Absolutely. God made our hearts, and we're restless until we have that personal relationship with him."

Lee seemed to melt as Betty talked. "Augustine, right?"

"Yes. We've been studying him in my Ancient History course online."

"Always learning," Lee winked. "I like that about you."

Willow knew Lee had his heart set on Betty and could see why. A woman with a voracious mind to learn was attractive. The more Betty went on about this Augustine, Willow saw her in a new light. And the Mennonites as well. How many Amish were in Mexico with his parents? Not many. Mennonites did so much of the legwork for Amish ministries, due to all their restrictions.

"I'll run upstairs and grab your stuff," Lee informed. "You travel like a minimalist, so I'll be down in a few minutes."

"Don't forget the scarf," he quipped. "Need it to stay warm."

"You have one from your friend in Smicksburg," Betty said as Lee mounted the steps two at a time. "Don't need to wear two."

"She made me another one...warmer."

Betty seemed to clam up, crossing her legs and shaking the dangling one. Pulling her sweater closer as if in a chill, she faced Willow bravely. "So, what do you think of my letter?"

"Your letter? Which one?"

"My last one." Betty's face slowly but surely turned a deep crimson. "You know, the one where I told you what I thought of you."

She was terribly uncomfortable, and Willow wanted to ease her. "I read all your letters."

"And?"

"And I think you…wear your heart on your sleeve, like my sister says."

She nodded and stared at the floor. "And how do you feel?"

Stunned, he felt his forehead. "Think the fever's easing a bit."

"You know what I mean…"

But he didn't. "How's things going with Lee? You two make a nice couple."

She groaned. "We're not dating. It's what my letter was all about. I don't prefer him because…Do I have to spell it out?"

When Betty shot up and paced the floor, it reminded Willow of his *daed*. *When nervous, pace. Work out the nervous energy.* "Betty, what' wrong?"

She clenched her fists, and if she were a teakettle, steam would be coming out her ears. "I told you I cared about you. I've never done such a thing, never so bold. But Willow, you think so little of yourself, or you're too humble to see your good qualities I've come to love."

Love? "What did you say?"

"Love. I said it. I love so much about you, Amish man." She covered her face in shame. "I cannot believe I just said that, but I do need to say it straight out with you since you don't get it."

Lee appeared, a duffle bag slung on his shoulder, and his eyes soon met Betty's. "Did I miss something?"

"*Nee*, nothing at all," Willow assured.

Betty seemed to wilt right there before him, and then she meandered out of the room, head down.

"What's wrong with her?" Lee asked.

Willow felt fatigued, due to all the emotion. Betty cared for him? She was way too good. Educated, pretty, a woman admired by many men at church, but she didn't see it. They saw her inner and outer beauty, but not her. Was he like her, too humble to see his good qualities? Did he deserve someone like Betty? "Lee, do you still care about Betty?"

A smile split his face. He didn't need to say anything more. "Hopeful, but something's holding her back."

Willow lay his head on the pillow. "You could get any girl in the church."

"I don't want any other girl in the church." Lee offered Willow a hand up. When Willow took it, he felt like a faithless friend to this man who was obviously smitten.

"Let's go buddy," Lee said. "No need to stay here another night."

Chapter 2

After a few days of rest, Willow felt somewhat at home at the Yoders. Being dropped off by them for work was mighty kind, but he regretted facing Mr. Peters. The man had done so much for him, and he up and left without even saying good-bye or when he'd be back to work.

As he neared the massive house, dawn still breaking across the winter sky, compassion for Cheri filled him. Seeing her pace the floor of the living room through the glass windows, book in hand, most likely studying for a test, he just couldn't help but want to solve her mysterious behavior. This girl was pegged by the town as someone who would never change. Could new surroundings help her? *Hannah would be a gut influence*, he thought. *Ach, when will I ever stop thinking of that girl back home?*

He rounded the house to find Mr. Peters playing fetch with his lead dog of his sled team. "Hello," he said, feeling about as big as a speck of snow.

He didn't look at him but said a good morning.

"I didn't plan to go without any explanation. My friends from the Mennonite Church insisted I leave."

Throwing out a stick, Mr. Peters sighed. "Cheri likes you just like we thought. Well, you've be a good influence on her, but we're concerned." The white dog that nearly blended into the falling snow dropped the stick at his master's feet. "We know the rumors around town about Cheri. I'm sure you have by now, too. Her being an…immoral girl."

"*Jah*, I have, but I feel for her," Willow blurted.

Beaming, Mr. Peters slapped his back. "I knew it. I knew you'd come to see the good in her."

His heart sunk. "Mr. Peters, I don't care for Cheri in a romantic way, but as a concerned…friend. I think she needs help."

"We've tried counselors," he was quick to spit out. "They do no good, only drain the pocketbook."

Did he dare tell him about Hannah? Or maybe Cassia could straighten Cheri out. "Well, I came up here. How about she takes a visit to Smicksburg and get a chance in a small town where she wouldn't be judged?"

Mr. Peters arched his back and thrust the stick. "She has an aunt who's offered a similar situation, but Cheri won't go. Stupid of me to think having someone Amish here could straighten her out."

Having someone Amish here? "Maybe Hannah could come up here," Willow thought aloud.

"Hannah's your sister?"

Trying to hide his affection and longing for Hannah, he leaned over to form a snowball and tossed it around. "A friend."

"A friend who's single I'm guessing?"

"*Jah*, she's my sister's best friend. Hannah has self-respect, something Cheri needs."

Slouching and as weary looking as the dog returning the stick, Mr. Peters complied. "Can you ask her to come stay with us? Soon? Cheri gets low around Christmas."

"Sure will," he said, the thrill of seeing Hannah and getting her away from Andy seeming mighty appealing.

~*~

Hannah jumped on her tiptoes as the kindling caught fire in Willow's woodstove. When a few amber flames made a steady glow, she threw on several small sticks and topped it with a log. Hopefully the house would be snug in five minutes or so.

By the glow of oil light, she observed how much cleaning would be required of her for this day. Tired from keeping up chores at home and at Willow's, she decided to sit and organize the business papers in Willow's desk. She rubbed her hands as she went through them, until one with pink flowers made her heart stop. *What on earth? Looks like a love letter.* Or maybe a business letter she needed to read. Against her better judgement, she opened the envelope to read:

Dear Willow,

You've only been gone for three weeks and I've missed you more than I imagined. The mission at the church is doing well, another Amish man showed up needing advice from the Mennonites. We all wished you were here to answer his questions since you've recently jumped the fence. Remember when you didn't know what that meant? Well, you do now.

Willow, I have a confession. I've been asked to court several men at church but have said no because I'm looking for that special one God has intended for me. If you can read between these lines, I think you can guess what I'm suggesting. I care about you, Willow. Please come back to us soon. I've never met such a gentle soul as you and well, I'll be praying hard you're right back up here where you belong. So much to do in the Mennonite Church. I admire your parents being Amish and reaching out to Outsiders. Seems rather unusual since the Amish are such a closed bunch, not like us Mennonites. Not like you, Willow Byler.

Love,

Betty

Hannah gasped for air and held the letter to her heart. Jealousy struck her near dumb. How could this girl be so bold? Were Mennonite women so open with their feelings?

She bit her lower lip, a chill running down her spine. Why couldn't she be open with her feelings? Hannah didn't know her own mind, that's why. And fear, her old enemy, had her paralyzed.

She gazed at this little place Willow built; it was dear to her. He'd protested about her coming to clean, saying she was a cleaning nut, but she needed to be here. Was it because she felt close to Willow? But he didn't even say good-bye and hadn't even written a short note of thanks for the scarf she'd made. Apparently, Willow had some leanings towards being Mennonite.

Hannah stood erect, and robotically started to straighten up the little house. She swiped away tears at the thought of thinking she knew Willow through and through, and here he was flirting with the Mennonites, one girl in particular.

She shoved the letter back in the desk, another letter with female handwriting falling to the ground. She quickly read:

Dear Willow,

I had to tell you before I popped. Dad was right in bringing you here to straighten me out. He told me his plan. What a good dad I have. I visited the Mennonite church. I'm reading my Bible now and see how sinful I was. You must think I'm a slut. I'm not, only really like you a lot. Don't live with Lee. It would be harder for me to see you.

Write back and let me know what you decide.

Love,

Cheri

Hannah was thankful she was sitting, because her legs would have given out. This girl had apparently seduced Willow and was apologizing for it. But did seeds pop into flowers overnight? An alarm system seemed to run through her. *Danger.*

She paced the floor. Who should she tell? Edmond? Maybe Edmond would go up and bring him home. Home where he belonged. Who could she get unbiased advice from? Not her *mamm*, since she sang the praises of Andy so often, she was starting to believe them. Andy? Would Andy go? As touched as she was that Willow yelled out his love for her in front of everyone right there on the street, maybe it made Andy see how *English* Willow was becoming and he could straighten him out. Her mind racing, she took deep breaths and counted to ten. When finished, a clear image of Granny and Jeb came before her. They'd know what to do.

~*~

Reed took a break from giving vaccines, walking off alone on a trail the locals assured him was free of poisonous snakes. The need to seek his Lord came mighty strong upon him. Something was wrong with his son. Something that needed tended to, but here he was in Mexico and Willow in Canada. Dorcas said their son needed to know his own mind as well as Edmond. Willow was at a crossroads and waiting for the good way to walk in. He slapped his dusty leg. "Willow should know by now what the Good Way is! It's the Amish way!" he rumbled in low tones. But fear for his son was consuming him, sometimes robbing him of the joy of helping hundreds of children. He thought of his Lord leaving the ninety-nine sheep to find the one who strayed. Was he supposed to go up to Canada?

He kicked a red stone down the path. Should he send money to Edmond and have him do his bidding? *Nee, Edmond's in his proving time.*

Exhausted from fear that seemed to come out of nowhere, Reed took a seat on a boulder that seemed to be right there for him. He had to calm himself down. First of all, fear was not from God. *God has not given us a spirit of fear but of power, love and a sound mind.* This strengthened him. His mind needed to calm down and be sound.

The line of children coiled around for miles. "Lord, help these people here in Mexico. I'm doing your work here and can't be in two places at one time. You are God with no limitations, but I do have many limits. I lift my son up to you. Edmond's right. He needs to know his own mind. If he's to be Mennonite, so be it. There're many fine Mennonite folk down here on this trip. Help the bond between us continue to grow. Give wisdom to Willow concerning his place in the world. You say in your Word you give us wisdom liberally and don't hold back, but we can't waver, being double minded and being unstable in all our ways. Lord, give my son not only wisdom, but a sound mind to take your wisdom and not waver. This is hard, Lord. I want Willow to be Amish. I imagine him with Hannah. That girl loves my son, but her *mamm* is pushing Andy on her mighty hard. Help Hannah have a strong decisive mind, too. I cast all my cares upon you, for you care for me. Amen."

He closed his eyes and let the heat and wind age his face. He didn't care. After a good talking-to with the Lord, he always waited for a scripture to pop into his mind or a settling to calm his heart. As he waited, he had a knowing deep down that everything was in control. God was in control and as he opened his eyes to see from afar, mothers in line, some nursing, he thought of Psalm 131 and recited it by heart.

Lord, my heart is not haughty, nor mine eyes lofty: neither do I exercise myself in great matters, or in things too high for me.

Surely I have behaved and quieted myself, as a child that is weaned of his mother: my soul is even as a weaned child.

CHAPTER 3

Cassia heard Hannah's usual three rapid knocks on the front door, and her heart lifted. Hannah, sweet bosom friend Hannah, had held her hand through the grief of losing her son, and continued to come and knit. They near bumped into each other at the door, and Cassia was quick to see Hannah was down in the mouth something awful. Well, it was time for her to be the one to hold her dear friend's hand. "*Ach*, Hannah, what's wrong?"

Unwrapping herself and placing her cape and bonnet on the coat rack, she blurted, "Nothing. Why?"

"Your face is flushed, and you look...angry. You look mad, Hannah. Have I done something to ail you?"

"*Nee*, not at all." Lifting her knitting bag up, she made her way to her usual chair and plunked down, pulling out soft angora yarn.

Cassia quickly got her basket and they began the ritual of tapping needles, sipping cocoa and chatting. Maybe it was all in her head that Hannah was upset. "So, Hannah, making another warm scarf?"

"Not for your *bruder*, that's for sure."

Cassia blinked in disbelief at her friend's sassy tone. "Well, you made him one long enough to go to the moon and back. He doesn't need another one."

Hannah chewed on her lower lip, the needles seeming too heavy for her hands. "He didn't even say *danki*."

"I'm sure he'll write. I think he's nervous deep down, us Bylers being in three countries right now. Willow won't admit it, but he's a homebody and just needs to prove to himself he can live away from family."

"*Ach*," Hannah snapped. "He's got leanings towards the Mennonites, is what."

Clearly Hannah was *furhoodled* today. The Winter Solstice, a day that had the shortest amount of sunlight was only three weeks away; was Hannah moody due to the weather? "Winter blues, Hannah? Why think such dreary thoughts about Willow? We had a chat on Thanksgiving and he's Amish for sure."

"Did he tell you about Betty and…Cheri?"

"His friends in Canada? Sure, he did. Why?"

"Do you know they both wrote to him when he was home for such a short spell and both care for him?"

Cassia's little *bruder* image of Willow was melting each and every day. He was a man. He seemed a bit standoffish at times, but everyone learning something new was wobbly on their feet. "I'm glad those girls can see the worth in Willow."

Hannah's knitting fell into her lap and she leaned her head on the back of her rocker. "Go on. Tell me how I'm the one for Willow and I need to wake up. Andy's not right for me."

Baffled, Cassia got up to put milk on the woodstove to heat. "More hot chocolate will lift your mood. Do you know chocolate raises the serotonin level in the brain? If we lack it, we get depressed in winter."

"I'm not depressed…"

"You're upset then. Tell me your troubles. I never would have made it through my grief if it weren't for you, dear sweet friend. We've gotten closer than ever. Tell me what ails you."

Picking up her knitting, Hannah crossed her legs and shook her foot, a nervous habit since a wee one. "I'm so unsettled about Andy. *Mamm* just won't give up the notion that we're engaged."

"You're not though. For real…"

"Well, at my age, I'd be daft to not take him seriously. I do want a family and he's Amish."

Cassia noticed the shadows that blanketed Hannah's face when talking of Andy. She also knew their family finances would be greatly lifted if Hannah married him. Esther did the most outlandish things when in grief. She overspent on her beloved husband's funeral and despite all warnings, she got a new dining room table and China cabinet. New dishes soon followed and then a new wringer washer. When she was about to buy the black stallion, Jeb stepped in and gave her a talkin' to. "Do you work for my *bruder* because you have to?"

"*Nee*, I love the dogs. I *redd* up his house after he comes home and go in to make sure it's clean. You know how mice show up in a quiet house."

"Well, that cat Willow bought you wasn't raised to be a mouser or you could just let Shadow stay there for a while."

Hannah cocked a brow. "How would you know if Shadow wasn't a mouser?"

"She's a purebred ragdoll is why." Cassia cupped her mouth. "Oops."

"Shadow's a ragdoll cat? They cost a fortune."

Cassia nodded. "Sure do, but that's just the way Willow is. He never does anything in halves."

Hannah's eyes pooled with tears. "Does what in halves?"

"Love," Cassia said gently. "You know he loves you. The whole Amish grapevine's faster than the *English* internet, and well, everyone heard about him telling you out on the road." Cassia pressed her yarn to her chest as she rose to fix the hot chocolate. "It was a shocker to many, but not me." Pouring scalding hot milk into mugs, she added a bit of cocoa and cinnamon, and placed them on the little table between them.

"A ragdoll's three-hundred dollars…"

"Willow paid a bit more," Cassia dared say. "But he never wanted you to know."

"He said it was a cat he *found*."

"Found in the newspaper and traveled to Pittsburgh to pick up. And then he made sure Doctor Fox examined the kitten."

Tears dripped down Hannah's cheeks. "I didn't know."

"He didn't want you to."

Looking like a ragdoll herself, all limp in her rocker, Hannah said faintly, "But he's not Amish, Cassia. I do care for Willow. I see he's a man now, not a little *bruder*. But he's leaning towards the Mennonites."

Cassia offered Hannah the embroidered handkerchief she'd received from her at knitting circle. "Well, if I get a letter telling me such nonsense, I'll believe it, but not until then. And, Hannah, if you care for Willow, please don't commit yourself to Andy. He's successful and all, bringing in lots of money with his carving business, but believe me, wait. I shiver to think of what my life would be without Martin."

"Andy's getting impatient and *Mamm's* exasperated."

"Well, you tell your *mamm* Willow's not a poor man and can take care of *yinz* just as *gut* as Andy if you…"

"If I what?"

Cassia wanted to scream out what she could clearly see. "If you admit you love Willow like I love Martin. There, I said it. You two have the makings of a great marriage."

"I know…"

"You know? And you still court Andy and don't encourage Willow at all?" Cassia quickly grabbed her hot cocoa, partly because she couldn't talk and sip at the same time."

"I did encourage Willow. What do you think the scarf was for? I didn't even realize it until after I made the second one. I do love Willow, but how can I encourage a man not yet baptized?"

Cassia's eyes became buttons and then little by little laugh-lines pinched them narrow. "I knew it. *Ach,* it was my prayer you'd wake up and see Willow for the man he is. Ever so happy! You'll be my sister-in-law!"

"But he has leanings towards the Mennonites, Cassia."

"Fiddlesticks," Cassia chimed. "He's Amish. Just up in Canada to keep his word to Mr. Peters." She wanted to skip around the room, but then remembered something. "You need to be honest with Andy. You don't love him. Tell him."

Hannah's face grew rigid. "I want *Amish kinner*. An *Amish* family. I can learn to love Andy."

Cassia wanted to throw a ball of yarn at her dear friend and shout 'Wake up!' but calmly said, "Just don't say yes to a marriage proposal until Willow's back home, okay?"

Hannah nodded but changed the conversation. A charity quilting bee was being planned. How many cardinals were at her feeder? Cassia knew her friend was in distress when she made small talk with her kindred spirit friend.

~*~

Hannah's day started off badly and it was now becoming worse. Andy was coming over to dinner again? Her *mamm* was making all his favorites. What her *mamm* was doing was making a fool out of her daughter. Was she so desperate to get her married off she'd break all the regular courting rules and intrude, inviting her so-called fiancé over three times a week?

Too annoyed and not trusting her tongue to not snap at her *mamm*, she said she needed some rest before dinner, and holed herself up in her room to sort through the day's mail. She noticed three handwritten letters, one with a postage stamp from Mexico. Dorcas knew she was a stamp collector and so she ripped into it first, several stamps falling out of the envelope. *Ach, I miss this dear woman!* She read the short note. All was well, but Dorcas was exhausted, the need being great and their time there so limited. The letter was only five lines long, the last one a plea for prayer for the children who had extended bellies and reddish hair, two signs of starvation. "Lord, bless Dorcas and Reed," she prayed, Shadow turning, looking a bit startled as the prayer broke the quiet of the room. She hugged her cat. "And bless their son who so selflessly let me believe this cat was no big expense. How could I miss it that she was a rare beauty, not your usual feline?"

The second letter was from her cousin in Ohio but the third had hard-lined male writing. She noticed it had a Canadian stamp. Willow! Ripping it open, she read:

Dear Hannah,

I miss you. Thanks so much for the scarf you made. I wear it often. I wanted to thank you in person but was sick and contagious when I left.

I have a big favor to ask you. Cheri Peters needs to learn some self-respect. Mr. Peters admitted he hired me in part because he thought a good Amish boy could straighten her out. Cheri's very flirtatious around men, and I think it's because deep down, she feels worthless. Her mamm is rarely home and she lacks a mentor.

I was wondering if you could befriend Cheri? I can pay for your train ticket up and you can stay with the Peters'. I know you'll be thinking of my dogs right about now, but Martin and Edmond can handle it for three weeks.

And I'd love for you to see how beautiful Canada is and meet some of my new friends.

Write back or call me at the number on the back side of this letter. My new address is beside it. I don't live with the Peters' anymore. Hannah, I'll be honest. What Betty and Lee call Cheri is Potiphar's wife. I had to flee like Joseph, if you know what I mean. But I still can't think badly of Cheri. I see a teenager in need of an example of the Godly Proverbs 31 Woman. You know, the perfect woman in the Bible Cassia used to compare herself too and fret because she can't cook. She's getting better, but the Thanksgiving dinner was another burnt offering.

Call me or write as soon as possible. I can make train arrangements on the internet. All you have to do is pack and get yourself up here.

Love,
Willow

Hannah kissed the letter. *I'll come up. But not for Cheri. For you, my dear Willow. To show you how far away from the Amish you've drifted. Be Amish…for me.*

Hearing her *mamm* call upstairs, reality set in. Who would stay with her *mamm*? It was the dead of winter. A funny idea popped into her mind. Andy! After all, she said several times a day he was like a son already.

~*~

After supper dishes were washed and dried, Esther placed a piping hot cherry pie on the table. "Your favorite, *jah*?"

"All your pies are my favorite," Andy said, licking his lips.

Hannah knew dessert was a good time to bring up the topic about Willow and her plans to rescue him. A spoonful of sugar helps the medicine go down, so she'd heard. "I got a letter from Willow today. He asked me to come to Canada to mentor the daughter of the family he's working for. He said I could do her some *gut*, so I'm going," she said, proud that she announced her plans, not asking for permission.

Andy's fork stopped short of his mouth. "Are you serious?"

Esther stood behind Andy, glaring at Hannah. "After Willow announcing to the world his foolish notion of loving you, you'd actually go and encourage him?"

"*Mamm*, I can read the letter aloud. It's not like that. And I'm old enough to make my own decisions."

Andy glowered. "No wife of mine would go traipsing off without my consent."

"I am *not* your wife," Hannah snapped. "And if you'd tie me like a dog to a leash, it will never happen."

Esther seemed to lose her balance but retrieve herself, reaching for a nearby chair. "Travel alone to Canada? We can't afford the train ticket."

Hannah's heart was beaming, feeling so free for some reason. Was it the encouraging letter from Willow? Did it give her courage? "Willow's buying my ticket."

"And you're accepting the money?" Andy asked, hurt etched into his countenance.

"Mr. Peters may be the one paying, since Willow's working for him. It's his daughter that needs help. I don't have all the details, but just know I don't have to pay."

"Do you have a passport?" Andy asked. "Can't cross into Canada without one."

"She doesn't have a passport," Esther informed, looking mighty content that Hannah's plans were foiled.

"Willow knows all about getting one expedited. I'll be calling him tonight to make arrangements."

Andy shot up. "You can't go by yourself. It's dangerous."

Was he actually worried about her safety? His eyes said yes.

"Why don't you go with her?" Esther interjected.

"*Mamm*, just the two of us travel? That wouldn't look right."

"I can get Sadie to go with us. I'll pay for our tickets."

Hannah was like an animal cornered, feeling confused and restless. "I don't know. The Peters only invited me."

Esther cheeks were two bright cherries, looking bewildered. "Well. When you talk to Willow tonight, inform him that you need a travel companion or two and see what he says."

Hannah knew she needed to talk to someone else before she even called Willow: *Granny*

CHAPTER 4

That night, the lanterns on either side of the buggy swayed, casting long shadows across the snow-covered fields, now at rest for the season. Rest. She needed rest. Her heart was restless, but she couldn't put her finger on what was wrong. Hannah pulled her cape taut as she exited the buggy and led her horse to the stalls. Glad to see the Weaver's buggy was taking refuge there, her unplanned trip over wasn't in vain.

She ran to Granny's needing not only a warm mug of tea, but an embrace. She knocked rhythmically on the front door, and soon an oil lamp illuminated Granny's face, revealing a lovely smile. Opening the door, Granny welcomed her and led her to the oak table where many a long discussion had taken place. Mentoring from this dear woman had saved Hannah many scrapes in life, as did the opposite. *Not listening to her.* She ignored Granny's suspicions about Freeman, only to have discerned his character quite right. He was Mennonite to his core, not Amish.

"Hannah, such a surprise. Late for us old folk. Jeb's in bed, but can I help?" She cupped her cheeks. "Problems with Andy…or Willow?"

"Both," Hannah admitted, awed at Granny's perception. She threw her outer garments in a heap on the bench at the long oak kitchen table and plunked herself down. "Men. So confusing."

Granny filled her tea kettle. "Not really that confusing. Sometimes we just need someone to talk things over. Now, tell me what's going on in that big heart of yours."

"Willow wrote and asked me to go to Canada. The family he's working for has a troubled teenager and Willow thinks I can mentor her. Mentor her like you do me, which helps heaps. Professional counseling has failed and well, Willow thinks I'm…a *gut* woman."

"That's all he said?"

"Well, he said I was like the Proverbs 31 Woman." Why Hannah added this information, showing pride, made her cheeks grow warm, but Granny seemed to ask questions without words. Her light blue eyes seemed to open Hannah's soul.

"So, Willow's saying you're the perfect woman. Praise indeed, Hannah. *Ach*, he's such a fine *man*."

The emphasis Granny put on 'man' Hannah clearly understood. "*Jah*, he's grown up quite a bit lately. But he's not baptized."

"Yet," Granny corrected. "We all went through *rumspringa* to know our mind. Now, Willow's convinced he's Amish but needs to make sure. The Mennonites are still tugging at his heart."

"Betty is," Hannah grumbled.

"Come again?"

"*Ach*, Granny, I need to confess something. I read a love letter this Betty from Canada wrote Willow. How bold to say she cared for him! He should be the pursuer."

Granny scratched her cheek. "That is bold. A visit from you would do him *gut*. Go to him. Need money from the *Gmay*?"

"*Nee*, Willow said he'd pay. Andy's the problem. He insists on going with me, along with Sadie. He said it wasn't safe to be on a train alone as a woman and offered to pay for their tickets."

Granny quickly dipped two tea bags into teacups and set them on the table. "I got sugar cubes," she announced, opening her sugar bowl and holding up little gold tongs. She grabbed a cube and placed it in her cup and handed them to Hannah.

"Where'd you get these?"

"At the Sampler. They carry lots of tea supplies now. New chintz cups are in. I love the pink. Anyhow, I agree with Andy. Don't travel alone. But he's being too bossy insisting he's the one to go with you. Isn't he busy at his little shop? Christmas is around the corner."

Hannah swirled her tea and took a sip. "He *should* be busy. Maybe sales are slow."

"You know, Roman's rocker shop is bustling, and the UPS truck comes almost daily to pick up orders. Ever notice any UPS trucks over at Andy's? Or boxes and packaging?"

"*Nee*. I wonder how they survive."

"And they were invited to several places for Thanksgiving but declined. Odd bunch, I say. Don't act Amish."

"What are you saying?"

"*Ach*, not accusing them of not being devout, but, well, Jeb's had to talk a few times with them about how green they seem about being Old Order. They seem more *English* than Amish at times, especially Sadie. She's as proud as a peacock, you'd think *Gelassenheit* wasn't common among the People."

"I see that in Sadie at times," Hannah agreed. "Not much humility."

"Edmond was told to submit and not go to Mexico. He struggled, but it's more important that he be Amish and not always have his way. We Amish don't put our own personal needs first, *jah*?"

Hannah nodded. "I wonder what Andy would say if I told him not to come to Canada with me. Sadie's enough so-called protection, don't you think?"

"You tell him to stay here and take care of his store. Earn his way among the People and stop taking." Granny clenched her hands and raised them to her forehead. "I didn't mean to say that."

"They ask for help? Why?"

"Always short on cash for some reason. Pretty shocking that Andy says he can afford a train ticket." Hunching over her teacup, she sighed. "We think the best, *jah*? I'm only saying there's something mighty different about the Smuckers but Jeb assures me it's nothing. Says the new mystery novel I'm reading isn't *gut* and to stick to Jane Austen and other classics." She sipped her tea. "He encouraged me to buy all I needed for tea parties, like Suzy has in her shop. People open up over tea."

Hannah arched her back, tension from the day settling in. "So, I'm not *furhoodled* after-all."

"What do you mean?"

"Well, Granny, I've kept one eye shut when around Andy. I thought it was my imagination but something's not right. He says he's Amish, and since the whole town thinks we're engaged, others keep saying how blessed I am to find such a nice man. But all along, deep inside, I get more suspicious. But is it wrong to be suspicious? The Bible says love thinks the best, hopes the best."

"*Jah*, it does, but marriage is the biggest decision you'll make. It's your partner for life we're talking about." Granny's eyes, filled with concern. "Hannah, be careful. Don't accept a marriage proposal from Andy until all suspicions are gone."

"I overthink everything, how can I ever be free from suspicions? How can I ever trust a man after Freeman's deceit?"

"Hannah, *ach*, you give Freeman too much credit. Remember Harvey, your pen pal romance? You were too understanding, compassionate-like –"

"Gullible," Hannah admitted.

"*Jah*, that's what I mean, but didn't want to say that word because you're a smart woman. You're just too nice.

Why not tell a fellow to go fly a kite and say you're not interested? On the other hand, why not tell someone how much you care when you do?" She reached across the table to poke Hannah's hand. "Why don't you do what Betty did and tell Willow you *love* him?"

Tell Willow I love him? Hannah knew it was late. This was a mistake. Granny was clearly too tired to give sound, traditional advice. Men pursued, not women! Trying to change the subject she asked, "Granny do you want to go up to Canada with me? You of all people can straighten out Cheri Peters."

"Me? *Ach*, Hannah, so sweet of you to ask. When are you leaving and how long will you stay?"

"A few weeks, I suppose. Until Willow and I come back home for Christmas."

Granny's face lifted as it glowed. "I like the sound of that. The two of you make such a nice pair and he loves you." She reached for Hannah's hands and squeezed them. "I can't leave for three weeks or Jeb will be one unhappy man. I'll start my Christmas baking soon." She winked. "The old man still licks the bowl." Her face shone like an angel. "Went to bed early, like I said, but I know why; he's looking at carving books and fusses until he finds the right Christmas present to make for me."

Hannah imagined Willow in his seventies and trying to make a present in secret. She'd knit him something and... *Hannah Coblenz, control your mind, for crying out loud! You're not marrying Willow!*

~*~

Hannah was too baffled that night to call Willow. Her imagination hadn't been running wild about the Smucker family. Passing the phone shanty, she made a beeline straight home, feeling chilled to her bones. What was she thinking going over to Granny's so late at night? But when she got home, she was not prepared to see Andy asleep in the rocker near the woodstove. She nudged him. "Andy, wake up."

"It's okay, *Mamm*. I'll do it."

Intrigued by what people said in their sleep, like Willow saying 'Cheri', she thought maybe she'd get some questions answered. "I can do it."

Andy gulped back tears. "*Nee*, too sick."

Hannah gasped, and stepped back. Sick? His *mamm* was sick? Every attempt Andy made to have Hannah get to know his *mamm* was always met with the fact that she was napping or under the weather for the day. Sick? How bad was it?

Andy began to cry in his sleep, breaking Hannah's heart. She nudged him, but he only took her hand and cried all the harder. *What to do? Ach, Hannah, you've opened a kettle of fish!*

"I can't leave you," he continued.

"Leave me?" Hannah asked.

"*Jah*, for Canada."

Guilt washed over Hannah and she shook Andy until he awoke. His eyes grew wet with tears and he looked at her like a lost boy. "Andy, you were dreaming. A bad dream."

"How do you know?"

"You talk in your sleep."

His eyes rounded as if his fingers were caught in a cookie jar. "What did I say?"

Hannah slowly sat in the rocker next to him, wondering all the while what to say. "Someone at your place sick? Sick enough to make you cry?"

"*Mamm*. She has many bad days."

"Why so many bad days? What does the doctor say?"

His chin quivered, and he looked at Hannah like an animal caught in a trap. "I can't say."

"*Ach*, Andy, it must be serious."

He nodded. "*Jah*, it is. But she's been having *gut* days all week now that she knows I'll be married. It's her…wish."

Her wish? "Andy. Why tell her we're engaged when we're not?"

"Makes her happy and that's *gut* for her immune system."

Hannah pressed a hand to her chest. How odd an answer. "And her immune system needs to be high because?"

"Reed Byler says so. I can't wait until he comes back from Mexico." He itched the back of his neck. "Reed knows *Mamm's* case."

This was all too mysterious. "Can you tell me what's going on? The whole town thinks we're engaged but it's to help your *mamm*? What's wrong with her?"

He leaned towards her. "I do want you to marry me, Hannah. I've become so fond of you. But I vowed not to tell anyone outside the family my *mamm's* condition."

So, this family secret is what made the Smuckers so elusive. Sympathy coursed through Hannah's veins. "I'm so sorry. Really. It must be something terminal or very bad." She'd never seen Andy so open and vulnerable, Hannah felt she could see into his soul. *He's been affected for a long while by his mamm's illness. So involved, maybe he put off marriage. And Sadie, what was she going through to keep mum about such a serious matter?* "Sadie seems almost proud, but she's hurting about her *mamm, jah?*"

Fresh tears covered his face. "*Ach*, she could be married by now."

"So why isn't she?" Hannah wanted to know.

"Her fiancé broke things off when he found out."

Hannah shot up a prayer before asking, "Does your family carry a genetic disorder?"

"Well, we weren't sure until Reed figured it out, but no. Not a genetic disorder, but Sadie won't take Skylar back. He never should have been so judgmental, like the rest of them."

Skylar? What an odd Amish name. "The rest of who?" Hannah continued to prod.

"Our group in Ohio…"

"But you said they were more liberal, more progressive…"

Andy glowered. "Doesn't mean they were understanding. What *Mamm* and *Daed* found here in Smicksburg is a rarity. It's like this town is…full of love. And *Mamm's* doing better."

Hannah, although thoroughly exhausted, had to get to the bottom of the Smucker secret and clarify a few things.

"Andy, you need to be honest with me. What's really wrong? You can't keep pretending we're engaged, telling the whole town, when we're not."

A shadow crossed Andy's eyes. "What should I tell my *mamm* then?"

Hope deferred makes the heart sick, Hannah remembered the Bible saying. Hope had such power. It helped Lily wait for Edmond when there wasn't a hint of him even coming back to the States. Hope energized a soul, but this was deceitful. "Andy, the truth is always best. You can tell your *mamm* you hope someday we'll wed but there's been a delay. Like a long pause, since I need time."

"I'll tell her nothing. If me being engaged makes her happy, she deserves it for a change. Her pain…is better." Andy shot up. "I better get home. Only stayed here to make sure you got home all right. Your *mamm* was worried."

Feeling guilty like a child sent to stand in the corner, Hannah caved. "I'm sorry. Didn't mean to make anyone worry."

"Where were you anyhow? Talking to Willow?" He glowered. "You shouldn't use the phone shanty that long."

"I haven't even called Willow yet. I was at Granny Weavers." Irritation ran through her. "I don't deserve to be rebuked. *Mamm* would have waited up herself if she was worried." She pointed to the door. "I'm tired. You better go."

He reached for her outstretched hand. "Like I said, I can pay for my train ticket and Sadie's, too."

Hannah backed away. "You spend the money on your *mamm's* care. I'll talk to Willow and see what he has planned."

"But your safety…"

"I'll be fine," Hannah said evenly and spun around to leave the room. Feeling suffocated now, she ran up the stairs to her bedroom, leaving Andy alone downstairs. She heard the outside door shut and fell on her bed totally exhausted.

Karen Anna Vogel

Chapter 5

"Mrs. Yoder, did anyone call over the past few days?" Willow asked.

"Now, I like being called 'Mom Yoder', but if you can't, just call me Emma." Her plump cheeks lifted. "Wait. Betty called about the church meeting. Thought she wanted Lee at first, but she did ask for you."

"Maybe Hannah wrote. Letters take time to arrive."

"Hannah a sister back home?" Mrs. Yoder asked.

"A friend. Someone like a sister. She's watching my dogs while I'm up here in the tundra."

"This winter's been awfully cold. Matthew said it's record breaking. But he said that last year. So much for so-called Global Warming," she quipped. "Now, I've worked with Ex-Amish for years and well, I'm glad we're getting time alone. You seem like you want to talk to Matthew and me, but then clam up. Why?"

Willow's brows raised. "I just moved in a week ago, but if I seem like a clam, I do have something on my mind. My parents are in Mexico and it seems like they're on another planet."

"Mexico? So, your parents left the Amish, too?" she asked, eyes round as saucers.

"They're Amish but took the train to California and then down to Mexico. My *daed's* a medical man."

She placed another shirt on the ironing board. "Amish don't see doctors. I know since I was Amish. Never had much medical care."

"Well, I've had plenty. Was the Amish settlement you were in super strict? Almost odd, really, to not appreciate *gut* medical care."

"Well, I suppose it was stricter. Being Mennonite was the happy balance for Matthew and me." She pat her tiny head covering that barely hid her bun. "I still dress plain, and with a car and electricity, well, everything is less burdensome. Take this electric iron. I love it. No more propane irons with the smell and mess." She wrinkled her nose. "I got headaches from the fumes."

Willow crossed his arms and prayed for patience. This was the second time Emma had expressed her dislike for Amish ways and it was grating his nerves. "Emma, the Bible says to respect all people. There's Orthodox Jewish people in Pittsburgh who wear black and have these long curly sideburns. When I was a wee one and poked fun at them, my *daed* gave me a *gut* talking to. Parents have the right to raise their *kinner* in the religion they choose."

Eye's wide, Emma sighed. "But, Willow, when you're a mature man, you can make up your own mind…"

"*Jah*, I know. And I have only a few more questions and I'm ready to be baptized into the Amish faith. I appreciate your concern, but please, respect my decision and don't talk about the Amish as something to run away from."

Her face fell, as did her shoulders. "Seems like you have a *gut* family. My childhood wasn't too happy. I left as soon as I could."

Willow had heard this all too often. "Well, I'm sorry for you, Emma. Did you tell your bishop or elders of any wrong doing?"

She quickly shook her head. "They say you have freedom to speak out, but you don't. It was a mind game. When I met Matthew, he felt the same and we both choose to have our own minds, not be controlled. Even God won't take away our free-will."

Willow sunk into a nearby chair. "Emma, didn't you have *rumspringa*, a running around time to know yourself? That's what the Amish really believe; to be convinced in your own mind so out of your own free will you choose to make the vow to the church."

"But Willow, there's an expectation. It's like doing bad on something your parents have worked so hard to mold you into. My father told my mom that she was a failure as a mom, when it was because of *him* I left."

Willow put a hand up. "Emma, I won't be turning Mennonite. I know it's the way you and Matthew see things, but please, don't try to sway me. For every negative story I hear about Amish leaving, I can give two *wunderbar* stories of people not leaving."

Emma hung the pressed shirt on a hanger. "I'm not trying to sway you, Willow. Lots of kids come through here and if they want to return to the Amish, we help them."

All Willow heard was 'kids' and he wanted to argue the fact that he was now twenty-three, not a teenager. He was relying on all the advice Edmond gave him. Stand at the crossroads and wait. Wait on God, who always knows where the good way is and walk in it.

"Now that Betty, isn't she the doll," Emma said, interrupting his thoughts. "You wouldn't turn Mennonite for her?" She cupped her mouth. "I'm sorry. I heard her talking at church and she has her hopes."

Willow shook his head. "I won't be turning anything for anyone but God."

"Will you be calling Betty back?" Emma asked. "Going to church tonight?"

"*Nee*. Need to go over to the Peters tonight and spend time with the dogs. Riding a dog sled for the first time today. Won't be home until late."

Wagging a finger, Emma warned, "Stay away from Cheri. She's trouble."

"She's hurting inside," Willow said, waving good-bye.

~*~

The flashlight on the window in the wee hours of the night was making Hannah downright irksome. When would Andy take her seriously? No flashing the light in her window ever again! But the light seemed to go to her *mamm's* and then hers. Was it an emergency?

She threw back quilts and ran to the window, opening it up. "Who is it."

"Andy. I need help."

His voice was loud and desperate. "Have you tried Granny and Jeb?"

"*Nee*. Don't want them to know."

Baffled, she didn't feel right going out in the middle of the night under such mysterious circumstances. But a knock on the door and her *mamm* soon at her side, calling out to Andy, telling them they'd be out in a minute, jarred her wide awake. "*Jah*, we'll come over to your place as soon as we can."

"I can wait."

"Are you needed at home?" Esther probed.

As if too much in shock to make a decision, he just stood there, the snowflakes collecting on his black wool hat.

"Go on home. We'll meet you." Esther grabbed Hannah's arm. "If my suspicions are right, we're in for a long night."

Hannah quickly dressed, wondering what her *mamm* meant about her suspicions.

~*~

Hannah slowly sat down, legs wobbly. "She's terminal?"

Andy, head in his hands on the living room sofa, didn't say a word. His shoulders had long since stopped shaking due to crying and he was like a wilted plant. She was relieved when her *mamm* came out of the first floor bedroom that Katherine Smith had lingered in for months. Her name was not Ruth Smucker at all but Katherine Smith. Ruth was her favorite Bible character and it sounded "more Amish". They'd come to Smicksburg where no one knew them to live out Katherine's last days and with hopes of a recovery. Live in a place that makes you happy? Katherine Smith had been told to go home, her battle with breast cancer was a losing one.

Hannah robotically turned to Andy. "Did Reed Byler know you're not Amish?"

His green eyes scolded her. "We're almost Amish. Going through a proving time in our own way. But, *nee*, Reed didn't know. No one does."

Esther pulled Hannah up and led her to a corner of the room. "Hannah, I'm sorry I held back my suspicions. Katherine had opened up to me a tad. Not that she wasn't Amish at all, but enough to take it to Jeb."

"Jeb doesn't know about this?" Hannah crowed. "They say they're Amish."

"Lower your voice, dear," Esther whispered. "I know this is hard, but remember, we have a dying woman here and a family in great distress." She cupped her mouth and leaned closer. "When we spent more time with the Smuckers, or Smiths, Katherine let out some details about her illness, but I thought they had permission by Jeb and the elders."

"For what?"

"They have all kinds of things forbidden by the *Ordnung*. I just thought we all needed to be patient with them, coming from liberal Amish out in Ohio. Imagine my shock when Katherine, too ill to sit up and write, told me what to write in a letter; a letter to a pastor of her *Englisher* church. She almost spilled the beans when I asked questions…but didn't."

Hannah knew she'd wake up any minute, this situation similar to some of her very odd dreams. "So, *Mamm*, let me guess. They read an Amish fiction book, thought it was all sunshine and roses, and when they got here, they realized it's not."

"*Ach, nee,*" Esther said. "They loved it more than they thought. Never had Katherine had such peace. Came to terms with her maker and is ready to step on into heaven. She learned so much from all of us and Andy wants to come clean and be Amish for real."

Deep within, Hannah wanted to laugh. Be it nervous laughter or not, this whole cockeyed night was becoming too bizarre. "So, Andy isn't Amish," she quipped. "Next thing you'll say is that the cow can jump over the moon!"

Esther took Hannah by the shoulders. "This is no light matter. What's come over you?"

Suppressing a giggle to beat the band, Hannah was able to say, "*Ach*, Freeman? Andy? Willow? Men? They're all *furhoodled* in the head. I say we start a yarn shop."

"What?"

"*Jah*, I'm serious. We can spin and be spinsters." This was just a dream, so why not make it completely uncanny?

"I need to get you home. You're in shock," Esther said, enveloping her daughter in an embrace.

~*~

"I don't want anyone to know about this," Esther told Hannah the next day as she poured maple syrup over pancakes. "I'll tell Jeb for sure, but no need to make the Smuckers the talk of the town when Katherine is so ill. It's not our way."

"The Smiths, not Smuckers," Hannah corrected.

Esther nodded. "We need to be Christian-like towards them. Katherine's faith is strong, but her husband's is lacking."

"Let me guess. His name is different, too."

"*Jah*. His name is Lincoln. Strange for a name, but that was one of the first scents I picked up on that they weren't Amish."

"How so?" Hannah asked.

"Well, he said he was named after an ancestor and well, it's Abraham Lincoln. He was a *gut* Christian man but not a pacifist, as we all know."

"He's related to Abraham Lincoln," Hannah said in monotone. "Andy said he thought he might be related to someone in the Martyr's Mirror." She pounded the table with a fist. "How could he be so deceitful?"

Esther held Hannah's hand down. "Maybe it was on his *mamm's* side. It was Katherine who wanted to be Amish, remember?"

Hannah put three teaspoons of sugar in her coffee. "She deceived us, *Mamm*. You do see that, *jah*?"

"I do. And you must be awful nervous about Andy's proving time."

Hannah shot up, her chair toppling over. "His proving time? *Mamm*, you're too sympathetic! You still think Andy's the one for me!"

Esther picked up Shadow and stroked the long gray fur. "I'll talk to Jeb today and see what he has to say."

Hannah felt her entire body tremble. "I will never marry Andy Smucker, or Smith, or whatever his name is. I need someone steadfast and honest!"

Esther's face grew pensive. "I know, Hannah. I know." She gingerly rose to retrieve a letter from the China cupboard. "I got this from Willow. It's one line."

"You read my mail? And you hid it?"

"Came only two days ago. I forgot."

Not convinced and perturbed beyond measure, she took the paper and read:

Dear Hannah,
Why haven't you called me? Please call. I have a plan.
Love,
Willow

Her eyes stared at the words "love." He said he loved her. *Ach, Willow, please come back and don't be Mennonite!*

"Call him today, Hannah. And if you need someone to go with you to Canada, I'll go. Maybe I can help that wayward girl he wants you to mentor."

Hannah forced a smile. "And you won't bring up Andy?"

"*Nee*, and neither will you. Reed and Dorcas are down in Mexico and don't know and Katherine's condition is growing worse than ever. Willow may write them and tell their story. I'd rather they be home to hear about it." She wrung her hands. "And, remember, this is a crucial time for the Smiths. They may see Jesus in us Amish. Keep mum."

Hannah smirked. "You sound like a Baptist."

Esther straightened. "I've learned a thing or two from them."

~*~

Hannah heard Willow's confidence wither when she asked if her *mamm* could accompany her. "She offered."

"I'm surprised, is all."

"Why?"

"Well, I was so rude to her when I was home. She's mighty forgiving. Meant to write but I came up sick and stayed pretty bad for a week or so."

Hannah held her chest. "*Ach*, Willow, you're so sweet."

"It's the least I could do as an apology. Maybe send her something from the Sampler, but like I said, I left sick."

"All's forgotten, Willow. More men need to have such tender hearts. Or consciences, I might add."

Hannah heard a woman's voice ask, "Is that Betty?" *What on earth?* Indignant, Hannah's dander got a bit too high. "Willow, maybe your Betty friend can mentor Cheri. Why ask me?"

"B-Betty?" he stuttered. "She tried without success. And Hannah…there's nobody like you." His voice lowered into a whisper. "I meant what I said about you being a Proverbs 31 Woman."

Touched beyond measure, Hannah found herself speechless.

"No one compares to you, Hannah."

He was serious. And his voice was filled with love, that she knew was unmistakable. "Willow, will you come home and take the vow to be Amish?"

He cleared his throat. "Can't talk now. No privacy. We'll talk when you come up. I'll buy your ticket online and you just go to the train station and show your passport. You did get a passport, *jah*?"

"*Jah*, but *mamm* didn't."

"Don't worry. Just do it online."

Online? He'd said it twice, so it wasn't her imagination. "Willow, we're Old Order Amish."

"*Jah*, and *Englishers* can do the work on the computer. Even Granny sells a few craft items on the internet. Suzy posts it."

"Well, I don't go for it –"

"Hannah, there's nothing in the *Ordnung* forbidding us to do paperwork on the computer. I'm not saying go to Walmart and buy a computer."

She knew she was being unreasonable; fear, her wretched companion, was gripping her. Fear that Willow was turning fancy. "Just this once. How long will it take for her to get it?"

"Expedited in eight days. There's a canister under my bed with some money in it. Use it for the fees. May be over a hundred bucks, but Hannah, I want you here."

The plea in his voice made her heart turn to putty. "Okay, Willow. I'll find the money and *mamm* and I will pack right quick. Anything you want from Smicksburg? Anything from the herb shop?"

He snickered. "*Nee*, nothing but you."

He was becoming so bold, and she liked it.

Karen Anna Vogel

Chapter 6

A few days later, Jeb wished that Reed Byler would get himself home and quick. Facing a woman who aimed to boost her immune system by being in a peaceful place, living among the Amish, seemed odd to him. What were the signs of total decline? He'd stayed at bedsides of many who were passing, holding one hand while the other was holding onto Jesus to pass the great divide, but he needed to gently confront this family. Gentle and confront didn't seem to fit. "Deborah would know what to say," he told his horse as he led it to the hitching post. "But that woman never says no to a ride to Punxsy-Mart." His heart warmed. *Buying what she needs to bake Christmas cookies.*

Andy opened the side door, a broom in hand, sweeping the little snow that fell last night. "My sister just made muffins. *Gut* time to visit."

Jeb swallowed hard. "Well, this isn't an easy visit. Is your *daed* around?"

"*Nee*, he's…out. But I have a few questions if you don't mind."

"Did you say confessions?" Jeb asked, hoping that his way was paved, him not having to drag the truth about their identity out.

Andy's green eyes darkened. "*Nee*, questions."

"*Ach*, maybe both I'm supposing," Jeb said as he mounted the steps and entered the kitchen. Through a doorway to another room he saw Sadie, book in hand, reading a book out loud. Was she reading it to her *mamm*? He drew closer to see the words *Holy Bible*. Lord, how would you handle this situation? I'm too blunt and don't see any gray areas. A lie is a lie, but this woman seems to have had a cause. A desperate cause.

"Do you want some coffee and pie? *Mamm* made one this morning," Andy asked.

Spinning around, nearly losing his balance, Jeb gawked. "Your *mamm* made a pie? This morning?"

He lifted up a lattice-topped pie. "It's cherry. Want some?"

Muddled, Jeb couldn't help but stare at Andy. "I thought she was sick. On death's door."

"She had a *gut* morning. We all have bad days, *jah*?"

Something irked Jeb, knowing now that Andy wasn't Amish and using such Pennsylvania slang words. Standing right in front of him lying. Yes, he was being deceitful and righteous indignation got a hold of him. "Esther Coblenz came by with a report." He yanked out a chair and sat, looked hard at the pie set before him. "Now, this may come as a surprise to you, *yinz* not being Amish, but I'm not a fool."

Andy's shoulders fell, and he collapsed into a chair. "Felt like we were."

"Were what?"

"Amish. *Mamm*... I mean, my mother wants to be. We're living plain. Messed up a few times but we did really good for her sake." He fidgeted with the shirt cuff. "I'm ready to take the vow."

Ach, Lord, what would Jesus do? He lowered his head, hands folded. *Lord, help me.* "We have lots of back-peddling to do. Your family came here to help your *mamm* battle cancer, *jah*? Boost her immune system?"

"*Jah*, we did. But like I said, we lived plain, and I think we're going to continue. *Mamm's* health took a nose-dive but she's much better today. Those herbs Reed Byler gave her did their work."

Jeb scratched his head. "Like my wife says. Mold grows in dark places, so let's air this out. Now, you're not Amish for starters. If I pull my buggy around, it doesn't make me a horse, *jah*? So, wearing our clothing and living without modern conveniences doesn't make you Amish. You're Amish the day you bow the knee and take the vow to the People."

"And I will," Andy assured. "Living plain and seeing that we liked it, that it's a better way, could be part of our proving time, right? The Amish are so forgiving, we just thought that we'd tell all when the time was right." He sighed. "Esther shouldn't have said anything."

Jeb threw up a hand. "That statement tells me you don't know a fig about Amish life. We keep each other accountable. If we see someone straying, we tackle sin right on."

Andy crossed his arms. "Sin? We didn't sin. We were just trying the Amish life out. And if we didn't want to convert, we'd just ask forgiveness."

Jeb cracked knuckles as he felt his heartbeat bang up against his ribcage. "Your behavior was deceitful, so we'll be dealing with the *sin* of lying first. I know how some of these *Englisher* preachers say to just forgive and act like nothing's happened –"

"He throws our sins away and doesn't remember them. Far as East is from West," Andy informed.

Jeb stared at the floor until he found some composure. "God doesn't have amnesia, for crying out loud. Beliefs like yours don't keep Christians from sinning."

Andy's face reddened and then his neck did in turn. "You keep saying sinning. My *mamm* is ill. Why keep talking about sin?"

"Because if you don't deal with it, it'll ruin your life. Now, a falsehood is a sin. You can't…live a lie. And that's what you're doing."

"He's right, Andy. No more lying."

Jeb turned to see the thin frame of Katherine Smith. Her face was like an angel as she removed her black apron. "We won't be wearing these clothes until we're deserving of them."

Jeb rushed to her. "*Ach*, I'm so sorry you're ill. The People care about your family, and maybe I needed to say that before anything."

She handed him her apron. "These past few months have been my happiest."

"You could have many more," Andy said, his voice cracking.

"I may. That Reed Byler's good at medicine, but so is the Amish way of life." She motioned for Jeb to take a seat. "But, I have a plan."

Relieved that someone did, Jeb obeyed and dug into his pie, anxiety giving him quite a sweet tooth.

"Freeman, the Mennonite man came over to see us. I think he's sweet on Sadie. Anyhow, he shared how we can live plain as Mennonites. Even drive a car. My husband's in agreement on giving up his horse and buggy," she said with a faint smile.

"But Freeman was asked to leave his Mennonite Church. I talked to the pastor," Jeb inserted.

"He confessed that. Said the feeling was mutual. His beliefs are more in line with more progressive Mennonites. He said they come in every flavor of ice cream."

Jeb cupped his mouth to hide his disapproval.

"Andy, I think we can all fit into Freeman's new church."

"New church?" Jeb blurted, and then coughed up a storm. Hitting his chest to make the pie go down easier, he blinked uncontrollably. "What new church?"

"The one Freeman and a friend are starting in Plum Creek. With a car we can get there in no time. Only fifteen miles away."

Andy stood as if in protest. "*Mamm*, I like being Amish. The real Amish, not fake Amish."

"Wait now," Jeb got out. "Mennonites came before Amish, so we're not at odds. We Amish broke off, not wanting to adopt modern ways. Ways that make life be in a rush and all, but if this family wants to be Mennonite, they're a plain group with *gut* thinking. Reed and Dorcas write me that many are Mennonite on their mission trip."

Katherine glowed. "I like how they keep the Sabbath holy. No one does that anymore."

Jeb nodded. "Lots to be said about the Mennonites." He pat her hand. "And if it helps you, body and soul, I encourage it."

Andy threw his hands up. "But I want to marry Hannah. No women like her around anymore!"

Katherine's brow creased. "You still can. Right Jeb? Andy and Hannah are engaged. If my son wants to be Amish, I won't interfere."

Jeb moaned and took Katherine's hand. "Your son can't propose to an Amish woman until he's baptized, so their so-called engagement is off. I think he needs to find a *gut* Mennonite woman."

Katherine's face grew pale. "But he loves Hannah. I'm sure there's a way for them to wed, one being Amish, the other Mennonite."

Jeb was mighty glad he'd been married to a woman who rubbed off his rough edges right at this point, as he wanted to scream, 'Hannah would be shunned. And Amish marry Amish.' But he calmly asked, "Where do you get some of these notions about the Amish?"

She pressed a hand to her chest. "I read Amish fiction all the time."

~*~

Son,

Your mamm and I are still here in Mexico, as you know. I read something the other day that helped me with my struggle to leave. Jah, I told you I'd battle discontentment and temptation. Temptation, at my age, to leave the Amish and be a real medical man. But that's all it is: a temptation. Our Lord was tempted, but didn't sin, so I aim to do the same.

King Solomon had it all. Hundreds of wives, (in that area, I'm content with my one sweetheart), wealth, education and on and on. He had a hungry mind to learn, too, but it left him empty. He said it all was vain and chasing after the wind. We both know you can't catch the wind, so his life was futile.

This helps me see what's what. If I moved here in a state of discontentment, I'd just bring my baggage down on the train. Nee, I've learned to be content. Paul wrote this to the Philippians from prison:

"I have learned in whatever state I am, to be content in it. I know how to be humbled, and I know also how to abound. In everything and in all things I have learned the secret both to be filled and to be hungry, both to abound and to be in need. I can do all things through Christ, who strengthens me."

So, Old Kind Solomon from ages past is helping me see that he made a mess of his life by thinking the grass is greener on the other side. You know what we Amish say to that. Fertilize your own grass to make it greener, and that's what I plan to do. When I get back, I plan to volunteer my time, my knowledge to those really in need, Amish or English. The Baptists have some wunderbar gut outreaches I'll be giving my time to. There're needs all around us back home.

Don't go thinking I'm saying this to sway you to live back in Smicksburg. Son, I've met lots of Mennonites on this trip and they're solid God-fearing people. Not what I had planned for you, but not my will, but God's be done.

Your loving daed

Willow didn't look up at Betty, Emma, or Lee who sat around the kitchen table nibbling on cookies, listening as he read. His watery eyes might show.

"Well, Willow," Emma started, "I have to say that shocks me to no end. If my father hadn't ruled with an iron fist, I may have stayed Amish."

Lee looked across the table at Betty. "Me neither. What about you?"

Betty blinked back tears and then oddly scowled at Willow. "You're *daed's* really Amish?"

Willow realized for the first time, sitting among this group of Ex-Amish, how much freedom he'd grown up with. "*Jah*, my *daed* believes in respecting our God-given free will. Now, he's not perfect, my sister almost leaving the Amish for an *Englisher* made him mighty cranky, but in the end, he would have respected my sister's decision if she left. Cassia wasn't baptized."

Emma, ever the hostess, replenished hot chocolate into empty mugs. "And how about you, Willow? Have you decided about being Mennonite or Amish?"

Willow stared at the letter. "*Jah*."

Chapter 7

A week later, Hannah stepped down the train steps and was instantly slapped by wind that lifted her outer black bonnet. Holding onto the strings, she gazed across an ocean of smiling faces greeting loved ones with hugs and kisses. Visions of Willow scooping her up, twirling her around like the couple she'd just witnessed, made her nervous and oddly shy. She needed to stop acting like an old spinster and show her tender, more vulnerable side. That was Cassia's parting advice. She did care for Willow now more than ever. Why did it take being so hurt by others to appreciate Willow? She bent down to rub her leg, it ever so stiff from the long ride. She scanned the now dispersing crowd. Where was Willow? Her *mamm* grabbed her by the arm, skidding across an icy patch. "*Mamm*, I don't see Willow. Did we get off at the right stop?"

Before Esther could reply, a beautiful young woman made her presence known. "You must be Hannah," she chirped. Grabbing Esther's little suitcase, she added, "And you're her mother?"

"*Danki.* I'm Esther. And you are?"

"Cheri, Willow's fancy-free friend." She twirled around, her white wool coat swooshing around her skin-tight jeans.

Feeling rather frumpy in her Amish attire, Hannah wished for the first time she could wear something beautiful. Something to make Willow think she was beautiful. But here she was in black boots, a long maroon dress and black apron under a drabby black coat.

"Can I carry yours too?" Cheri asked Hannah. "I'm pretty strong and you're…you know, older."

Hannah's mouth gaped, and she looked to her *mamm* for help.

"*Ach*, Hannah's fit as a fiddle. Can split wood like a man."

She tilted her head in suspicion. "Willow told me to go to the station and help his old friends. Get them to my place safely."

"Where is Willow?" Hannah couldn't help but be blunt.

"Fancy-Free doesn't have a car, *jah*? And you're staying with me, right?"

Esther took over, assuring Cheri they were grateful and took her by the elbow to nudge her to where the rest of their luggage was. As they walked towards the end of the train, Hannah's heart plunged into her feet. This girl called Willow 'Fancy-Free'? And he didn't run for his life? He came back to Canada for more praise and flirtation by this immoral girl. "Willow, how could you be so dumb? So naïve?"

~*~

That night, when Hannah was ready to call it a day, Willow finally stopped by to greet them. Feeling neglected, she kept rather quiet. She watched as Willow told Mr. Peters his progress with a yellow Lab he was training for search and rescue. He'd had a friend hide a mile away and given the dog his scent and off went Lucy, running as if she were saving her own life, to find someone in danger. Willow smiled so broadly, seeming rather proud of himself. Cheri near danced around him as he told the story. Mr. Peters pat Willow's back, saying he'd get extra pay for a job well done.

Esther was in the kitchen sharing recipes with Mrs. Peters, who begged for help making something quick and easy. This whole house full of glass seemed ready to crash somehow. Everything was too fast-paced, and since Willow seemed to be enjoying talking about dogs, she slipped upstairs, wanting to cry her eyes out. What a cold country, cold family! The cold got into her bones somehow, her knees aching still. Was she getting old? Arthritis?

She'd brought a few books along, her constant reliable companions, and opened an Amish Christmas romance she'd bought from the rack at the train station. *Romance. Was there any in her future at all?*

A knock on her door startled her, but when Cheri asked her to open it, she said she was feeling ill and was headed to bed. "Willow wants to talk to you," Cheri said in a whiny pleading voice. If she was to mentor this girl, that was the first thing she'd nip in the bud. Whining was a form of manipulation, she was taught as a child. Just talk plain and simple. "Not right now," she said evenly.

She was relieved when there was no retort and flopped down on the bed, staring at the massive ceiling fan. Why is everything so big in this house? Whatever happened to small and quaint?

A louder pounding on the door made her fear she'd offended precious Cheri and she had told her father. Mr. Peters seemed nice but not a man to be told no to. "Hannah, open up. It's me."

It was Willow's sweet voice. Naïve as he was or a hidden flirt for coming back into this house, she nervously opened the door. "Come in."

He drew her close and planted a kiss on her forehead. Pushing him away, she edged away. "I'm not like that Cheri girl, Willow Byler."

His eyes were round whoopie pies. "I was checking for a fever. Hannah, what's wrong with you? I've never seen you so touchy." He neared her and took a hand. "It's me, Willow. Aren't you glad to see me?"

She was sore at him for not being at the train station and being out with his dog the whole day of their arrival. What could she say? "I'm glad to see you but –"

"But?"

"I don't know. I'm tired and, well, sore. My knees ache something fierce. My wrists, too."

He gave a knowing look. "It's the air up here. Really cold." He smiled. "Bone cold. Takes some getting used to."

He was so near and so concerned, she wanted to lunge at him, give him a bear hug and tell him just how much she missed him. How absence makes the heart grow fonder, but she was too suspicious. He flirted with Cheri right before her eyes. As he stared down at her, she turned. "Seems like your friend Cheri thinks you're the best thing since ice cream. Why?"

Willow clucked his tongue. "Hannah Coblenz, I paid *gut* money for you to come here to help her. Everyone thinks she's beyond hope, but I don't."

Hannah spun around. "Why do you care so much?"

The light in Willow's eyes went out and he slouched. "Well, my *daed* never gave up on a patient. And I guess I see her as someone who's sick."

Hannah saw that old tenderness. Willow was helping Lily up after falling on the ice and skinning her knees. "I'm sorry. The ride up must have made me a tired old woman."

Willow slowly put a hand on her shoulder. "Come with me downstairs and have some hot chocolate. Mrs. Peters is learning to make it from scratch without the help of her microwave."

As Willow urged a laugh out of her, she threw her arms around him. "I'm so glad to see you."

He pulled her tight. "Me, too."

~*~

When Esther saw Hannah walk side-by-side with Willow into the kitchen, her eyes were opened as if for the first time; *Willow was a man*. A greatly respected man by the Peters. And it appeared that Hannah didn't see him as a wee *boppli bruder* anymore. *Nee*, she had a glow about her cheeks. Did she love Willow Byler? *Ach*, how meddling she was, pushing Andy in between them! How could she make it up to her daughter?

Esther knew Andy pleaded with Hannah before they left, insisting they write, of all things. Should she intercept Andy's letters? No, that wasn't right. She had to trust her daughter's judgment; Hannah had little tolerance for deception. An outright lie the Smith's had spun, no matter if Katherine was getting better, a miracle of sorts, her immune system ramping up by living a plain life. But two wrongs never made a right. Sadie's sassy attitude had ceased, too, after a few visits with Freeman. Well, she hoped they had a *gut* Mennonite church plant, whatever that meant. Plant a church. How odd.

As she stirred the next pot of cooked milk, adding powdered cocoa and sugar, she watched Willow lead Hannah near the large blazing fireplace. But Cheri was soon on their heels, yapping up a storm. Would they ever have time to talk?

A plan formed in Esther's mind. A lesson learned from Granny Weaver. *Anyone can act, but how they reacted told the true story.* She'd have Hannah and Willow react so they could plainly see what was in their hearts. She asked Mrs. Peters if she'd be okay scooping Christmas cake batter onto the cookie sheet alone, and even though nervous, Mrs. Peters agreed to Esther taking a "break" by the fire. "We'll make butter cookies tomorrow," Esther added.

"Don't want to get thick around the middle with all these sweets."

Esther wondered if the Peters had any Christmas traditions like regular *Englishers*. Not one decoration up yet or any presents being made. "It's going to be Christmas and you've got to get your baking done, *jah*?"

Mrs. Peters shrugged. "Not a very old-fashioned person, baking at Christmas like you. I do buy a few things from the bakery."

Esther bit her lip, wanting to say what joy baking gave her and how popular it was among the Amish community. She was missing baking frolics among her friends right now; it made her heart sink a bit. *So is my dear Dorcas, being in Mexico. We'll have our own. Ach, how their friendship almost unraveled over Willow!*

She dusted off her apron and approached the trio staring at the flames, Cheri was telling Hannah about the history of the house, how many windows and whatnot. "*Ach*, Willow, this house seems to fit you better than that little tiny thing you have back home."

Willow's brows knit together. "This house is fancy."

"And aren't you? I mean, you seem mighty cozy being up here and all, and you're not baptized, so you can choose."

Hannah eyes bugged. "*Mamm*, Willow plans to add on to his house. It's only for him now but…"

"But what?" Esther probed.

"He'll get married someday and, well, add on. And it's built according to the specifications of the *Ordnung*."

"What's an Ord…whatever?" Cheri shifted. "Don't tell me the Amish have to approve your house."

"*Jah*, we have to. No fancy roofs, doors," Esther motioned to the exposed beams and carved wood staircase. "We can't have anything fancy like this."

"But why?" Cheri giggled. "Seems ridiculous to have such rules."

"Because we don't try to outdo each other," Hannah stated, looking to Willow for support.

"*Jah*, we have all things in common. And work crews know how to build the simple structures. Makes things less complicated."

Hannah was glowing as if what Willow just said was from divine revelation.

"But Willow," Esther continued, "you kept saying you couldn't wait for us to see how beautiful this house was."

Cheri boldly slipped an arm through Willow's. "He felt comfortable living here until the Amish back in Smicksburg told him he had to live with Mennonites."

Hannah pulled at Willow's free arm. "We thought it best since he'd have more…"

"Have what?" Cheri asked. "Unhealthy pies and cakes? The Amish use lard still, which I can't believe. We only use it to feed birds in winter. My mom's a dentist and we're low on sweets here."

Esther could feel the hair on the back of her neck rise. "We bake because it's part of our heritage. We eat pie for breakfast because we can all bake them. Everyone knows how to make hot chocolate from scratch."

Hannah gasped. "*Ach*, Cheri, my *mamm's* trying to say we bond over food. Over baking together. *Mamm* and I bake cinnamon rolls, muffins, pies, all kinds of things, just to spend time together. Sometimes we have a group of women bake and end up taking it all to church for the menfolk." She smiled at Esther. "Some of my happiest times are baking with my *mamm*."

Cheri covered her mouth as her eyes pooled tears. "Really?"

Taken aback by the pain in Cheri's face, Esther never thought making Willow and Hannah react would work on Cheri as well. "Don't you have any hobbies with your *mamm*?"

Mrs. Peters, who could overhear the conversation, joined them. "Cheri has hobbies, but she's more like her dad. Follows him around like a shadow."

"But surely there's something you two do together. Do you knit or give tellin's?"

Mrs. Peters appeared confused. "Give a what?"

"A tellin'," Hannah said. "It's storytelling. I like to tell the stories about my ancestors."

Mrs. Peters gave a dismissive glare. "Who has time for that? I work full-time."

Cheri inched closer to Willow. "I'd like to know more about my ancestors. Mother, could you share what's in all those photo albums?" she asked, pointing to a row of white binders stacked in a built-in cherry-stained bookcase."

"No," Mrs. Peter's snapped. "That was long ago and…Cheri you're making something of yourself in college. We don't waste our time, right?"

Cheri seemed to want to hide behind Willow now. Esther thought this whole scene rather pathetic. The scripture came to her mind that it was better to eat herbs in a house full of love than choice meats in a wealthy house with strife. Strife, discord, and lack of love had most likely driven Cheri to seek love elsewhere. Esther would be sharing this with Hannah later on tonight.

CHAPTER 8

Even though Esther's plan to get a reaction out of Willow had backfired, she was tenacious and now as she and Hannah entered Lord's Mennonite Church to volunteer, her mind went into overdrive. She prayed that Willow would not take her encouragement towards this church…and Betty…and step out and say what he really believed. And propose to her daughter as a baptismal candidate for Christmas. It was her earnest prayer.

But her heart sunk when seeing Willow seeming to hang on every word a beautiful Mennonite woman spoke; she assumed this was Betty. Esther glanced at Hannah, who seemed to still have Cheri on her mind. When the wayward teenager decided at the last minute not to come into the church, but just drop them off, Hannah was shaken. Could they really help the Peters family?

A few men raced towards them, so they could deposit the bags of groceries into their strong arms. One with an accent Esther thought was German struck up a conversation with Hannah. And praise be, Willow sprinted back to them.

"Hannah, this is Lee, my *gut* friend. And this is her *mamm*, Esther."

"Nice to meet you. Willow's told me all about you."

"*Ach*, don't believe the not-so-*gut* parts," Esther quipped.

The girl he left standing alone joined them. "And I'm Betty, Willow's good friend, too." She flashed a dazzling white toothy smile at Willow. "So, how was your trip up?"

Hannah was blushing something fierce, appearing not able to talk, so Esther just said fine. "Willow," she ventured, "you seem right at home here in this church among your new friends."

Lee slapped his back. "Doesn't he look good? Came in like a homesick pup, but not anymore."

Willow elbowed Lee. "Enough dog jokes."

"No, it's too much fun. When I saw the Lab he's training to search and rescue, it put its tail between its legs. Willow came here all slouched like that, and he walks tall now."

"God doesn't like a proud look," Hannah said, sounding a tad bit too judgmental. "And he walked just fine in Smicksburg."

Esther knew she had to hear from Willow what he had to say, from the heart. She needed a reaction. "Willow, I agree. You look better among the Mennonites. So many nice young people not married yet. Willow's like an old bachelor in our parts."

"Amish marry so young," Betty informed. "We Mennonites go to college and, well, have different views, right?"

"Right," Esther continued, even though it pained her. "And Willow comes from a family of real educated folk, so if he turns Mennonite, he may be able to go to college, too."

Lee slapped his back again. "Can still sign up for spring term. He should be a veterinarian, is what I think. Or a vet tech."

Willow's confused eyes met Esther's in a most concerning way. "You're encouraging me to leave the People in Smicksburg?"

Hannah cleared her throat loud and clear. "I'm not, even if *Mamm* is." She cupped a hand to whisper into Esther's ear. "What are you doing?"

"Reaction," Esther mumbled.

Hannah's brows furrowed. "Stop."

"Esther, can I talk to you private-like? Hannah, you can hear what I have to say," Willow said. He motioned for them to go to what Esther assumed was the altar. A big dark barn wood cross hung behind a podium of sorts. Willow pat a padded bench and Esther sat down. Hannah stood, arms crossed.

Willow slid next to Esther. "I'm sorry. I know I didn't act too Amish, being so rude to you. I meant to come by and apologize, but I got real sick. But here I am, still Amish in my heart, and I'm asking for forgiveness for how rude I was towards you. I let my dander get too high, like Granny always says. I was jealous of Andy. I know you think he's better than me."

Esther wished she was a bug, so she could crawl under the carpet. "*Ach*, I was rude, too. Comparing isn't *gut*."

"Especially when Andy isn't exactly an angel," Hannah grumbled.

"*Nee*, he is not." Esther said under her breath.

"What did he do? Get another modern convenience?"

Hannah sat next to Willow and stared at the cross. "We all sin and fall short, *jah*? No one's perfect."

Esther, relieved that Hannah didn't spill the beans about Andy just yet, relaxed a bit. Being Reed's patient, if they got word of the Smith's deception, it may ruin their missions trip. "Have you heard from your parents?" Esther probed.

"*Jah*, and *Daed* helped me heaps." Turning to Hannah he repeated the word "heaps." What did he mean?

Betty and Lee walked past them with boxes marked 'Altar decorations. Xmas.' As Willow made small talk with Hannah, she watched as Lee cut open boxes and pulled out fake garland, poinsettias and wreaths. They placed white candles on the two little tables placed on either side of the altar and the way Lee looked at Betty revealed all; he cared for this girl. This girl who kept glancing towards Willow.

"Willow, just point to where the kitchen is and we'll get some pies started. You go help Betty."

Willow's face screwed up. "Why? Lee's doing a *gut* job."

"Well, she keeps looking over at you. Must need help."

Hannah's eyes rounded as did Willow's.

Slouching, Willow pointed to a side door. "Go through there and you'll smell bread. The church makes batches every Monday. Follow your nose."

Hannah's lips pursed. "I'll catch up with you, *Mamm*. Willow and I were talking…"

She pointed to Betty. "She needs him."

Willow looked like he'd just picked up heavy weights. "Go on, Hannah. We'll talk later."

The hurt in Hannah's eyes Esther could hardly bear, but she only had two weeks to get Willow to "know himself."

~*~

Over the next few days, Esther's behavior gave Willow sleepless nights. Why was she pushing Betty on him? Why was it awkward to talk about Andy? His Mennonite friends who met regularly for Bible study mentioned how downcast he seemed since they arrived and charged that once again, the Amish were too oppressive a bunch for him.

So, he took refuge in dogs once again. Maybe he could live in the dog kennel since it was heated. Or maybe the boathouse? He'd come to love ice fishing and then warming up in the quaint little house. When he got home, he hoped to make something similar, so he could be up early with the fish. He could just see the look on Jeb Weaver's face, the yearning to want to sleep over and Granny calling him old man, and that he'd nearly drowned once long ago while ice fishing.

Homesickness ran him down without warning and he charged towards the kennel. He was made for more than just taking care of dogs. He wanted a wife and *kinner*…with

Hannah. But, Esther acted so odd, it only meant one thing. She didn't want to break his heart and tell him about Hannah and Andy.

He let Lucy out of her kennel and after a good rubdown, he stuck a piece of material under her nose. "Go find it, girl." The dog rushed towards the Peters where he'd left the other half of the pillowcase. In the future, Lucy would be given a piece of clothing and she'd have to find the "match"; the scent of the missing person. He'd have to make this harder, but she was doing pretty well for a beginner.

Chasing after the dog, she all too soon found the cloth stuck near the garbage cans on the side of the garage.

No one seemed to be home at the Peters and he recalled Hannah saying she was taking Cheri shopping. Or did he hear her right? Mrs. Peters and Cheri. A mother-daughter day out. Seemed like Hannah was trying to get Cheri to have the bond that she had with her own *mamm*. He doubted this could work, but he trusted Hannah's judgment. Well, not when it came to men…

He took the ratty pillowcase from Lucy, told her to stay, and entered the house knowing where they kept the microwave hot chocolate. He needed a quick warm-up.

Taking off his boots, he made his way to the kitchen and right there on the granite counter, in full view, was a letter addressed to Hannah… with a return address to Andy Smucker. So, he could teach a dog to track a scent, but he was too stupid to pick up on all the clues Esther had thrown his way.

~*~

For the life of her, Hannah couldn't believe how aloof Willow acted among the Mennonites. She wanted to give him a good talkin' to in Cassia's place, but she rarely saw him. Last night when she'd gotten home from an exhausting shopping spree, walking a mall the size of Pennsylvania, listening to Mrs. Peters worries about giving too short a notice to take a day off, was unnerving. Willow talked to Mr. Peters about his beloved Lucy when they got home, ignoring her as usual. Was it wrong to be jealous of a dog?

She hoped to see him today when they visited the house that took in Ex-Amish. The folks who ran the place said a teenager wanted to go home but was too afraid. Rubbing shoulders with Amish may help him bridge the gap back home.

Cheri, as usual, dropped them off before heading to college. Cheri. A most unusual bright spot in her life at present. Her *mamm* was right; Cheri had failed to bond with her own *mamm* so she had no foundation for healthy relationships. Mrs. Peters was also too demanding and intense. Couldn't she just relax for a minute and laugh?

She hugged Cheri good-bye, the teen tensing, but then pulling Hannah close. "We'll talk tonight?"

"For sure," Hannah said. "If you can make the popcorn in a pan and not a microwave."

Cheri laughed. "Did it twice without burning it."

Hannah followed her *mamm* to the large two-story house and before Esther knocked, the door flung open and they were greeted by a frazzled woman. "I'm so glad you're here. I'm Emma, as you probably know. I'm sorry, but tension's brewing in the living room and I have to get back."

She ran off and Hannah and Esther followed. The pitch of shouting frightened Hannah. Willow lived here? *No wonder he's always out with the dogs and a nervous wreck.*

"*Nee*, you're not going back there," a muscular teen shouted. "*Daed* will tan your hide."

"*Nee*, I wrote to Uncle Adam. He'll go with me to the bishop."

Hannah noticed both Betty and Lee were spectators. Why not stop this fight? But of all things, Lee got up and stood between the brothers. "Now, Johnny, you chose to leave the Amish. Let Mike decide for himself."

"It's like living in a prison," Johnny scowled. "I don't want him going back."

"It was prison to you because you never listened to any rules since you were born!" Mike screamed.

"How do you know? I'm five years older and you weren't born yet."

Mike huffed. "I heard it from the older *bruder*. You're breaking *Mamm* and *Daed's* hearts."

"They don't have hearts, Mike. They only want to control."

Hannah took hold of her *mamm's* hand and she was visibly shaken.

When Betty stood up, saying she agreed with Johnny, and how set free she was when she left the Amish, it made Hannah weak in the knees. How unfair! She wanted to shout out that they were proud…and prejudiced. But women didn't speak out so boldly in mixed company. Or did the Mennonites allow these brawls? What would Granny do? Speak up, too! Hannah flung off her cape and untied her bonnet. "I'm Amish. So is my *mamm* here. And *jah*, we believe in rules. Rules guide us, teaching us right from wrong." She intentionally avoided eye contact with Betty and walked towards Mike. "Ever hear of *Rules of a Godly Life?*"

Mike nodded, seeming relieved that someone came to his aid.

"Amish read these rules often. But they don't tell you what kind of clothes to wear or how long to grow your hair. Actually, the man who wrote them wasn't even Amish."

A hush fell over the room.

"*Jah*, a man not even Amish, but a true Christian, wrote these rules and they're broken down into three categories: words, thoughts and works. What if we had no fences?"

"The animals would escape," Johnny grumbled.

"So do your words, and yours are not only coming out too fast, but being hurtful." Hannah felt perspiration beads forming on her forehead, but she continued. "You think wrong about the Amish, too. We measure our words, *jah*? We think long before we hurt someone with them." She wanted to pound her foot but remembered to breathe. "And, above all, we aren't prejudiced."

Esther stood near Hannah. "Willow Byler came here because of a pure heart and no biases. But from the reports I've heard, many here have a chip on their shoulders about Amish folk. You all best be examining your hearts." She laced her fingers through Hannah's. "Now, we've come to help, but no sense in staying if minds are already made up."

Without a word, Mike went over to Emma and whispered something in her ear. Emma, with a trembling voice said, "Esther. Hannah. You've done more work here than I thought possible. We do come across as if we help Ex-Amish. We praise those who leave and not the ones who want to return. Mike here wants to go home. Can we all say we believe the Lord above is guiding him?"

"Never," Johnny yelled.

The room was quiet for a while, but one by one, the group got up, and gave Mike a hug or handshake. Hannah noticed Betty was mechanical, not heartfelt at all when giving Mike a quick side-hug. And it dawned on her. Was she making Willow unfeeling? Was she turning him from his People in Smicksburg? From her?

Feeling bolder than ever, she approached Betty. "Where's Willow? I came over to help here...but to see him, too."

Betty shrugged. "Probably out with his girlfriend."

"Girlfriend?" Hannah blurted. "He has a girlfriend?"

"Yes, didn't you know?"

Hannah's heart beat so hard, dizziness caused her to find a chair.

"Lucy," Betty informed. "We all say Willow's girl is Lucy."

Lucy? Who was she. And then it dawned on her it was his dog. But why was Betty so snippy? Was she jealous of the time Willow spent with the dogs.? What right had she to expect his attention? Were they courting?

CHAPTER 9

*W*illow stood at the bottom of the steps, out of sight of anyone in the living room. But he could hear the feud between Johnny and Mike, and it was getting old. Grow up, Johnny, he wanted to say, but just stared out the window watching the nuthatches and downy woodpeckers feed at Emma's daily feast of peanuts, sunflowers, and suet. He prayed that Johnny would see how immature he was and crossing the line; God gave man free will and he needed to stop trying to take Mike's away through threats and plain old bullying.

To his utter shock he heard Hannah boldly talking. He couldn't make out all her words since her voice was softer. It had quite a sting to it though. But the group grew quiet and he heard her talk about *Rules of a Godly Life*. He didn't think she had it in her to stand up and proclaim her beliefs. But why shouldn't she? Hannah was Amish and did her part in reaching out and being a light in a dark world. He was so proud of her. He thought she was too outspoken and headstrong but blamed it on Esther. 'The apple doesn't fall far from the tree,' he'd reasoned. But now here were Esther and Hannah reaching out to the Mennonites and Peters.

He'd seen a real difference in Cheri since Hannah spent a bit too much time with her, ignoring him completely. But women talked four times as much as men, he'd read, so maybe it was time well spent. Cheri wasn't as sarcastic and seemed more at peace with herself. When she came back to the kennels, she made no attempt to seduce him but politely asked him how he was doing, of all things. Did he need anything? In a nutshell, Cheri was beginning to think of others. She was acting like Hannah.

He heard Betty whine about him spending too much time with Lucy. She was right. He was out in the woods, getting his job done and praying for firm direction. He'd been at a crossroads for weeks and being out in the crisp air, he'd waited on God, looked for the good way. And he found it for sure and certain.

Not in the mood to make small talk with everyone exiting the living room, he mounted the steps, two at a time and shut his bedroom door. Words seemed to bubble up and he needed to write the good news to his *mamm* and *daed*. Getting paper and pen, he settled in at his desk to write:

Mamm and Daed,

How are you two? I hope your missions trip comes to a close without you both wanting to bring home a brood full of orphans.

I'll be home for Christmas and it's not just for a visit, but to settle down. Daed, your letter about battling discontentment helped me see my restlessness is just part of the human condition. And my friend Betty is learning about a guy named Augustine who said that we're all restless until we rest in God. I've been mighty restless, but it had nothing to do with being Amish or Mennonite. I've never rested in God, but always tried to figure everything out. So, I take walks at night and sit and watch the night sky and found that the heavens declare the glory of God, like Psalm 19 says.

I've read Romans a dozen times and chapter 1 verse 20 got me thinking about it so much I memorized it. It says:

For the invisible things of him from the creation of the world are clearly seen, being understood by the things that are made, even his eternal power and Godhead.

Well, I have to confess, I used Betty's computer to look up 'eternal power' and 'Godhead'. I thought the cold air was freezing my brain or something because I kept feeling like God was walking right out there in the woods with me, like Adam in the garden. But, God is real and I can see his eternal power, which in the Greek is dunamis. Guess what other word comes from dunamis? DYNAMITE! Mamm and Daed, don't think I'm going daft, as Granny says, but I had a real God encounter in the woods. I know God's love in a real way.

I looked up 'Godhead', too, and in the Greek it is theos. And I couldn't believe what that meant! It means 'God's nature.' Do you see it? We can see God's nature by creation and, well, nature itself. Now, I'm not talking like I see God in trees and such nonsense, but his nature.

Maybe it's too hard to explain but what I'm trying to say is my hesitation to being Amish had nothing to do with the Amish, it was about Christianity. I knew it all in my head, but I knew deep down it had no power to keep me Amish. Like Jeb says, it takes lots of *faith to be Amish. Lots of dying to our wants and so-called needs. And I found it in Jesus. Jah, I found Jesus, Daed, and don't be laughing that he was never lost. But I was.*

Hope this letter doesn't upset you. I'm not going to walk around barefoot holding up signs saying the end of the world is coming. Well, Amish don't wear shoes much in summer, so maybe it can be a summer pastime. (Just kidding) No, I'm more stable than ever and know who I am, too. I found myself here in the woods. Lots of things surfaced, but I can share when I get home.

Hannah and Esther seem to be helping the Peters daughter, Cheri. Mamm, I know Esther made you feel guilty for traveling so far from home. Don't you find it comical she's up here in Canada? She took to Outsiders right quick and it made me realize the Amish aren't so backwards after all.

Love you both,
Willow

Dorcas held the letter to her heart. "Nice letter and I'm so thrilled he's coming home, but why talk about this Betty when Hannah's up there?

Reed pat her shoulder. "He only used her computer and talked about Augustine of Hippo."

Dorcas squinted. "A hippo? He said he saw God in nature but…did he go to a zoo or something? Watch animals there?"

Reed bellowed out a laugh which lasted a bit too long. Dorcas nudged him to stop, which he attempted to do, unsuccessfully.

"Well, no matter if he found God in the woods or at the zoo, I'm glad he got his awakening, epiphany of sorts and is a steady Christian now."

Reed coughed and cackled until he found his voice again. "You're right, love. And I can tell you think I'm laughing at you, but I'm not. Augustine was from a place called Hippo." He pursed his lips. "Doesn't say much about Hannah. I wonder if she'll go through with marrying Andy Smucker."

Dorcas' brow creased. "In all my letters back home, I've inquired about Ruth Smucker's health with no reply. I fear the worst."

"She's terminal but sticks to her radical diet and herbal therapy. Maybe it spread to the liver. *Ach*, that would not be *gut*."

"Well, we'll find out next week when we go home."

Reed brightened. "For your Christmas baking time." He rubbed his hands in anticipation. "There is a time for everything under heaven and Christmas baking time, *ach*, well, it's the best."

Dorcas laughed and fell into his open arms.

~*~

That night, with a crackling fire with cocoa along with her knitting needles, Hannah could not ask for more. How her soul craved comfort and rest. The spiteful scene between Johnny and Mike kept replaying, as did Betty acting irritated that Willow was neglecting her. When she came, she feared Cheri would drain her to no end, not Willow and his Mennonite friends. Yes, it wasn't homey at the Peters, but she saw improvement, and Hannah, being task oriented, liked results.

Right now, Cheri was sitting next to her learning how to knit. Across from them on the other overstuffed leather couch was her *mamm* and Mrs. Peters, leaning close to each other as Esther taught crochet. Getting Mrs. Peters to sit down was an accomplishment and right now, she even seemed to be enjoying it. Hannah glanced over at the white binders that seemed to haunt Mrs. Peters when Cheri inquired about her ancestry. Could they help Cheri?

As the howling wind slapped snow against the massive windows, Hannah spoke up a bit. "Mrs. Peters, what nationality are you?"

All eyes landed on Hannah as if she spoke a word out of season.

"I'm half German and half Irish. Why?"

Hannah knit a bit faster. "Did they immigrate from Germany and Ireland, or are your relations long time Canadian folk?"

Mrs. Peters set down her crochet hook. "Long time Canadians. Why do you ask?"

Her tone was so snappy Hannah felt like she needed to apologize. "Sorry if I'm being nebby. We Amish know our ancestry. Most are German, Dutch, some even Swiss, but we don't have any Swiss in us."

"Mom has historical pictures of this area in those binders," Cheri informed, "but she's never given a telling. Mom, you should give an Amish telling."

Cheri bounced in animation, but Mrs. Peters did the opposite. She became a stiff board. "Some are historic, but others are just old family pictures."

Cheri skipped over and pulled out one binder and started to flip through. "This is a family picture. Funny I never wondered about these photo albums before." She sat on the hearth and looked at the pictures, making comments like, 'Well this one had a bad day. Looks mean." Hannah went back to her knitting and leant her ear to the crackle of the fire and the wind. Nature had a way of calming her. She decided right then she'd explore the area, recording birds she'd most likely never see in Smicksburg.

"Mother, who are these little girls?" Cheri ran to her mother, slipping the picture in front of her crochet project.

Mrs. Peters snatched the picture and stared at it as her countenance fell. Her face grew pale as she gripped her stomach. Esther put a hand on her shoulder. "Are you all right?"

Mrs. Peters glared up at Cheri. "When do you ever listen to what I tell you? Put his back!"

Cheri shrank back in fear. Hannah wanted to chide Mrs. Peters for being so mean but felt too sorry for her. It appeared she'd seen something mighty painful from the past. Poor Cheri. It was so obvious her *mamm* had erected many walls around her. Walls that ruined a relationship between mother and daughter.

Cheri sat next to Hannah, telling a joke she'd heard at college. So spry for someone hurting. What walls Cheri had up. She pretended to listen to the joke and even smiled at the end, but her heart just ached for this girl.

And then the whole concept of 'hurt people, hurt people' came to her. Was the picture of someone deceased? Hannah knew she could relate to Mrs. Peters when it came to loss. "Mrs. Peters, the picture upset you because of pain, I'm thinking. My *daed* passed away almost two years ago. Sometimes I get angry when I see Willow with his *daed*.

Jealous that my *daed* was taken so young, but I figure we know in part down here. We don't see the whole picture, *jah?*"

Mrs. Peters shot up. "We Canadians don't open up like this. We're strangers."

Cheri shot up as well. "Yes, Mother, we Canadians do open up, just not you. You're a clam, or crab or whatever it is that closes up. Why can't you be nice like…"

"Your father?" She let out a sarcastic laugh. "He's too nice to you. Spoils you rotten."

"All you do is criticize him. No wonder he's always out with his dogs. They at least show him some respect."

Esther wiped her forehead with her handkerchief. "This is *gut.*"

All eyes landed on Esther in confusion.

"You heard me right. This is *gut*. Not arguing but cleaning out a wound." Esther's wide-eyes begged for Hannah to tell the all too familiar story of the cleansing wound lesson.

"*Jah*, when you have dirt caught under a wound, it needs to be opened up again so infection doesn't set in. Very painful, but needful." She dared to face Mrs. Peters. "We were having a *gut* time here until you saw that picture. Seems like you need some healing? Need to talk about it? No need to yell at Cheri because most likely she has nothing to do with your…wound."

"Do you know I'm a doctor?" Mrs. Peters cried out. "You're an Amish girl half my age with an eighth-grade education, and you're trying to tell me about some kind of wound?" She rose, clenching her yarn like a rag doll. "I don't have time for this." She glanced at Esther. "I don't think crocheting is for me. Good night."

"Mother, don't be so rude to Hannah!" Cheri begged. "She's becoming like a sister to me. And I think what she says is true. We need to talk about our problems."

Mrs. Peters put up her nose. "Now you're becoming outspoken, too?"

Cheri grimaced. "I'm finding my voice, Mother."

Rolling her eyes and clucking her tongue in disgust, she spun around and marched out of the room and made the house shake as she stomped up the steps.

Hannah knew she'd been wrung out by this emotion filled day, but did she speak out of turn? To someone who was her elder. "*Mamm*, I didn't mean to be rude."

"You weren't," Esther said. "I should have told the story about a wound needing cleaned, but I missed your *daed* as soon as you brought him up. Cat caught my tongue."

"*Ach*, I'm sorry, *Mamm*. We talked about this last night. Christmas makes you miss him."

"It's *gut* to talk about your *daed*. Keeps his memory alive. You'll have to tell your *kinner* lots of telling's about him."

Cheri crossed her legs and let one fly like a whirligig. "My mom is such a crank. I'm sorry she treated you like you were an idiot, Hannah. She does it to me all the time." She set her face like flint, staring ahead. "Can't wait to get out of this cuckoo house!"

Hannah had a suspicion that part of the root of Cheri's immoral behavior was to escape. Find a nice man like her *daed* and move away. Find a man like Willow…who wouldn't want a man like him?

CHAPTER 10

Hannah reread the short letter she wrote to Andy:

Andy,

I don't want to hurt you, but I need to be truthful. I love someone else. I think it's the reason I could never open up to you, or truly court you. This man I love seems to love another, so I'll remain a spinster. It's not Freeman. I've heard through letters that your family will be attending his new church, so I don't want you being upset with him. Freeman will make a good pastor.

I wish I knew my heart when we first met. I'm sorry if I gave you hope. You're a fine man. If you turn Amish, like you say you will, do it because it's your calling. You'll find a better girl to marry than me. Someone who will love you with all her heart. I can't and I'm sorry.

Hannah

"Well, Hannah Coblenz, you've just committed yourself to spinsterhood," she said to the dresser mirror. A big mirror compared to the hand-held ones they were allowed to use. She noticed how pale she looked. She really needed to get outside, get some fresh air and sunshine.

A light rap on her door and then Cheri popped her head in. "Hannah, my mother's car is still here. She never misses work. And the door to her bedroom is locked."

"Can you ask your *daed* to check on her?"

"He doesn't have a key."

A key? She locked her husband out of their bedroom? But then again, some *Englishers* she'd heard had separate bedrooms. How odd. "What do you want me to do?"

"Well, I'm afraid I made her go over the edge about the picture. Maybe she's dead."

Hannah cocked one eyebrow sky high. Cheri was given to dramatics, but this took the cake. "So, you think she's dead because of the picture? Like she had a heart attack or something?"

Cheri's eyes brimmed with tears. "Can you see if she opens for you?"

Hannah saw the panic in Cheri. "Of course, I'll try." She followed Cheri down the long hall, noticing through a window a pair of cardinals. *Hurry, hurry, hurry*, their calls to each other seemed to say. She recalled when Willow left in a huff and she wondered if she should hurry after him. She was glad she stuck to her principals. Willow was so love struck with Betty they spent all waking hours together. Where else would he be? How could he ask her to come the whole way up to Canada, and then ignore her completely? She had to somehow move on and live a life without Willow Byler. Why it took her until it was too late to see she loved him, she'd never know.

Cheri pointed to the white door with an intricately carved golden doorknob. "Mrs. Peters?"

A faint 'Yes' was heard. Cheri held her hand over her heart and started to speak until Hannah hushed her by placing a hand over Cheri's mouth.

"Can I come in?"

"Door's not locked."

Hannah turned the knob and stared at Cheri, whispering, "Let me take care of this. Don't come in."

"Why?" Cheri whispered back.

"You had a bad quarrel last night." She put an index finger to her lips and slipped into Mrs. Peters' bedroom. Oddly, it was decorated in bright pinks and yellows, happy colors. Mrs. Peters wore dowdier colors than the Amish. "Cheri's afraid something's wrong. Your car's still here."

"Not…feeling too…well," she said, a sob catching her words.

"*Ach*, why're you crying? Is it because of me? I was so outspoken last night."

Mrs. Peters motioned for Hannah to sit in the chair near her bed. Hannah obeyed.

"The truth hurts. That picture sent me over the edge emotionally. You see, I had a little sister once. And that was a picture of the two of us."

"And something happened to your sister?" Hannah prodded.

"I killed her," Mrs. Peters said hollowly.

Hannah stared at the woman before her. She killed her sister? How on earth could this be true? "How? I don't mean exactly how you did it, but why? And…"

"If you leave a child in a hot car unattended, it's called neglect and parents go to jail. I should have gone to jail. I neglected her."

Not knowing what on earth to say, Hannah sat and waited for her to continue.

"My mother never got over it. Told me it was my fault."

Hannah was moved with compassion and leaned to take Mrs. Peters's hand. "How old were you when she died?"

"Seven. Old enough to go to school and know better. I just loved my cat more…"

Cats. Finally, something in common. "I have a cat and care for it a lot, but I would never let some seven-year-old watch it."

"Why?"

"Cats are really adorable. I'm an adult and lose track of time cuddling with her."

Mrs. Peters's eyes widened. "I did that all the time. Mother said I was in another world…and that's what killed my sister."

As Mrs. Peters cried, her body shook, and Hannah soon found herself rocking the poor woman back and forth like a child. "Your mother blamed you for your sister's death?"

"Yes!" she screamed. "Yes. How could a mother blame a child for so long? And my whole life, I've carried this pain." She beat her heart with a fist. "I vowed I'd do something to make her proud. When I graduated first in my class at dental school, she never even came to my graduation. When I opened my practice, she kept her old dentist." She stared dazed at Hannah. "I'd never do that to Cheri. I've worked my tail end off so she'd never be poor, like we were. When my sister died, my dad took to the bottle and we had no money." She raised her hands. "I built this house so my daughter would never have to be poor."

Hannah hugged her tight, rubbing her back, trying to calm her. This was a gaping wound that needed to be cleansed. "Does anyone know about your sister?"

"No," she said in a child-like voice. "Too painful."

Hannah heard Cheri behind her cry out, "Mother? Are you okay?"

"Run and get your *daed*, Cheri. Quick." As soon as Hannah said this, Mrs. Peters collapsed in her arms.

~*~

Willow rubbed Lucy behind the ears as she caught another scent. "*Gut* girl. You'll rescue somebody someday for sure."

He knew he'd been avoiding Hannah too long and, wanting to preserve the relationship, he headed over to the Peters'. He'd valued Hannah since he drew breath and had to learn to somehow stay connected to her as Andy's wife. *I can do all things through Christ who strengthens me*, he thought.

Being here in Ontario had settled his heart in many ways. For one thing, he was Amish to his core, like his *daed* suspected. His shyness had dissolved by being forced to meet new people. And he knew that still small voice of God all the better. He'd waited at the crossroads long enough and was ready to go home. His parents would be back soon, and he hoped to wrap things up with Lucy. Staying to ride sled dogs lost its appeal for some reason.

Yes, he'd taken a spin on the sled, but it was more fun to watch.

His mission was over up here. Cheri was less flirty; Hannah's influence helped her.

He threw a stick ahead and Lucy ran to catch it in mid-air. What a powerful dog. How he'd miss her.

As he walked up the driveway to the Peters, he was shocked to see Mrs. Peters screaming about something, while Mr. Peters forced her into the car. *What on earth?* Cheri was crying, and Hannah stood there without even a cape, hovering over Cheri like a mother hen.

He made a beeline to them. "What's going on? Is someone hurt?"

Hannah glared at him. "Not now. Not a *gut* time."

"I give up," Mr. Peters panted out. "We need to call an ambulance or something."

Mrs. Peters oddly stopped sobbing and meekly got into the car and fastened her seatbelt. "It's time."

Hannah led Cheri to the lamppost while the car skidded down the long driveway. Willow made an attempt to ask what was going on, but Hannah was preoccupied with Cheri as she urged her to go back inside and get warmed up. Willow followed them and looked for Esther. He searched downstairs, but she was nowhere to be found. And then it dawned on him that someone was in the backseat of the Peters' car. *Esther?*

He'd known this family and cared for them deeply. Why didn't Mr. Peters ask him to help? He stopped and instantly chided himself for throwing a pity party at such a time as this. This was not about him. But, it didn't help that

Hannah was being her usual bossy self and basically told him to leave during a family crisis. "Hannah Coblenz!" he yelled louder than calling for one of his coon dogs.

She soon appeared at the top of the steps. "Willow, what are you doing here?"

Confused, he screwed up his face. "What's going on? I've never seen the Peters so upset."

Hannah sighed. "Mrs. Peters got dizzy; had chest pains. She went to the hospital."

Willow stared in disbelief. Hannah was lifeless and unfeeling. She gave no indication if she was concerned about Mrs. Peters. Or was there a wall up between them and he couldn't see his so-called Proverbs 31 Woman? He doubted this wall would come down anytime soon, unless he asked if he offended her. Like the Good Book said to do. "Hannah, have I offended you in any way?"

"*Jah*," she sneered. "Ask me to come up here and then ignore me. I cannot wait to get back home to Smicksburg. To…"

To Andy, he thought. He reached for her hand, but she recoiled. "Hannah, no matter what, I'll always love you."

She clenched her fists. "Save it for Betty," she yelled, and then Cheri ran down the steps with a backpack and pillow. "I'm staying with my mother no matter how long it takes. Willow, did you hear about my mother's heart attack?"

Willow frowned. "I heard she had chest pains. Maybe a panic attack, *jah*?"

Cheri ran to Willow and gave him a bear hug. "Maybe just a panic attack. Willow, you always have a way of calming me down."

Hannah's ice-cold eyes sent shards through Willow and he took his cue to leave. Hannah was as cold as ice.

~*~

Esther massaged Mrs. Peter's hand. "See, no heart attack. But I dare say your heart's been cleansed? A wound healed?"

Still in a hospital gown and lying in bed, Mrs. Peters started to cry again. "And I never told a soul. Why do you think I did that? I'll be in therapy for ages."

Esther knew Reed Byler treated many with anxiety and herbs and minerals could help, but there was One higher than any name given to anything who could help. "You need to talk to the Great Counselor."

"Sure do. Need to pay big bucks for the mess I am."

Praying as she rubbed the soft skin, Esther prayed that Mrs. Peters would understand that even though her earthly parents had failed her, she had a parent who was perfect who could heal all hurts. Feeling like it wasn't the best of times to go through the ABC's of the gospel message, the Christmas song sung at the town light up night oddly came to her mind. "Can I sing you a Christmas song we sing in our little town back home?"

She nodded, although clearly taken aback.

Tears blurred Esther's vision. "I miss my husband and learned it last year. It comforts me. Now, I'm not the best singer, mind you."

Mrs. Peters stared as if waiting in anticipation.

Love came down at Christmas,
Love all lovely, Love Divine,
Love was born at Christmas,
Stars and Angels gave the sign.

Worship we the Godhead
Love incarnate, love divine
Worship we our Jesus
But wherewith for sacred sign?

Love shall be our token,
Small gift until something greater is given
Love shall be yours and love be mine,
Love to God and all men,
Love for plea and gift and sign.

Mrs. Peters bit her lower lip for a spell and tears pooled. "We used to sing that in church." She stared at the linoleum floor. "My dad held me tight up in his arms. I was high enough to see the choir." She covered her face. "How can I remember that?"

Esther had only her own life experience to share. "When my dear husband died, I tried not to think of him and did it for a few months after his death. But I got sick a lot, as I recall. Hannah was concerned. Got me going to a knitting circle where women open up about their troubles and pray for each other. So, I went and talked about my loss and the memories flooded back in. All the *gut* and not so *gut* times. I think I sealed myself up because if I was honest with anyone, I was mad at God."

Mrs. Peters shook her head. "Me, too. Me, too. I've hated him for years. A lifetime."

"And you know deep down that there's a God in heaven who loves you, don't you, but you can't face him because —"

"He wasn't fair to me. Oh, Esther, he wasn't fair to me!" she crumbled into a pathetic sob, a sob a child would wail out and soon a nurse was in the room, Mr. Peters on her heels.

Ach, Esther, what have you done?

~*~

Willow went back and forth from the lake house to the main house several times to see if Hannah and Cheri had gotten back from the hospital. He needed to reason with a woman who was acting unreasonable. *Save what for Betty?* What kind of reply was that when he told her he'd always love her; she knew what kind of love he meant, too. If she cared, she'd have reciprocated his affections by now. Maybe Hannah didn't realize she was leading him on. And all day, he'd been convicted that he was doing the same to Betty. He needed to put a stop to it and tell her he was leaving for Smicksburg. He'd be Amish, his crossroad experience was over, and he realized how much he loved his close-knit family. Maybe he'd marry later in life like Edmond and Martin. Maybe his bride was only thirteen and needed to grow up.

But one last attempt to talk to Hannah he was about to try; the truth would set him free. Free to let go and be patient that maybe in years, he'd have the family he'd envisioned. A desire to have a family much like his own he believed God birthed in his heart, a dream, a vision.

Thankful for a full moon to help light his way to the house, he saw one lone lamp in the living room. He could make out that it was an Amish woman sitting near the fire and his heart raced. *Lord, give me the words.* Ringing the doorbell, he looked over the hill to the lights of the small town. Pretty enough to be a puzzle, he thought. How he'd miss this place, but it wasn't home. It became home for Betty and Lee, but not for him.

The door opened and Esther, appearing worn out, welcomed him in. "No one's here but me. Watching the house. Cameras everywhere and an alarm system, but they said to make it look lived in." She motioned towards the kitchen. "I think they wanted me to leave the hospital after making Mrs. Peters cry. You were helpful though, calming Cheri about it being a panic attack. That's just what happened."

"Glad I could help," Willow said.

"She was diagnosed with anxiety, not the kind we all experience from time to time. It's personal and maybe Mr. Peters will share with you when he gets back." She tapped the granite counter top. "Bring up a stool and I'll make you something hot to drink. Chocolate, tea or coffee."

"Chocolate. *Gut* for the nerves. I came by to talk to Hannah."

"She went with Cheri to a church in town. Not Mennonite but one where Cheri has friends." A warm smile slid across Esther's weary face. "Cheri's become a believer in Christ. The hospital chaplain talked to her, but it's been your example, Willow Byler, that had much to do with it. Bringing Hannah, someone who's been dealing with grief here to find the root of Cheri's immoral behavior, gave her something to help pull lots of poison out of Cheri. Not real poison, not drugs or anything, but pent up anger and lots of things that kept her from seeing a loving God." Esther raised a hand. "Like I said, no drugs. Don't want to mess up anything more today."

Willow scratched his chin. "We all get misunderstood sometimes. It's why I want to talk to Hannah." Seeing the countertop strewn with all kinds of papers that needed to be categorized, Willow collected dog sled brochures and other items marked for the kennel, things he knew Mr. Peters would give him. He detected a letter with female writing. The Peters emailed everything, no handwritten letter had he ever seen here. Did his *mamm* write from Mexico again? But upon closer inspection, he saw a letter written to Andy Smucker. He just stood there, staring at it. "So, when's the wedding?"

Esther opened the microwave, stirred his chocolate and looked at him dumfounded. "Who's wedding?"

"Andy and Hannah's? Here's a letter to him. Saw one from him come in. Not being nebby, but I'm not blind."

"They're writing?" Esther asked, clearly surprised.

He nodded. "Really don't know what she sees in him. He treats her like a child."

Esther's eyes watered. "You deserve someone who will adore you. I adored my husband and we had many happy years."

Willow sipped his chocolate. "Christmas brings back lots of memories, *jah*?"

"*Jah.* It really does."

"Well, I'll pray for you." The chocolate slid down like silk and he slurped the last drop. "Well, I'm headed back home. Need to have a talk with Betty. I'm heading home."

Esther cocked her head. "Sorry I can't be as *gut* a company as Hannah. You best be going over and talk to Betty."

Willow could see bags under Esther's eyes, mixed with a heap of confusion. He'd clear things up in the morning. "*Gut* night."

"Sleep tight."

CHAPTER 11

Cheri flopped on her bed. "Could it really be true? Hannah, tell me yes."

Hannah couldn't help but laugh in delight. "*Jah*, all the preacher said was true."

"Tell me that scripture about snow and being white like Snow White," Cheri cupped her mouth. "I'm too emotional, huh?"

"*Jah*, you are but it's okay. The pastor at church tonight said that even though we have sin as red as scarlet, we can be made as white as snow."

"So all my sins…even sexual sins, are forgiven?"

Hannah sat near Cheri. "Now, Jesus said to the woman caught in adultery he didn't condemn her, but go and sin no more. We're forgiven and because of that, we should be grateful and want to serve God with all our hearts."

"What does condemn mean? Being condemned to prison? Hell?"

Hannah was tired but tried to find a synonym. "Look down on. God doesn't hold our sin against us. It's like he wipes the chalkboard clean."

Cheri snickered. "You Amish still use chalkboards?"

Hannah smiled. "*Jah*, we do." She took Cheri by the shoulders. "Now, I have something serious to tell you. Don't try to be a Christian on your own. Wolves prey on animals that are on their own, *jah*?"

Cheri hugged her middle. "We have coywolves up here. I've seen them. Really creepy."

Hannah's forehead pinched. "They're creepy because they're on the prey for a defenseless animal. One that has left the flock. Understand? Cheri, you're all excited about being a Christian, being forgiven, but promise me you'll be faithful to going to your church."

"But you didn't like the guitars and drums…"

Hannah snickered. "I almost fainted seeing them there, but King David played a harp. It's not the most important thing. Learning to love God is. And you do it through reading his love letter to us."

"Love letter?" Cheri questioned.

"The Bible tells us of God's love for us. Read it faithfully and make some *gut* kindred spirit friends you can talk to about your faith. They'll keep you from being snatched off by a wolf."

"And by that you mean Satan?"

Hannah nodded. "We also have temptations, being human. We all have weaknesses…"

"You don't," Cheri said, defeat in her voice. "I can never be perfect like you."

Hannah hugged Cheri. "You've only known me for a short time. People close to me know I'm not perfect…for sure and certain."

~*~

Hannah stood in awe of the full moon and yearned for a nature walk. Being cooped up with Cheri in the hospital, and then talking about such deep emotional issues made Hannah crave nature. It calmed her. The moon was one thing fixed in space and a constant. She never had to wonder if it would be out or not.

She thought back to what her *mamm* told her about the moon. It has no light of its own but reflects the sun. Her *daed* brought out the best in her *mamm*. How she longed for companionship. But she had her *mamm*. Being Amish, she'd do her best to care for her as she aged. They'd grow old together.

Wondering if she was looking at the same moon, Hannah tip toed down the hall and knocked on her *mamm's* door. "*Mamm*, are you up?" She whispered.

The door flung open. "I can't sleep a wink. You've been writing to Andy? Why?" She pulled Hannah into her room. "He isn't marrying material, like the Baptist's say. Way too many red flags flapping about."

She appeared to be packing, many drawers open and a suitcase on the bed. "Are we leaving tomorrow? Did I get the dates wrong?"

"I'm just packing early," she said, plopping down on the bed. "I'm worked up. Why didn't you encourage Willow Byler more? He loves you, or at least he did."

Clearly spending much of the day with Mrs. Peters was too much for her *mamm*. "You're exhausted. We can talk tomorrow."

Esther jutted her chin. "I'd like to know why you wrote to Andy and didn't encourage Willow? He stopped by here to talk to you tonight. Seemed as cool as a cucumber, mighty confident. And I realized I messed up again!"

"Again?"

"*Jah*. My mouth is too big. I sang a song to Mrs. Peters. It's why they asked me to so-called watch the house. And then I sing the praises of Andy when Willow is the finest man alive, but it's too late."

Hannah knelt at her *mamm's* feet. "Slow down. Now, Mrs. Peters loved the song. She cried because she's been putting up a wall between God and herself for ages. *Love Came Down at Christmas* knocked a hole in the wall. And she talked to Cheri about lots of stuff and the whole family's going to start attending church together. I was like a fish out of water tonight; they sang to guitars and drums, of all things. But *Mamm*, your friendship with Mrs. Peters was like a balm. A real healing balm."

Esther's eyes brightened. "Really? But I did so little. Taught her a few things in the kitchen but not much more."

"You became her friend. A *gut* listening ear bosom friend."

"*Ach*, too much praise."

"Not enough. Now, what's all this about Willow and Andy? You're too troubled. Your cheeks are flushed."

"Willow, like I said, is mighty confident." She touched Hannah's face. "He's changed. Said he was going home...to Betty. Asked when you and Andy were getting married without any feeling except, I don't think he likes Andy much."

Hannah's intuition had been right. Willow had been away due to his commitment to Betty. A pain lodged like a pit in her heart. How she'd live without Willow Byler... the one man who brought the best out in her was taken. And if he called this area home, that meant he was staying and turning Mennonite. Sorrow mixed with anger over her pride made her want to jump out of her skin. "*Mamm*, I need to take a walk."

Esther caught her arm. "It's too late."

"I took night walks in Smicksburg all the time. I'll go to the lake house and back. I promise I'll only be gone for fifteen minutes."

"At least take a flashlight. Hannah?"

Not wanting her *mamm* to see her tears, darted out of the room and bundled up for a brisk walk. A very brisk walk.

~*~

Willow jerked out of sleep when someone rapped on his bedroom door. "Come in."

Lee ran across the dark room, the light of the cell phone lighting his path. "It's Hannah's mom. Hannah's out in this storm."

Willow grabbed the phone. "Esther?"

"*Ach*, Willow, Hannah's not back from her walk."

Willow ran to the window, snow slapping the glass so hard he couldn't see how many inches fell. He turned back and grabbed the phone. "How long's she been gone?"

"Hours," Esther sobbed. "She said she'd only go to the lake house and back but she's not back yet."

"What time did she leave?"

"*Ach*, nine? Not sure. Willow, do something."

Willow eyed Lee's phone to see ten-thirty. "I'll come by with Lucy. Meet me at the door with something Hannah's worn lately. Something with her scent."

Willow heard Esther make a hysterical plea to forgive Hannah. She's not marrying Andy. But he wasn't sure what he heard, her voice was shaky, and he wasn't awake. And he needed to find her. This was a deadly storm.

~*~

Hannah, exhausted from walking in circles, looked up once again to find the moon, to no avail. It hid behind the curtain of snow. Hoping to see even a shadow of the lake house would be some comfort. *Crack!* Hannah's feet wobbled. Fear ripped through the core of her being. Was she on the lake? "God, help me!" She cried out to the deafening wind. It howled at her, as if teasing, taunting. *What a fool you are, Hannah Coblenz.* Paralyzed with fear, she mounted in place. Ice cracked beneath, and she was sure she'd be plunging deep into the lake soon. Visions of her *mamm* finding her dead, on the heels of her *daed's* death jolted her and she ran.

Solid ground? She tapped a toe ever so gently. "Solid ground!" She knelt down and hugged it. "*Danki,* Lord! You are my shepherd! You lead me through the shadow of death!" she cried out. "Lead me on further! Back home!"

With no visible light, not even the stars, she wondered where in the world she was? Right near the lake or miles away? Had she been on the lake or a frozen puddle? Why had she been so stubborn and not taken a flashlight like her *mamm* advised? As snow continued to stack on her, covering her, burying her, she cried out, "Help me!"

She knew she had to stay awake and keep moving but fatigue was washing over her in waves. After digging with her mittens down enough to know she was on solid ground, Hannah wiggled her toes and shook her hands, clasping them shut and opening them again. Keep your circulation going until help comes. *Mamm must be frantic*, she thought. And then it dawned on her. Did her *mamm* fall asleep? Maybe no one knew she was out in this wretched storm.

Lord, you see me out here. I'm a lost sheep. You leave the ninety-nine safe ones and find the one in danger. Send me help! Tears dripped down her cheeks…and they felt warm. She let them flow onto her fingers. *Lord, I can't lose my fingers. I'd never knit again.*

She lifted her arm, her cape like a wing, and shielded the swirling snow as she tried to make out anything at all. As she squinted, she made out two glowing eyes. She screamed in fright as they got closer, larger, and then a vicious bark sent her into a screaming fit. Wolves!

~*~

"Hannah! It's Lucy!" He yelled but by the light beaming from his head flashlight, he saw her topple over. As Lucy licked Hannah's lifeless face, Willow scooped her up and ran to the boat house. "*Ach*, God, she has to be all right! I can't be too late!"

He flung on the light switch but with no heat except a woodstove, he ran to the storage bench to get a thick wool blanket and commanded Lucy to lay near Hannah. He checked her pulse. It was strong. She must have fainted. He kissed her cheek and then waited to hear her breathe. "God, *danki!*" he yelled. Kissing her again, he ran to the woodstove and threw in kindling, paper, and a log. Striking a match, he blew until it caught, and he shut the glass door and ran back to his girls. So proud of Lucy he was, he kissed the top of her head as well.

He carried Hannah to the couch and rubbed her fingers. "Hannah, wake up." An image of her stepping onto the lake, her heavy cape and dress saturated and then frozen, her sinking to the bottom of the lake while drowning made him gasp for air. *She's okay now!* Hannah was dry. She was right here with him. And Lucy was near her and would help warm her up. Wake her up…

How long had she been laying there? Panic set in. She was clearly breathing but had she been asleep, freezing to death in his arms? He slapped her cheeks. "Wake up! Hannah, please, wake up!"

"Ouch," she whimpered, slapping him back with what little strength she had.

Willow laughed and cried together. "Hannah, it's me, Willow." He drew her up into his arms. "*Ach*, Hannah, I love you so much. Thought you were dead."

"W-Wolves," she shuddered. "Lock the door."

He smoothed her disheveled hair on her face back under her *kapp*. "It was Lucy, not a wolf."

"Your dog?"

"*Jah*, my dog. Hannah, you almost went out on the lake. Just the thought of it makes me sick. Makes me realize again how much I love you. No one loves you like I do."

Hannah's light blue eyes focused clearly and twinkled. "What did you say?"

"I love you. Don't marry Andy. He's not –"

She leaned into him. "I love you."

He swallowed and shook his head. Was he dreaming? He clearly saw the flickering flames in the woodstove. He felt the warmth of Hannah in his arms. "You love me? As your *wee bruder* or...as a man?"

"Marry *me*, Willow. Be Amish. Please."

"Okay, now I know I'm dreaming. I've had this dream before!" he blurted.

She reached up and kissed him. "Did I kiss you in a dream?"

A smile slid across his face. "*Jah*, I'll wake up soon."

Hannah cupped his cheeks and kissed him fervently, lacing her fingers around his neck.

Willow had indeed dreamt of this moment and it was happening. Hannah saw him as a man. A man she could love. And she asked him to marry her. What a bold, outspoken girl! He kissed her cheek, forehead, and nose. "I accept your proposal."

Her eyelashes fluttered. "My proposal? *Nee*, you have to ask me. It's tradition. And I'm not a forward –"

He kissed her soundly. "*Jah*, you are. And I love you, you stubborn girl. You *wunderbar*, headstrong woman!"

Epilogue

Dear Lee,

I'm sure you'll pass this letter around to Betty and the whole house. Hannah and I told the family about our engagement on Christmas Day. No one was surprised, since we're seen together often and I can't help but grab Hannah's hand tight. It took me ages to get her to be mine and sometimes I fear she may dart. It's my old low self-worth kicking in again. When I see Hannah's beauty, inside and out, I have to remind myself I am worthy of such a gift from God. He loves me that much and gives GOOD gifts to his children.

I'm glad Betty finally saw you for the great guy you are. Keep me posted on how things progress. Or maybe I should look for a wedding invitation in the mail?

Hannah and I are planning on building on to my little house. She wants the pond out back drained though. Can't say I blame her. One of our wee ones may be like her and wonder off on a snowy night. I know it was the prayers of the folks at the house that led me to her that night I sometimes have nightmares about. But I wouldn't change Hannah's strong-willed nature for anything. She's not a passive woman. I always thought them dull.

We plan on expanding the kennel, too, and will train service dogs. It's amazing what you can train a dog to do, but I won't bother you with all the details.

We'll have forty acres and plan on tapping into the many maples and have a syrup farm. Hannah's wanted that for as long as I can remember. She loves to bake and can make me maple cookies, pies, cakes, you name it. She thinks she's getting her way starting a maple syrup farm, but we both know who wins in the end. (Wink, wink)

About Andy and his family. Well, they're Mennonites like you. Andy actually talks to me real civil-like. Maybe he always had but my jealousy didn't let me see it. My newfound faith has opened my eyes to all the goodness in Smicksburg and beyond. Hannah and I plan to go with my daed down to Mexico on his next missions trip. Going up to Canada stretched us in many ways. (I think we both have a bit of my daed's travel fever.) Daed hopes to go once a year. Mamm won't go back. She cried most of the day on Christmas because of how rich we are and how she wanted to bring home some of the kinner. Edmond, will go, too. I told you about him, the Englisher doctor turned Amish. He and Lily plan a wedding in January of all things. Smack dab in the middle of winter. Hannah says it's not traditional and wants a November wedding during wedding season. She'd dreamt of it her whole life and I'd do anything to make my Hannah happy. My Hannah. I love saying that.

Thanks for checking in on the Peters from time to time. Cheri's on the worship team playing her flute? That was good news. Sounds like Mrs. Peters is doing good. She writes to Esther, Hannah's mamm, real regular-like. Keep in touch, buddy.

Tell everyone I said a belated Merry Christmas!
Willow Byler

DISCUSSION GUIDE

1.) Willow has a quiet temperament, not needing to be around people all the time. He wants to be more like 'outspoken Hannah'. But we see Hannah struggles with fear, even though she appears very confident. A wonderfully healing verse for me was a few lines from Isaiah 53:5:

The chastisement of our peace was upon him; and with his stripes we are healed. (KJV)

That may sound like Old English, but I love the poetic feel of the King James Version. Chastisement is another way of saying 'scolding', like reprimanding a child. But think about it, Jesus was reprimanded so we could have peace. Oh, sigh of joy! A big sigh of relief! Who wants to be constantly scolded in their minds? Well, we can be our own worst enemies. I was until I learned that Jesus died for me to have peace. It means 'shalom'. When traditional Jewish people greet each other they say "Shalom," meaning "Peace be with you." I want that! It's a struggle some days and it's why I read the Bible daily.

Great peace have those who love your law, and nothing can make them stumble. Psalm 119:165

2.) Willow and Hannah feel rejected by each other. Hannah occupies herself with helping Cheri, the reason she's in Canada in the first place. Willow stays outside with the dogs, enjoying nature and seeking God. We all can feel left out, marginalized or plain rejected at times. When these feelings plague you, who can you reach out to? You're blessed when you reach out to others. Or maybe you need to go outside and see the nature of God….in nature?

3.) Cheri's mom can't connect with her, and basically, she's starved for attention. Sometimes books blame it all on dad when a daughter becomes immortal, but where's the mom modeling good behavior? Teaching her self-worth? Self-respect? Who has modeled this in your life? How can you be a model to others?

4.) Mrs. Peters hides from her childhood pain by being a workaholic. As a grown woman, it may seem ridiculous that she hasn't connected the dots by now, but it took opening up to a friend that set her free. Poor Esther! She thinks she made things worse, when in reality, her friendship was the source of healing. Have you ever stopped a friend from giving TMI (too much information)? Sometimes it's a nice way of saying, "I'm in a hurry and don't have time to talk." If so, take this friend seriously and chat later. There is such healing in talking through a problem.

5.) Reed Byler fights discontentment. Is that shocking? It's reality. We all do. It's part of the human condition. A friend told me (rebuked me) once that I was the most discontent person she'd ever met. Since this friend hardly ever criticized, I took notice when she said this. I spent a year studying how to be content. I literally learned to be content, like the Bible says we need to do. We need to learn it. I read scriptures and many books and let it sink in over a year. Do you battle discontentment? If not, how about fear? Loneliness? Isolation? Boredom? Depression? These are all top women's issues in America. Maybe choose which one to tackle first and take a year and battle it head-on. I've found it's the only way to get real results. *Ach*, patience is a virtue!

6.) What do you think of Dorcas Byler? Isn't she a peach? The real Amish woman who inspired this character, the herbalist's wife who runs the herb shop in Smicksburg, has many great qualities. Supportive wife, loving mom and a woman who could not believe she stepped foot in Mexico. I told her I'd add the part about needing new shoes being her first excuse/reason not to go on the trip. She laughs about it still.

Dorcas is an encourager. She doesn't get much praise or acknowledgement, but continually props up those who do. In what ways can you support loved ones to be the best 'them' they can be? Not trying to change them, but nurturing.

7.) Who has been your favorite character in this series? I'd love to hear from you. Visit

www.karenannavogel.com/contact Sometimes a whole new stories springs from a much-loved character. Granny Weaver is so loved; she just keeps stepping into scenes as I write them!

Reader Friends,

While writing the last book in this series, a reader friend died who taught me much about giving. Maggie Holz, from Cleveland Ohio, crocheted my two grandchildren outfits, stuffed toys and made me so many needlepoint pins, if I put them all on my refrigerator at once, it would be hidden.

I now have two grandsons due to be born two months apart and I miss this encouraging woman. She was in chronic pain and made craft items to give as gifts. By reaching out to others, she got her mind off her pain. If you want to read about Maggie, she became a character in Amish Knit & Stitch Circle: Smicksburg Tales 4.

If you've met someone as rare as Maggie, could you share their story with me? I love putting real people (names changed to protect the humble) in my stories, passing along inspiration to my readers.

God bless you all and stay in touch at
www.karenannavogel.com/contact or
https://www.facebook.com/VogelReaders

Amish Recipes

Esther's Christmas Baking Recipes

Christmas Butter Cookies

1 cup soft butter

½ cup brown sugar, packed

2¼ cups flour

Cream butter until it resembles whipped cream and slowly add the sugar, beating well. Add flour gradually and blend thoroughly. Wrap in waxed paper and chill for several hours. Knead dough slightly on floured board and then form into a smooth ball. Roll to about ⅛ inch thick and cut to desired shapes. Place on ungreased cookie sheets and bake in moderate oven at 350 degrees for approximately 12 minutes.

Belsnickel Christmas Cakes

1 cup sugar

½ cup melted butter

2 eggs

1½ cups flour

½ tsp. baking soda

pinch of salt

Pour melted butter over sugar in a bowl and beat until smooth and creamy. Add the eggs, beating one at a time, into the mixture. Sift the baking soda through the flour and then salt. Add to the cake mixture. Stand the dough in a cold place for an hour. Roll out on floured board, quite thin. Cut into small rounds or other shapes. Sprinkle with sugar and bake in hot oven at 400 degrees for 10 minutes.

Karen Anna Vogel

About Author Karen Anna Vogel

Karen Anna Vogel is dusting off book outlines written thirty years ago when she was running after her four preschoolers. Having empty nest syndrome, she delved into writing. Many books and novellas later, she's passionate about portraying the Amish and small-town life in a realistic way. Being a "Trusted English Friend" to Amish in rural Western Pennsylvania and New York, she writes what she's experienced, many novels based on true stories. She also blogs at *Amish Crossings*

She's a graduate of Seton Hill University, majoring in Psychology & Elementary Education, and Andersonville Theological Seminary with a Masters in Biblical Counseling. Karen's a yarn hoarder not in therapy, knitting or crocheting something at all times. This passion leaks into her books along with hobby farming and her love of dogs. Her husband of thirty-seven years is responsible for turning her into a content country bumpkin.

Visit her at www.karenannavogel.com/contact

Karen's booklist so far (2018)
Check Amazon author page for updates.

Continuing Series:

Amish Knitting Circle: Smicksburg Tales 1

Amish Knitting Circle: Smicksburg Tales 2

Amish Knit Lit Circle: Smicksburg Tales 3

Amish Knit & Stitch Circle: Smicksburg Tales 4

Amish Knit & Crochet Circle: Smicksburg 5

Standalone Novels:

Knit Together: Amish Knitting Novel

The Amish Doll: Amish Knitting Novel

Plain Jane: A Punxsutawney Amish Novel

Amish Herb Shop Series:

Herbalist's Daughter Trilogy

Herbalist's Son Trilogy

At Home in Pennsylvania Amish Country Series:

Winter Wheat

Spring Seeds

Summer Haze (Yet to be released)

Autumn Grace (Yet to be released)

Novellas:

Amish Knitting Circle Christmas: Granny & Jeb's Love Story

Amish Pen Pals: Rachael's Confession

Christmas Union: Quaker Abolitionist of Chester County, PA

Love Came Down at Christmas

Love Came Down at Christmas 2

Love Came Down at Christmas 3

Non-fiction:

31 Days to a Simple Life the Amish Way

A Simple Christmas the Amish Way

How to Know the Love of God

God loved the world.

For this is how God loved the world: He gave his one and only Son, so that everyone who believes in him will not perish but have eternal life. *John 3:16*

God loves you!

"I have loved you, my people, with an everlasting love. With unfailing love I have drawn you to myself.
Jeremiah 31:3

"That He gave His only Son
Who is God's son?

"Jesus told him, "I am the way, the truth, and the life. No one can come to the Father except through me.'" — John 14:6

That whoever believes in Him

Whosoever? Even me?

No matter what you've done, God will receive you into His family. He will change you, so come as you are.

""I am the Lord, the God of all the peoples of the world. Is anything too hard for me?" — Jeremiah 32:27

"At that time the Spirit of the Lord will come powerfully upon you…You will be changed into a different person." — 1 Samuel 10:6

Should not perish but have eternal life

Can I have that "blessed hope" of spending eternity with God?

"I have written this to you who believe in the name of the Son of God, so that you may know you have eternal life."- 1 John 5:13

To know Jesus, come as you are and humbly admit you're a sinner. A sinner is someone who has missed the target of God's perfect holiness. I think we all qualify to be sinners. Open the door of your heart and let Christ in. He'll cleanse you from all sins. He says he stands at the door of your heart and knocks. Let Him in. Talk to Jesus like a friend…because when you open the door of your heart, you have a friend eager to come inside.

Bless you!

If you have any questions, contact Karen at karenannavogel@gmail.com

Made in the USA
Middletown, DE
28 April 2021